THE GOLEM of HOLLYWOOD

THE GOLEM *of* HOLLYWOOD

JONATHAN KELLERMAN *and* JESSE KELLERMAN

G. P. PUTNAM'S SONS

NEW YORK

PUTNAM

G. P. PUTNAM'S SONS
Publishers Since 1838
Published by the Penguin Group
Penguin Group (USA) LLC
375 Hudson Street
New York, New York 10014

USA · Canada · UK · Ireland · Australia
New Zealand · India · South Africa · China

penguin.com
A Penguin Random House Company

Library of Congress Cataloging-in-Publication Data

Kellerman, Jonathan.
The Golem of Hollywood / Jonathan Kellerman and Jesse Kellerman.
p.   cm.
ISBN 978-0-399-16236-7
1. Golem—Fiction.   2. Murder—Investigation—Fiction.   3. Suspense fiction.
4. Horror fiction.   I. Kellerman, Jesse.   II. Title.
PS3561.E3865G65   2014   2013051043
813'.54—dc23

Printed in the United States of America
1   3   5   7   9   10   8   6   4   2

Book design by Gretchen Achilles

THE GOLEM of HOLLYWOOD

CHAPTER ONE

Heap had followed the girl for days.

The watch was an important part of it, the most delicious part: sinking into the background while that wonderful brain of his roared in high gear, eyes, ears, everything finely tuned.

People tended to underestimate him. They always had. At Eton: two nights locked in a broom closet. At Oxford, they laughed, they did, the horsefaced girls and the cooing boys. And dear Papa, Lord of the Manor, Chancellor of the Purse Strings. *All that school and you a bloody office boy.*

But underestimated is close to unnoticed.

Heap capitalized on that.

She could be any girl who struck his fancy.

Eye the herd.

Cull.

The bright-eyed brunette in Brussels.

Her virtual twin in Barcelona.

The early work, glorious countryside afternoons, honing his technique.

The unmistakable tingle came on him like a fit of sick. Though Heap wasn't fool enough to deny that he preferred a certain species: dark hair, sharp features. Lower class, not too bright, not bad-looking but well shy of pretty.

Smallish body, except he demanded a big chest. The soft, yielding pressure never failed to excite.

This one was perfect.

HE HAD FIRST SPOTTED her walking east along the Charles Bridge. He'd been skulking round for two weeks by then, taking in the sights, waiting for an opportunity to present itself. He liked Prague. He'd visited before and never left disappointed.

Among the jean-clad magpies, the wattled American tourists, the leather-voiced buskers, and the minimally talented portrait artists, she had stood out for her modesty. Limp skirt, tight hair, focused and grim, she hurried along, cheeks carved out by the midmorning glare off the Vltava.

Perfect.

He tried to follow her but she melted into the crowd. The next day, he returned, hopeful, prepared, attentive. Opening his guidebook, he pretended to reread a gray box headed *Did you know?* The bridge had eggs mixed into its concrete for added strength. Good King Charles IV had commandeered every last egg in the kingdom, and they had obeyed, the stupid, slobbering masses, showing up to place them obsequiously at his royal feet.

Did Heap know?

Yes, he did. He knew everything worth knowing and much besides.

Even the guidebook underestimated him.

She passed again at the same time. And the day after that. Three days running he watched her. A girl of fixed habits. Lovely.

Her first stop was a café near the bridge. She donned a red apron, cleared tables for change. At dusk, she left Old Town for New Town, exchanged the red apron for a black one, bussing trays and refilling steins at a beer hall that, by the smell of it, catered to the locals. Photos of the entrées in the window showed sausages smothered in that vile, muddy sauce they put on everything.

From beneath the trolley stand, Heap watched her flit here and there. Twice passersby paused to ask him a question in Czech, which Heap took to mean that he appeared, as ever, unremarkable. He replied, in French, that he spoke no Czech.

At midnight, the girl finished mopping up. She doused the restaurant's lights, and a few minutes later, a window two floors up blinked yellow, and her pale arm drew the blind.

It would be a squalid rented room, then. A sad and hopeless life.

Delicious.

He considered finding a way into her flat. Blitzing her in her own bedroom.

Appealing notion. But Heap despised senseless risk. It came of watching Papa burn thousands on football, cricket, anything involving imbeciles and a ball, pouring the fortune of centuries down the grimy throats of bookmakers. Never the most discriminating chap, Papa. How he loved to remind Heap that it would all be gone before Heap saw a penny. Heap was nothing like him and therefore deserved nothing.

Someday Heap would let him know what he thought of that.

To the task at hand: no sense changing the pattern. The pattern worked. He'd take her on the street like the others.

Leaving an empty-eyed shell propped against a dustbin or a wall, waiting to be discovered by some privileged citizen of the free world.

Heap examined an unmarked door to the right of the restaurant, six anonymous buzzer pushes. Never mind her name. He preferred to think of them numerically. Easier to catalog. He had the librarian's spirit in him, he did. She would be number nine.

ON THE SEVENTH NIGHT, a Thursday, Number Nine went up to her room as usual but reemerged soon after, a feather duster in one hand, a folded square of white cloth in the other.

He gave her slack, then followed north as she crossed into Old Town

Square, uncomfortably alive with pedestrians. He clung to shadows on Maiselova as they entered Josefov, the former Jewish quarter.

He had come this way days before, while reacquainting himself with the city. It was the thing to do, see the old Jewish places. Dutifully he had elbowed through the revolting gawking swarms, tour guides prattling about Slavic tolerance while their charges snap snap snapped away. Heap didn't care enough about Jews as a group to summon genuine loathing. He regarded them with the same contempt he had for all lesser humanity, which included everyone except himself and a select few. Those Jews he'd known at school were self-satisfied twits laboring to be more Christian than the Christians.

The girl turned right at a shambling yellow wreck of a building. The Old-New Synagogue. Curious name to go along with a curious design. Part Gothic, part Renaissance, the result a rather clumsy porridge, homely crenellated roof and skimpy windows. Far more old than new. But then Prague had no end of old buildings. They were common as streetwalkers. He'd drunk his fill.

An alleyway unfurled along the synagogue's south side, ending at a wide set of ten steps that in turn ran up to the shuttered shops of Pařížská Street. Heap wondered if Nine was headed there, to tidy up at one of the boutiques.

Instead she went left at the foot of the steps, disappearing behind the synagogue. Heap crept along the alley in crepe-soled shoes, reaching the steps and stealing a glance.

She stood on a small cobbled terrace, facing the rear of the synagogue, into which was set an arched iron door, rudely studded. A trio of rubbish bins constituted the exterior decor. She had flapped open the white cloth and was tying it around her waist: yet another apron. Heap smiled to imagine her closet, nothing but aprons in every color. So many secret identities she had, each more wretched than the last.

She picked up the feather duster from where she'd laid it, against the wall. She shook it out. Shook her head, as well, as if banishing drowsiness.

Industrious little *charwoman*. Two full-time jobs and now this.

Who said the work ethic was dead?

He might have taken her right then, but a duet of drunken laughter came bounding along Pařížská, and Heap continued slowly up the steps, watching the girl peripherally.

She withdrew a key from her jeans and let herself into the synagogue through the iron door. The lock clanked.

He took up a vigil beneath a lamppost, opposite the synagogue's dark visage. A series of metal rungs in the brick ran up to a second arched door, a shabby wooden echo of the iron one, thirty-five feet off the ground and opening illogically onto thin air.

The garret. *Did you know?* There, the world-famous (according to whom, Heap wondered) Rabbi Loew had conjured the golem, a mythical mud-creature who roamed the ghetto, protecting its inhabitants. The selfsame rabbi had a statue of himself in a grand square, he did. While following the girl, Heap had pretended to stop and take its picture.

Hideously undignified, really. Mud was one step above shit.

The legend had become the wellspring of a gaudy commercialism, the monster's lumpy form cropping up on signs and menus, mugs and pennants. In one particularly rank bistro near Heap's hotel you could buy a brown-sauce-soaked Golem Burger and wash it down with Golemtinis enough to rot your liver.

People would pay for anything.

People were disgusting.

The laughter of the couple had faded in the warm wind.

Heap decided to give it one more night. More foreplay made for a better climax.

FRIDAY EVENING, the Old-New was a busy place, worshippers filing in, some stopping to talk to a blond man stationed out front with a walkie-talkie. With smiles all around, and everyone afforded entry, the attempt at security struck Heap as a bit of a sham.

Nevertheless he'd come prepared, his better suit (his only decent suit since Papa had screwed tight the tap), a mild white shirt, and his old school tie, plus inoffensive flat-lensed specs. Approaching the entrance, he hunched to take off some height, blousing his jacket, eliminating the bulge of his inside pocket.

The blond guard was more of a boy, hardly out of nappies. He shifted his body to block Heap's progress, addressing him in a throaty, vulgar accent. "Can I help you?"

"I'm here to pray," Heap said.

"Pray," the guard said, as if that were the strangest reason to visit a house of worship.

"You know. Give thanks. Praise God." Heap smiled. "Perhaps it'll help."

"Help?"

"World a mess and all that."

The guard studied him. "You want to come into the *shul*?"

Dense little turd. "Indeed."

"To pray for the world."

Heap lowered the level a few notches. "That and personal good fortune, mate."

"You are Jewish?"

"I'm here, am I not?"

The guard smiled. "Please, you can tell me: what is the last holiday?"

"Sorry?"

"The most recent Jewish holiday."

A furious moment while Heap ransacked the files. A light sweat broke out on his forehead. He resisted the urge to wipe it away. Aware that he was taking an awfully long time, he coughed up what he had. "Well, then, that would be Passover, would it not?"

The guard said, "Passover."

"Reckon so, yes."

The guard said, "You are British."

There's a clever lad. Heap nodded.

"I can see your passport, please?"

"One wouldn't think one would need it to pray."

The guard made a show of taking out his keys and locking the synagogue door. He gave Heap a condescending pat on the shoulder. "Wait here, please."

He sauntered off down the street, murmuring into his walkie-talkie while Heap swam in the red tide of his mind. The sheer nerve: to *touch* him. He puffed his chest against the bulge. Stag bone handle. Six-inch blade. *Ought to give thanks of your own, mate.*

Twenty yards hence, the guard stopped at a doorway. A second man materialized and the two of them conferred, appraising him openly. The sweat kept oozing. Sometimes the sweat was a problem. A drop ran in Heap's eye and stung and he blinked it away. He knew when he wasn't wanted. He could be patient. He left the guards talking and went on his way.

EVERY MAN HAS HIS LIMITS, though. After six more days without a fair chance, he was aroused to the brink of madness, and he decided that tonight would be the night, come what may, and how lovely it would be.

By three a.m., she'd been inside the synagogue for over two hours. Heap slouched in darkness near the steps, listening to distant bleats from somewhere well beyond the Jewish quarter, rolling the knife handle between his fingers. He began to wonder if she'd snuck in a brief nap. Busy girl, she must be falling off her feet.

The iron door screamed on its hinges.

Number Nine stepped out toting a sizable plastic tub. She turned her back to him, headed for the rubbish bins, hoisted the tub and dumped it out noisily, clanking cans and rushing paper, and he unfolded the blade (oiled and silent, a welcome release it was, like his lungs filling with fresh air) and moved on her.

Halfway to her, a muffled clap froze him in panic.

He glanced back.

The alley was empty.

As for the girl, she hadn't noticed the noise; she continued about her business, raking out the last of the rubbish with her fingers.

She set the tub down.

She untied her hair and began to regather it, and her raised arms formed a wide-hipped lyre, oh lovely lovely shape, and his blood boiled afresh and he started forward again. Too eager: his shoe caught the cobblestone and sent a pebble clicking toward her and she went rigid and turned, her mouth already poised to scream.

She didn't have time enough before his hand mashed against her lips and he twirled her, her back to his belly and his stiffening prick. Practical hardworking girl, she kept her nails cut short; hard rounded calluses clawed ineffectually at his arms and face before a deeper prey instinct took hold of her and she sought his instep to stomp it.

He was ready. Number Four, Edinburgh, had done the same. A sharp little heel; a broken metatarsal; a good pair of loafers, ruined. Heap had learned his lesson. He had his feet splayed as he braced against her. He twined his fingers in her hair and yanked her head back to form a graceful convexity of her gullet.

He reached up to stroke the blade.

But she was a resourceful lass, and it seemed she must have fingernails after all, because she made a spittly hiss and he felt a hideous stab in his eye, like an awl driving through the lens and the jelly to scrape his optic nerve. False colors gushed. The pain made him gag and loosen his grip on her hair and his hand went up to protect his face. He had prey instincts, too.

Her distorted form broke away from him and ran for the steps.

Groaning, he lurched forth, grabbing at her.

Another hiss; another stab of pain, his other eye, driving him stumbling into the rubbish bins, both eyes streaming, the knife flung from his hands. He could not understand. Had she shot him? Thrown something at him? He blinked forcefully to clear the blurriness and he saw the girl reaching the top of the steps, disappearing round the corner onto Pařížská, and her waning form brought the awareness of a dawning catastrophe.

She had seen his face.

He struggled to his feet and started after her, and from behind he heard a hiss and pain knocked him flat, as if someone had buried a claw hammer in the base of his skull, and as he pitched against the hard ground, his fine roaring brain grasped that something was happening to him, something wrong, because the girl was long gone.

Sprawled on his stomach in scattered rubbish, he opened his tearing eyes and saw it, half a foot away, a coin-sized spot, glittering blackly on the cobblestones.

A hard-domed insect, shimmering antennae, long black thorn sprouting from its head.

It charged him, driving itself into the center of Heap's forehead.

He screamed and swatted at it and tried to stand up, but the thing kept coming at him, fast and vicious, the growl of its wings audible in every direction, like a cattle prod touched to Heap's neck, his spine, the backs of his knees, herding him away from the steps and backing him into the wall of the synagogue, where he balled up with his arms thrown over his head.

Abruptly, the assault broke off, and the night went still save a faint wooden clapping noise. Heap waited, shaking. Puncture wounds seeped along his hairline, blood trickling along the side of his nose and into his mouth.

He uncovered his head.

Down on the cobblestones, the bug squatted, peering up at him.

Full of hate, Heap rose to his full height.

Raised his foot to crush it to pulp.

Brought his foot down.

Missed.

It had dodged and was waiting, several inches to the right.

He tried again, and again it moved, and again, and they engaged in an absurd little wrathful dance, Heap stamping and jerking while the foul creature darted in mocking circles.

At last he came to his senses. He was chasing an insect, and meanwhile the girl who had seen his face was God knows where, saying God knows what to God knows whom.

He had to leave. Now. Never mind his things. Catch a taxi straight to the airport and depart posthaste for jolly old, never to return to this awful place.

He turned and ran and crashed into a wall.

A wall that hadn't been there before.

A wall of mud.

Broad as an avenue, taller than the synagogue, soaring upward like some manic cancer, climbing, expanding, ballooning, reeking of stagnant waters, rotting fish, mold, oily reeds.

He slipped and fled in the opposite direction, hitting another wall.

And then it surrounded him, the mud, mud walls, a city of mud, a megalopolis, vast and dense and formless. He raised his gaze to an indifferent sky, the stars blotted out by mud. Weeping, he cast his eyes down to the earth, where mud black as dried blood began to creep across his shoes, starting at the toes and inching upward. He screamed. He tried to lift his feet and found his shoes cemented to the stones; tried to kick them off but the mud had reached his ankles and grasped his shins and begun to climb. It was the source of the smell, viscous and putrid. It was an absence of color and an absence of space, an aggressive burning emptiness swallowing him alive.

He screamed and screamed and his voice came back close and wet and dead.

The blackness rose to his knees, grinding his bones in their joints; it moved up his thighs like too-tight stockings rolled incrementally up, and Heap's bowels opened of their own accord, and he felt his genitals pressed, slowly, back up into his body cavity; he felt his abdomen cinched and his ribs snapped and his windpipe collapsing and his innards forced up into his neck, and he ceased to scream because he could no longer draw breath.

In the wall of mud, two slits yawned, a pair of cherry-red holes at eye level.

Studying him. As he had once studied his own prey.

Heap could not speak, but he could move his lips.

He mouthed, "No."

The answer came: a weary sigh.

Muddy fingers closed around him and squeezed.

As Heap's skull popped free of its spinal moorings, millions of neurons made their final salvo, and he experienced several sensations at once.

There was, of course, pain, and beyond that, the agony of insight. His was a death without benefit of ignorance, for he understood that he understood nothing, that his sins had not gone unnoticed, and that something unspeakable waited for him on the other side.

Finally there were the fugitive images that imprinted themselves on his fizzling, fading brain as his gape-mouthed head spun in the air: a night sky flocked with gentle clouds; the saffron glow of the lamps along the riverbank; the door to the synagogue garret, flapping open in the breeze.

CHAPTER TWO

The brunette puzzled Jacob.

First off, his memory of last night—a stunted memory, admittedly—featured a blonde. Now, in the light of morning, sitting at his kitchenette table, she was clearly dark-haired.

Second, while he could recall some frantic groping in a sticky vinyl booth, he was pretty sure he had gone home alone. And if he hadn't, he couldn't remember it, and that was a bad sign, a sign that the time had come to cut back.

Third, she was museum-quality gorgeous. As a rule he gravitated more toward average. It went beyond low standards: all that need and vulnerability and mutual comfort could turn the act more than physical. Two people agreeing to make the world a kinder place.

Looking at her, so far above his pay grade, he decided he could make an exception.

The fourth thing was that she was wearing his *tallis*.

The fifth thing was that she wasn't wearing anything else.

He smelled fresh coffee.

He said, "I'm sorry I don't know your name."

She placed a hand on her throat. "I'm wounded."

"Please try to be forgiving. I can't remember much."

"There isn't much to remember. You were absolutely coherent and then you put your head down and it was lights-out."

"Sounds about right," he said.

He slid past her to fetch down a pair of handmade mugs, along with a lidded jar.

"Those're pretty," she said.

"Thanks. Milk? Sugar?"

"Nothing for me, thanks. You go on ahead."

He put the jar and one mug back, pouring himself a half cup, sipping it black. "Let's try this again. I'm Jacob."

"I know," she said. The *tallis* slipped a few inches, exposing smooth shoulder, delicate collarbone, a side swell of breast. She didn't put it back. "You can call me Mai. With an *i*."

"Top of the morning to you, Mai."

"Likewise, Jacob Lev."

Jacob eyed the prayer shawl. He hadn't taken it out in years, let alone put it on. At one point in his life, the idea of covering a nude body with it would have smacked of sacrilege. Now it was just a sheet of wool.

All the same, he found her choice of covering profoundly weird. He kept the *tallis* in the bottom drawer of his bureau, along with his disused *tefillin* and a retired corps of sweaters, acquired in Boston and never shown the light of an L.A. day. If she'd wanted to borrow clothes, she would've had to dig through a host of better options first.

He said, "Remind me how we got here?"

"In your car." She pointed to his wallet and keys on the counter. "I drove."

"Wise," he said. He finished his coffee, poured another half cup. "Are you a cop?"

"Me? No. Why?"

"Two types of people at 187. Cops and cop groupies."

"Jacob Lev, your manners." Her eyes brightened: an iridescent brown, shot through with green. "I'm just a nice young lady who came down for some fun."

"Down from?"

"Up," she said. "That's where you come down from."

He sat opposite her, careful not to get too close. No telling what this one was about.

"How'd you get me into the car?" he asked.

"Interestingly, you were able to walk on your own and follow my instructions. It was strange. Like having my own personal robot, or an automaton. Is that how you always are?"

"How's that?"

"Obedient."

"Not the word that springs to mind."

"I thought not. I enjoyed it while it lasted, though. A nice change for me. Actually, I had a selfish motivation. I was stranded. My friend—she *is* a cop groupie—she left with some meathead. In *her* car. So now I've spent three hours chatting you up, I've got no ride, the place is closing, and I don't want to give anyone any ideas. Nor do I relish forking over money for a cab." Her smile brought her into brilliant focus. "Abracadabra, here I am."

She'd chatted him up? "Here we are."

Long languid fingers stroked the soft white wool of the *tallis*. "I'm sorry," she said. "I got cold in the middle of the night."

"You could've put on some clothes," he said, and then he thought: *moron*, because that was the last thing he wanted her to do.

She rubbed the braided fringes against her cheek. "It feels old," she said.

"It belonged to my grandfather. His grandfather, if you believe family stories."

"I do," she said. "Of course I do. What else do we have, besides our stories?"

She stood up and removed the *tallis*, exposing her body, a masterwork, shining and limber as satin.

Jacob instinctively averted his eyes. He wished like hell he could remember what had happened—any part of it. It would provide fuel for fantasies for months on end. The ease with which she stripped bare felt somehow less seductive than childlike. She sure enough didn't appear ashamed to show herself; why should he be ashamed to look? He might as well take her in while he had the chance.

He watched her reduce the *tallis* to the size of a placemat with three precise folds. She squared it over a chairback, kissing her fingertips when she was done—a Hebrew school habit.

"Jewish," he said.

Her eyes took on more green. "Just another *shiksa*."

"*Shiksas* don't call themselves *shiksas*," he said.

She regarded his straining boxer shorts with amusement. "Have you brushed your teeth?"

"First thing I do when I wake up."

"What's the second?"

"Pee."

"What's the third?"

"I guess that's up to you," he said.

"Did you wash?"

"My face."

"Hands?"

The question threw him. "I will if you want."

She stretched lazily, elongating her form, unbridled perfection.

"You're a nice-looking man, Jacob Lev. Go take a shower."

He was under the spray before it had warmed, vigorously scrubbing pebbled skin, emerging rosy and alert and ready.

She wasn't in the bedroom.

Not in the kitchen, either.

Two-room apartment, you don't need a search party.

His *tallis* was gone, too.

A klepto with a fetish for religious paraphernalia?

He should have known. Girl like that, something had to be off. The laws of the universe, the balance of justice, demanded it.

His head throbbed. He poured more coffee and was reaching into the cabinet for bourbon when he decided that it was, no question, time to cut back. He uncapped the bottle and let it glug into the sink, then returned to the bedroom to check the sweater drawer.

She'd replaced the *tallis*, snugging it neatly between a blue cableknit and the thread-worn velvet *tefillin* bag. As a gesture, it seemed either an act of kindness or a kind of rebuke.

He thought about it for a while, settled on the latter. After all, she'd voted with her feet.

Welcome to the club.

CHAPTER THREE

He was still crouching there, naked and perplexed, when his doorbell rang.

She'd had a change of heart?

Not about to argue.

He hurried over to answer the door, preoccupied with cooking up a witty opening line and hence unprepared for the sight of two huge men in equally huge dark suits.

One golden brown, with a wiry, well-trimmed black mustache.

His companion, squarer and ruddy, with sad cow eyes and long, feminine lashes.

They looked like linebackers gone to seed. Their coats could have doubled as car covers.

They were smiling.

Two huge, friendly dudes, smiling at Jacob while his cock shriveled.

The dark one said, "How's it hanging, Detective Lev."

Jacob said, "One second."

He shut the door. Put on a towel. Came back.

The men hadn't moved. Jacob didn't blame them. Guys their size, it probably took a lot of energy to move. They'd really have to want to go somewhere. Otherwise don't bother. Stay put. Grow moss.

"Paul Schott," the dark one said.

"Mel Subach," the ruddy one said. "We're from Special Projects."

"I'm not familiar," Jacob said.

"You want to see some ID?" Subach asked.

Jacob nodded.

Subach said, "This will entail opening our jackets. And offering you a glimpse of our sidearms. You okay with that?"

"One at a time," Jacob said.

First Subach, then Schott showed a gold badge clipped to an inside pocket. Holsters held standard-issue Glock 17s.

"Good?" Subach said.

Good, as in, did he believe they were cops? He did. The badges were real.

But *good*? He thought of Samuel Beckett's response when a friend commented that it was the kind of day that made one glad to be alive: *I wouldn't go that far.*

Jacob said, "What can I do for you?"

"If you wouldn't mind coming with us," Schott said.

"It's my day off."

"It's important," Schott said.

"Can you be more specific?"

"Unfortunately not," Subach said. "Have you eaten anything? You want maybe grab a muffin or something?"

"Not hungry," Jacob said.

"We're parked down by the corner," Schott said.

"Black Crown Vic," Subach said. "Get your car, follow us."

"Wear pants," Schott said.

THE CROWN VIC KEPT a moderate pace and signaled without fail, allowing Jacob to stay close behind in his Honda. His best guess for their destination was Hollywood Division, until recently his home base. A northward turn on Vine scuttled that theory, though, and as they headed toward Los Feliz, he fiddled with rising unease.

Seven years on the job, he was green for Robbery-Homicide, the beneficiary first of a departmental memo prioritizing four-year college grads, and second of a plum spot vacated by a veteran D keeling over after three decades of three packs a day.

That he had performed admirably—his clearance rate was consistently near the top of the department—could not erase those two facts from his captain's mind. For reasons not entirely clear to Jacob, Teddy Mendoza had a king-sized hard-on for him, and a few months prior, he'd called Jacob into his office and waved a manila file at him.

"I read your Follow-Up, Lev. 'Frangible'? The fuck are you talking about?"

"It means 'fragile,' sir."

"I know what it means. I have a master's degree. Which I believe is more than you can claim."

"Yes, sir."

"You know what my master's is in? Don't look at the wall."

"That would be communications, sir."

"Very good. You know what you learn to do in communications?"

"Communicate, sir."

"Bull's-fucking-eye. You mean 'fragile,' write 'fragile.'"

"Yes, sir."

"They didn't teach you that at Harvard?"

"I must've missed that class, sir."

"I guess they don't get to that till sophomore year."

"I wouldn't know, sir."

"Refresh my memory: how come you didn't finish Harvard, Harvard?"

"I lacked willpower, sir."

"That's the kind of smart-ass answer you give someone when you want to shut them up. Is that what you want? To shut me up?"

"No, sir."

"Sure you do. I ever tell you I had a cousin who got into Harvard?"

"You've mentioned that in the past, sir."

"Have I?"

"Once or twice."

"Then I must've told you he didn't go."

"Yes, sir."

"Did I say why?"

"It was cost-prohibitive, sir."

"Expensive place, Harvard."

"Yes, sir."

"You had a scholarship, if I recall."

"Yes, sir."

"Lessee . . . An athletic scholarship. You lettered in Ping-Pong."

"No, sir."

"Varsity nut juggling . . . ? No? What kind of scholarship was it, Detective?"

"Merit-based, sir."

"*Merit*-based."

"Yes, sir."

"Merit-based . . . Hunh. I guess my cousin didn't have as much merit as you."

"I wouldn't assume that, sir."

"How come you got it, and he didn't?"

"You'd have to ask the financial aid office, sir."

"Merit-based. See, in my mind, that's a lot worse than not getting a scholarship. In my mind, that's the worst thing, when you have something and you piss it away. No excuse for that. Not even a lack of willpower."

Jacob did not reply.

"Maybe you could finish up online. Like a GED. They got a GED for Harvard? You should look into that."

"I will, sir. Thank you for the suggestion."

"Till that day comes, though, you and I, our diplomas say the same thing. Cal State Northridge."

"That's true, sir."

"No. It isn't. Mine says *master*." Mendoza kicked back in his chair. "So. Feeling burnt out, are we?"

Jacob stiffened. "I don't know why you'd think that, sir."

"I think it cause that's what I heard."

"Can I ask who you heard it from?"

"No, you may not. I also heard you're thinking about putting in for some time off."

Jacob did not reply.

"I'm giving you the opportunity to share your feelings," Mendoza said.

"I'd rather not, sir."

"Work's got you down."

Jacob shrugged. "It's a stressful job."

"Indeed it is, Detective. I got a whole bunch of cops out there who feel the same way. I don't hear any of them asking for time off. It's almost like you think you're special."

"I don't think that, sir."

"Sure you do."

"Okay, sir."

"See? That's it. Right there. That's *exactly* the kind of tone I'm talking about."

"I'm not sure I understand, sir."

"*And again.* 'Not sure I gah gah gah gah gah.' How old are you, Lev?"

"Thirty-one, sir."

"You know what you sound like? You sound like my son. My son is sixteen. You know what a sixteen-year-old boy is? Basically, he's an asshole. An arrogant, entitled, snotty little asshole."

"I appreciate that, sir."

Mendoza reached for his phone. "You want time off, you got it. You're being transferred."

"Transferred where?"

"I haven't decided. Someplace with cubicles. Fight it if you want."

He didn't fight. A cubicle sounded fine to him.

Strictly speaking, *burnout* wasn't the correct term. The correct term was *major depression*. He'd lost weight. He prowled his apartment, exhausted but unable to sleep. His attention drifted, words dribbling from his mouth, syrupy and foreign.

These were the outward signs. He knew them well, and he knew how to hide them. He drew up a curtain of aloofness. He spoke to no one, because he couldn't be sure how short his fuse was on any given day. He ceased to nourish his few friendships. And in the process he made himself out to be exactly what Mendoza thought he was: a snob.

Not as obvious, and harder to conceal, was the dull sorrow that shook him awake before dawn; that sat beside him at lunch, turning his ramen into an inedible repugnant wormy mass; that chuckled as it tucked him in at night: *Good luck with that.* It revealed the raw injustice of the world and made a mockery of policework. How could he hope to correct a worldly imbalance when he could not get his own mind right? His sadness made him loathsome to himself and to others. It was a sick badge of honor, a family inheritance to be taken out every few years, dusted off, and worn in private, a tattered black ribbon, the needle stuck through naked flesh.

Up ahead, in the Crown Vic, he could see the outlines of the two men. Apes. Heavies, in case things got heavy.

It was all he could do not to wheel right around and go home. Special Projects had to be a euphemism for fates best avoided.

It sounded like what you got when you thought you were special.

Maybe he hadn't vetted them thoroughly enough.

He could send a text, let someone know where he was going. Just in case.

Who?

Renee?

Stacy?

A jittery message to the ex-wives would make their respective days. *Mr. Sunshine.*

Renee's title for him, imbued with nuclear scorn. Stacy had adopted it, too, after he'd made the mistake of telling Wife Number Two about Wife Number One's nagging and Wife Two came to empathize with "the crap you put her through."

Everything turned to shit in the end.

So he was bound for someplace unpleasant. What else was new.

Determined beyond all reason to enjoy the ride, he eased back in his seat, nudged his mind toward Mai. He put her in street clothes, then removed them, piece by piece. That body, injection-molded, freakishly proportional. He was about to rip the *tallis* off when the Crown Vic made a sharp turn and Jacob swerved after it, hitting a pothole.

The sign said ODYSSEY AVE, an ambitious name for a grimy, two-block afterthought. Wholesale toy dealers, import-exports with Chinese signage, a shuttered "Dance Studio" that looked as if no feet, agile or otherwise, had crossed its threshold in ages.

The Crown Vic pulled over outside a set of rolling steel doors. A smaller glass door was inscribed 3636. A man in the dress of LAPD brass stood on the sidewalk, shading his eyes. Like Subach and Schott, he cut an imposing figure—towering, gaunt, pallid, with two frothy white tufts over his ears, suggestive of wings. He wore ash-gray pants, a luminous white shirt, a service firearm in a lightweight mesh holster. As he approached the Honda and bent to open Jacob's door, the gold badge around his neck swung forward, clicking against the window, COMMANDER in blue enamel.

"Detective Lev," the man said. "Mike Mallick."

Jacob got out and shook his hand, feeling like a different species. He was six feet tall, but Mallick was six-six, easy.

Maybe Special Projects was where they put the freak shows.

In which case, he'd fit right in.

The Crown Vic honked once and drove off.

"Come on in, out of the sun," Mallick said, and he glided into number 3636.

CHAPTER FOUR

Mike Mallick said, "Lev, would you say times are good or bad?"

"I'd say that depends, sir."

"On what?"

"Individual experience."

"Come on, now. You know better than that. For us, the creatures that we are, times are always bad."

"Yes, sir."

"How's life in Valley Traffic?"

"Can't complain."

"Sure you can. Basic human right."

The room was, or had once been, a storage garage. Concrete walls breathed acrid, nose-pinching mold. It was icy, cavelike, windowless save the glass door, free of furniture but for a crooked halogen lamp turned a quarter of the way up, its cord snaking off unseen.

"What're you working on?" Mallick asked.

"Fifty-year citywide data analysis," Jacob said. "Car versus pedestrian accidents."

"Sounds stimulating."

"Without a doubt, sir. It's a regular diamond mine."

"My understanding is you needed a break from Homicide."

This again? "As I told Captain Mendoza, I was speaking out of frustration. Sir."

"What's his beef with you? You steal his lunch or something?"

"I like to think of Captain Mendoza's style as a form of tough love, sir."

Mallick smiled. "Spoken like a true diplomat. Anyhow, you don't have to justify yourself to me. I get it. It's natural."

Jacob wondered if he'd been picked for some sort of experimental psychobabbly program; a puppet to trot out for the press, help dispel LAPD's well-earned reputation as an orgy of paramilitary machismo. *And we gave him a bag of kittens, too!* "Yes, sir."

"I hope you don't plan on making a career of it," Mallick said. "Traffic."

"Could do worse," Jacob said.

"Actually, you couldn't. Let's not kid ourselves, okay? I talked to your superiors. I know who you are."

"Who am I, sir?"

Mallick sighed. "Turn it off, would you? I'm here to do you a favor. You've been temporarily reassigned."

"Where?"

"Wrong question. Not where, who. You'll report directly to me."

"I'm flattered, sir."

"Don't be. It's got nothing to do with your skills. It's your background I'm interested in."

"Which part of it, sir? I'm a pretty complex guy."

"Think tribal."

Jacob said, "I'm assigned because I'm Jewish."

"Not officially. Officially, the Los Angeles Police Department actively and enthusiastically promotes diversity. In matters of case assignment, we maintain a strict policy of race blindness, gender blindness, ethnicity blindness, religion blindness."

"Reality blindness," Jacob said.

Mallick smiled and offered a scrap of paper.

Jacob read an address with a Hollywood zip code. "What am I going to find there?"

"Homicide. As I said, you'll report to me. This is a sensitive matter."

"The Jewish angle," Jacob said.

"Call it that."

"The vic?"

"I'll let you form your own impressions."

"Can I ask what's so special about Special Projects?"

"Everybody's special," Mallick said. "Or hadn't you heard."

"I have," Jacob said. "I haven't heard of you."

"As a unit, we don't feel it's appropriate for us to get overly involved in the day-to-day," Mallick said. "It enables us to move faster when we're really needed."

"What do I tell Traffic?"

"Let me handle them." Mallick walked to the glass door, held it open. The sun turned his white shirt to a mirror. "Enjoy the view."

JACOB's GPS PUT 446 CASTLE COURT at the northernmost reaches of Hollywood Division—north of the reservoir, west of the Sign—and estimated a travel time of fifteen minutes.

It had lied. Half an hour in, he was still climbing, the temperature gauge on the Honda spasming as he pushed past mid-century boxes, some remodeled, others flaking. Cross streets appeared in thematic spurts, Astra and Andromeda and Ion, followed by Eagle's Point and Falconrock, then Cloudtop and Skylook and Heavencrest. Evidence of multiple real estate developers, or a single one with ADD.

The road writhed and forked, civilization thinning along with the oxygen, until the asphalt petered out and the GPS announced that he'd arrived.

Another lie. No crime scene in sight. Nothing but a continuing ribbon of rocky soil.

He drove on.

"Recalculating," the GPS said.

"Shut up."

Pebbles spat against the undercarriage, and the Honda rattled over buckling earth on rotten shocks. It felt like he was being punched in the kidney by an angry, relentless toddler. He had to take it down to five miles an hour to avoid a blowout. The surrounding land was weedy, desolate, cratered, scrubby; devoid of human structure because there was no place level enough to accommodate any; devoid of life, seemingly, until he spotted a pair of horny squirrels flaunting their sexuality beneath a spiky thicket.

He wasn't the only one to notice: in an instant, a bird was circling overhead. Large one, probably a raptor. Ready to turn the amorous couple into brunch.

The eagle of Eagle's Point? The falcon come down from its Rock?

The bird began to bank, and Jacob craned to watch the drama unfolding, his attention drifting. Then a crest raised him up and slammed him down and he beheld a shallow mountaintop depression, a couple of wind-whipped acres of dirt and stone, bounded to the south and east by a steep, curving canyon.

A stark gray cube cantilevered out over the city like a faceless gargoyle. He'd arrived.

Total travel time: fifty-one minutes.

"Recalculating," the GPS said.

"Eat me," Jacob said, and turned it off.

There was none of the postmortem party that took place when agencies converged. No black-and-whites or unmarkeds, no Coroner's van, no tech crew. Just a necktie of yellow tape fluttering from the doorknob, and a silver Toyota askew on a concrete parking pad. Crypt card on the dash. Woman perched lightly on the hood.

Mid- to late thirties, she was slim, graceful, nice-looking despite—or perhaps because of—a toucan-beak nose. Wide charcoal eyes shone; long, lush hair the same color; skin like freshly ground nutmeg. She wore jeans and sneakers, a white coat over a flame-orange sweater.

THE GOLEM OF HOLLYWOOD

She stood up when he got out of the car, spoke his name when he was three feet away.

"In the flesh," he said.

Her hand was warm and dry.

The badge clipped to her breast pocket said DIVYA V. DAS, M.D., PH.D.

He said it was nice to meet her. She yawed her head skeptically.

"You might want to reserve judgment," she said.

Indian English in her voice: musical, coy.

"Nasty?" he asked.

"When aren't they?" She paused. "You've never seen anything like this, though."

Like the garage on Odyssey Avenue, the house showed signs of long abandonment: water stains, rodent droppings, close air saturated with filth.

The light was nice, at least. He could appreciate that. The architect had exploited it to its utmost with sweeping glass panels, at present crying out for a washing, yet clean enough to offer a 270-degree panorama of hills and sky.

Beneath a veil of smog, the city winked and snickered.

Jacob had long believed that every last square inch of Los Angeles had been fought for and claimed. Not here.

Perfect place to kill someone.

Perfect place to leave a body.

Or, in this case, a head.

It was in the living room, lying on its side, centered precisely on a faded oak floor.

Exactly two feet away—a measuring tape had been left in place—was a greenish-beige mound of what looked like a jumbo portion of spoiled oatmeal.

He looked at Divya Das. She nodded permission, and he came forward slowly, his own head filling with white noise. Some guys could stand around in the aftermath of a massacre, cracking jokes and popping

Cheetos. Jacob had seen plenty of bodies, plenty of body parts, and still, the first sight always knocked him sideways. His underarms felt clammy, and his breathing had grown shallow, and he suppressed his rising gorge. Suppressed the thought that a nice Jewish boy with an Ivy League education (or part of one, anyway) lacked the stomach to work homicide. He reduced the scene to shapes, colors, impressions, questions.

Male, anywhere from thirty to forty-five, ethnicity unclear; dark-haired, beetle-browed, snub-nosed; an inch-long nub of scar tissue on his chin.

Decapitation had taken place where the throat would have met the shoulders. Aside from the vomit, the floorboards were spotless. No blood, no leaking brain matter; no dangling blood vessels, tendons, or muscle meat. As Jacob made a circuit on his haunches, he saw why: the bottom of the neck had been sealed. Rather than ending in a ragged tube, it pinched together, as though pulled tight with a drawstring. The surrounding tissue was smooth and plasticky, bulging with the pressure of fluid and death-bloat, the domain of higher thought turned to a gore-bag.

The rats had left it alone.

He dragged his attention from the head to examine the fetid heap twenty-four inches to the left. It glistened surreally, like a gag item fished from the ninety-nine-cent bin at a novelty shop.

"The green means bile, indicative of rather severe emesis, explosive. I took samples for analysis and I'll scoop up all of it when you're through. But I wanted you to see it as it appeared."

He said, "Explosive vomit in one neat pile."

She nodded. "You'd expect spatter, speckling, clumps."

Jacob stood up and backed away, pulling in air. He looked out the window again.

Sky and hills, for miles.

"Where's the rest of him?"

"Excellent question."

"This is it?"

"Show a little gratitude," she said. "It could be a foot."

"How'd he vomit without a stomach?"

"Another excellent question. Given the lack of spatter, I assume that the actual vomit*ing* took place elsewhere, and that it was brought here, along with the head."

"For decoration," Jacob said.

"Personally, I prefer carpet," she said. "But that's me."

"How'd they close the neck up?"

"Three for three, Detective Lev."

"So I didn't miss any tiny stitches."

"Not that I can see. I'll want a better look at it, of course."

"Blood?"

"Only what you see."

"I don't see any," he said.

She shook her head.

"No drips leading from the door."

"No."

"Nothing outside."

She shook her head again.

"It happened somewhere else," he said.

"I would call that a reasonable conclusion."

He nodded. Looked again at the head. He wished it would shut its eyes and close its mouth. "How long's he been here?"

"Hours, not days. I arrived at one-fifty a.m. A uniform handed it off to me and was quick to excuse himself."

"Did you get his name?"

"Chris. Something with an *H*. Hammett."

"Did he say who called it in?"

She shook her head. "They don't tell me that."

"And who else has been by since?"

"Just me."

Jacob wasn't a stickler for procedure, but this was rapidly going from weird to troubling.

He checked his watch: it was close to ten. Divya Das looked trim and bright-eyed. She certainly didn't look like a woman who'd been toiling solo over a crime scene for eight hours.

He noticed that she was on the tall side, as well.

"Let me guess," he said. "You're Special Projects."

"I'm whatever the Commander needs me to be," she said.

"That's nice of you," he said.

"I try," she said.

"They really want to keep this quiet, don't they?" he said.

"Yes, Jacob. They really do."

"Mallick said I'm here because of my background," he said. "What's Jewish about this?"

She said, "In here."

The kitchen dated from the fifties. Functionless, no appliances, cheap frames for the cabinets, counters cut from the same budget wood, warped and splintering at the edges. The suggestion of water damage, but no smell of mold. To the contrary: the room felt bone-dry.

In the center of the longest counter was a burn mark.

Black shapes, etched in charcoal.

$$\text{צֶדֶק}$$

Divya Das said, "This means something to you."

A statement, not a question.

He said, *"Tzedek."*

"Meaning."

"Meaning," he said, "'justice.'"

CHAPTER FIVE

Not having planned to spend his day off this way, Jacob resorted to using his cell phone to photograph the scene.

"I took my own before you arrived," Divya Das said. "I'm happy to share if yours don't come out."

"Appreciate it."

He photographed the head and the vomit and the lettering in the kitchen. The house's isolation had made it seem larger from the outside; aside from the kitchen and the living space, there was a medium-sized bedroom, an adjoining bathroom with a composting toilet, and a small studio with a shelving unit and a crude wooden desk jutting from the wall, picture window overlooking the eastern slope.

"Anything else?" she asked.

"No, go for it."

She went to her car and came back with what looked like two over-sized vinyl bowling bags, one teenybopper pink and the other lime green, as though she'd raided wardrobe at Nickelodeon. She donned gloves, carefully placing the head inside a plastic bag, double-wrapping it, and transferring the bundle to the pink bag. She scooped the vomit into a snap-top container using a plastic spatula. Stomach juice had burned a matte amoeboid patch in the varnish. She nudged loose the few dried flecks using a smaller, thin-bladed spatula, and placed the lot of it into the green bag.

"Remind me never to have pancakes at your place," he said.

"Your loss," she said.

Swabbing the remaining stain with a clear liquid, she transferred the green-stained cotton into an evidence bag.

A few more swabs produced clean cotton. She collected those as well. They went into the green bowling bag.

"You don't seem very grossed out," Jacob said.

"I hide it well," she said. Then she grinned. "Confession time. The vomit's mine."

He laughed.

"Next," she said.

In the kitchen, she dabbed delicately at the wood-burned message. "Good to go."

"Nothing in the rest of the house?"

"Two rooms," she said. "Bedroom, bathroom, no furniture, no movables. I went over it thoroughly."

He asked about the toilet and she shook her head.

"You're positive," he said.

"Quite," she said. "And to be frank, it's an experience I would prefer not to relive in the retelling."

She hefted her hideous luggage and he walked her to the door.

"It's been somewhat of a pleasure spending the morning with you, Detective Lev. Let's do it again, what say?"

JACOB SEARCHED the surrounding hilltop.

No footprints, tire tracks, or other signs of human intrusion. Hostile soil and bleached stone and ground-hugging, drought-tolerant plants.

He crab-walked around the back end of the house, moving south and east as far as he could before the slope got too severe. He estimated the drop into the canyon at four or five hundred feet. The upper third of that was bare dirt, nothing to grab on to if you fell. You'd build up one hell of a head of steam before you hit bottom, an impenetrable pubic tangle of chaparral and scrub oak. He doubted the hardiest K-9 could manage the descent without breaking a leg. It was terrain custom-made for disposal: set a body tumbling and go to bed that night feeling easy.

He made a note to check a map of the area for other access points. The western edge of Griffith Park, perhaps. Still, he had to figure that any corpse thrown down there would be picked clean long before some unlucky hiker got lost enough to stumble across it.

Justice.

He scrambled back up to the house, the sun baking his hangover, the pain bringing the irregularities of the situation out in bold relief. It wasn't impossible to conceive of a skeleton crew being sent to handle a murder, even an atypical one. LAPD, like every city agency, was understaffed, underfunded, overworked. Someone—Officer Chris Hammett or Divya Das; someone further up the chain—had recognized the etched characters as Hebrew, known enough to get antsy.

Jewish victim?

Muslim victim?

Jewish perp?

He imagined the brass at a hastily assembled meeting, panicked fantasies of urban ethnic war. Scrambling for ass-cover.

Get a Jewish D.

Do we have anyone like that?

Good morning, Yakov Meir ben HaRav Shmuel Zalman.

Bye-bye, protocol.

He had a solid notion of what Special Projects meant now: shut your mouth and follow orders.

If he ever cleared this one, would he be asked to don a yarmulke at the press conference?

Wrap himself in his *tallis* to address the media?

If. Biggest word in the English language.

Inside the house, he examined the letters burnt into the kitchen counter.

Wood-burning stamp, battery-op? Hobbyist killer? Merit badge in decapitation?

Would that kind of thing work to seal the neck? He'd have to ask Divya Das about it.

He thought about her. The accent was attractive.

Then he thought about Mai.

Then he thought: *Get a life.*

He stepped outside and dialed his own extension at Valley Traffic. The phone rang ten times before Marcia, the normally cheerful civilian receptionist, answered warily.

"I just finished packing up your stuff."

Mike Mallick didn't screw around.

"Where are you sending it?" Jacob asked.

"Chen had me leave it in his office. Come get it at your leisure. Why are you calling?"

"I was hoping to touch base with him."

"I wouldn't. He's less than thrilled with you. He seems to think this is a habit of yours."

"What is."

"Bailing."

"It wasn't my choice," he said.

"Hey, I don't care. I mean, I *care.* You used to brighten my day, Lev."

"You'd be the first to say so," he said.

Marcia laughed. "Where are you headed?"

"Caught a case."

"What kind?"

"Homicide."

"*Re*-ally. I thought you were finished with that."

"You know how it goes."

"I don't. Anthony's been trying to move from Central Burglary to Van Nuys Homicide for a year and a half so he doesn't have to commute like a maniac. No go. Total freeze. Tell me how you swung it and I'll be your best friend."

For a moment he considered asking if her husband was circumcised. With a name like Sangiovanni, though, it was probably a moot point. "Not my choice."

"We didn't bore you enough with our puny little vehicular mishaps?"

"I miss them already," he said.

"Then I'll expect to see you back here as soon as you're done."

"Your mouth to God's ears," he said.

He did another outdoor search, taking his time, finding nothing.

Overhead movement against the two o'clock sun caught his attention. The bird was back, circling to Jacob's south, descending gradually.

Do your thing. Show me what you're after.

As if responding, it swooped. Flattened its descent, speeding diagonally.

Aiming directly at Jacob.

When it was about forty feet above the ground, it pulled up and began turning loops. Big and black and shiny—not a raptor. A raven? He squinted, unable to get a bead on it. It was moving fast and the sun was strong. Not a raven, either: the wings were too stubby, and the body oddly flat.

For nearly a minute it traced haloes far above him. He waited for it to touch down. Instead it shot off into the eastern sky, over the deep canyons. He tried to follow its trajectory. No cloud cover, nowhere to hide. Even so, it vanished.

CHAPTER SIX

The Crown Vic was parked outside his building, Subach and Schott in the front seat. Jacob nodded to them as he eased into the carport, and they met him at the door to his apartment, each man carrying a cardboard box.

"Merry Christmas," Schott said. "Can we come in?"

They set the boxes down in the living room and—without obtaining consent or announcing their intentions—began rearranging the furniture.

"Feel free," Jacob said. "Really, don't hold back."

"I do feel free," Schott said. "It's the defining feature of humankind."

"That and the capacity for speech," Subach said. He lifted Jacob's coffee table with one paw. "Otherwise we're no better'n a buncha animals."

They disconnected the television and DVR, stacking the media console atop the couch, which they had shoved into the corner. That left a low bookcase, its shelves home to a collection of wooden-handled tools, oiled and polished. Wire brushes, scrapers, styluses, knives, loop-end trimmers.

Jacob transferred them, two by two, to his bureau. Schott bent to admire them.

"Nice. You a woodworker?"

"My mother's," Jacob said.

"She's a woodworker?"

"Was. A sculptor," Jacob said.

"Talented family," Schott said.

Subach appeared, carrying the denuded bookcase. "Where do you want this?"

"Where it was," Jacob said.

"What's your second choice?"

Jacob waved vaguely in the direction of his closet.

While Schott returned to the car for another box, Subach pried open a flat-packed pressboard desk. He settled down cross-legged in the living room and began laying the pieces out, rotating the diagrammed instructions this way and that, shaking his head.

"Fuckin Swedes, man," he said.

Jacob went to the kitchen to make coffee.

An hour later, they were done.

A swivel chair. A brand-new computer, a blue pleather three-ring binder leaning against it. A compact digital camera and a smartphone. A compact multifunction printer, tucked against the wall, on the floor. A wireless router and a humming battery pack.

"Welcome to your new office," Schott said.

"Mission Control," Subach said, "J. Lev Division. Hope it works for you."

"I was thinking I could use a new look," Jacob said.

"Sorry about the TV," Subach said.

"It's better," Schott said. "No distractions."

Subach indicated the router. "Secure satellite. The phone, too."

"You won't be needing your old cell," Schott said.

"What about personal calls?" Jacob asked.

"We'll reroute them to the new one," Schott said.

"All the numbers you'll need are preprogrammed," Subach said.

"Does that include pizza?" Jacob asked.

Schott handed him an unsealed envelope. Jacob took out a credit card, pure white plastic, orange Discover logo, embossed with his name.

"Operational expenses," Subach said.

"Does that include pizza?"

The men did not reply.

"Seriously," Jacob said. "What the fuck is this?"

"Commander Mallick thought you'd be better off working from home," Schott said.

"How thoughtful."

Subach made a pained face. "May I remind you, Detective, you let us in of your own free will."

Jacob examined the sat phone. It was a brand he had never heard of. "Should I assume you'll be listening?"

"We won't tell you what to assume," Schott said.

Subach pulled out the desk's keyboard tray, pushed a button. The computer screen glowed darkly. There was a chime, and the desktop popped up, tiny icons displayed in a tight grid: everything from NCIC to police departments in major cities to missing persons databases to ballistics registers.

"Fast, comprehensive, broad reach, no passwords, no permission slips," Schott said.

"You'll like it," Subach said. "It's fun."

"I bet," Jacob said. He looked at the binder.

"Your murder book," Subach said.

"Some things are best kept old school," Schott said.

"Any questions?" Subach asked.

"Yeah," Jacob said. He held up the credit card. "What's the limit?"

"You won't hit it," Subach said.

"I wouldn't be too sure about that," Jacob said. "I eat a lot of pizza."

"Anything else?" Schott asked.

"About thirty thousand," Jacob said.

Subach smiled. "That's good. Questions are good."

———

AFTER THEY'D GONE, Jacob stood there for a moment, wondering if a drink would make it harder or easier for him to accept his new reality.

For most of his adult life, he'd been a high-functioning alcoholic, although sometimes *functioning* was the operative word, and sometimes it was *high*. Since his transfer to Traffic, he hadn't been drinking as much—he hadn't needed to—and it bothered him that he'd blacked out last night.

Now that he was back in Homicide, he supposed he was entitled.

Stop, wagon-driver! I want to get off.

He brewed fresh coffee and got the spare bottle of bourbon from beneath the sink and added an unhealthy slug.

Each sip blunted his headache fractionally, and he began to think of Mai.

It was raining weirdos.

He killed the drink and killed its twin and had a seat at his new desk.

Opening up the browser, he plugged in a query. The computer was indeed responsive.

Commander Michael Mallick had a handsome wife and two handsome daughters.

He was an alumnus of Pepperdine University, class of '72.

The final standings of several amateur golf tournaments suggested that he ought to consider taking up tennis.

File photos had him talking to reporters, announcing the arrest of a local terrorist cell plotting to bomb the office of a state congressman.

So maybe Jacob was after a Jewish terrorist, after all.

The idea embarrassed him. His people. Collective responsibility.

How long did you have to be on your own before they ceased to be your people?

Anyhow, how would Mallick know who the bad guy was?

And if he did know, why hadn't he told Jacob?

Questions are good.

But for a cop, answers were better, and Jacob had the unsettling thought that Mallick preferred to have him spinning his wheels.

A sensitive matter.

Protecting someone?

Maybe the whole thing really was revenge from Mendoza. Make Jacob look dumb, lower his clearance rate, keep him subservient.

He shook his head. He was getting paranoid.

He looked up Officer Chris Hammett in the PD directory. He dialed him on his personal cell. It wouldn't go through. His home phone worked fine, though, and he used it to leave the officer a message—a small act of defiance, little better than a tantrum. They hadn't explicitly forbade him from making calls on the landline, and moreover he assumed that they were listening in, as well.

He searched for *Dr. Divya V. Das.*

A native of Mumbai, a graduate of Madras Medical College. Her Facebook page was set to private. She'd done her doctorate at Columbia University.

The *V* stood for *Vanhishikha.*

He could squander the rest of the day on the Internet, reading about other people, and get no closer to closing his case. Murders weren't solved by technology. They were solved by people, and persistence, and enough caffeine to disable a yeti.

The sat phone's directory listed Michael Mallick, Divya Das, Subach, and Schott.

All the numbers you'll need are preprogrammed.

In other words, no consults allowed. Jacob felt his headache returning.

As far as he could tell, the camera was a normal camera.

He opened the pleather binder.

Blank pages, his job to fill them.

But not empty, not completely. A tooth of paper peeked up from the rear slit pocket.

A check made out to him, written on departmental Special Account, signed by M. Mallick.

Ninety-seven thousand ninety-two dollars.

One year's salary, before taxes.

CHAPTER SEVEN

Badly needing air, he stuffed the Discover card and the sat phone in his pockets and walked the four blocks to the 7-Eleven on Robertson and Airdrome.

Except for a year in Israel, another in Cambridge, and a brief, unsuccessful bid by Stacy to graft him to West Hollywood, Jacob had always lived within the same one-mile radius. Pico-Robertson was the hub of west L.A.'s Orthodox Jewish community. His current home was on the second floor of a dingbat, three blocks from the dingbat he'd lived in after college.

He sometimes felt like a dog tugging on its chain. He never did tug that hard, though; breaking free required energy he didn't have.

In a sense, he was ripe for hush-hush undercover work. He lived an undercover life, walking familiar streets wearing a stranger's face. Sometimes a childhood acquaintance would buttonhole him, wanting to catch up. He'd smile and oblige and move on, knowing what they'd be saying about him at lunch on Saturday.

You'll never guess who I ran into.

He's a what?

He married who?

Divorced?

Twice?

Oh.

We should have him over.

We should fix him up.

Steadily his childhood friends had filled their expected positions of prominence. Doctors, lawyers, dentists, people engaged in ambiguous "finance" activities. They married each other. They took out mortgages. They had robust, adorable children.

For this reason, it didn't bother him that he'd devolved into a cliché: the hard-drinking loner cop. It didn't bother him, because it wasn't *his* cliché.

And even if he avoided the community, he felt comforted that it thrived.

Someone had faith, relieving him of the burden.

More important, he had his father to think of. Sam Lev would never leave, and by extension, neither would Jacob.

A reason for staying, and an excuse.

Their corner of the neighborhood had always been low-rent despite proximity to South Beverly Hills and Beverlywood, with their tony mini-mansions. His grade-school classmates engaged in an arms race over the latest Jordans or Reebok Pumps. Jacob got off-brand back-to-school Velcro specials, once a year, Memorial Day weekend. The Levs didn't own a television until the Gulf War, when Sam bought a crappy black-and-white so they could keep count of the Scud missiles pelting Israel. As soon as the hostilities ended, the set went out on the lawn, for sale. Nobody wanted it. Jacob hauled it out with the trash.

The mere fact that he was an only child made him an outlier. Free-spirited, deeply pious, his parents had met and married relatively late in life, raising Jacob in a kind of intellectual and social bubble, without the large extended family that swaddled his peers. The grandparents and uncles and aunts and cousins who made sure you were never, ever alone.

Jacob was often alone.

Now, pushing through the doors at 7-Eleven, he thought about his TV, disconnected and slumped on the sofa. His father would be thrilled.

The clerk greeted him by name. He did most of his shopping there.
Bachelor's diet.

Bachelor *cop's* diet. He needed to start living better.

He bought two hot dogs and four bottles of Jim Beam.

The clerk, whose name was Henry, shook his head as he scanned the
liquor. "I say this as your friend. Go to Costco."

"Duly noted," Jacob said. He dug out his wallet, started to give Henry
a twenty—then reconsidered and handed him the Discover card.

While he waited for it to ring up, he glanced at the ATM. He had the
check in his wallet, too—he hadn't wanted to leave it at home—and he
smiled to himself, imagining the machine belching smoke and exploding as he tried to deposit a hundred grand at once.

"It's not going through," Henry said.

No limit, my ass. Jacob couldn't pretend to be surprised. It was LAPD.
Of course they'd use some company like Discover. He paid in cash, took
his dinner, and left.

He made this trip five or more times a week, and his pace was carefully calibrated so that he'd finish the hot dogs right as he reached his
building. Two blocks shy, his pocket began to buzz. He crammed the
remaining fourth of the second dog in his mouth and fished the sat
phone out, hoping for Officer Chris Hammett.

His father.

Jacob tried to quickly chew a too-big bite, coughing as he answered.
"Hello?"

"Jacob? Are you all right?"

He swallowed, painfully. "Fine."

"Is this a bad time?"

Jacob pounded his chest. ". . . no."

"I can call back."

"It's fine, Abba. What's up?"

"I wanted to invite you for Shabbos dinner."

"This week?"

"Can you come?"

"Dunno. I might be busy."

"Work?"

Jacob assumed that his lack of observance was a disappointment to his father, for whom working on the Sabbath was inconceivable. It was to Sam Lev's credit that he'd never showed outward disapproval. On the contrary, he expressed a shy but morbid fascination with the terrible things Jacob related.

"Yup," Jacob said.

"It's interesting, I hope?"

"Right now there's nothing much to discuss. I'll let you know as soon as I can."

"About the case?"

"About dinner," Jacob said.

"Ah. Please do. I need to know how much food to get."

"You're not planning on cooking."

"That wouldn't be very hospitable, would it."

Jacob smiled.

Sam said, "I'll ask Nigel to pick up takeout."

Jacob considered that better than having Sam burn his house down, but not by much. His father lived on a tight budget. "I'm asking you to please don't put yourself out."

"I won't until I know you're coming."

"Right. Well, I'll call you if I can make it, okay?"

"Okay. Be well, Jacob. I love you."

Sam was a gentle man but sparing with his affection. To hear him state it plainly took Jacob aback. "You too, Abba."

"Call me."

"I will."

Jacob turned onto his block. The hot dog still felt lodged in his chest, and he was tempted to crack open one of the clinking bottles and wash it down.

A dinged white work van had taken the place of the Crown Vic.

CURTAINS AND BEYOND—DISCOUNT WINDOW TREATMENTS

Midway up the stairs, Jacob changed course. Rather than take the bottles into the apartment, he stashed them in the Honda's passenger-side footwell and drove back toward the murder house.

THE OFFERING

Her older brother says, "You are mine, for I am elder."

Her twin brother says, "You should love me, for you arrived on my heels."

Her older sister says, "You are ungrateful and must humble yourself."

Her twin sister says, "You are willful and must submit."

Her father says, "You remind me of one I once knew. She flew away."

Her mother frowns and says nothing at all.

Of herself, she says, "I am mine and I will do as I please."

ONE YEAR HAS PASSED since Asham's sisters wed. Now the harvest has come again—a great bounty, thanks to Cain's wooden mule—and their father declares that they will bring their offerings soon.

"And then you must choose."

"I choose nothing," Asham says.

Eve sighs.

"It isn't right to be alone," Adam says. "Every creature finds its mate."

"'Its'? Am I an animal?"

Nava, bent over the loom, snorts.

Adam says, "If you won't make a decision, we will allow the Lord to make it for you."

"I thought you and He weren't on speaking terms," Asham says.

Yaffa feeds the fire, clucks her tongue. "Don't be rude."

"Your vanity is a sin," Adam says.

"You say everything's a sin."

"Things cannot go on as they have," Adam says.

"They're grown men," Asham says. She turns to her sisters. "Tell your husbands to stop behaving like children." She picks up the carrying gourd and starts out.

"I'm not done talking to you," Adam says.

"I'll be back later," Asham says.

WHENEVER THEIR FATHER SPEAKS of the garden, his voice droops with sorrow. Knowing nothing of the early days, Asham feels not sadness but wonder that things could be any different than they are. Her greatest pleasure is to walk alone, plucking flowers, grass caressing her bare knees. The land smiles on her. As a girl she would annoy her parents by coming home with her face caked in mud and her hands teeming with bugs and worms and snakes that she has been warned never, ever to touch. They are her companions, the earth's hidden majority, the displaced and the disdained.

Today the valley sings of spring, and she hums in harmony as she tramps through the fields, the gourd swinging by her side, keeping time. She sips air sweet with pollen and savory with solitude.

And why shouldn't she be vain? Not terribly much, but she's not going to pretend she doesn't see how her brothers look at her. And would be lying if she said she didn't find their rivalry flattering, in some perverse way. Though she thinks it would be wicked if that were her only reason for holding out. She knows them. She knows that choosing one will rupture the fragile truce that exists because she has steadfastly refused them both.

What kind of creator creates a world out of balance?

Asham does not share all of Cain's doubts about the Lord's perfection, but neither can she content herself with the simple obedience preached by Abel and their father.

Two by two they exist.

Father and Mother, Cain and Nava, Abel and Yaffa.

And her.

She is the odd number, extraneous, a joke perpetrated by a cruel god.

Runty and irate, she arrived last, moments after Yaffa, in a gush of blood. Their mother speaks of the birth as if she still feels the pain.

In that moment, I understood my punishment.

She does not speak this way of any of her other children, only Asham. Leading Asham to wonder: was the punishment the agony, or her very existence?

TWILIGHT FINDS HER HUGGING her knees beneath the canopy of a carob tree. Against a sky of purple and gold, soot-colored lumps come over the hill.

Abel, returning with the flock.

Asham watches his regal shape grow. Her twin is fine and fair with fluffy golden hair; he looks, in fact, not dissimilar to the animals he tends. Though she has never heard him raise his voice in anger, there is nothing weak about him. She has seen him carry four stragglers at once, digging his fingers into fleece, lifting while they bleated and protested.

Across the meadow, she can hear him clicking his tongue and stamping his crook, urging the sheep homeward.

The dog sprints ahead to scout.

Asham lets out a low whistle, and the animal pricks up its ears. It bounds through the foliage and into her arms, licking her face. She holds it close and puts her finger to her lips.

"I know you're out there."

Asham smiles.

"Both of you," Abel says. "I can hear you."

"No, you can't," she calls.

He laughs deeply.

She releases the dog and it bolts forward to lick its master's hand. Asham crawls out and shows herself. "How did you know it was me?"

"I know you," he says.

"You're out late."

"I could say the same about you."

"I didn't want to go home," she says, hefting the sloshing gourd on her shoulder. It wobbles on a handle made of spun flax—Cain's invention.

"Let me," Abel says, taking the gourd as easily as if it were empty.

The light has left the trees, and the night stirs, prey and predator alike seeking cover. Fireflies flash and extinguish. The flock tightens of its own accord, and the dog barks at any who stray. Abel listens to Asham relate the discoveries of the day, showing him with her hands the size of the iridescent beetle she caught this morning.

"Don't exaggerate," he says.

"I'm not," she says, jostling him.

"You're spilling my water," he says.

"Sorry—your water?" she says.

"Now my leg's all wet," he complains.

"Last I checked, I drew it."

"I'm carrying it."

"I never asked you to," she says.

He clucks his tongue at her. It makes her feel like she's one of his sheep.

She says, "Father says we'll bring the offerings next week."

"It'll be good to give thanks. The Lord has been generous."

Depending on her mood, his piety either charms or irritates her. At present she wants to hit him again, in earnest; he knows as well as she does that Adam has set her a deadline.

They fall silent. Not for the first time, she wishes Abel would be the one to lead the conversation. Talking to him is like floating in a lake.

Talking to Cain is like thrashing in a whirlpool.

"I'm expecting another lamb any day now," Abel says.

"Can I help?" she asks.

"If you'd like."

Asham's sisters are mystified by the satisfaction she takes midwifing the ewes. Nava, particularly averse to manual labor, makes snide comments.

A man in a woman's body. That's you.

The gory frenzy thrills Asham, though, and until her brothers settle their differences, accepting a lamb into her arms is the closest she'll come to motherhood.

Abel says, "I wish you'd make up your mind."

"And if I choose him?"

"Then I hope you'll reconsider."

"Don't be greedy," she says.

"It isn't greedy to love someone," Abel says.

"Yes," she says. "It is. There's nothing greedier."

THE ALTAR IS HIGH atop the Mountain of Consideration, one day's journey from the valley floor.

It is a pilgrimage fraught with disappointment: the closer they draw, the more landmarks they reach, the clearer the memories of previous failures. Cain has often argued that they're wasting good food. They ought to face the fact that they are praying to no one, and that their survival depends solely on their own efforts.

The idea terrifies everyone else, including Nava. Only Asham can see any value in it.

She knows what it is like to rely on herself.

It was in this same spirit that Cain built the wooden mule, in defiance of Adam's warnings. When the crops came up plentiful and fat, Cain hurled the sheaves at his father's feet and crowed.

You are cursed. Not by Heaven, but by your own lack of imagination.

However stern Adam's rebuke, Asham observed that he did not hesitate to eat from Cain's harvest.

The journey began at sunrise; by midday they are trudging along, weak from having fasted. Abel carries his offering on one shoulder and guides Yaffa with his free hand. Cain and Nava lean on carved walking sticks. The wind whips Asham's hair, and she lags behind, breathless with anxiety. If she feels especially jumpy, it's with good reason. With the brothers still at loggerheads, her father has declared that she will be given to the one whose offering draws favor.

She's not sure how seriously to take this threat. He has made similar pronouncements in the past. But the zeal with which he charges up the hill—Eve following him like a shadow—tells her this time will be different.

Cain falls in next to her.

"Cheer up," he murmurs. "What's the worst that can happen? Me. Lucky you. Anyhow," he says, giving her a dig in the ribs, giving her a heretical wink, "I wouldn't worry too much."

She wishes she shared the confidence of his unbelief.

It seems an accepted truth that Cain is the clever one, Abel the handsome one. To her it's never been quite so clear. That mode of thinking—the assertion that if one person is blessed with one talent, the other must have an equal talent; the idea that equity inevitably prevails—grates hard against her experience. It's true that she finds Abel easy to look at. But she can just as easily look away, knowing that she can always come back to him, and find him unchanged.

There is beauty in imperfection.

Beauty in its evolution.

On the surface, her brothers would seem mismatched to their pursuits. Better Abel to preside over the land, Cain to cope with the bloody realities of livestock. But Asham knows better. For the most part, sheep are self-contained. They reproduce themselves. They emerge fully formed. They allow Abel to ply his benevolence from a comfortable distance.

Farming is different. It is hand-to-hand combat, a constant negotiation with an unwilling partner. It is the slaughter of weeds, the massacre of thorns and thistles. It drafts unruly trees and drills them into orderly rows, inducing them to produce fruits that are larger and bigger every season. And it is there, on the line between coaxing and coercion, dreaming and plotting, that Cain thrives.

"Here," he says, handing her his stick. "You look like you could use it."

He leaves it with her and goes ahead to walk beside Nava, glancing back to wink at Asham again. She thinks he is more handsome than anyone will admit. His scaly green eyes ripple like rising grass. His dark brow holds the force of storm clouds that frighten and sustain them all. For better and for worse, he moves her.

EXHAUSTED, THE FAMILY HUDDLES together on their knees. A year's worth of weather has erased the traces of their last offerings, and as Adam raises his hands in supplication, praying that their gifts be accepted with favor, the howling wind drowns him out.

He finishes his prayer, and they rise.

Cain offers first, a bundle of leftover flax. Adam ordered him to bring wheat, but Cain refused, arguing that the crops were his, to be distributed as he pleased. *Grow your own and you can do what you like.*

He places the limp, fibrous mass atop the stone altar. Nava pours out a libation of foul-smelling retting water and they reconvene at a distance, watching the heavens for a sign of forgiveness.

The heavens remain expressionless.

Cain smiles sourly. The silence vindicates him, even as it robs him of a wife.

Abel has brought his finest newborn lamb. Three days old and unsteady on its legs, it could not manage the walk, and he has bound it hand and foot. As he carries it to the altar, it raises its head in search of its mother, wailing miserably when it cannot find her.

Yaffa burrows into Asham's shoulder.

Abel sets the lamb down and leans over it, soothing it, stroking its belly.

Cain says, "Get on with it."

Abel's hand trembles as he raises the slaughtering stone. He glances back at Asham, as if seeking her permission. She looks away and waits for the scream.

It does not come. She looks again. The lamb is squirming. Abel has not moved.

"Son," Adam says.

Abel shakes his head. "I can't."

Eve moans softly.

"Then let's go," Nava says.

"We can't leave the poor thing here," Yaffa says.

"It cannot come down," Adam says. "It is consecrated."

That is precisely the sort of obscure logic that drives Cain mad, and he makes an exasperated noise and strides forth to snatch the stone from Abel's hand.

"Hold it down," he says.

Abel is wan, useless.

Cain turns to the rest of the family, appraising them one by one before addressing Asham.

"Help me."

Her heart punches.

He says, "Do you want to be finished here, or not?"

As though compelled by an outside force, she approaches the altar.

The lamb squeals and kicks and she cradles its hot body.

"Keep it still," Cain says. "I don't want to cut myself."

She grasps the lamb's feet. It bucks wildly. Terror has doubled its strength and she nearly lets go. Cain grabs it.

"Listen," he says. His voice is gentle. "It'll be over in a minute. The tighter you hold him, the better it'll go for both of us. For all of us. Tight. Tighter. Good. Good."

Asham shuts her eyes.

Warmth jets across her arms.

The kicks slow and then cease altogether.

She swallows back vomit.

"It's over."

She opens her eyes. The dripping stone hangs by Cain's side, and he is gazing testily at the mute sky. Abel stares in horror at the lamb's carcass.

Though weak herself, Asham rises, takes him by the hand, and leads him away.

THEY HAVE NOT DESCENDED FAR when the top of the mountain explodes.

The sound splits Asham's skull and the light blinds her and she is cast down and awakes to Yaffa screaming and Eve lying in Adam's arms and Abel cowering and Nava groaning in pain.

Asham's ears ring.

Where is Cain?

Rolling gales of dust pour down the mountain. She hears coughing and the babble of her mother, unhinged. Where is Cain? Asham starts crawling up the hill, calling his name, overwhelmed with relief when at last she spies his compact, muscular shape, erect and visible against a greasy plume of smoke, rising from the blast-scorched stone.

He is staring at the altar.

The smell of charred flesh and singed hair is overpowering.

It begins to rain, cool drops against Asham's upturned face.

"Mercy," Eve says.

Yaffa has crawled over to Nava and is pressing her bleeding arm. Adam falls to his knees to pray.

The rain thickens, lashing loose chunks of the hillside, sending muddy currents sluicing toward the valley.

They are all shocked, but none more so than Abel, who blinks rapidly, rainwater streaming into his open mouth, his golden curls a sodden mass.

"Mercy," Eve says. "Mercy."

Cain hears her. He turns back, blows water from his nostrils. "What does *that* mean?"

He faces the altar again. Asham cannot tell if he is pleased or horrified, who is victor, who vanquished.

DAYS LATER, THE TOP of the mountain continues to chuff smoke, a thin black line twining into the sky. It is still drizzling, the earth still drenched, the judgment a riddle.

Having regained his composure, Abel contends in his smuggest voice that the offering was his and therefore the favor shown to him—a statement that draws whoops of derision from Cain. The storm, Cain insists, was nothing more than a coincidence, and besides, favor was clearly shown to he who carried out the deed.

Bitter words rush in to fill the void.

The inability to interpret a sign would seem to indicate to Asham that it is no sign at all.

Sick of listening to them fight, she reiterates that the choice is hers.

The men, shouting, pay her no mind.

ABSORBED IN HIS LABOR, Cain does not notice her approaching. She reaches the edge of the field where it borders the orchard, and he stands up from behind the wooden mule, grunting, black chest hair flat with sweat.

"Don't sneak up on me like that."

"I wasn't sneaking," she says.

"I couldn't hear you," he says. "Therefore, you were sneaking."

"If you can't hear me, that's your problem."

He laughs, spits. "What brings you all the way out here?"

She regards the wooden mule. Deftly carved, sleekly proportional, the grips grown shiny where Cain rests his hands to steer, it is a marvelous object, turning the earth ten times as fast as Adam can. The real mule yoked to it swishes its tail rhythmically, causing the mosquitos at its rump to scatter and contract.

Sometimes she wonders what her parents' life was like before Cain arrived. More peaceful, surely, but also frustratingly basic.

She would admire him so much more if he did not demand it.

"Hard at work," she says.

"No time to waste. New cycle."

She nods. It has rained on and off for weeks, leaving puddles in the churned earth. The breeze coming through the orchard brings fig and lemon, cloying and cutting.

"I wanted to ask you something," she says.

"All right."

"On the mountain," she says. "You chose me to hold the lamb."

He nods.

"Why."

"Because I knew you could do it."

"And how did you know that?"

"Because," he says, "you're like me."

Asham has no ready answer. She could say *No, I'm not, I'm nothing like you.* She could cite the womb she shared with Abel. She remembers the blood spurting and the twitching of the lamb as it died, and it repels her to know that Cain could see that in her and bring it out.

But she cannot blame him, can she, if it was there all along.

He moves closer to her, an intoxicating mineral reek.

"We could build a whole world together," he says.

"The world already exists."

"A new one."

"You have Nava for that."

He makes an impatient noise. "I want you."

She starts to move away from him, and he grabs her arm.

"I'm begging you," he says. "Please."

"Don't do that," she says. "Don't ever beg."

He flushes red, and his face swells, and he pulls her to him, crushing his lips against hers, his stubble shredding the skin on her chin, his humid chest an animal skin thrown over her. His tongue stabs through her teeth; he would suck the life from her, and she works her hand between their bodies and shoves him back, sending him stumbling into the mud.

"What are you doing?" she says.

"I'm sorry," he says, rising.

"I'm sorry," he says again, and he throws himself atop her.

In an instant he has torn her robes off, and she screams and kicks, and they wallow in the sucking, squelching mud. Stones bite her naked back. She pounds his arms, strains at his chin as if to snap his head off, but he slaps her and shakes her and roars his dominance. He will not be denied; she will be his, he will possess her.

Overhead, dark birds puncture a blazingly clear sky.

She gropes in the mud for a stone, opens a jagged chasm in his forehead that sheets blood into his eyes. He bays and releases her, clutching at his face, and she wriggles free and runs.

She runs, naked, maddeningly slowly, her feet sinking into the mud, her limbs gowned in clay. She clears the edge of the field and breaks through a wooded patch and plunges across another field—fallow, muddy, slowing her further—and more woods and then the pasturelands begin. He's behind her. She can hear his feet slapping the wet ground, and she scrambles, chest burning, up a hillside; she reaches the crest and below sprawls the soft wonderful gentle flock and the frantic spot of the dog and Abel, tall and golden.

She screams for help and Cain tackles her.

Down they tumble, grabbing at each other instinctively, turning over and over, again and again slammed against the ground, their mud-covered bodies picking up leaves and twigs and grass, their noses touching, his eye sockets rimmed with blood, his forehead a bloody valley, blood and mud soaking his forelocks.

At the bottom of the hill they come to a rest, broken and slashed and coughing plant matter. The dog's barks race over the pasture, and a long shadow enfolds Asham.

Abel says, "You will be repaid for your wickedness."

Cain wipes his mouth. The back of his hand comes away red. He spits. "You know nothing."

"I know what I see." Abel tosses down his crook. He kneels, scoops Asham into his arms, and starts to carry her away.

He has taken five steps when the crook splinters on the back of his skull.

The earth here is drier, thirstier, unforgiving as Asham falls and cracks her own head against it. Her eyes cloud and her ears dull and her limbs do not work and her tongue lolls like a slug in her mouth; she can do nothing other than watch them struggle. It shouldn't last long, and it does not. Abel is larger, and stronger, and Cain, brought to his knees, begs for mercy while the sheepdog snaps and snarls.

What will you tell Mother.

Such a brazen ploy. So simple. She would never fall for it. But she knows that Abel will, because he, too, is simple, and she watches, immobile, as his anger melts and he extends a hand to his brother and Cain rises up.

CHAPTER EIGHT

It was late by the time Jacob finished canvassing the neighborhoods below Castle Court.

He started at the bottom of the hill and worked his way up. The type of folks who elected to live thirty-plus minutes from the nearest supermarket were also the type of folks who didn't take kindly to night-time visits. Those who answered were reluctant to open the door, and those who did hadn't seen anything. By general consensus, the murder house was an eyesore, abandoned as long as anyone could remember.

Number 332, the final stop before the road went to dirt, hid behind a high stucco wall bristling with pigeon spikes and brooding CCTV cameras.

Jacob craned through his car window, cajoling the homeowner over the intercom. For ten minutes he sat staring at the gate, a forbidding sheet of rust-finished steel, while she phoned the department to verify his badge number.

A motor ground; the gate shunted aside on recessed tracks. Lowering his brights, he wound up a crushed-stone driveway through tussocks and cacti toward yet another mid-century modern, well maintained, an asymmetric white cuboid forced into the terrain.

She was waiting by the front door in an emerald flannel bathrobe, a woman in her mid-fifties with scowl lines that broadcast across ten feet of darkness. He prepared to be told off.

Instead she introduced herself as Claire Mason, pressed a half-gallon mug of bitter tea on him, and escorted him through a tight, short entry hall into a living room with a buffed concrete floor and forward-sloping windows, like the prow of a spaceship as it plowed over an urban lightscape. Abstract Expressionist art crazed the walls. The furniture had been designed for skinny people with no children.

She batted away his questions with her own: Was she in danger? Should she be on the lookout for anything in particular? Should she call a neighborhood watch meeting? She was the president. She had moved out here to get away from all that.

He said, "Do you happen to know anything about the house up the road? Number 446?"

"What about it?"

"Who lives there?"

"Nobody."

"Do you know who owns it?"

"Why?"

"This is really interesting," he said of the tea, which tasted like it had been brewed from guano. "What is it?"

"Stinging nettle," she said. "It prevents bladder infections. I own a gun. I don't keep it loaded, but listening to you I'm thinking I might have to start."

"I really don't think that'll be necessary."

Eventually he quelled her agitation and steered the conversation around to the security cameras. Through the kitchen—onyx, more cement—to a converted pantry, replete with canned goods and alarm panels and a shortwave radio. A bank of monitors cycled through various exterior angles. The chair cushion showed the two-humped indentation of long, fond hours kept.

"Very impressive," he said.

"I can access it on my phone and iPad, too," she said, settling in.

In her needy preening, he recognized the paradox at the heart of any paranoiac: the validation that persecution provided.

"How long before the footage deletes?" he asked.

"Forty-eight hours."

"Can you give me the road, yesterday, about five p.m. on?"

She brought up a window broken into eight panes, each showing a virtually identical blank strip. She clicked the counter, entered the time, set the playback to 8×, and hit the space bar.

Except for a change from full color to night-vision green, the windows remained static.

It was like the worst art film ever made.

"Can you speed it up a hair?" he asked.

She increased to 16×.

A shape zapped across the screen.

"What was that?" he asked.

"Coyote."

"Are you sure? Can you go back?"

She rolled her eyes, rewound, set playback to 1×.

Sure enough: a shaggy, scrawny animal, slinking along with its tongue out.

"I'm amazed you could tell," he said.

Claire Mason smiled dreamily at the screen. "Practice, practice, practice."

UP AT THE MURDER HOUSE, he sat in the Honda, listening to the tick and clank of the overworked engine as it cooled. Every visit was taking years off its life. Between the Discover card and the advance on his salary, he supposed he could spring for a rental.

Anyone coming here by car would have to pass Claire Mason's cameras. But he hadn't seen tire tracks anywhere on the property, no crushed vegetation.

On foot? Hiking in, circumventing the road, head in a sagging Trader Joe's bag?

A helicopter?

Jetpack?

Magic carpet?

Alakazam!

Oddly, the house looked less bleak than it had during the day, its menace effaced by a wide field of stars. Wind carried the snicks and clicks and hoots of animal life, abundant and invisible, creatures that come out at night.

He took his flashlight from the glove box, but didn't need it to find his way to the front door. He didn't need it inside, either. Moonlight mixed with city glow flooded the open air.

It felt significant to him that the place was both totally isolated and totally exposed.

You'd expect a body dump to be chosen with secrecy in mind. The staging reeked of exhibitionism, though, and those two facts in combination hinted at a desire for a specific audience.

Who owned this place?

Who knew about it?

He checked the sat phone for a missed call from Hammett. Frowned. No reception. These things were supposed to work anywhere.

He walked around, waving the phone, one bar dancing in and out. He managed to pin it down outside the master. He waited for a message icon to appear, but there was nothing.

The air was surprisingly free of death funk, and on the whole, he noticed that he felt less creeped out than he would have thought. Jacob was no mystic, but he did believe that people were drawn toward spaces that reflected their personalities, and that the soul of a residence and the soul inhabiting it grew progressively overlapped over time.

Here, he sensed a kind of serenity, verging on Zen calm. It would be a good place to write, or draw, or sculpt—an atelier in the sky, ideal for the rare artist who could afford it.

Or someone with money, posturing as an artist.

In Jacob's experience, the vast majority of bad guys took the path of least resistance. That was what made them bad guys: an overwhelming need to do whatever they wanted while expending as little energy as possible. Most criminality was a pathological form of laziness.

This guy, though. He had a sense of style. Repulsive, but distinct. Maybe he truly was different, or thought he was. There was a second variety of criminal, less common but flashier. The Rippers, the Ed Geins, the BTKs. They went the extra mile to make the papers. A notable subtype being the Hitlers and the Stalins and the Pol Pots.

Both types were dangerous. The first because they were careless, the second because they were careful.

Jacob wandered into the studio and stood before the east-facing window, thinking about the house he'd grown up in, the corner of the garage taken over by twenty-five-pound boxes of clay, jars of paint and glaze, a small electric kiln, a drying rack hidden behind a drop cloth. The wonky three-legged stool she sat on. No potter's wheel. Bina Lev had worked freehand.

He had a vague notion of a youthful flirtation with the avant-garde. No physical evidence of that period remained, though, and by the time he got old enough to conceive of his mother as an individual with ambitions, hers had imploded. The woman he knew strictly produced ritual objects—goblets for holding the Sabbath wine, menorahs, spice boxes for the *havdalah* ceremony. She hauled them to weekend fairs, sold them on consignment at local Judaica stores. You couldn't exactly call it pragmatic, her choice to forsake art for craft. It wasn't like she made any money. And there was bitter irony for Jacob in learning that these items were now considered collectible in some circles, owing to their scarcity.

The Internet would have served her well. Poor timing.

Poor timing, all around.

Shortly after her funeral, Sam, nearly comatose with grief, decided to put the house up for sale. It was a simple enough matter getting rid of the furniture, but he begged off cleaning out the garage. Jacob stepped in. He was used to feeling like the sole adult.

He bought a roll of contractor bags and went about the business with methodical rage, half-finished candelabra thrown in indiscriminately alongside unopened cases of Amaco Low Fire Lead-Free. He disjointed the drying rack and gave the pieces to his neighbor, who had a working fireplace. A pawnbroker offered him thirty dollars for the kiln, a sum so meager that it brought remorse down on him like a bootheel.

Fifty with the tools.

Jacob said no, thanks, he'd decided to keep those.

He took his thirty bucks and went back to the garage, combing through the bags in search of anything worth salvaging. He'd done an unfortunately thorough job of venting his anger: mostly it was shards and dust.

A few items swathed in newspaper had survived. A couple of coffee mugs. A double-handled cup for washing hands. A *mezuzah*. A lidded jar with strong, thin walls whose exact function he could not determine. He placed them carefully in a duffel bag lined with towels.

One well-padded bundle turned out to be several dozen smaller pieces, individually wrapped. Curious, he pulled away a corner of the paper and was startled by the appearance of a tiny, alien face. He unwrapped the rest of the pieces and discovered more of the same.

He had long assumed that his mother's switch to plates and cups had something to do with Judaism's disapproval of depictions of the human form—an outgrowth of the ban on idolatry.

Or maybe she had given herself an out, on a technicality: certainly, the things in his hands weren't *human* in any conventional sense. Gray, mottled with black and dark green, strongly organic, they shimmered, and their limbs writhed as though to escape.

Bina had invited people to handle her creations. Even the simplest pieces responded to touch.

These appeared to resent it.

Surrounded by junk on the floor of the broiling garage, his hair sticking up, he'd stared at the figurines, wondering if and how he'd misjudged her.

He wrapped them up and put them in the duffel.

He'd borne this sad legacy through two marriages and countless apartments, nailing up the *mezuzah*, putting the washing cup by the kitchen sink, filling the jar with sugar. He took his coffee black, but it gave him something pleasant to offer a lady friend in the morning. They oohed and aahed at his good taste.

The potter's tools he displayed in the bookcase: they were objects of beauty in themselves, their smooth wooden handles glowing from within. He could look at them and be reminded that life was fragile and strange and brief. For some reason, that made him feel good.

The figurines creeped Renee out so badly that he'd moved them to a safe deposit box.

Probably not worth the monthly rental. Anyway, nobody around to protest now, and as he peered down into the pleated canyon, he thought that he ought to go retrieve them.

A black hand smacked the glass.

He crashed backward, Glock up, shouting orders at an empty room.

Silence.

The thing that had made the noise—it was outside, clinging to the window.

Squat, domelike. Black segmented underbelly. Flittering wings tonguing the glass.

He shook his head and laughed at himself. He'd almost put two bullets in a bug. Twenty hours without sleep or proper nutrition could do that to you.

He holstered his gun, left the house, and jogged to the Honda. He reached down and grasped one of the liquor bottles. He took a few sips, leaving himself just shy of impairment, just enough control to get home, drink more, and fall asleep.

THAT NIGHT, he dreamt of an endless garden, lush and dripping. At its crowning center stood Mai. She was naked, her arms open to him. He stretched for her but he could not reach her, and the chasm between them ached, for he understood that on the other side lay a homecoming.

CHAPTER NINE

Up early, wired, Jacob hacked away at the keyboard, nursing a cup of spiked coffee and neglecting an Eggo waffle.

The murder house belonged to a trust, which belonged to another trust, which belonged to a holding company in the Cayman Islands, which belonged to a shell corporation in Dubai, which belonged to another holding company in Singapore, for which he found a number.

He calculated the time difference, debated whether there was any point calling in the middle of the night, decided it was worth a try to see if the number even worked.

A woman answered in accented English, and a tortuous series of questions revealed that he was speaking not to the holding company but to an answering service whose sole reason for being was to divert nosy callers from obtaining information about the holding company. He was in the midst of conjuring his most persuasive self when the sat phone jumped: Officer Chris Hammett.

Jacob hung up on Singapore without saying good-bye.

Hammett sounded young and bewildered. "Sorry I didn't get back to you sooner, Detective. I was kind of—I got held up."

"Not a problem. How're you doing?"

"Honestly?" Hammett exhaled. "Still kind of freaked out."

"I don't blame you. I saw it."

"I mean, seriously. That is some fucked-up shit."

"No kidding. You mind telling me how it went down?"

"All right, well, I got up there about midnight—"

"Before that," Jacob said. "Where were you when the call came in?"

"Down Cahuenga, near Franklin. Dispatch said they got a woman calling in to report something suspicious."

"A woman?"

"That's what they told me."

"What did they say?"

"Just that there was something needed attention at that address."

"Name?"

"Nope. Said get someone to get on up there and check it out. I was closest." Hammett paused. "I'll be straight with you, sir: it took me a while. The signs're for shit and I almost ran off the road. I didn't get there till maybe an hour later."

Jacob's annoyance was tempered by sympathy as he imagined himself trying to find the house for the first time at night. "And when you did?"

"I didn't hear nothing or see anything out of the ordinary. The door was open a couple inches. I poked my head in and shined my light down the hall, and there it was."

"The head."

"Yes, sir." Hammett described his search of the house and his discovery of the letters in the kitchen counter. "I called in and my captain had me send over a picture. I guess he must've kicked it up the chain, cause pretty soon after that, the crypt doctor showed up. She said she'd take it from there."

"Anything else you think might be relevant?"

"No, sir. But—question for you?"

"Go ahead."

"Is this, like, something I need to be concerned about?"

"How do you mean?"

"Yesterday when I came in the station there was some guys waiting to talk to me from some department I never heard of."

"Special Projects," Jacob said.

"That's the one."

"Big guys."

"Like, circus big."

"Mel Subach. Or Paul Schott."

"Actually, it was both of them. Schott did the talking, though. He took me aside and implied that it was in my interests to keep what I'd seen on the DL. That's why it took me a while to get back to you, sir. I didn't want to overreach. I called him up and asked about you and he said go ahead, just after that, pretend it never happened. Don't get me wrong, I can sit on it."

"Thanks," Jacob said. "You've been very helpful."

"Anytime. I hope you get him."

"Your mouth to God's ears," said Jacob.

"Pardon me?"

"Have a nice day, Officer."

JACOB E-MAILED MALLICK to update him, adding that he was having trouble with the credit card he had been issued. He e-mailed 911 dispatch to request a copy of the call, got dressed, and headed down to his car. While backing out, he noticed that the window treatment van hadn't moved since yesterday evening.

BY NINE A.M. he was back at the scene, walking the grounds with a topo map printed off Google. He'd brought his new camera. It had a nice hefty zoom lens, as close as he was going to get to the bottom of the canyon without a pickaxe and crampons and a whole lot of rope and determination.

He went inside the house to rephotograph it, starting with the letters burnt into the kitchen counter.

They were gone.

For a moment, he did not move. Then he turned around, thinking he'd misremembered their location.

The rest of the countertops were clean.

The original photos were on his personal cell—the useless one, back in his apartment. He estimated where the mark had been, bent close to inspect the spot, taking care not to touch it. He couldn't see evidence of sanding or scraping or erasing, not there or anywhere else.

Maybe Divya Das's swab had caused the mark to degrade. But that was only possible if it was superficial, and what he remembered seeing was incised into the surface of the wood. Restoring a perfectly even surface would require replacing the entire countertop.

Message delivered, they'd come back to remove the evidence?

He straightened up, acutely aware of the stillness.

He shut the camera off and put it in his pocket, drew the Glock, crept through the living room, the master, the studio.

Deserted.

Outside to recheck the perimeter.

He was alone.

He fetched his fingerprint kit out of the trunk of the Honda and went back to the kitchen. He snapped a host of photos of the now-pristine countertops, then dusted, coming up blank.

The good news was that if someone had been here doing renovations while he slept, Claire Mason's security system would have caught them. He left the house and drove back down the hill.

"You're back," she squawked through her intercom.

"Couldn't stay away."

The gate motor growled to life.

In daylight he could appreciate the scope of the property. It was an ode to human ingenuity, an oasis of modernity in that barren, prehistoric setting: three-car garage, electric blue pool, desert landscaping, weathered brick paths branching through terrain artificially gentled and tufted. Stark steel I-beam sculpture, patinated to match the front gate. The peaked glass brow of a greenhouse poked up from behind a neat grove of fruit trees. He wondered what she wanted with so much home-grown produce. Given what he knew of her, he could easily figure her for an end-of-the-worlder, preparing for the worst, erecting walls to keep out the ravenous hordes that would inevitably turn up in times of shortage, licking their lips, ready to feast upon the rich.

She met him wearing the same flannel bathrobe, and he suffered through another giganto helping of tea.

"Twice in twelve hours," she said. "How can you tell me I shouldn't be concerned?"

"Due diligence," he said. He gestured to the view. "Lovely place you have here."

"It's a rental," she said.

In the security room she played back the previous night's footage—static, except for the arrival and departure of Jacob's car.

"Is there another way up? Fire road, or something that's not showing up on my map?"

"The area to the north is public land. You get oddballs coming through. Hikers. That's why I have the cameras."

"Right," he said. *That, and cause you're bonkers.*

Having her on duty was like running a twenty-four-hour stakeout: he left his card with her, asking that she contact him if she saw anyone go up the hill.

For the next two hours, he tooled around Griffith Park, failing to find any way to access the canyon. A brief consult with a park ranger confirmed as much. Unless Jacob could convince Special Projects to call in a rappel team, a body down there was staying put for the foreseeable future.

ALL THOSE TRUSTS and blinds and holding companies stank of money. Keywording the Castle Court address pulled up nothing, not even the expected Zillow or other real estate sites. An afternoon at the desk brought Jacob to the home page of a USC professor interested in the social history of the Southern California upper class. The prof had undertaken to scan in decades of Blue Books, getting as far back as 1926 and as far forward as 1973. OCR made the directory searchable.

Jacob found what he needed in the 1941 edition.

The house belonged to a Mr. and Mrs. Herman Pernath. Mister was a principal architect at a firm that bore his name. The couple had two children, Edith, sixteen, and Frederick, fourteen.

The *L.A. Times* archive yielded obituaries for Herman in 1972, his wife two years before that. Daughter Edith Merriman, née Pernath, had died in 2004.

A search for Fred Pernath brought up an Internet Movie Database entry with scores of special effects credits, the sort of Z-grade gorefests Jacob figured didn't get made anymore. But there were titles as recent as three years ago, indicating that Pernath was alive and well, and another search yielded a phone number and an address in Hancock Park.

Jacob called him on the sat phone, explained who he was, and asked if he could find out more about the house on Castle Court.

"What's there to find out?"

"Have you been there recently?"

Pernath's laugh was wooden. "Not since it became mine."

"When was that?"

"What's this regarding, Detective?"

"It's an ongoing investigation," Jacob said. "Who else has access to the house?"

"How was it you found me?"

Jacob didn't like people who answered questions with questions. They reminded him of his grade-school rabbis. "Look, Mr. Pernath—"

"You want to talk to me, you can come here."

"A phone conversation would be fine," Jacob said.

"Not to me," Pernath said, and he hung up.

CHAPTER TEN

Fred Pernath lived on June Street, north of Beverly Boulevard, in a stately Georgian at odds with the Neutra-like stylings of Castle Court. Jacob did detect a certain similarity in the lack of upkeep. Every other home on the block had been landscaped, repainted, reroofed. Pernath's gutters sagged; brown smeared the front lawn.

One look at the man himself went a long way toward ruling him out as a suspect. He was pigeon-chested and emaciated, leaning on a cane whose tip squeaked against the hardwood as he beckoned Jacob in and hobbled off into the gloom.

Like its exterior, the house's overflowing interior stood in contrast to the emptiness of Castle Court. Jacob didn't see any severed heads, but he might well have missed them, lost among the quivering electric sconces, the still lifes in carved gilt frames, the Chinese vases sprouting dusty silk flowers. Ornate, polished furniture impeded easy passage—reverse feng shui—every space remotely horizontal clustered with gewgaws.

Amid the dizzying visual thicket, no family photos.

They went to Pernath's study, wallpapered with ghoulish posters and production stills. Jacob sank into a depleted loveseat, declining with considerable reluctance Pernath's offer of whiskey. He watched enviously as Pernath poured from a crystal decanter and crossed the room to open a built-in cabinet containing cut-glass bowls of nuts and a severed head.

Bloody and ragged and gazing out eyelessly.

Jacob leapt up.

Pernath glanced at him incuriously. He plucked the head by its hair and hurled it at Jacob, who caught it.

Rubber.

"For a cop, you seem a tad high-strung," Pernath said.

He took out two bowls of cashews, setting one in front of Jacob.

"Apologies if they're not at the peak of freshness," Pernath said, folding himself behind a formidable oak desk.

From up close, the head was obviously fake, the paint job meticulously crafted to look correct at a distance of about fifteen feet—Monet meets Grand Guignol.

His heart still tripping, Jacob said, "You do that for all your guests?"

"You're not a guest." Pernath popped a cashew in his mouth. "You might want to get on with it," he said. "I am eighty-four."

Jacob sat down in the loveseat. "Tell me about the house."

Pernath shrugged. "It was my father's. He came from money, owned property all over the city. Houses, factories, raw land. It was a great deal of real estate, and when he died, that made for a great big fight." He sipped whiskey. "The truth is I didn't need the money. But my sister decided she had to have it, so naturally I decided I wouldn't let her."

"She's deceased, your sister."

Pernath cackled. "That's how I won. I had a fifth column: Virginia Slims." He sat back in his chair, which was large and creaky and studded with brass nailheads. In its grip he resembled a dried leaf. "*Technically*, I won. Lawyers gobbled up two-thirds of the pie. I kept the properties that brought in income and sold the rest. Made out like a bandit. The house was part of a larger plot that my father subdivided. He built it. His design."

"He was an architect."

"He was a pig," Pernath said. "But, yes, he did draw. Personally, I've never cared for his work. Bit antiseptic for my liking."

Jacob glanced at a stuffed monkey suspended from the ceiling. "So I gathered."

Pernath chuckled and got up to pour himself another whiskey.

"That house," Jacob said. "It brings in income?"

"Not a cent."

"Then why not sell? Seems to me it's wasting away."

"That's exactly the point. Let it rot. Every time I think about it falling apart, I get a nice fuzzy feeling inside." Pernath stoppered the decanter and hobbled back to his chair, making a detour to reclaim the rubber head, which he cradled in his lap like a shih tzu. "It was supposed to be a haven for him, someplace he could go to dip into the well of creativity. I don't think he so much as lifted a pencil there. He was *creative*, after a fashion, and no doubt he did a lot of *dipping*. Every secretary or office girl he ever hired saw the inside of that place—or the ceiling, anyway, while he bounced on top of them. It's amazing he didn't crush anyone to death. He was a pig, in every sense of the word. He destroyed my mother."

"Why not tear it down, then?"

"Oh, well, I would *never*. It's architecturally *significant* . . ." Pernath finished his second drink in one swallow. "Call it a monument. To adultery."

"You haven't been by since you inherited it."

"Why would I?"

"Who else has access?"

"Everyone. I leave it unlocked. Anyone who wants to come in, that's their problem. The more curses heaped upon that place, the better."

Jacob frowned. That wasn't what he'd wanted to hear.

"What kind of crime are you investigating, Detective? Something ugly, I hope."

"A homicide."

Pernath's throat clicked. "Ugly as it comes. Shame. Whodunnit?"

"If I knew, I wouldn't be talking to you."

"Who died?"

"I don't know that, either."

"What do you know, Detective?"

"Not much."

"That's the spirit," Pernath said. He tilted his glass. "Embrace ignorance."

Jacob, thinking of the missing photos, said, "You have other family in town?"

"My ex-wife's remarried, although I hesitate to call her family. She lives in Laguna. My son's in Santa Monica. My daughter's in Paris."

"Do you see them often?"

"Not if I can help it," Pernath said.

"So it's just you," Jacob said.

"Me," Pernath said, stroking the fake head, "and Herman."

PERNATH'S CHILDREN HAD INHERITED their grandfather's preference for clean lines. Greta ran a gallery in the Marais that sold stripped-down works rendered edgy through the use of materials like chewed gum and donkey urine. Richard was an architect whose work consisted of steel-and-glass skeletons. Jacob clicked through his portfolio, reflecting on the generational pendulum, everyone rising up to slaughter their fathers' tastes.

In any event, both seemed successful in their own right, busy people with busy lives.

Dead end.

A database search for similar crimes generated a short list of beheadings but nothing that matched his: no sealed neck, no burn marks (disappearing or otherwise), no Hebrew. Usually the bad guy was mentally ill and had been caught quickly. One offender had staked the head of his elderly aunt in the backyard and danced around it, singing "We Are the Champions."

The most rational beheader—so to speak—was a Pakistani in Queens who had strangled and decapitated his teenage daughter for texting racy photos to a classmate.

Religious fervor brought out the best in people.

Justice.

Jacob perused the files on Jewish terror groups in the United States.

Broadened his parameters to include any example of Hebrew at the scene of a homicide.

Broadened them to include any burns.

Broadened them to include the word *justice.*

Nada.

He sat back, stomach growling. It was nine forty-five p.m. His untouched breakfast waffle sat on a cold plate beside the computer, its surface glazed with syrup and caulked with congealed butter. He scraped it into the kitchen can. He knew the fridge was bare, but he checked it for form's sake before walking down to 7-Eleven to buy a couple of hot dogs.

JACOB DOUBTED HIS PERP would risk a second revisit of the scene, especially now that the message had been erased. But he had no fancy evening plans, and it seemed worth a few hours of his time. He drove up to the hills and eased the Honda onto the shoulder fifty yards past Claire Mason's driveway. He uncapped a beer, racked the seat back, and waited for good luck to strike.

Shortly before three, he started awake, whanging his elbow against the steering wheel. His back was stiff, his mouth dry. He had a full bladder and a raging erection.

Crickets tittered at him as he got out to take a piss at the side of the road. He'd been dreaming of Mai, naked in the garden, closer to her yet still unable to touch her. While he waited for his penis to relinquish her image, and soften up, he considered the meaning of the distance between them. His missed opportunity, perhaps. But that very incompleteness, the tension it created, had a pleasurable aspect to it. He thought of her playful ease with her own body, the way she hid nothing from him, making the erotic innocent.

He could use some of that in his life. His work over the past seven years had forged a link in his mind between sex and violence. He didn't like it, but there it was. If a woman like Mai wanted to come along and redeem him, he had no objections.

At the same time, he knew exactly the kind of chick who hung out at 187.

You're a nice-looking man, Jacob Lev.

He wondered if she'd ever go back there.

One way to find out.

CHAPTER ELEVEN

The owners of 187 were a pair of ex-cops who knew what cops wanted: strong booze, loud music, and a kitchen that stayed open until four-thirty a.m. to accommodate guys coming off the mid-p.m. shift, at two forty-five. For maximum grit, they'd rented a subdivided warehouse, sandwiched between a sandblasting company and an auto body shop on Blackwelder Street, an industrial zone south of the 10.

The door was unmarked, the handle a welded tire iron. He hauled it open and bass thundered out, rattling chain-link and razor wire.

The nearest residences were two blocks east, across Fairfax, which might or might not put them beyond the sonic blast zone.

Good luck getting anyone to serve a noise complaint.

The floor thronged with law enforcement and those who loved and lusted for them. Female cops seldom bothered, making 187 a popular choice for civilian women slightly past expiration date.

Jacob paused near the entrance, scanning for Mai.

She'd stand out in this crowd.

Plenty of cleavage. Plenty of tramp stamps rising above low-riding waistbands as the bearers bent to aim for the corner pocket, to whisper, to lick an earlobe.

No Mai.

It was tough for him to imagine her here. She must've felt like raw rib eye. Tougher still to imagine her finding him, chatting him up.

Taking him home? That was impossible to imagine.

Another dead end. Time to go.

But the PA was blasting Sublime, and he felt too keyed up to sleep.

He fought his way to the bar, three-deep with boozers and flirters. An hour before closing, desperation reigned, couplings forming and imploding like some frantic game of human Tetris.

Behind the bar, Victor was already pouring him a double bourbon. Loyalty born of bad habits. Jacob pictured his own funeral: a tearful crowd of bartenders and convenience store clerks.

Victor set his drink down and turned to collect another order.

"Yo," Jacob yelled, waving him back. "You remember a girl was in here couple nights ago?"

Victor gave him a look like *they made you a detective?*

"She left with me," Jacob said.

Victor laughed. "You're not narrowing it down none."

"She came with a friend. Hot as hell, if that helps."

"We don't allow that kind," Victor said. He tapped the rim of Jacob's glass. "Four more, I bet you find someone who looks just like her."

He hustled off to confront demands.

Jacob sloshed the bourbon, watching it cling to the side of the glass, feeling no desire whatever to have a drink.

But high-functioning alcoholism demanded dedication.

He tipped the liquor back, tossed a twenty on the bar, turned to go, ran smack into a pillowy chest.

His usual midweek prize, soft around the edges, hard in the face; bleached, un-picky, and deep into her cups.

She pouted. "You spilled my drink."

He sighed and signaled to Victor.

HE WALKED HER TO HER CAR, pointed out his own, and told her to follow, adding, "Drive carefully."

She snickered. "Who's gonna pull me over?"

In his kitchen, he stood with his pants around his ankles, a drawer handle poking his bare ass, a bottle of Beam in hand to swig from whenever his enthusiasm waned.

She paused from going down on him to shoot him a stern look. "Don't pass out on me."

"Yes, ma'am."

"No whiskey dick, either. Hang on, I need to pee."

Her knees cracked as she stood up and left the room.

Jesus Christ, he thought.

He heard the stream. Loud. She'd left the bathroom door ajar.

"Very classy," she yelled.

"Can you get a condom, please? Bottom drawer left."

The toilet flushed, the sink ran, and she reappeared, sans jeans, shirt open, flapping the condom like a sugar packet.

"You have roaches," she said.

Though he knew it wasn't fair, he couldn't help but compare her to Mai.

Maybe she was what he needed to help him forget.

Uncomplicated.

He sat down on a kitchen chair, rolled the condom on, gave his thigh a slap.

"At your service," he said.

She stumbled over and positioned herself over him, her breasts swinging in his face. She was about to lower herself when she paused and kicked at something on the floor.

"Uch. You need Raid." She kicked again, let out an annoyed yelp. "Fuck."

"What."

"Fucking thing bit me."

"What?"

"Whatever," she said, plopping down on his lap.

She gasped.

Another satisfied customer.

He took hold of the flesh at her hips and started to swivel her back and forth atop him and then he realized that she was gasping still, and it didn't sound like she was having any fun.

He looked up and saw her eyes rolled back into her head, her head lolling, chin to chest, drooling.

This was a first for him. He'd been known to pass out mid-act but he'd never been the other party. Feeling slighted, he gave her a shake. "Hey."

She slumped forward against him, her body seizing violently.

He swore and tried to hold her up and she pitched backward off his lap onto the linoleum, bashing her head against the fridge door and landing with her legs spread.

He dropped to his knees, ready to do CPR.

She was blinking up at him, white with terror. "What's happening."

"You tell me," he said.

She stared down at her own genitals; at his; at his face.

She scrambled from the kitchen.

He followed her into the bathroom, watched her hop into her clothes. "Are you sure you're all right? You hit your head."

"I'm fine," she said.

As she raised her foot to tug on her heel, he noticed a red welt on her left instep. "Are you allergic to something?"

She didn't answer.

Then she said, "It felt like you were stabbing me."

He said, "I . . ."

He stopped. He didn't know whether to apologize, or . . . what. He felt he should make an effort to get her to stay, at least until she was good to drive. He started to say so and she waved him off, grabbing her purse and rushing out into the milky morning.

From the window he watched, unnerved, as she sped away.

He dressed and got down on hands and knees to hunt for roaches.

He couldn't find any, not there or in the bathroom.

All the same, he tied up the trash bag containing his old waffle and took it out to the thirty-three-gallon cans at the side of the building.

He walked to 7-Eleven, bought one can of bug spray and one box of roach motels.

Thinking that the bug bite theory didn't have much going for it.

Her eyes white. Her breath whistling.

It felt like you were stabbing me.

Maybe she had a condition. Dryness. After all, she'd gone with Extra Lubricated.

A funny thought popped into his head. The Hebrew word for penis: *zayin*.

Also the seventh letter of the Hebrew alphabet: ז.

Also the word for weapon.

The shape had it. A blade or an axe or a mace.

His was the dick of death.

A schlongsword.

Excockabur.

He started to laugh. He couldn't help himself.

He went around setting out the motels, spraying poison until the apartment was well and truly fogged. He threw open the windows and went to get cleaned up.

CHAPTER TWELVE

The sat phone was dinging as he stepped from the shower, a voicemail from his father, a text from Divya Das: *ring me*.

Today was Friday. He hadn't given Sam an answer about dinner tonight. "Hey, Abba."

"Did you get my message?"

"I'm swamped. Can we reschedule?"

A brief pause. "Of course."

"I'm sorry I didn't tell you sooner," Jacob said.

"You do what you need to do," Sam said. "Have a good Shabbos."

"You too." Jacob disconnected the call and thumbed the directory for Divya Das.

"Good morning, Detective."

"I got something for you," he said. "You got something for me?"

"Indeed. Are you free to meet up?"

"Name it," Jacob said.

She gave him an unfamiliar address in Culver City.

He told her he'd be there in fifteen minutes.

The white work van was parked across from his building. He had a faint recollection of it being there the night before. He was far from sure. He'd been drunk, focused primarily on getting his lady friend up the stairs without her pitching over the railing. If he was right, though, the vehicle hadn't left the block in several days, shifting from space to space.

Somebody had a lot of curtains to put up.

He jogged over to peek through the windshield.

Tools, rods, boxes of fabric.

No hulking dude on a headset monitor.

He told himself to stop acting ridiculous.

En route to Culver City, the sat phone rang: his father again. Jacob let it go to voicemail.

The address Divya Das had given him turned out to be a pink stucco apartment complex fronting an unsavory stretch of Venice Boulevard. A homeless man slept on the grass beneath a hopeless sign touting one-, two-, and three-bedroom vacancies.

Jacob parked on a side street, cut the engine, and played the voicemail from his father.

Hi, Jacob. I don't know if you listened to my previous message, but please disregard it. I'll manage.

He hadn't listened to it. Now he had to.

Hi, Jacob. You've probably got your hands full, since I haven't heard from you. Not to worry. I have everything prepared, except for one thing: Nigel accidentally brought me two challahs instead of three and I wanted to ask, if it's not too great an inconvenience, maybe you might have time to pick up another. I like poppy seed, but—

Jacob stopped the playback and dialed him.

"Jacob? Did you get my other message?"

"I got it. Can I ask you something, Abba?"

"Of course."

"Was that an honest attempt to absolve me of picking up the challah, or was it intended to make me feel guilty?"

Sam chuckled. "You think too much."

Jacob rubbed one gummy eye. "What time's dinner?"

DIVYA DAS HAD APPROACHED her generic white Sheetrock walls as a blank canvas, embarking on a charmingly random spree of color and texture. A neon orange throw revived a battered sofa; the dining table was a fifties-era TV set topped with glass. Laminated prints of gods and goddesses brightened the living room: elephant-headed Ganesha, Hanuman the monkey god.

He meant to tell her about the missing letters, but she began chatting with him, inviting him to sit at the breakfast bar and setting out a plate of cookies and a steaming mug.

"There we are," she said. "Proper tea."

He took a mouthful. It was scalding.

"Shit," he gasped.

"I was about to say," she said, "you might want to blow on it."

". . . thanks."

"It's essential to use fresh, clean water and to bring it right up to the boil. Americans consistently neglect that step, with disastrous results."

"You're right," he said. "It tastes much better with a third-degree burn."

"Do you need me to call an ambulance?"

"Some milk would be nice."

She got it for him. "I'm sorry I don't have something more substantial to offer you."

"Don't be. This is the most complete breakfast I've had in months."

"I shall have to tell your mother."

"You'll have to shout pretty loud," he said. "She's dead."

"Oh, my," she said. "I'm so sincerely sorry."

"You didn't know."

"Well, I ought not to make assumptions."

"Don't sweat it. Really." To spare her further embarrassment, he pointed to the fridge door, magnets pinning snapshots. "You and yours?"

The centermost photo had Divya embracing an elderly woman in a red sari. "My *naniji*. This one"—a host of people arrayed on either side of an elaborately bedecked couple—"is from my brother's wedding."

"When did you move to the U.S.?"

"Seven years ago," she said. "For graduate school."

"Columbia," he said.

"Have you been checking up on me, Detective?"

"Just Google."

"Then I'm sure you know everything you need to know."

There were others photos, too, that she apparently did not think required explanation. They showed her in far-flung locales, engaged in mildly risky activities: strapped into a rock-climbing harness; in ski suit and goggles; among girlfriends woozily hoisting margarita glasses.

No kissy photo booth strip; no thick-haired man in surgeon's scrubs, clutched around the waist.

She said, "I hope I didn't bother you, calling on you early."

"I was up."

"I wanted to catch you before I had to leave for the day. I know it's unorthodox to meet here, but it's for the best. I've had to tread lightly. My immediate superior isn't very gung-ho about your severed head. Right now we've got several pathologists away at a convention, and the bodies are piling up."

"What's that mean, not very gung-ho?"

"I believe his exact words were, 'I haven't got time for curiosities.'"

"It's a homicide."

"He tried to convince me it's a relic from a museum."

"With fresh vomit?"

"I didn't say he was successful," she said. "Or sensible. But I know better than to waste time arguing. He can be rather authoritarian, especially under stress."

"So you called me here to apologize for not working my case?"

She smiled, causing a gold stud in her left nostril to twinkle. He hadn't noticed it before.

She said, "I'm afraid I've been a bit naughty."

HER APARTMENT WAS a two-bedroom. The door to the first was ajar, giving Jacob a glimpse of a bed piled with embroidered pillows.

The second had been set up as a mini pathology lab. Heavy-duty plastic sheeting protected the carpet. A dissection tray sat on a folding table; a desk hosted a microscope; there were bins labeled for scalpels and forceps and hammers, a biohazard container, an air purifier, and a two-thousand-count box of nitrile exam gloves.

Jacob looked at her.

She shrugged. "Beg, borrow, and steal. Nothing fancy, mostly surplus. I've been refining it since my student days. No mean feat getting it through customs, believe you me."

"It's nice to meet someone as OCD as me," he said.

"It helps to pass the time," she said.

And explains in part why you're single. Jacob liked her more and more.

In the closet, a wire rack displayed five vinyl bowling bags—the pink and green versions she'd had with her at the crime scene, and three others in orange, black, and red.

"Very *Sex and the City*," he said.

She pointed to the green bag. "Emesis." The black one. "Fingerprints." Red. "Blood." Pink. "Gobbety bits."

"Orange?"

"For when I go dancing," she said. "It's my favorite color. Tell me: how would you know anything about *Sex and the City*?"

"Ex-wife," he said.

"Ah," she said.

He wondered if he'd erred, because in the next breath she was back to business. "I didn't want my boss looking over my shoulder, so I brought the material here—"

"Material?"

"The head. Vomit, too. They're in the freezer."

"Remind me never to have ice cream here, either."

"If I might continue, please. The vomit wasn't very useful. It was so laced with acid that it actually began corroding my glove. And I confess I still haven't been able to determine what sealed the neck. The skin isn't blistered or scorched in keeping with a blast of high heat. I suspect it's some form of tissue adhesive, such as hospitals use to aid in wound repair."

"Someone with specialized knowledge," Jacob said. "Access to medical supplies."

"Possibly. Although you can order transglutaminase over the Internet. Chefs use it. They call it meat glue."

"A mad doctor or a mad chef."

"Or none of the above. That's not the interesting part, though. I took tissue from the head and snuck into the Coroner's lab to extract DNA and run it through CODIS. I wasn't expecting much, but I wanted to be thorough. It's your lucky day, Detective. You're familiar with the Night Creeper, I presume."

Certainly he was.

"Well, you've got him. Or, rather, his head. Or, rather, I do. In my freezer."

Jacob, dumbstruck, watched her give a shallow curtsy.

"Ta-da," she said.

THE LAND OF NOD

On the morning of Asham's departure, her father again tries to dissuade her.

"You'll never find them."

"I won't if I stay," Asham says.

Eve mumbles to herself.

"Our place is here," Adam says, gesturing to the valley walls. "You have no right to leave. Seeking knowledge that isn't yours is the source of all evil. There's no worse sin."

"You think?" Asham says. "I can come up with a few."

"He's right," Yaffa says. "Please."

Asham looks at her ruined sister. Her golden hair has turned to weeds; blue veins worm across her face. She has refused to cast off her widow's garb, refused to work, spending her days cross-legged on the dirt floor, picking listlessly at the skin on her hands.

With Cain fled, and Nava gone with him, the burdens have fallen heavily upon Asham, leaving her to draw the water, cut the firewood, gather the food and cook it; leaving her to grit her teeth while Yaffa keens.

Where is my beloved?

Where is his vengeance?

Asham wants to shake her.

Your beloved is gone.

His vengeance is yours for the taking.

But it requires that you stop crying.

It requires that you stand up, and act.

Asham says, "You don't know what's out there."

"That's the point," Adam says. "And if you do find them? How many must I lose?"

"It's justice."

"Justice is the Lord's to dispense, not yours."

"Tell that to your dead son," she says.

He slaps her.

In the silence, Eve's murmuring is like a shout.

Yaffa says, "You don't need to go. I don't want you to hurt him."

"What hardness is in you," Adam says, "that you cannot forgive when she can?"

Asham, remembering the scream of an unbodied soul, says, "She wasn't there."

SHE CARRIES LITTLE. Spare sandals; a blanket of wool and another of flax; a small gourd; a slaughtering stone.

All products of Cain's ingenuity.

She could not pursue him without his help.

Knowing that they cannot be without a source of fresh water, she follows the river upstream, away from the family's sheltered nook in the shadow of the Mountain of Consideration. The next morning she arrives at a sharp bend, the farthest boundary of their cultivation. Past that, their father has said, it is forbidden for man to venture—forbidden to think about venturing.

She remembers a day long ago, standing beside Cain, staring at the opposite bank.

How can a thought be forbidden?

He will have exploited superstition.

In his position, she would do the same.

She wades to the other side.

The valley winds, narrows, widens again. Hacked vines scabbed with dried sap point the way, and she seeks blackened patches—the remnants of campfires, each of which represents a day of their progress. Behind her, smoke threads from the top of the Mountain of Consideration, which shrinks and drops below the horizon. Vegetation rushes in unchecked. The land's cheery face slackens to indifference and then to a hostile frown. Even the wildflowers appear malignant and overbright. Strange animals stare, unblinking, unafraid. Distant shrieks steal her breath. Skeletons, picked clean, hurry her on.

When Asham was a girl, her parents talked about the hideous fate that awaited anyone who strayed too far. Unimaginable cold, rivers of fire that boiled away flesh, leaving bones for wild beasts to gnaw on. Seizing out of a nightmare, she would feel Yaffa beside her, also trembling, and the two of them would cling together, mewling.

It was Cain who consoled them, Cain with his angry logic.

How would they know what's out there if they've never been?

The Lord told them.

Did you hear him?

No, but—

They're just trying to scare you.

I am scared.

Which one is it? Beasts? Or fire? Or cold?

All three.

Fine, then. We'll go one by one. First: anything that can melt your flesh or freeze you solid can do the same to a beast. And heat and cold cancel each other out. So at worst it's one at a time, not all three. And say your bones do get gnawed on. Who cares? You'll already be frozen. Or burned. Either way, you'll be dead, and you won't feel it.

By that point in the argument, Yaffa had her hands clamped over her ears, begging him to stop. Asham was giggling uncontrollably.

And say they are telling the truth he went on. *They're not. But say they are. You're safe as long as you're here. Isn't that what they said? Right. So. You have nothing to worry about. Go back to sleep and stop kicking me.*

That he so long acted as her source of reason makes it all the more difficult for her to understand his crime. Not an hour passes in which she doesn't see his senseless, swollen face.

Now he is the source of her nightmares.

Rage is a fruit that grows larger with every bite. When she is hungry, she eats of it. It is the drummer that never tires. When she wearies, she marches to the pounding of its fists. Each step is consecrated, the long run-up to an altar. She will offer her brother up as an atonement for himself, save him, redeem him. It will be as much an act of mercy as of justice.

ON THE TWENTY-SIXTH DAY, she surpasses the tree line and beholds a new mountain, unfathomably huge, its summit lost in the clouds.

She weeps.

Because she is so tired and yet must ascend.

Because something so beautiful could exist without her ever having known.

The river has been growing steadily, so that its width is now doubled. It roars down the mountainside, carving the stone, hurtling off ledges and exploding into mist. She spends much of the initial stage of her climb soaked, her teeth chattering. Between that and the thinning ground cover, building a fire becomes an ordeal.

From what she can see, Cain and Nava had the same problem.

On the thirtieth day, she kneels before the wreckage of the wooden mule, grieving to see such a marvelous creation reduced to charcoal.

He went about it wisely, of course, breaking the wood up and parceling it out bit by bit, stretching its use to four days, leaving nothing for her to burn.

She wraps herself in blankets and struggles on. The valley's lushness is forgotten here. There are no trees, no soft places to lie, only gravel that causes her to lose her footing, boulders that deflect vicious gusts of wind at unexpected angles, threatening to sweep her off into space.

She could not have imagined how cold it could get.

Perhaps her parents weren't lying, after all.

The hard ground obscures the trail, and increasingly she finds herself confronting an inscrutable expanse of gray stone. She puts herself in Cain's place and asks: *Where would I go?*

And when she looks again the correct path seems to glow before her.

And invariably she comes to a black patch beside a stumpy, denuded shrub, the most logical spot to build a fire in this illogical place.

She can do this because he spoke the truth.

She is more like him than she realized.

ON THE THIRTY-THIRD DAY, the ground turns a dazzling white.

Asham bends down to scoop some up; gasps, entranced, as it dissolves.

She has no word to describe its radiance.

She licks her palm.

It's water.

The river, too, has begun to crust over, and later that day it disappears, and she realizes she has come to its place of origin, which Cain talked about as if its existence were a certainty, and which her father dismissed as an impossibility.

She has not eaten in two days. She gobbles white by the mouthful, cold etching down her throat, and walks on.

No matter how hard she sucks in air, her lungs never seem satisfied. Her head spins and she pants silvery clouds as she climbs through the starlit night, afraid to stop and sleep.

Dawn reveals a vivid splash of red against the gray landscape. She cannot understand what it is until she's standing right next to it, and even then she must pry open her mind to admit the reality of the horror.

It is the mule—the living one. Its head and tail are missing. Its hide is flayed and chunks of flesh are carved away from the bone.

Unnatural carnage; the work of man.

Starving, she falls upon the carcass with a stone, slices off half-frozen shreds.

Her first taste of animal flesh is a revelation. The texture and flavor make her feel as though she has bitten off and is chewing her own tongue.

It nauseates her and yet she craves it. It fills her belly and reignites her rage.

A jagged flap of hide dangles from the mule's underbelly. Asham removes it and holds it against herself, warming it to pliability. She hacks it in half and wraps the pieces around her numb feet. Another strip, cut from the neck, she drapes over her own neck and shoulders.

She breaks the mule's ribs and uses them to skewer scraps of flesh.

The animal toiled without complaint to bring their harvest. It is feeding them still.

She spends half a day burying its useless remains.

On the thirty-sixth day, she reaches the pass.

The summit remains cloaked, but she can see down a sheer corridor of blue-white walls to daylight. She staggers along blessedly level ground. From within the walls come pings and cracks and snaps, muffled, and she hurries toward the light, and the sounds grow louder, and she begins to run, but she cannot outrun them, and the air trembles terribly and the mountain bellows its displeasure.

SHE AWAKENS in the dark.

Her last memory is of a rushing wall of white, then an all-encompassing cold.

Now she feels parched. She kicks off the blanket and frigid air hits her skin and freezes the tears in her eyes, and she shivers, groping for the blanket regretfully. She thinks if she cannot find it, she will die. She cannot find it. But a hand touches her shoulder and the blanket draws up to her chin and a voice commands her to sleep. She obeys.

AWAKENING WITH A CLEARER HEAD, she sees that she is in a cave filled with a pulsing, gelid light. There is no fire. The glow comes from the stones themselves, slick with radiant slime.

A man stands over her, tall as a tree, gaunt as a reed, wearing luminous white garments.

He says, "You are hungry," and hands her a steaming gourd. Asham raises it and touches it to her lips. Expecting heat, she chokes it out: it's some sort of gruel, water and grain, and it's cold as white. Once she gets a taste, though, hunger storms forth to claim its due, and she cannot stop herself. She drinks the mixture down without pause. It is salty and thick and nourishing. She hits the bottom of the gourd to get out the last drops, licks the sides clean.

The man says, "More?"

She nods, and he pours from a shining vessel. The second bowl she savors. Grateful. And cautious, and confused. She has never seen anyone other than the members of her family. Until this moment, she has been given no indication that anyone else might exist.

He says, "You were burning with fever when I drew you from the snow."

"Snow?"

The man smiles slightly. "My name is Michael. This is my abode. You may stay here until you've recovered your strength, and then I'll see you down to the valley."

She pauses, the gourd halfway to her mouth. "I'm not going to the valley."

The fluctuating light plays over Michael's face, causing his features to shift and fade, so that her eyes cannot catch hold of them. One moment he is young and smooth, the next ancient as stone.

Asham says, "I'm going over the mountain."

"Your brother is far away," he says. "It would be wiser to go home."

"You've seen him."

Michael nods.

"Where is he? Was Nava with him?"

"You can still turn back. You will be given another."

"I don't want another."

Michael says, "It is not the will of the Lord."

"Maybe not," she says. "But it's mine."

FOR SEVEN DAYS he tends to her, and on the eighth day he bids her to rise. He provisions her with water, dried fruit, and nuts; he dresses her in clean flaxen garments and gives her a multicolored fur, soft and strong, light and warm. It comes from no animal she has seen, but she is coming to accept the extent of the world beyond her experience. She knows nothing.

He blesses her in the name of the Lord and says, "Come."

The cave is far deeper than she realized. Through tunnels, stepping over frozen pools, the temperature rising. A spot of white appears in the distance and Michael stops and turns to her, his ageless face creased with sorrow. She feels as if she is seeing him for the very first time.

"Evil crouches by the door," he says. "It will wait for you all your life, unless you master it."

Accustomed to the low light, she emerges blinking into the sun. The air is cool, dry, spicy, rotten. She raises her face gradually, taking in the earth beneath her feet, lightly dusted with snow; the downward slope of the mountain, white giving way to tan, smooth giving way to pebbly; spiky plants rippling with flies; the edge of the sere plain, and then the plain itself, vast, brown, and flat, cracked and smoking beneath a colorless sky, infinite as cruelty itself.

CHAPTER THIRTEEN

Jacob knew about the Creeper; every L.A. cop did.

Cold for two-plus decades, the case was a favorite of true crime shows for its grisly particulars: nine single women raped, tortured, and slashed.

Every few years, some lazy freelancer dug it up to rehash the lack of progress.

Jacob had been eight or nine at the time of the murders and could remember a paralyzed city. Locks double-checked, no walking to the store, rent-a-cops at drop-off, pickup, recess.

He doubted other kids had noticed.

Exactly the kind of thing he noticed, attuned as he was to an unpredictable world.

Divya Das said, "You look rather more put out than I'd hoped."

"No," he said. "No, I—I'm . . . stunned, I guess."

"As was I."

"You're absolutely sure it's him?"

"The profile matches every instance where DNA was recovered, seven out of nine. This was offender DNA, mind you, not incidental fluid. Semen from the victims' vaginas and, at one scene, nonvictim blood, presumably the killer injuring himself in the struggle. It didn't hit anyone in the system, though, so in a way I suppose this finding raises as many questions as it answers. Nor does it tell us who killed him, or why."

"That I can answer," he said. "Justice."

Divya Das nodded.

He'd been so caught off guard by the news that it only now struck him how swiftly she'd obtained her results. In his experience, the turn-around time on DNA was seldom less than a couple of weeks. He asked her about it and she shrugged. "Friends in high places."

"Special friends in special places," he said.

She smiled. "You said you had something to tell me?"

". . . yeah."

He told her about his trip to the house and showed her his photos of the restored countertops. "I was thinking maybe the stuff you used might've caused it to fade, or . . ."

She took the camera, said nothing.

"You swabbed it," he said.

She nodded.

"And?"

"I examined it for traces of caustic agents. It appears to be an ordinary burn. Anyone could have managed it with a wood-burning pen."

The same thought he'd had. "Which would leave a mark."

She pursed her lips at the photo. "Not if it was sanded down."

"Yeah, but it didn't look that way to me," he said. "You can—here."

He took the camera, scrolled back to a photo taken along the plane of the wood. "If there was a dip in the surface you'd see it. But there isn't."

"Perhaps it was sanded down uniformly," she said.

He hadn't considered that. There was a reason: it sounded prepos-terous.

No more so than someone replacing the countertops wholesale, though.

"I guess," he said. "Any other thoughts?"

A silence.

"None that will help," she said.

"Maybe I should be looking at contractors," he said.

She smiled politely.

"One way or the other," he said, "someone was there. I dusted for prints and didn't find crap. It's definitely possible I missed something."

"I can go back, if you'd like."

"Would you, please?"

She nodded.

"Thanks," he said. "Be careful."

"I will."

"I can accompany you."

"That's not necessary," she said. The smile had dried up; he sensed his cue to leave. It seemed particularly self-defeating, then, the urge he felt to touch her, to tell her that he wanted to see her more, to learn her, to know the woman in the refrigerator photographs. He slapped himself back into line by thinking of the girl from the bar, the boiling whites of her eyes as she lost consciousness.

He said, "If you think of anything else."

She nodded again. "I'll let you know."

ON HIS WAY HOME, he stopped off at Zschyk's, the kosher bakery. He pulled a ticket from the dispenser and waited among the crowd of housewives and their housekeeper proxies. After his conversation with Divya Das, he regretted having accepted his father's dinner invitation. A lost evening. He ought to be running down leads.

He supposed he could drop off the challah and cancel. It didn't seem fair to keep jerking the poor guy around, though.

He could predict his father's response.

Please. Don't give it a second thought.

The worst part was knowing that Sam really was hell-bent on not playing the guilt card. Meaning whatever guilt Jacob felt was self-generated. He hadn't progressed toward adulthood as completely as he liked to think.

The counterwoman called his number, took his order, handed him a warm bag. By the time he arrived back at his apartment, the Honda had filled with a rich, yeasty aroma, and he decided running down leads could wait.

His vic was a very bad guy who'd gotten away with nine murders.

Now he was dead. Justice. No need to hurry unduly.

He tossed the challah down on his desk and sat to think.

He'd pegged Mr. Head as thirty to forty-five. For the guy to have committed the murders in the late eighties, he would have to fall closer to the high end of the estimate. So he'd been off. He was used to that. The land of Tighten and Tuck devalued first impressions; the best way to figure a person's real age was to look at their hands. Hands didn't lie.

It would help to have some hands.

It would help to have a body.

Whatever his precise age, Mr. Head had gotten off clean for a long time.

Apparently, not everyone agreed that justice delayed is justice denied.

A person who knew the Creeper's secret, judged him for it, did not care to wait around for the system to play catch-up.

Tzedek.

Like much of biblical Hebrew, the word had multiple shades of meaning. The same letters formed the root of the word *tzedakah*, charity.

The mingling of the two concepts struck Jacob as novel, even contradictory. In English, charity and justice stood in opposition. Justice was the letter of the law, the pursuit of absolute truth, the demand for punishment.

Charity mitigated justice, softened it, introduced the variable of mercy.

The murder of a murderer could be considered an act of justice or an act of charity.

Justice for the dead. Justice for their families.

Charity for future victims.

Charity, even, for Mr. Head himself, sparing him from engaging in more evil.

What differentiated between the two Hebrew words was the feminine suffix, the letter *heh*—itself a symbol for the name of God.

Tzedakah, he supposed, could be considered a womanly form of justice.

That recalled Portia's courtroom speech from the *The Merchant of Venice*. A plea for mercy, delivered by a woman, dressed as a man.

The letters of *tzedek* also gave rise to the word *tzaddik*: a righteous individual, one who performed good deeds, often in secret, without expectation of recognition or reward.

The doer of justice; the doer of charity.

Did that say something about how Mr. Head's slayer saw himself? Herself?

Why not? Hammett said it was a woman who'd called it in.

Jacob checked his e-mail for a response from 911 dispatch, saw a bunch of spam. He started to write to Mallick, telling him what he had, then scrapped the draft. He didn't really know what he had.

Plugging *Night Creeper* into the *Times* archive brought up seven hundred hits. Jacob narrowed his search to those from the appropriate period, curious to see if any of the vics had overtly Jewish surnames.

Helen Girard, 29.

Cathy Wanzer, 36.

Christa Knox, 32.

Every one of them young, well liked, attractive; every one of them the cornerstone of an exponential tower of ruined lives. Wanzer was blond, a massage therapist who worked out of her home. Girard and Knox, both brunettes, left grieving boyfriends, devastated parents.

Patricia Holt, 24.

Laura Lesser, 31.

Janet Stein, 29.

The parade of happy faces was sapping his motivation to solve his crime.

He circled Lesser and Stein.

Inez Delgado, 39.

Katherine Ann Clayton, 32.

Sherri Levesque, 31.

Convenient for a Jewish vic to equal a Jewish avenger. That was wishful thinking, though. And by themselves, names told him very little. There were Jews with non-Jewish names and non-Jews with Jewish names. There were mixed families. There were friends. There were folks who followed a stranger's case, got interested, and then invested, and then involved far beyond what was reasonable. It happened to cops all the time.

He had to start somewhere, though.

He read about Laura Lesser. A psychiatric nurse. Pretty, like the rest of her unfortunate sorority.

Janet Stein owned a small Westwood bookstore. Memorial held at the funeral chapel of Beth Shalom Cemetery.

Same place his mother was buried.

One definite Jewish victim.

He returned to the archives, found a follow-up article from '98, ten-year-after piece of rubbernecking. A D named Philip Ludwig had picked up the torch, vowing to revisit every lead, utilize every resource, including the FBI's newly operational Combined DNA Index System.

In another follow-up, six years later, he sounded less optimistic.

My hope is that whoever committed these crimes is now dead and can't cause any more tragedy.

The reporter asked if that didn't deny closure to the victims' families.

I don't know what the hell that means.

The article went on to say that Ludwig was headed for retirement at the end of the year. What, the reporter asked, did he intend to do with his free time?

Take up a hobby.

Given the guilt and disappointment seeping through, Jacob was willing to lay even money that, for Ludwig, "hobby" meant sitting around and indicting himself.

Jacob found him living in San Diego—too far to drive and make it back in time for dinner. He called on the sat phone and left a brief message.

He considered starting to track down victims' families, decided to wait until he heard what Ludwig had to say. That left the day open.

CHAPTER FOURTEEN

First came the hipsters, colonizing Silver Lake and Los Feliz and Echo Park, so that these days you were as likely to see a gourmet taco truck run by mustachioed culinary school grads with earlobes stretched to hula hoops as you were an actual taquería.

Then real estate developers who'd hit the ocean and run out of raw material sniffed the trend and headed back inland to perform CPR on downtown. They built luxury "green" high-rises with fitness centers and underground parking, and attempted to lure buyers with the promise of a burgeoning nightlife. In Jacob's view, they were kidding themselves. Real wealth would always flow westward. Lacking a center, Los Angeles would always be seventy-two suburbs in search of a city.

Even the most ardent downtown boosters steered clear of Boyle Heights. It claimed one of the city's highest homicide rates; crossing over the trickle of river via the Olympic Boulevard bridge, Jacob saw drugs dealt openly and handguns flashed with a smirk.

Beth Shalom Memorial Park attested to the neighborhood's long-fled Jewish community. It was actually three cemeteries—Garden of Peace, Mount Carmel, and House of Israel—wedged between the 710 and the 5. Only the first still accepted new burials; the latter two had been full since the seventies.

Entering Garden of Peace, he saw EST. 1883 carved into the gatepost and wondered how much room they had left.

The dead kept on stacking up, relentless as debt.

The man at the front office had the chatty sheen of the newly hired. He wrote down the plot numbers for Janet Stein and Bina Lev, marking them roughly on the map. "You know Curly's here."

"Curly."

"Like from the Three Stooges?" The guy asterisked a section labeled *Joseph's Garden*.

"Thanks," Jacob said. "I'll bear it in mind."

The day had turned mushy, and his shirt stuck to his back as he walked the lawns to Janet Stein's crypt inside the Hall of Memories.

A stained-glass window cast an array of pinks and purples on the terrazzo. There was no air-conditioning—it wasn't like the residents needed it—and flowers languished in their holders, layering the floor with more color in the form of shed petals.

He found her in the middle of the corridor.

JANET RUTH STEIN
NOVEMBER 17, 1958–JULY 5, 1988
BELOVED DAUGHTER & SISTER
DEATH BE NOT PROUD

The quote from Donne intrigued him. More typically, you'd expect a passage from the Bible. Jacob supposed it was fitting for a lover of literature, and it gave him another degree of kinship to her. Before coming, he'd looked up Janet Stein's former bookstore. Like most brick-and-mortar sellers, it was shuttered. He stood in communion, trying to telegraph to her that the man who had cut her down young was gone in a terrible way. It made him feel silly and useless.

TO BUY HIMSELF SOME TIME, he went to find Curly.

The headstones of Joseph's Garden were upright, carved with symbols signifying the deceased's status in the community, or occupation. A pair of hands, raised in priestly blessing, for a Kohen. For a Levite, a cup pouring water. Lawyers got scales and doctors got caduceus staffs. Movie moguls—there were several—got reel-to-reel cameras. Palm trees swooned in perpetual infatuation. Jacob could tell from the lack of pebbles placed atop the headstones that there had been few recent visitors to these parts.

Curly had been accorded slightly more attention. Atop the grave, someone had laid out, in pebbles:

NYUK

NYUK

NYUK

Laughing, Jacob left his own pebble and walked on.

He wandered around for a while, swirling around the section containing Bina's plot, like a ship caught in a slow-turning whirlpool. The relative newness of Esther's Garden was reflected in its more modern headstones, black granite set flush with the grass. From a distance it evoked a tilled field. He found himself stooping to read markers, to place a pebble on those that had been neglected. The sun was ferocious, and he hadn't brought a hat or water. It was half past two; he could beat traffic back to the Westside, but only if he left right now; he still had to shower and get over to his dad's. He really should come back later, when he had more time to devote to her.

He couldn't stall forever. He reached the correct row. Hers was the ninth plot in.

פ"נ

בינה פרל בת יהודה חיים

BELOVED WIFE & MOTHER

BINA REICH LEV

MAY 24, 1951–JULY 11, 2000

תנצב"ה

He didn't care to think how long it had been since his last visit. His father went several times a year: on the anniversary of her death, of course, and also before major holidays. Nigel drove him, helped him make his way to the grave.

A son's job. Sam had never asked.

Jacob wasn't about to volunteer.

Her gravestone was unadorned, strange for a woman who could only express herself through her art, the uneasy coexistence of piety and radical independence, asymmetry and order.

Look at her work and you saw a creator whose contradictions made her beautiful.

Look at her and you saw a cipher.

Jacob's friends' mothers drove carpool to soccer games and whipped up elaborate Friday night dinners with fatty beef, potatoes, and a half stick of margarine. At her best, Bina Lev was scatterbrained, introverted, perfectly capable of sending her son to school wearing mismatched shoes or toting an empty lunchbox.

She was not often at her best.

And he was a logical child, brutally so. He understood cause and effect. He could look at the photo albums and parse the gaps. Her first hospitalization had come when he was a toddler.

Bouts of depression were hard, but at least he could slog along in peace. Mania was the real terrorist, holding all of them hostage. She argued with voices. She broke things. She stayed in the garage for days without eating or sleeping. Eventually she would reemerge, having created dozens and dozens of new pieces; she would drop into bed, never attempting to explain herself, not to Sam and certainly not to Jacob.

In retrospect he understood that she was trying to shield him from the ongoing avalanche of her mind. At the time, however, he'd felt as if he were staring up an insurmountable slope, silence denying him any context for her deterioration.

It was not swift. It was not merciful.

His sole consolation that he hadn't been around to witness the worst of it.

At the start of his senior year of high school, the head rabbi spoke to Jacob's class about the value of taking time off before college to study in yeshiva. Some boys were dismissive, others skeptical but open to persuasion, and some, like Jacob, already had their bags packed.

He couldn't get far away fast enough.

Every six weeks or so, he'd call home from Jerusalem on a scratchy pay phone and hear the desperation mounting in Sam's voice.

I'm worried about her.

But Jacob was eighteen, high on freedom, and bursting with righteous indignation. He was eight thousand miles away.

What do you want me to do about it?

College provided a whole new set of excuses not to come home. His newly minted girlfriend invited him to have Thanksgiving dinner. Her family had a place on Cape Cod and she wanted him to experience a real Christmas. Then she ditched him for a hockey player and he spent the money meant for his spring break flight to go to Miami with his roommates, also smarting from being dumped.

She's asking for you.

She had never asked for him before.

Let her ask a little more.

He stayed in Cambridge that summer, working as a research assistant to an English professor whom he hoped to enlist as a thesis adviser down the line. He wangled a stipend and a dorm room that came with a campus extension that never rang until it did.

OFFICIALLY JUDAISM SHUNNED SUICIDES, condemning the soul to an eternity of wandering and forbidding the survivors to observe the laws of mourning. But there was a workaround, the rabbi explained.

We assume that the deceased was not of sound mind—a prisoner of their illness, if you will—and therefore not responsible for his or her actions.

If anyone fit that description, it was Bina. But the suggestion that they needed a loophole to grieve enraged Jacob, and he would later point to it as the shining example of why he'd had it with religion.

Don't throw everything away because of one fool Sam said.

It wasn't one fool, though. All four of Jacob's grandparents had died before he was born, and his first hands-on experience with the mourning process convinced him that he would never go through it again. The rigidity, legalism, the miming of emotion. Tearing one's clothes. Sitting on the floor. Not bathing. Not shaving. Praying, and praying, and praying again.

To me it's a comfort Sam said.

It's inhuman Jacob said.

For seven days the two of them sat in the dusty living room while strangers paraded through, offering hollow support.

She's in a better place.

She would want you to be happy.

May the Lord comfort you among the mourners of Zion and Jerusalem.

Just him and Sam, nodding and smiling and thanking these assholes for their wisdom.

When he got back to school, his voicemail was full up with condolence calls that he deleted mechanically. He didn't know then that he was establishing a template for years to come: the periodic shedding of attachments, his deciduous heart.

The voicemail said, "Tuesday, July 11."

The day of: his father, presumably, calling to tell him something he didn't need to hear again. He started to thumb DELETE but the voice that filled his ear wasn't Sam's.

It was Bina's.

Jacob she said *I'm sorry.*

He couldn't say which was worse: that he'd been too busy to answer her call, or that it was the first and only time he could remember her apologizing.

He squeezed down his thumb.

"SIR? WE'RE CLOSING SOON."

Jacob stood up, brushed the grass from his pants, looked down at the stone one final time.

A large black bug skittered to the center of the granite and stopped.

Jacob frowned, crouched to shoo it away.

The bug dodged, ran a slant, paused at the stone's upper right corner.

The light was different, and he was viewing the insect's top side rather than its belly, and he was no entomologist.

But to him it looked like the same one he'd seen at the murder house.

Had it gotten into his car?

Ridden home with him?

You have roaches.

Jacob had known more than a few vermin in his time. This was far bigger than any cockroach he'd seen. A drunk woman might not be in a position to make comparisons, though.

"Sir? Did you hear me?"

Jacob reached slowly for the bug, expecting it to dart off.

It waited.

He laid his hand on the stone and let the insect crawl onto his fingers.

Lifted it up to examine it.

It stared back at him with bulbous, bottle-green eyes.

A spade-shaped head, adorned with a menacing horn; jagged, pro-truding jaws. Remembering the red welt on the bar lady's foot, he almost flung the insect away. But the jaws opened and closed gently, and he felt no threat. He fished his cell phone from his pocket to take a picture, and it appeared to comply: posing, rearing up to reveal its lacquered abdomen, its numerous legs flimmering.

"Sir." It was the man from the front office. "Please."

The insect parted its armor, extended gossamer wings, and flew away.

"Sorry," Jacob said.

They walked back toward the gate.

"I thought you'd left hours ago. I almost locked up. That wouldn't've been fun for you. We don't open again till Sunday."

"Depends on your definition of fun," Jacob said.

The man looked at him strangely.

"Enjoy your weekend," Jacob said.

CHAPTER FIFTEEN

The apartment complex Sam Lev had lived in for the last twelve years belonged to a wealthy co-parishioner named Abe Teitelbaum. Abe and Sam had known each other since their twenties; they were long-time Talmud study partners, which explained how Sam had come to occupy the superintendent's unit.

God knew he didn't do any actual superintending. His expertise was limited to a memorized list of phone numbers. Called upon to confront a broken toilet or a faltering A/C, he'd say, "Right away," depress the hook-switch, and dial the appropriate handyman.

Nonetheless, Abe took pains to frame the arrangement as a job rather than an act of charity, paying Sam a nominal salary and refusing to take rent, claiming that it had been deducted from Sam's paycheck.

The apartment was tiny, fronted by a stamped concrete patio furnished with a pair of sooty plastic chairs and an equally uninviting bistro table. A terra-cotta planter contained a barren clod of potting soil. Jacob paused amid the splendor to silence the ringer on his phone and withdraw a suede yarmulke from his pocket. The leather was stiff and dry, permanently creased into a taco shell shape from having been folded and crushed at the bottom of a drawer. He tried without success to iron it out against his leg, then pinned it on with clips, conscious of its weight and the jutting peak. In his mind's eye, he looked like a crested parrot.

Sam was slow in answering his knock. Worried, Jacob knocked again.

"Coming, coming . . ." The door opened. "Good Shabbos."

His father wore a baggy gray suit, white shirt, black loafers, and anomalously large red sunglasses. The skinny end of his necktie stuck out below the fat end, and Jacob tamped down the urge to reach out and fix it.

"Sorry I'm late. I got stuck downtown and traffic was horrendous."

"Not at all. I just got back from *shul*. Come on in."

Jacob made his way carefully across the living room. Cardboard boxes stacked two deep and four high housed a motley library, traditional Jewish texts as well as countless works of physics, philosophy, philology, astronomy, and mathematics. There were also a number of books whose unorthodoxy Jacob had only recently come to appreciate: classics of Sufism and Buddhism, Christian mysticism and gnosticism. In third grade he had scandalized his teacher by bringing in a copy of the Tibetan Book of the Dead for show-and-tell, resulting in a conference with Rabbi Buchbinder, the *rosh yeshiva*.

Eyes that read such nonsense should go blind.

On the car ride home, Jacob had sat curled up in the bucket seat, quaking in anticipation of ghastly consequences. They came to a stoplight and Sam reached over to take his hand.

Not everyone who wears the title of rabbi deserves it.

But he said—

I know what he said. He's a fool.

At nine, this was a mind-boggling revelation.

The light turned green. Sam eased off the brake.

You can't be afraid of an idea he said. *Follow the argument, wherever it leads.*

Another decade passed before Jacob realized that his father had been quoting Socrates.

But the weight of evidence seemed to fall in Buchbinder's favor, because in the interim, Sam really *did* start to go blind. It began a few years after the show-and-tell incident: a sludgy spot at the center of his field of vision that gradually crept outward, sucking up shape and color. He saw better in low light, and had taken to wearing sunglasses, indoors and out; he kept the living room curtains drawn and the track lighting dim; he alone could navigate his library, by following the map in his mind; and while his vision appeared to have stabilized, that could always change: the condition was considered chronic and incurable and, best of all, heritable.

Yet more for Jacob to look forward to as he got older.

Insanity?

Blindness?

Why choose . . . when you can have *both*?

He said, "Someone walked you home, I hope."

Sam shrugged.

"You went on your own?"

"I'm fine."

"It's not safe."

"Fine," Sam said innocently. "I'll drive."

"Hilarious. Have Nigel take you."

"He does enough."

Jacob placed the bakery bag on the dinner table, which was laid with a white stainproof tablecloth, wine, and two crooked place settings. He stepped into the kitchen, sniffing. His father wasn't so good at reading the oven knobs.

No burning.

No nothing.

"Abba? Did you put the food in to warm?"

"Of course."

Jacob lowered the oven door. Foil-wrapped pans sat on cold racks.

"Did you remember to turn the oven on?"

A pause.

"Nobody's perfect," Sam said.

THEY BEGAN WITH *Shalom Aleichem*, a song welcoming the Sabbath angels. Jacob then fell silent, listening to Sam's mellow baritone as he intoned *Eishet Chayil*, the closing section of the book of Proverbs, a hymn to the woman of valor.

> *Grace is false, and beauty is vain.*
> *A woman who fears God—she is praised.*
> *Give to her of the fruit of her hands,*
> *and her deeds will praise her at the gates.*

It angered and awed Jacob that, after so many years and so much heartbreak, his father was still singing to Bina.

"Your turn," Sam said. He reached for Jacob's head but hesitated. "If you want."

"Go on. I can use all the help I can get."

As a young boy, he would listen to the parental blessing, mumbled from on high, the words of a marble-mouthed angel. Sometimes Sam would smile and crouch down so that Jacob could place his hands on Sam's head and reciprocate with a solemn string of nonsense Hebrew. *Kama rama lada gada Shabbos amen.*

Now they stood with their faces inches apart, close enough for Jacob to smell his father's Irish Spring, to be momentarily hypnotized by the flicker of his lips. Physically, Jacob favored Bina's side, her dense, charcoal hair, delicately salted at the temples; her fluid jade eyes, even more unearthly than his; the open, questioning features that, on his face, plucked a maternal chord in women, endearing him to them at a glance, and later becoming a source of ire.

Don't look at me that way.

What way?

Like you don't know what I'm talking about.

Sam, on the other hand, was angular, whittled, with decisive bone structure and a mildly bulbous forehead—a brain outgrowing its housing. Jacob thought it was good his father had found an outlet in his writing; otherwise the theories and concepts and other bits of nuclear theologic cognition would pile up, pressure mounting, skull swelling and swelling until it ruptured, spraying gray matter and words of Torah over a half-mile radius.

Sam had removed his glasses. The disease had not caused any outward change; as ever, his eyes were a glossy brown, verging on black. They trembled, half closed, as he murmured.

> *May God make you as Ephraim and Menasheh.*
> *May God bless you and guard you.*
> *May God light up His face to you and be gracious to you.*
> *May God lift His face to you and establish for you peace.*

Sam pulled him in and gave him a wet kiss on the forehead. "I love you."

Twice in one week.

Was he dying?

Jacob filled one of Bina's ceramic goblets to the brim with red wine, setting it carefully in Sam's hands. The wine sloshed across Sam's knuckles as he recited *kiddush*, dripping onto the white tablecloth and diffusing, a lavender diaspora. They drank, washed their hands with another of Bina's cups, and sat to break bread: hunks of challah dipped in salt.

Electing to skip the cold soup, they went straight to the main meal. Sam insisted on playing waiter, setting out platters of roast chicken, sweet potato, rice pilaf, cucumber salad.

"What it lacks in temperature, it makes up for in quantity."

It was indeed a lot of food, and Jacob felt touched. His father didn't have money to spare. Before his weakening vision had forced him to stop, and he'd taken on his so-called superintendent duties, Sam had scrounged a living doing freelance bookkeeping and tax prep, usually for elderly neighbors and always at a deep discount. His indifference to the material world was, like his continuing devotion to Bina, a source of admiration and frustration for Jacob.

"Everything's delicious, Abba."

"Can I get you anything else?"

"You can sit down and eat, please." Jacob forked a piece of Jerusalem kugel, sweet and peppery and springy to the touch. "So. What's up?"

Sam shrugged. "The usual. Scribbling."

"What're you working on?"

"You really want to know?"

"I'm asking."

"Maybe you're just being polite."

"You say that like there's something wrong with being polite."

Sam smiled. "Since you ask, it's a supercommentary on the Maharal's *Chiddushei Aggados* to *Sanhedrin*, with special attention given to the themes of theodicy and reincarnation."

"I smell bestseller," Jacob said.

"Oh, definitely. I'm thinking we get Tom Cruise to play the Maharal."

Sam was ordained—although he wouldn't permit anyone to call him rabbi—and not a few of the books piled up around the apartment bore his authorship: lengthy, esoteric tracts written in longhand in composition books. Whenever he completed one, Abe Teitelbaum paid to print a few dozen copies, which Sam then sold.

That was the theory. Invariably, Sam ended up giving the books away to anyone who showed the slightest interest, trying, unsuccessfully, to reimburse Abe out of his own pocket.

As Sam launched into a summary of the latest work, his elegant pianist fingers flying, Jacob fixed on a smile and set his head on auto-nod.

He'd heard most of the ideas before, or some version of them. His father considered Rabbi Judah Loew, the Maharal, his cardinal commentator, and had been talking and writing about him as long as Jacob could remember. The guy could do no wrong. The guy had special powers. The guy was the *gadol hador*—the greatest Torah mind of his generation. He was a *lamed-vavnik*, one of the thirty-six hidden righteous men who sustained the world. He was Abraham and Einstein and Babe Ruth and the Green Lantern rolled into one, at once mythical and intimate, like some highly exotic fruit hanging off the far end of the family tree; the fourth cousin who never shows up to reunions because he's building affordable solar-powered housing in Guatemala or pearl diving off Sri Lanka, and whose absence turns him into the sole topic of conversation.

One of the few recollections Jacob had of Bina showing a maternal instinct was when Sam decided to read to him from a book about the Maharal's creation of the golem of Prague. The cover art featured a monster with glowing, jaundiced eyes, stretching a bearish hand after some hapless, unseen victim. It had scared the bejesus out of Jacob, then four or five. He'd run in his pajamas to Bina, who gathered him up and turned on Sam ferociously.

Read him a normal book, like a normal child.

In hindsight, it did seem a questionable choice for a bedtime story.

A shrill electronic plaint interrupted his thoughts and paused Sam's monologue. Jacob fumbled out the sat phone. He was sure he'd turned it off. He flicked the ringer switch, but the phone shrieked a second time.

"You should get that," Sam said.

Jacob flicked the switch back. The goddamned thing kept ringing. "It can wait."

"It might be important."

Hot with shame, Jacob tripped through the cardboard maze, stepped out to the patio.

"Hello?"

"Detective Lev? Phil Ludwig."

"Oh—hi."

"I'm catching you at a bad time?"

"No, it's, it's fine," Jacob said, eyeing Sam through the ragged lace curtain. His father had laid his cutlery across the edge of his plate and was sitting with his hands crossed on his shallow stomach, gazing placidly into oblivion. "Thanks for getting back to me."

"Yeah. What can I do for you?"

"I caught a case that relates to one of your old ones, and I wanted to pick your brains."

"What case would that be?"

"The Night Creeper," Jacob said.

Ludwig said nothing for a solid ten seconds. When he next spoke, his tone was guarded—close to hostile. "Is that a fact."

"Seems that way."

"Relates how?"

"I think I may have your offender," Jacob said.

Ludwig exhaled. It sounded labored.

"Detective?" Jacob asked.

"One second."

The phone clattered down, and Jacob heard grunting, like the guy had accidentally swallowed a cigarette butt.

"Detective? You okay?"

Ludwig came back on. "Yeah."

"Is everything all right?"

"Well—I mean, Christ. *I* don't know. You tell me."

"I was hoping to swing by and talk to you," Jacob said.

"You have him? I—shit. I thought you were gonna tell me you had another DB."

"I do," Jacob said. "Your offender."

"Jesus Christ," Ludwig said. "You're kidding."

"I wouldn't kid about that. Tomorrow okay?"

They arranged to meet at eleven a.m. Before they got off, Jacob again asked if Ludwig was feeling well.

"Don't worry about me. Listen up: you'd better not be yanking my chain here."

"Hand to God," Jacob said.

"Cause you are, I'll break your fucking neck," Ludwig said.

CHAPTER SIXTEEN

I apologize," Jacob said, reseating himself. "It's this new phone. I tried to silence it, but for some reason it won't turn off. Anyhow, sorry. I hate to disrupt your Shabbos."

"You're not. It's absolutely permitted. Your work is no different from a doctor's."

"Nobody's going to die if I don't answer the phone."

"Can you say that with certainty?"

"In this case, yes." Jacob resumed eating, noticing that Sam hadn't taken more than a couple bites of his own food. "Abba? You're not sick, are you?"

"Me? No. Why? Do I look sick?"

"You'd tell me if you were."

"Of course."

"You've barely eaten."

"Have I?" Sam squinted at his plate. "I guess I got distracted."

"You were telling me about the Maharal."

"Enough about that. I don't want to spoil the ending." Sam's smile acknowledged the absurdity of Jacob—of anyone—reading his book. "I'd much rather hear about you."

"Not much to tell. Busy."

"So I gather. Anything exciting?"

"You really want to know?"

"I asked." Sam's dim left eye winked. "Although maybe I'm just being polite."

Jacob laughed. "Touché. Well, all right. I'm not sure how much I should discuss."

"As much as you want," Sam said.

"Right," Jacob said. For the first time in his career, his work touched upon Sam's area of expertise, however tangentially. To say nothing felt artificially tight-lipped, almost unjust. "This homicide I've got, it's a weird one."

"Homicide," Sam said.

Jacob nodded.

"I thought you'd been reassigned."

"They re-reassigned me."

"I see," Sam said. He didn't sound pleased. He began pushing slices of cucumber around, rearranging them into a watery green mosaic. "And?"

"And . . . so, they put me on this because they found some Hebrew letters at the scene."

A silence.

"That's," Sam said, "that's unusual."

"No sh—no kidding."

"What did the letters say," Sam said.

"*Tzedek.*"

Another silence.

"You're still not eating," Jacob said.

Sam put down the fork. "Is that what the call was about?"

"My case is connected to an old one. The victim has an ugly past."

"How ugly?"

Jacob shifted. "I shouldn't . . . I mean. Pretty ugly. Let's leave it at that."

"And now someone killed him," Sam said. "To render justice."

"That's more or less the size of it. To be honest, the whole thing makes me kind of uncomfortable."

"Why?"

"I guess I don't want my avenger to turn out to be Jewish," Jacob said. "It's not like I'm responsible for him, but . . . You know."

"And if he is Jewish?"

"If he is, then he is. Follow the argument, wherever it leads."

Sam appeared not to notice Jacob quoting him back to himself. "If you can't be objective," he said, "you should recuse yourself."

"I didn't say I can't be objective."

"It sounds to me like you have doubts."

"A decision I can make for myself, thanks. Anyway, he might not be Jewish, just trying to leave that impression."

"I don't understand," Sam said. "You said you were done with Homicide."

"I told you. They asked me to come back. Ordered me, actually."

Sam said nothing.

"Abba. What's wrong."

Sam shook his head.

"Look," Jacob said, "I'm not going to beg you."

"I'm remembering how unhappy you were," Sam said.

Jacob had made an effort to hide his depression, and now he bridled, feeling caught out. "I'm fine."

"It wasn't good for you," Sam said.

"Leave it alone, please."

"You can't ask them to find someone else?"

"No. I can't. They want me precisely because I'm Jewish. Seriously, I don't want to discuss it anymore, all right? It's a done deal and it's not Shabbos table talk."

Sam had often used the same rationale to block an objectionable topic of conversation; as before, he gave no sign of recognition. He nodded abstractedly, blinked, smiled. "Dessert?"

SECONDS AND THIRDS of tea and cake left Jacob groaning. "I surrender."

"But look how much is left."

"There's no obligation to eat the entire thing in one shot."

"I'm going to make you a doggie bag," Sam said.

"Not a chance. You keep it for the week."

"I'll never finish all that," Sam said. "You have to do your share."

"I think my share was done with my fourth piece of kugel."

"Shall we *bentsch*?"

"Sure."

Sam passed him a small prayer booklet, a white satin cover stamped with blue letters.

Bar Mitzvah of
Jacob Meir Lev
פרשת שופטים
ד׳ אלול תשנג
AUGUST 21, 1993

"Old school," Jacob said.

Sam fluttered his fingers in the direction of the library. "I have a box of them sitting around somewhere."

"They belong in a museum." *Of apostasy.*

They recited the grace after meals.

"Thanks for dinner."

"Thank you for taking the time . . . But Jacob? I meant what I said, before. You shouldn't minimize the importance of what you do. It's an ancient calling. It's in your Bar Mitzvah section. *'Shoftim v'shotrim.'*"

"Judges and policemen. Hey, maybe I should've been a jurist instead. Give you bragging rights, 'my son the Supreme Court Justice.'"

"I'm proud of what you are."

Jacob said nothing.

"You do know that, don't you?"

"Sure." It was the first time he could remember his father expressing an opinion, positive or negative, about his line of work. Lev family culture didn't foster typical professional-class expectations, but neither did it encourage a cop's life, and Jacob assumed that his choice had made for a source of disappointment, similar to his loss of faith.

Now the burst of earnestness made him squirm, and he steered the conversation away. "Here's a question for you. The case got me wondering about the idea that justice and charity spring from the same root. *Tzedek* and *tzedakah*."

"That's true in an imperfect world."

"Ah?" Jacob said. "Say better."

"What we call justice is a creation of human beings, and since we ourselves are creations, limited by definition, what we create is flawed. There's an enormous difference between Godly judgment and man's version. You might call it the defining difference. Human justice, like every aspect of this world, is tailored to meet our needs and suit our capabilities. In a sense, it's the opposite of pure justice . . ."

Jacob listened with half an ear as Sam got himself worked up into a rhythm. There was a reason his father was the rabbi and he the cop, and while it would be reductive to say that his career path had been forged in opposition to Sam's airy worldview, a childhood bent over books, both secular and religious, had lent allure to the notion of getting one's hands dirty.

". . . perceive as opposites in this world, for example justice and mercy, are in fact unities in the mind of God—it goes without saying that I mean that metaphorically—which, speaking of, relates to what I was saying earlier, about dialectical truth . . ."

Jacob could appreciate now that his mother must have felt the same way. In her case, the urge to escape into concreteness was literal: he remembered her fingernails, edged with brown clay that would dry and flake off in little crescent moons. A tiny accidental cosmos, accumulating in the linen closet, the pantry, waiting for the day she cleaned up the house and herself, a day that never came, so that Jacob would eventually lose patience and get out the vacuum himself.

He was both of them, neither of them—a phenomenon no less mysterious for its frequency.

Sam paused. "I'm prattling again."

"No, no . . ."

"I am, I can see you."

"See what."

"You're smiling."

"I can't smile because I'm happy?"

"I'd love for you to be happy," Sam said. "Nothing would make me happier. But I'm not sure that's why you're smiling."

"What you just said is very you."

"Who else would I be?"

Jacob laughed.

"At any rate. It's good that we never face real judgment in this world. No man could withstand the scrutiny of the Divine gaze. Every last one of us would melt like wax before fire."

"Yeah, well, I don't want to think about what I'm in for when I die," Jacob said.

"I thought you didn't believe in any of that," Sam said.

He said it so casually that it took Jacob a moment to grasp the import of what he was being confronted with. He said, "I don't know what I believe."

Sam's eyes creased behind his sunglasses. "It's a start," he said. "Now let me go fix you that doggie bag."

CHAPTER SEVENTEEN

He'd had too much to eat: his dreams blew in strong, almost sickeningly tactile. It was the garden again, and Mai again, receding as he pursued her, locking him in infinite desire.

He woke up drenched, looked down, and saw that he'd been masturbating in his sleep.

He rose groggily to finish the job in the bathroom.

Couldn't manage it. Tried to conjure her face.

No use: she vaporized.

Tried instead to conjure up some of his greatest hits.

No use.

He sat on the edge of the tub, watching his penis wilt in his hand. Turn on the TV, and ad after ad made it sound like it was a perfectly normal problem, for any man, at any age. But it was a new experience for him, and he didn't like it in the slightest.

He took the coldest shower he could stand.

By eight-thirty he was on the road to San Diego, a gas station burrito stuffed in the cup holder, fiddling with the stations to drown out reverberations of confusion and shame.

For once the freeway lived up to its name: he cruised, arriving at the Point Loma Marina fifteen minutes early. He parked and got out and took in a chestful of brine and diesel. Across the harbor, the Coronado Bridge threaded through the fog; a naval destroyer lay in for repairs. Gulls circled tauntingly. Jacob bent over the splattered call box to punch in Ludwig's number, willing the D to hurry up before he got bombed.

Ludwig's boat was a twenty-five-foot weekend cruiser named *Pension Plan*. On deck stood a keg-chested man in his early sixties, blond hair leached to white, a blue Hawaiian shirt open three buttons deep, exposing a rooster-red V of sunburnt flesh. He'd kept his stache, yellowed at the fringe by nicotine.

They shook hands and went below, occupying opposite ends of a garishly upholstered banquette set with watery iced tea.

"Clean swap," Jacob said. "I'll tell you what I've got and hopefully we can both close."

"You first."

Jacob had expected as much. He read Ludwig's skepticism as a product of having been burned before by similar claims. He wanted to help almost as much as he needed help in return.

All the same, he had his own territory to protect, and he cherry-picked in describing the scene, leaving out most of the bizarro elements and making the crime sound like a run-of-the-mill rage killing.

"I wondered what he did to piss someone off that bad," Jacob said. "Now I know."

Ludwig's fingers worked thoughtfully.

"Don't go sniffing around those families," he said. "They've been through enough."

Jacob let that pass. "Did you ever work up a suspect profile?"

"FBI gave us their opinion. White male, twenty to fifty, intelligent but underemployed, trouble with interpersonal relationships, meticulous. The usual garbage. I always did think that was—I mean, wow. 'Trouble with interpersonal relationships.' That is . . . that is insightful. That is some *superb* fuckin analysis, right there. 'Trouble with . . .'" He shook his head. "Whatever. Any of that fit your guy?"

"I don't know. I don't know who my guy is."

"What's he look like?"

Jacob showed him a photo of the head; Ludwig whistled. "Ouch."

"Bells?"

"Nobody we ever talked to."

"He couldn't've been that meticulous," Jacob said. "He left behind DNA."

"Not too many guys thinking about that in 1988," Ludwig said.

He stared at the photo, momentarily transported. Then he sagged disappointedly.

"Well, he's white," he said, tossing it down. "They got that much right."

"Who was the original D?"

"They had a whole big R-H task force, but the lead was a guy by the name of Howie O'Connor. Maybe you heard of him?"

"Don't think so."

"Grade-A prick. Good cop, though. They forced him out a couple of years after the task force folded. Some witness claims he felt her up, they tell him take a hike pending investigation. A week later, he eats a bullet. Sad stuff."

"What was his theory?"

"Far as I know, he didn't have one, or not a strong one. I never talked to him directly. I only know what was in the file, and O'Connor wasn't the kind who made up stories to fit his assumptions. The general consensus was a drifter, a guy who moves around without anyone ever really seeing him. Remember, this is happening right around the time they nailed Richard Ramirez. People see what they're conditioned to see."

"How's that sit with you?"

Ludwig shrugged. "I caught the case around when the big news was CODIS, media's going on like now we've got this magic thing's gonna solve every last coldy-moldy piece of crap taking up space in a file cabinet."

"You never got a hit," Jacob said.

"Not a one. I reran the profiles, first weekly, then monthly, then on the anniversaries of each killing. I went back and interviewed everyone who was still alive. Nothing had changed. Nobody arrested in the interim. Nobody straining at the seams with guilt. Nothing to deliver on the big promises. My commander implied that nobody would think ill of me if I buried it."

"You didn't."

"I did what I could without getting myself noticed," Ludwig said. "Then my wife got sick and I bowed out."

"Who owns it now?"

"Hell if I know. Nobody, probably. Nobody wants to touch it, cause in the first place they'd know they ain't gonna solve it, and in the second place they'd know they gotta deal with me calling them up and chewing on their ass about it whenever I get bored."

Jacob smiled. "They must love that."

"Oh, they're used to me. I have plenty of time and unlimited long distance. They treat me like a senile old goat, which if you want the truth is what I am."

"Anyone else at LAPD I should talk to?"

"No one name jumps out at me. You know how it is."

Jacob nodded. There was no tragedy so large that it would not fade, first from the headlines, then from the mind of the public, and finally from the minds of those charged to prevent its like from happening again. By the time it trickled down to a guy like Ludwig, it would have been all but erased from institutional memory, the smarter cops averting their eyes, looking out for simpler and more fruitful tasks.

What to make of Ludwig, then? The one who pursued the fleeting?

Admire him.

Pity him.

Wonder if he's you, in thirty years.

Ludwig fired up a cigar and leaned back. "Honesty time. What's your angle?"

"None," Jacob said.

"Hey, now. Don't bullshit a bullshitter. You didn't drive a hundred twenty miles to enjoy my boat."

"Put yourself in my position," Jacob said. "What would you think?"

"What do I think? I think your vic was a bad guy and he probably did a bunch of bad things in addition to killing those girls. I think he maybe did some of those bad things to other bad guys, because that's who bad guys like to hang out with: other bad guys. They get together and do bad things. It's like Satan's bowling league. Then one time you drop a ball on your friend's foot, or maybe a whole bunch of feet, and he, or they, do what bad guys do, or at least this variety of bad guy. They get mad and chop someone's head off."

"You find that satisfying?"

"I find pot roast satisfying," Ludwig said. "I find that plausible."

Jacob said, "There's something I didn't tell you."

Ludwig was expressionless, rolling the cigar in his mouth.

"Whoever waxed my guy left a message," Jacob said. "'Justice.'"

Ludwig said nothing.

"*Now* put yourself in my position. What do you think?"

"You didn't think it was worth mentioning that?"

"What do you think now?"

"I thought this was a clean swap."

Jacob did not reply.

Ludwig sighed. "Probably I'd think the same thing as you. But look. I'm telling you, I know every single one of those girls' families. It wasn't none of them did this."

"What about friends? Boyfriends?"

"A little credit, please. Those were the first guys that got looked at. O'Connor squeezed them. As did I, multiple times. They don't fit."

"Maybe they don't fit the original murders, but they might fit this. In fact, if they did fit the originals, I'd lean toward ruling them out, because what kind of sense does that make?"

"They don't fit *any* murders," Ludwig said. "I mean it. Leave them the hell alone."

A silence.

Jacob was about to apologize when Ludwig said, "Which profile did you match?"

"Pardon?"

"There's two," Ludwig said. "Which one."

Jacob said, "Two what."

Ludwig smiled. "Right. Okay."

"What," Jacob said again.

"There were two DNA profiles," Ludwig said. "Anal semen and vaginal semen. Completely different."

"Shit," Jacob said.

"Yup."

"Two guys?"

Ludwig chuckled smoke.

"And you didn't think it was worth mentioning *that*?" Jacob asked.

"Fair is fair, Detective."

"You have an interesting notion of fairness."

"I acquired mine same place you did: the Los Angeles Police Academy. And what's unfair? You said clean swap and that's what you got. Your bullshit for mine."

Jacob shook his head. "Anything else you want to share?"

"I'll tell you the identity of my secret crush."

"Look—"

"It's Salma Hayek."

"The word 'justice' was burnt into a kitchen countertop," Jacob said. "And it was in Hebrew."

"What the fuck does that mean?"

"Your guess is as good as mine."

"I don't have a guess," Ludwig said. "Hebrew?"

"Nobody told me about two guys," Jacob said.

"Yeah, cause that information was never released, not even internally. You have to read the case file. Have you read the case file?"

"I haven't had a chance yet."

Ludwig sighed. He stubbed out his cigar, drained his iced tea, and stood up. "You kids."

CHAPTER EIGHTEEN

They caravanned to a cul-de-sac in El Cajon, septuplet ranch houses worshipping a teardrop of molten asphalt. Jacob could understand why Ludwig preferred the boat: it was easily fifteen degrees hotter out here than it had been down by the water.

Inside, the blinds were drawn, the air-conditioning going full bore. Ludwig stooped to pet a languid sheepdog before leaving Jacob in the kitchen.

"One minute."

While Jacob waited, he checked out the photo propped next to the coffeemaker. The Ludwigs had bred for maximum blond: missus was as towheaded as mister, and the boys they'd produced looked like a Nelson cover band. Fresh tulips above the sink implied that Mrs. L had made it through whatever illness had caused the D to take retirement. Some woman was resident, anyway. Girlfriend? Second marriage? Jacob knew better than to ask. All happy families might be alike, and every unhappy family unhappy in its own way, but since there *are* no happy families, you never can tell.

Ludwig clomped in, schlepping a cardboard file box. He dumped it on the kitchen table and arched his back. "I made copies of everything before I left."

"Need a hand?"

"Yeah, okay."

There were thirteen boxes, one for each of the victims and four overflow. As Jacob ferried them from the garage, he noticed a curtained corner, a workbench and plywood table visible through a crack.

It reminded him of his mother's old setup, and he remembered Ludwig's comment to the reporter who'd asked how he planned to spend his free time.

Take up a hobby.

Jacob remarked on it to Ludwig, who snorted.

"That clown didn't print the rest of my answer. He goes, 'What hobby?' And I go, 'I dunno, something mindless. Like journalism.'"

Jacob laughed.

"Got to keep busy," Ludwig said, and he pulled the curtain aside.

What lay beyond was not the stuff of carved ducks. It was more like Divya Das's second bedroom, or a hybrid of the two.

There were hand tools, hardware, clamps, a glass cutter, a Shop-Vac— their purpose evident in several half-constructed shadowboxes.

There were also specimen jars, tweezers, magnifying glasses. Shelves of thick books with weak spines and USED stickers. *The Handbook of Western Butterflies. North American Lepidoptera. The Audubon Society Guide to Insects and Spiders.*

Jacob picked up a shadowbox containing three monarchs and a hand-lettered placard that read *D. plexippus.*

"Beautiful," he said.

"I told you, I'm bored. I never knew a thing about any of this until I moved down here. I never had the time. These days, it's all I have. Do yourself a favor. Stay in L.A."

LUDWIG SAID, "Anyway, that's the way it makes sense to me."

They were at the kitchen table, the dog at their feet, coffee cold, boxes exploded, paper towers occupying every chair except the two they were sitting on.

"A power struggle," Jacob said.

"Guys working in pairs, you've got a leader and a follower. There's always going to be internal tension. Twenty years of staying quiet, that's no small thing. Figure them arguing about something, going back and forth at each other, this and that, and one of them gets nervous and goes, 'I've got to take him out before he takes us both down.'"

"You think the message was a blind," Jacob said.

"It worked, didn't it? You're here asking about the victims. Or try this on: Guy A feels remorse, but instead of going to the cops he turns around and kills guy B. In his mind, that's justice."

"The cop who responded to my scene said it was a woman who called it in," Jacob said.

Ludwig said, "You're full of surprises, aren't you?"

"To me that's a reason to revisit some of the victims' families."

Ludwig nodded slowly. "Okay, maybe. But these people have suffered, you keep that right smack in the front of your mind."

"Promise," said Jacob. "Any suggestion where I should begin?"

A silence.

Ludwig said, "I hesitate to even mention this."

Jacob said nothing.

"One of the vics had a sister who was mentally ill. We never considered her for the original killings because, in the first place, she had no history of violence, and in the second place, we were only looking at men—we had semen. I guess it's not impossible to fit a crazy woman to yours. Just cause she's had some problems—"

"I know," Jacob said. "I get it."

"She'd have to succeed in tracking the guy down where we failed, and if she's anything like I remember, that's out of the question."

"Fair enough," Jacob said. "Let me talk to her, at least."

"Go easy, would you?"

"I promise. What's her name?"

"Denise Stein."

"Janet Stein's sister," Jacob said.

Ludwig nodded.

Jacob said, "Did you ever look at anyone who spoke Hebrew?"

"Someone Jewish, you mean?"

"Not necessarily."

"Who else speaks Hebrew?"

"A classically trained priest, a Bible scholar. You come across anyone like that?"

Ludwig was laughing. "Maybe I should be looking at you, Detective Lev. No. I don't remember anyone like that. If there was, it'd be in there somewhere."

Warily, Jacob regarded the mess.

Ludwig said, "Best of luck. Don't forget to write."

THEY REPACKED THE FILE BOXES and loaded them into the Honda: four in the trunk, two belted in the passenger seat, and seven stacked in the back.

A station wagon pulled into the driveway, and a slightly older version of the woman from the family photo got out, carrying a Gap bag and a supermarket rotisserie chicken.

"He's taking it off my hands," Ludwig said to her, thumbing at the boxes.

She beamed at Jacob. "My hero."

Her name was Grete. She insisted Jacob stay for dinner. While they ate, she asked if Jacob intended to take her husband's bugs, too. "Pretty please," she said.

"She won't let me bring them in the house," Ludwig complained.

"What sane human being would?"

"I think it's good to have a hobby," Jacob said. "Better that than gambling."

Grete stuck out her tongue at him.

"Listen to the man," Ludwig said. "He's a bright one."

Jacob showed him the photos of the insect from the cemetery.

"Any idea what that is? I think I have an infestation."

Ludwig put on his reading glasses. "I can't tell the scale."

Jacob demonstrated with his fingers. "About yea."

Ludwig arched an eyebrow. "Really. That big . . . ? Well, tell you what: e-mail them to me, and I'll think on it. Don't get your hopes up, though. It's black, it's shiny, it's got six legs. Could be a lot of things. You know how many species of Coleoptera there are? About a hundred jillion. They once asked this biologist what his study of nature had taught him about the Creator. He said, 'God has an inordinate fondness for beetles.'"

"Can we please, *please* talk about something else," Grete said.

Jacob asked about their kids.

The younger son was at UC Riverside, the elder a sous chef in Seattle.

"You must eat well when he comes home."

"I won't let him in my kitchen," Grete said. "He destroys it. He'll use every single pan I own to make a salad. He's used to other people cleaning up after him."

"Like father, like son," Ludwig said.

CHAPTER NINETEEN

Northbound traffic was bad, Sea World day-trippers returning to Orange County. Jacob burned most of a tank feathering the gas pedal. Behind and beside him, the boxes thumped and listed and threatened to topple, and every time he glanced in the rearview and confronted an expanse of tan cardboard, the magnitude of his new burden fell heavily on him.

Best of luck. Don't forget to write.

Thanks, Philly.

Three exits shy of LAX, a Sigalert put an accident ahead. Jacob killed the radio and settled in to wait, using the quiet to turn over his discussion with Ludwig.

The D's bias could stem from an honest belief that the family members were innocent. It could also be sensitivity to the suggestion that he had screwed up the first time around. Jacob sympathized. Anyone could benefit from a pair of fresh eyes. That didn't make looking through them any fun. He wondered how well he'd take it if a young punk with half his years and twice his energy showed up to interrogate him about his most outstanding failure.

Minus Ludwig's sales pitch, however, the Psychopath vs. Psychopath scenario held less appeal. Both versions—Jacob dubbed them Nerves and Remorse, respectively—had major shortcomings.

Remorse, because what defined a psychopath was lack thereof. It was far more common for a guy to get caught bragging than confessing.

Nerves suffered the same problem. Psychopaths didn't get anxious. Jacob knew of no calm so profound and chilling. It enabled them to engage in behaviors that would cause an ordinary person to pass out.

Also: a nervous man didn't waste time on symbolism.

Unless Ludwig was right, and the point was to juke the cops.

Psychopath trying to look like an avenger. *Ha-ha: I control everything.*

Maybe. But Jacob's instincts rebelled. He'd seen the severed head, seen the message. As gestures, they were at once too subtle and too theatrical not to be genuine.

These were telegraphs, direct from the heart.

A twisted heart, but one that felt, deeply.

A heart that longed to communicate.

Then his mind pretzled: double fake-out? Avenger trying to look like a psychopath trying to look like an avenger?

Vice versa?

How far up the theoretical beanstalk did he want to climb?

In a way, the process he was engaged in—inflating ideas to their extremes, then kicking them for soundness—drew on skills cultivated in Hebrew day school and yeshiva. Argument proceeded by putting forth a law, then presenting challenges and contradictions to it. Sometimes those challenges were resolved. Sometimes not. Sometimes the reasoning behind a law was roundly demolished but the law itself retained in practice.

It was an idiosyncratic method, a mash-up of pure logic and faith-based exegesis, insisting on the truth of many truths. You argued not to find an answer, but to argue well.

For that very reason, the method had its limitations when applied to the real world. He didn't think his superiors would be content with a series of penetrating questions.

Or would they?

Questions are good.

The basic refutation to the Psycho vs. Psycho theory was the woman on the 911 call. Ludwig had to agree that she couldn't be one of the original killers, not unless there was a third person never accounted for, and such an explanation flew in the face of parsimony. Two killers was already pushing it. Two plus a female was beyond farfetched.

Jacob laughed to himself with an unexpected memory: an old friend who kept a running list of English words that sounded like Yiddish.

Farfetched.

Far-flung.

Melts.

Inspiring Jacob to create his own list, English that sounded like Talmudic Aramaic.

Derisive.

Houdini.

Time to add a new one.

Beheaded.

The Prius in front of him stopped short, and he jammed on the brake, his brain popping and fizzing. He couldn't remember feeling this keyed up in years. He'd never get to sleep tonight without a drink.

The Venice Boulevard exit crept into view. He could be at 187 in fifteen minutes. He clicked on his turn signal.

It felt like you were stabbing me.

He clicked the signal off.

Remembered that it was the same exit for Divya Das's apartment. Clicked the signal back on.

Remembered the pull he'd felt toward her.

Off.

Remembered the news of the second offender. He'd need to call Divya on business, regardless. Good enough reason to drop by.

On.

Unannounced? At ten-fifteen on a Saturday night?

Off.

This was starting to feel like a passage of Talmud.

Tractate "Loneliness."

On.

Chapter "He Who Bangs His Coworker."

Off.

The driver behind him was probably reaching into his glove box for a handgun.

Jacob swerved into the exit lane.

HE PHONED FROM THE SIDEWALK, apologizing in advance for the disturbance. Two stories up, her face popped into view. He couldn't tell if she was smiling.

She'd left her front door ajar, and he found her in the kitchen, filling a kettle. Chopsticks pinned a black snake of hair; a bulky red terry-cloth robe emphasized the delicacy of her throat and wrists.

"I woke you up," he said.

She rolled her eyes and set out a plate of cookies. "You must consider me an absolutely enormous loser to think me asleep at this hour. To what do I owe the pleasure?"

He recounted his visit with Ludwig. Her reaction to news of the second killer was more subdued than he'd expected.

"Mm," she said. She sat down behind the breakfast bar. "That does complicate things, rather."

"That's it?"

"Well, I don't reckon it makes them *simpler*."

He blew on his tea until she clucked her tongue at him.

"If it's Snapple you wanted, there's a Vons on the corner."

But she was smiling, and she hadn't bothered to re-cinch her robe. Beneath it were pale orange surgical scrubs: more freebies scrounged from the Great Pathology Labs of the World.

"I was thinking you might be able to dig up that second profile for me," he said.

"I'd be happy to. Be patient, though. You know as well as I do that it's much faster to work backward from a known sample."

"Even if you call your friends in high places?"

"Unfortunately so. I'm not friends with everybody, and before we arrive at that point, we've got to track down where it's filed. Tell you what, I'll start first thing tomorrow morning."

"Don't bother. It can wait till Monday."

"I thought this was urgent," she said.

He shrugged. "I feel bad eating up your whole weekend."

"But we've already established that I'm an absolutely enormous loser."

"You don't need to tell me about that," he said. "I'm here, aren't I?"

"Yes," she said. "So you are."

The edge of the breakfast bar bit into his ribs, making him aware that he was leaning toward her.

Divya said, "I googled you."

He raised an eyebrow.

"Turnabout is fair play," she said.

"And? Anything interesting?"

"I hadn't realized that you were a fellow Ivy Leaguer."

"I'm not. Never graduated."

"Ah. Well. I've gone and put my foot in it again, haven't I?"

"It's all right. It was a valuable year. Or so I tell myself, cause I'm still paying it off. Anyhow, it worked out. I ended up finishing at CSUN. Same shit, different packaging."

"Why did you leave?"

"It was right after my mom died," he said. "I didn't want my dad to be alone. He's not a hundred percent—he's got vision problems, and . . . I just thought it would be better."

"That's kind of you," she said.

"Yeah, maybe."

"What's there to doubt? You did what a son ought to do."

"Yeah," he said. "Except, that's not really what happened."

She said nothing.

He said, "It's true that I wanted to be around to help him out. But that makes it sound like I came to rescue him, which is bullshit, cause he can pretty much handle himself." He paused. "I left for me. I was messed up and depressed and I couldn't hack it. I didn't turn in any work for half a semester and they took back my scholarship and threw me out. I mean, they were more polite about it. The way they phrased it was more along the lines of, 'We're inviting you to take a leave of absence until you're ready.' Technically, I can still reenroll." He laughed and shook his head. "What about you?"

Her eyes were wide with compassion, and she was biting her lip, as if to hold back platitudes. "Me?"

"Why'd you leave home?" He thought that true compassion, at that moment, would be to agree to change the subject. She seemed to come to the same conclusion, for she smiled and said, "Fleeing adulthood."

"Ah."

"My parents are very traditional. They had an arranged marriage. It worked for them. Naturally they can't understand why I wouldn't want one. Time's running out. Now they're petrified I'm never going to get married. The last time I went back, my mother sat me down and asked if I'm a lesbian."

He smiled, sipped tea.

"For the record, I'm not."

"Not my business one way or the other," he said.

A silence.

Once again he was grateful for the breakfast bar, resentful for the breakfast bar.

He said, "Listen, I don't know what your deal is—"

But she was already looking down, shaking her head.

He grinned. "That has to be some kind of record. I didn't even finish my sentence."

"I'm sorry if I gave you the wrong impression," she said.

"It happens. I'm sorry, too."

She knotted her hands. "You don't understand, though."

"I'm a big boy. I get it."

"No," she said. "You don't."

A silence.

She said, "I'm not like you, Jacob."

In her mouth, with her accent, his name sounded more like the Hebrew version, Yakov.

"Different can be good," he said.

"Sometimes, yes."

"But not in this case," he said.

"It's not as though I'm particularly happy about it."

"Then you're right. I don't understand."

"Whether I'm happy or you're happy is not the real question."

"I think it is," he said. "I think that's the only question."

"Do you? Really?"

"What else is there?"

She didn't answer.

He said, "People like you and me, we see suffering every day. We see death. I don't know what that's taught you. To me, it's the moment, this moment, that counts."

She smiled wistfully. "If not now, when."

He blinked. "Yes."

She sighed, pulled her bathrobe tight, stood.

"I'll call you when I have something to report, Detective Lev."

Back on the sidewalk, Jacob watched her window, waiting for the light to blink out. When it did, the sudden darkness yielded a sky full of cold stars.

ENOCH

Asham learned as a girl to mark the days by the cycle of the sun, but in a featureless land, a seasonless land, risings and settings mock her.

She stops counting. Then she forgets that a count ever existed.

She forgets where she is going. Forgets why she wanted to go there.

It isn't a question of failing resolve; she simply cannot recall what was done or who did it. She forgets there was something to forget.

Her own voice says *Go home*.

She doesn't know what that means.

One day she is no longer looking for her brother or her home but for the tree-tall man Michael. She will fall at his feet and beg him to end her torment.

If he is as merciful as she remembers, he will do it gladly.

Perhaps she misremembers, though. Perhaps she imagined him.

The heat pummels her. The world flickers and glints.

She travels at twilight like the rodents whose eyes flash in the dusk. Snakes molting against the stones teach her to scrub her limbs with sand. She darts lizardlike after lizards, stomping their heads and sucking out their hot slick innards.

Seeing people, she runs toward them. Like the pools of cool water that appear when the sun is high, their faces evaporate as she draws near. Beckoning hands sprout spikes. In fury she slashes them open, licking at the astringent moisture inside.

Every day is the same.

Every day, the earth shakes.

The first time she felt it, she thought it was her own body trembling. A bone-splitting crack, followed by the appearance of a jagged cleft in the otherwise uniform plain, showed her the truth. She was too confused, and it ended too quickly, for her to feel genuinely frightened.

The next time, however, her mind was primed. She felt the movement and heard the roar and began screaming and running in circles until it ended. There was no place to hide, no reason to think she could.

The wrath of the Lord was upon her.

When, after days without number, a new shape appears on the horizon, she initially takes it as another mirage.

Rather than shrink and dissolve, however, the shape grows larger and sharper as she approaches, casting a lengthy rectangular shadow.

It is a lone wall, fissured and wind-worn. Made not of lashed branches, like the walls of her family's hut (for a happy instant she remembers that; remembers them), but of dried clay—the same ocher clay she stands on, the same clay she has wandered forever.

Somehow it has been summoned up from the bed of the plain, commanded to take shape and to remain erect.

She studies the seams between the blocks; scrapes at the wall's surface, grit collecting under her fingernails.

More blocks demarcate the intended outline of the structure. The other walls have collapsed, if they ever stood. There is no roof. It appears as though the builder gave up midway through.

The symmetry, the ingenuity: she is looking at Cain's handiwork.

Why would he abandon his efforts?

She has her answer that afternoon.

Curled up in the shadow of the wall, she jolts awake with the angry earth. Luck saves her, for she has not managed to move before the wall buckles and heaves away from her, collapsing into rubble.

Eventually the shaking stops, and she uncovers her head and rises in a cloud of fine clay dust. The pile of broken blocks sighs as it settles, disappointed to have missed her.

Had she slept on the other side—or had the wall chosen to fall toward her—she would surely be dead.

The futility of building on such fickle ground is clear to her. Cain must have understood, too. He will keep going until he finds a more sensible place to camp.

She experiences a stab of kinship.

Kinship rekindles memory.

Memory rekindles hatred.

She waits till evening to strike out, the anger in her heart reborn.

SEVERAL MONTHS LATER, she finds the second hut.

All that time she has been walking in a straight line, away from the setting sun. She has done so because it's what Cain would do. She turns her thoughts to his, and signs of him begin to reappear, and the path glows anew.

She will not falter again.

Within days, the sameness of the plain gives way to isolated stands of trees. Grass appears, first furtively, then with confidence, and then overwhelmingly, swarming forth like so many locusts. Thorny grass; sticky grass; a grass that makes Asham's mouth feel cold and another that smells spicy and makes her itch for a week if she is so unwise as to brush against it.

Against this pale terrain, the black stains of campfires long abandoned stand out, and the glowing path leads her to the broken skeleton of a medium-sized beast, its bones finely scored by a stone blade.

The cut marks are efficient, the product of a practiced hand.

Deep in the grasslands, the earth no longer stinks or smokes or shakes. The weather turns mild enough to sustain streams and ponds. They return a horrifying reflection when she kneels to drink: flaking skin lies tight against her bones. Her scalp shows through where clumps of hair have fallen out.

The second hut, when she comes to it, is no surprise. She has been sensing it for some days. Nor is she surprised to observe Cain refining his methods. Three thick walls, a mat of woven grass, a pile of unused clay blocks.

Animal bones abound, some of them fashioned into tools she cannot identify. She selects one the length of her arm, its point menacingly honed, before setting out again.

EACH OF THE NEXT two huts is larger and more elaborate than its predecessor. The fifth is more impressive still; it's more than a hut, really, consisting of several outer structures arrayed around a dominant central building.

Curiously, while the smaller buildings contain the by now familiar signs of habitation—seed husks, bone tools, ash—the largest building houses nothing but a towering clay pillar, painstakingly worked smooth.

Something important occurred here. It is not like the Cain she knows to build without a practical purpose in mind.

And having built, it is not like him to run.

He must know that she is behind.

That night, she sits before the fire with a handful of berries. Since entering the grasslands, she has returned to surviving on plants.

How disturbed she is, then, to find herself yearning for a taste of flesh.

And how convenient to turn and find a bloody hunk before her.

Without hesitation she buries her face in it. Quiveringly fresh, unimaginably delicious, and best of all, it never runs short: new flesh grows in to fill in the cavities where she tears at it with her teeth. Her stomach swells to bursting but she cannot stop eating, not until she hears her name called and looks up to see that the meat is not a detached slab but a living limb.

It is Cain's thigh, raggedly joined to his body at the socket.

He gazes at her kindly. *Satisfy yourself.*

She awakes from the dream with her face and neck wet: saliva has pooled in the hollow of her throat and dried across her chin.

WHILE TRAVELING ONE EVENING, she feels a wet sensation and glances down to see that she has cut her thigh. She didn't feel it happen, but as soon as she probes the wound and discovers its depth, it begins to throb. A long trail of red drops follows her. She tears a strip of soiled linen from her blanket, binds herself up, and presses on.

Within minutes, the fabric is saturated and dripping. She grimaces and hurries ahead to a small clearing, easing down to retie the linen. She jerks it tight, steadies herself to stand, pauses.

She is not alone.

Unseen bodies ripple the grass. She reaches for a stone and whips it into the grass with a shout. The movement stops.

A low growl follows. Another in reply.

Silence.

They're moving again.

She hurls another rock. The rippling of grass tips continues, undeterred. Her first shot missed. They know she cannot harm them.

She stands, clutching the bone spear in one hand, her injured leg with the other.

Waits.

Black snouts appear, twitching greedily.

Tongues swing from yellow spotted faces set in round skulls. Idiot grins.

She counts four, five, six, seven. They are bony, haloed by fleas. They stand as high as her waist. She would tower over them, if she weren't bent awkwardly, holding her bleeding leg.

The largest one raises its snout and begins to laugh.

It is a demon sound.

The rest of the pack joins in, a mad cackling chorus.

The first attack comes from behind and is meant to test her. She swings the spear, raking the ground but missing the animal by a wide margin. It sinks into the grass, laughing.

The others laugh, as well.

They are enjoying themselves.

You go first they seem to be saying. *No, please. I insist.*

A charge for her flank: she swings, making contact with the side of the spear. The animal yelps and bolts, and in its wake come two more, one for her leg, the other leaping at her throat.

She screams and stabs and slices and moments later an animal lies whimpering, its belly leaking offal, one leg scrabbling as it tries to push itself to safety.

She limps to it and kneels and drives the spear through its throat, silencing it for good.

She yanks the spear free and stands, her arms running red.

The leader growls.

They've underestimated her.

They all come at once, from every direction, and soon she has been punctured and bitten and clawed insensate, no longer feeling pain but a numb disappointment that she should fail so ingloriously, to such inglorious adversaries. It's not like her to go without a fight.

She fights.

She takes another creature and a third but they are too numerous and too coordinated, she can smell their fetid breath as she falls and pulls into a ball and they try to snap her spine through her neck and she flexes in terror as they must have known she would and snouts burrow into her belly which tightens in anticipation and she waits to die and then there is a howl, deeper and stronger than the howls of the beasts devouring her.

Instantly the air clears; instantly it refills with movement. A white cloud hovers over her, leaps over her, circles her; it snarls and lunges at her attackers, driving them back, laughing, into the grass, until the last of them is gone and she is alive.

Their cackles fade.

Quiet panting.

She uncurls.

Aside from the two she killed, a third beast lies savaged, its head nearly torn off.

Beyond it, a familiar shape stands watching her.

Abel's sheepdog, its mouth smeared with gore.

She reaches for it with a trembling hand.

It trots forward and licks her bloody palm clean. Stands back.

She struggles to her feet, steadies herself on the spear.

The dog crosses the clearing, pausing to make sure she follows.

THE DISTANCE THEY TRAVEL ought to take no more than half a day. In her current state, it takes two. Her thirst never seems to abate, and she stops frequently to rebind her wounds. The smallest have already scabbed. Others sting in the open air but are dry.

It's the gash on her leg that worries her. It continues to ooze blood as well as a greenish slime that reeks of rot. The pain roots into her flesh, knotting up close to the bone, an ache that expands and contracts in time with her heartbeat. Her skin burns, tender to the touch, and the swelling has climbed to swallow her knee, slowing her further.

Sensing that she is not well, the dog keeps its distance, walking far enough ahead to urge her on, close enough to ward off danger. It's limping, too; one of the beasts must have bitten it. She tries to show how sorry she is for having dragged it into a fight. She apologizes, aloud.

It never betrays impatience. It never seems to tire, patrolling as she sleeps.

On the second day, it leads her to the rim of a new valley, a smaller, drier version of the place she grew up.

What it cradles transfixes her.

A massive complex of clay buildings stretches on and on and on, a rough tan rash cut at regular intervals by open passages allowing free transit from one place to the next.

Transit for the hundreds of people therein.

The dog barks and begins its descent.

The slope is severe and rocky and Asham is light-headed. Her wounded leg can bear weight for only a moment before agony shoots up through her groin and into her torso. She balances with her hands, reaching the valley floor with palms scraped raw.

The dog knows where it's going. Otherwise, she would be instantly lost in the maze of buildings. Ranging from modest to grand, they reflect their inhabitants, who are young and old, fat and thin, diversely dressed, with skins milk-white or tar-black and every shade in between.

Their reactions to her are identical: they drop what they're doing to gawk. What a spectacle she must present, filthy and half dead. As she limps along, a crowd collects behind her, their whispers a gathering storm of mistrust.

A man steps out to bar her way.

"Who are you?"

She says, "My name is Asham."

More men appear beside him, each armed with a bone spear, similar to hers but made longer by the addition of a wooden handle.

"What crime have you committed?" the man asks.

"None."

"Then why have you come here?"

"I don't know where here is," she says.

The people murmur.

"This is the city of Enoch," the man says.

"What's a city?"

Laughter. Asham's leg pulses with pain. Her throat sticks to itself. She has not drunk in hours—a mistake.

"I was attacked by beasts," she says. "The dog saved me and brought me here."

"And why would it do that?"

"It knows me," she says. "It belongs to my brother."

Silence.

Then the crowd erupts, shouting at one another, at the man, at her. They surge forward to take hold of her, but the dog rushes to her side, barking and snapping, just as it did before.

The crowd withdraws, quieting to a resentful simmer.

"You speak truly," the man says.

"Of course I do," Asham says.

A smile plays at the man's lips. He bows and stands aside.

The crowd parts.

The dog leads her on.

Nobody touches her, but she can feel them following at a distance.

The dog turns to a clay building of surpassing size and perfection. It is magnificent to behold, as are the two bare-chested men guarding its stepped entrance. The dog skips up the stairs, pausing to bark at her before disappearing through the doorway.

Leg throbbing, she limps forward. The guards cross their spears, blocking her.

The crowd that followed her is murmuring again.

"Please let me pass," she says.

The guards do not bat an eye. They do not move a muscle, and there are a lot of muscles to move. She tries to peer around them, but they are broad as oxen and they shift to obstruct her view.

The dog comes wriggling out through the guards' legs, barking.

A voice from behind them says, "Open, please."

The guards slide apart to reveal a young boy dressed in clean skins. A bright yellow band encircles his head. A yellow flower hangs on a thong around his neck. His eyes are dark and curious.

The dog runs to Asham, wagging its tail and barking impatiently.

"Hello," the boy says. "I'm Enoch. Who're you?"

"Asham."

"Hello, Asham."

"Is this your dog?"

The boy nods.

"He's very nice," she says.

The boy nods again. "What happened to your leg?"

A clammy wave breaks over her. "I hurt it."

"I'm sorry," Enoch says. "Would you like to come inside?"

THE INTERIOR TEMPERATURE COMES as a shock. She begins to shiver. The room is cavernous, littered with carved wooden stools and broken up by doorways that open onto darkness. Torches along the wall partially relieve the dim.

"I've never seen you before," Enoch says. It's an observation made without malice. "Where do you come from?"

"Far away."

"That's interesting," he says.

She smiles despite her discomfort. "Do you have any water, please?"

Enoch takes the yellow flower around his neck and shakes it, producing a sharp sound.

A bare-chested man silently materializes in one of the doorways.

"Water, please," Enoch says.

The man disappears.

Asham is still staring at the flower. "What is that?"

"A bell, silly."

"I've never seen one before."

"Why not?"

"I just—I haven't. They don't have bells where I come from."

"Far away."

"Yes, far away."

"That's interesting," the boy says.

"Can I try?"

Enoch removes the thong and hands it to her. She shakes the bell, but the sound she produces is muted, nothing like the clear, piercing ring.

"No, no," he says. "Like this." He grasps the bell by its top and rings. "See?"

A new bare-chested man steps through a different door.

The boy giggles and hands the bell back to Asham. "Now you."

She rings.

A third bare-chested man appears.

"Does that happen every time?" she asks.

"Oh, yes. Try it and see."

Asham summons two more men, one of whom jostles the first man, hurrying in with a shining vessel that coughs water onto the floor. The three other men run to wipe it up, while the boy giggles and claps his hands and says, "Again, again," and Asham complies, ringing the bell, bringing yet more men and resulting in confusion and dancing and more spilled water, and then footsteps approach and all the men withdraw rapidly to the wall, standing at attention as a new voice, tight with exasperation, cuts through the commotion.

"I've warned you: if you can't stop that nonsense, I'm going to take it away."

He emerges wearing a cape of skin, and carrying a flaming staff, and immediately she sees how the years have changed him. He is harder and leaner, and though he wears his hair long, it has receded at the front, so that the cord of scar tissue bisecting his forehead stands out. The sight of it causes Asham to swoon.

"It wasn't me," Enoch says. "She asked to try it."

Cain does not reply.

"He's right," Asham says. Another wave of light-headedness overtakes her, more powerful than the last. She digs her fingernails into the flesh of her palm. "Don't blame him."

"Leave us," Cain says.

The bare-chested men disperse.

"You, too."

"Why?" Enoch asks.

"*Go.*"

The boy frowns but obeys.

Save the memory of the bell and the hiss of flames, the room is perfectly still.

Asham says, "You stole his dog, too."

Cain smiles. "You must be tired." He draws out a wooden stool. "Why don't you sit down?"

She cannot move. Her body tingles unaccountably. Her knees knock together.

The torches shrink. The room shrinks and spins.

She has so much to say.

She faints.

CHAPTER TWENTY

The Creeper's paper trail reflected the case's long and complicated history, as well as the march of technology and the passage of time.

There were black-and-white photographs, color photographs, photographs that had been digitally scanned and reprinted. Interview transcripts and autopsy reports and forensic reports, enough documentation to reconstitute a medium-sized forest.

The earliest reports were typewritten or stippled by a dot-matrix; then smudged, the result of being whipped too quickly from the mouth of an inkjet. Most recently, the laser print was faint, as department-wide cutbacks had turned the wait for a new toner cartridge into a Soviet breadline.

He counted forty-three different handwritings, some a single margin scrawl, a couple that filled page upon page—the key players on the LAPD end.

Howie O'Connor wrote in a blocky script that mirrored his nononsense approach. He was a grinder, a list maker, plotting the locations of the murders on a map to rule out a geographical pattern.

He was also bit of a bully in the interrogation room, cutting people off in mid-sentence when they strayed from answering his questions.

In Jacob's mind, this was a cardinal sin for a detective. The idea was to get the other guy talking, and to do that, you had to shut up, let the mind wobble where it wanted. The best interviewers were like therapists, silence their sharpest tool.

Google offered a couple of pictures that might or might not have been O'Connor. It wasn't an uncommon name. Nothing about a sexual harassment scandal. Hushed up or never publicized. These days they'd be blogging about it in Uzbekistan before the guy had time to zip up his pants.

Ludwig had called O'Connor a good cop; maybe the Creeper wasn't his finest hour.

Maybe the impatience and witness groping were both signs of the same malaise, a decent man anesthetized by horror and buried in bureaucracy.

Maybe the case itself had driven him over the edge.

Jacob put the brakes on that train of thought. An atlas of Howard O'Connor's psyche would tell him nothing about nine murders.

Aside from their youth and clean looks, the victims had little in common. They did not run in the same social circles. Cathy Wanzer and Laura Lesser both patronized a bar on Wilshire and Twenty-sixth, but everyone from boyfriends to bartenders swore up and down that the women didn't know each other, and after keeping an eyeball on the place for months, O'Connor had chalked it up to coincidence.

MO was another story. That was consistent.

All nine lived alone, in unalarmed one-level houses or ground-floor apartments with a larger-than-average amount of space separating them from neighboring buildings.

No sign of forced entry.

Looking back, Jacob could understand the intensity of the public panic.

A monster waltzing into your home, slaughtering you, vanishing.

Hard as it was to imagine by today's standards, prior to the fifth murder, nobody had thought to check the semen samples against each other.

Hence there was no hint that O'Connor had considered the possibility of two killers until frustratingly late in the game.

Jacob tried to bear in mind the constraints of the era. In 1988, DNA testing was new, fancy, expensive. Its admissibility in court was subject to debate; the decision to spend the time and money would have been far from automatic.

In 1988, the watchword was *end gang violence.*

The collective computing power of LAPD, circa 1988, could fit on Jacob's smartphone.

O'Connor deserved credit for requesting a test in the first place, more credit still for connecting the murders as quickly as he had.

It was evident in the files when Ludwig had taken over: Jacob recognized his neat handwriting from the monarch butterfly shadowbox. His touch was lighter than O'Connor's. He asked the right questions—which was to say, the questions Jacob would've asked—gathering up loose ends and snipping them off.

Whatever his advantages as an investigator, however, they were more than canceled out by the intervening decade. Memories had weakened, details blurred. People had died, or left town, or grown rigid with resentment at being asked to revisit the worst moment of their lives yet again. Some were outright hostile, refusing to talk until they saw evidence of progress.

His master list of interviewees ran to thirty-six pages. A handful of names were starred. Jacob didn't know if that meant they deserved special attention or could be ruled out.

Denise Stein was not among them.

The floor of the apartment was quilted with paper, bottles of Beam placed at strategic points, enabling Jacob to reach out and grab one without looking. He took a swallow and began crawling around, hunting for Howie O'Connor's file on the Stein murder.

O'Connor's remarks about Denise were brief. She'd been the one to find her sister's body. The detective considered her too ill to be a suspect.

Jacob guessed no one had taken the time to interview her at length.

No reason to. They wanted the Creeper, not the Creeper Avenger.

He sat at his desk, waved the mouse to clear away the screen saver.

Denise Stein was off the grid. No known address. No criminal record. The phone number Ludwig listed for her went to somebody else's machine.

Was she institutionalized? Jacob doubted a doctor or administrator would confirm that over the phone. He'd have to show up in person to plead his case, hoping he wouldn't be forced to jump through legal hoops.

He rummaged in the kitchen for anything within three months of its expiration date, returned to the living room with Lev's Special Shish Kabab: seven martini olives impaled on a bamboo skewer. He pulled them off slowly, chewed slowly, concentrating on their meaty texture to avoid looking at the crime scene photos stacked atop the coffee table.

He'd been saving those for last, wanting to first explore both Ds' perspectives thoroughly. Only then could he objectively assimilate the raw visuals.

A lie. He didn't want to assimilate them.

He stalled some more, tossing the skewer into the sink, wiping his hands on his pants, pouring himself another drink. Easing over sideways; using his peripheral vision to make an abstraction of the first corpse; and then he looked unsparingly at Helen Girard, seeing her as her boyfriend had encountered her on the afternoon of March 9, 1988.

Nude, legs spread, facedown, the bed pushed aside to make room for her on the floor.

The autopsy report noted friction abrasions at wrists and ankles, though she'd been unbound at the time of discovery. Diffuse bruising on her lower back suggested the killer had been kneeling atop her, yanking her head up to slit her throat down to the spine.

Arterial spray striped the baseboards, the bed-skirt, formed an oblong stain in the carpet that stretched toward a windowpane hazy with daylight.

The bulk of the blood had pooled around her, soaking into the pile, drying black, suspending her over a depthless chasm.

To forestall nausea, Jacob asked himself questions.

Why tie her up, then free her? Afraid of leaving evidence? A little fight to heighten the excitement?

Cheapskates unwilling to spring for more than one piece of rope?

He moved on to Cathy Wanzer.

Likewise prone on her bedroom floor, likewise tied and subsequently freed, throat cut.

Similar spatter pattern, a long arm of lifeblood growing from a matte black hole.

Another point of similarity: the rest of her apartment was pristine. She hadn't put up a fight. Maybe they'd told her they didn't intend to harm her, as long as she complied.

That changed with Christa Knox. Signs of a major struggle in the bedroom—a toppled nightstand, a closet door listing on a broken hinge—spilled into the living room, where her body was laid out, blood spreading erratically on the Spanish tiles, sending out tributaries and plugging gaps in the grout.

She'd awoken and seen them.

Known what was coming.

Tried to run.

Further proof of her will to live: her knees and forearms were severely bruised, a chunk of hair missing at the base of her skull.

She'd wrenched and kicked and died all the same.

No semen recovered.

They got spooked—too much noise?

Patty Holt was a wisp of a woman, but like Christa she had fought back, making it to her kitchen for her last stand. The nonvictim blood Divya had mentioned showed up along the broken edge of a ceramic plate.

Good for you, Patty.

Jacob didn't think it coincidental that the killers had next chosen to break pattern. By then the story was front-page news. They could no longer take stealth for granted.

So while the first four murders had occurred between midnight and three a.m., Laura Lesser died around ten in the morning after coming off a graveyard shift at the VA. Sitting in her den in pajamas, watching television, eating breakfast.

Jacob pictured her leaping up at the sight of two men.

Dropping her grapefruit juice.

A bowl of cereal had survived unscathed on the arm of the sofa.

Howie O'Connor had diligently recorded that its contents had turned to mush.

Alarmed by Laura's absence at work, her best friend and coworker dropped by, peeking in windows when her knocks went unanswered. The house had a second bedroom Laura used as a walk-in closet; piles of shoes had been kicked aside to make space for her body.

Shortly thereafter the city had gone into lockdown.

Four months of peace.

When the killers resumed, it was with a return to form, a nighttime break-in, gore and damage confined to Janet Stein's bedroom.

The following morning, Denise Stein let herself into the apartment with her duplicate key. She often crashed on her sister's futon when things got rough for her at home. The two of them had made plans to go shopping for jeans; seeing the bedroom door closed, Denise assumed Janet to still be asleep. She helped herself to a Coke, waiting half an hour before growing impatient enough to enter without knocking.

An already troubled young woman, walking into *that*.

What the hell was he going to say to her?

The seventh murder was mildly anomalous. Inez Delgado was the second victim whose body did not yield semen samples; her wrists showed no evidence of rope abrasions; and while she'd been found in her bedroom, the rest of her house had been trashed, too.

Jacob's initial impression was that she'd attempted to escape, knocking things over before fleeing back to the bedroom to try and lock herself inside.

Differences in the wound and spatter patterns put the lie to this. Inez had been stabbed in the abdomen fifteen times, painting the bathroom with blood and bile. Smear marks ran from there, down the hall, to the foot of her bed, where the relative lack of pooling around her throat led the coroner to suggest that it had been slit postmortem.

A need for consistency? Six cut throats demanded a seventh?

Katherine Ann Clayton was missing for a week before an upstairs neighbor called the landlord to complain about a smell.

Sherri Levesque, a single mother, had dropped her five-year-old at his grandparents' for the weekend.

Jacob's coffee machine clicked on.

Despite having worked through the night, despite having had minimal sleep in three days, he felt wired. That alarmed him; the only person he knew who could work uninterrupted for days on end was his mother, in the midst of a manic high.

There was no blood test for bipolar. No definitive genetic marker.

He tiptoed around folders and bottles to his bedroom and set an eight-thirty alarm.

Stripping naked, he slid between tangled sheets, stared at the popcorn ceiling.

Wide, wide, wide awake.

He couldn't disentangle how much of his agitation had to do with the crime scene photos, how much had to do with the physical side effects of being awake for so long, and how much stemmed from the anxiety of *knowing* he'd been awake for so long.

He sat up. Time for a nightcap.

Morningcap.

Whatever works.

CHAPTER TWENTY-ONE

Denise and Janet Stein's parents lived in Holmby Hills, their Dutch Colonial manse set back behind pittosporum hedges. Jacob rang the intercom. The maid came on to inform him that nobody was home.

"Try the club."

He turned to face a woman with pink flotation-device lips, pink Juicy Couture tracksuit, a Yorkshire terrier on a pink leash with a pink Swarovski-studded collar.

"They're there every afternoon," the woman said.

The dog crouched to lay a turd on the Steins' front lawn.

"It's Denise I'm looking for," he said.

The woman smiled abundantly. "I'm sure they can tell you where she is."

The club, it emerged, was the Greencrest Country Club, two miles west on Wilshire. Jacob thanked her. As he drove off, he glanced in his rearview, calculating what percentage of the woman was biodegradable and frowning to see that she'd left without picking up after her dog.

His badge couldn't get him through the gate.

He called Abe Teitelbaum.

"Yakov Meir, my wayward boy. How are you?"

"Hey, Abe. Still fighting the good fight. Yourself?"

"Putting up no resistance whatsoever. And your father the *lamed-vavnik*?"

"Anyone who thinks he's a *lamed-vavnik* is by definition not a *lamed-vavnik*."

"I didn't say he thinks it," Abe said. "*I* think it. And I don't think, I know. What gives?"

Jacob conveyed his predicament.

"Time me," Abe said.

While Jacob listened to hold music, he observed a remarkable change come over the fellow in the security booth. He reached lazily to answer the desk phone—then bolted from his chair, peering through the smoked glass, stricken with the fear of God.

Jacob smiled and waved.

At the count of eighty-one, the barrier arm went up.

Abe came back on the line. "Am I having any effect?"

"Like Moshe at the Red Sea," Jacob said.

"Peachy. Have a drink. Put it on my tab."

Greencrest had been founded by Jews denied membership in the city's venerable gentile country clubs. Candids of studio founders and comedians bygone plastered the walls. Policies had eased up in the seventies, but the dining room retained a distinctly synagogue-y vibe, populated by unsomber men and women who laughed heartily, ate with gusto, dressed well. Like the oak coffering the ceiling, they showed evidence of polish applied and admirably reapplied.

The manager who met Jacob at the door discreetly inclined his head toward a booth, where a woman in expensive knitwear sat drinking alone. "Please make it quick," he said.

Otherwise chicly made-up, Rhoda Stein had missed a spot at the base of her throat. The flamingo flush told Jacob that the colossal piña colada in front of her wasn't her first of the day.

She looked him up and down and said, "I gave at the office."

He smiled. "Jacob Lev, LAPD. May I?"

She waved indifferently.

He sat. "Is your husband around?"

"Sauna. Sweating out the toxins." Her swig left lipstick on the rim of the glass. "You must be new. I've never seen you before."

He nodded.

"Younger every year, they get." She dabbed her mouth with a starched napkin, leaving another smudge. "Well. What is it this time?"

Jacob said, "It's about Denise."

Rhoda Stein started visibly. "You mean Janet."

"Denise," he said. "I need to get in touch with her."

She stared at him.

From beyond a plate glass window, the plink of a driving range.

He said, "I know you've gone through a lot. I can't begin to imagine it. I want you to know that I'm a hundred percent committed to getting justice for Janet. And right now, the best way for you to help me achieve that is by helping me speak to Denise."

"I like that," Rhoda Stein said. "'Justice for Janet.'"

He waited.

"We started a foundation in her name. To promote literacy. Maybe we should've called it that instead. 'Justice for Janet.' Catchy. Not very optimistic, though. What do you think?"

He said, "I think this must be difficult for you."

"How'd you get past the guard?"

"It wasn't easy."

"Nor should it be," she said. "That's the point of a club: to keep the world out. Check your cares at the door, share a joke, a nice meal. Arturo makes a great piña colada, real fruit juice, not like some vulgar premixed resort swill. Care to try?"

"No, thanks."

She drank, dabbed, said, "You want to talk to Denise."

"I'm curious to know what she's been up to lately."

Rhoda nodded, nodded, kept nodding. She took another healthy swig and peered into her glass, sighing as though disappointed to find it half full.

"Such a shame to waste it," she said.

She threw the drink in his face, dabbed her lips, dropped her napkin on the table, stood up, and tottered away.

Jacob sat, stunned, his chin dripping.

But not for long. In the storied history of the Greencrest Country Club, enough drinks had been thrown in enough faces that a protocol existed. Within ninety seconds, a phalanx of tuxedoed men advanced, waving rags. They wiped down the tabletop and seats, removed the offending glass, handed Jacob a clean napkin and a glass of seltzer for his shirt.

As for the other club members, they'd seen it all before, too. They paused but briefly before returning to their eating and yakking.

"Hey. Pal."

A wizened man in a cashmere blazer had taken the toothpick out of his mouth and was beckoning him toward a nearby booth.

Jacob approached, mopping his neck.

The man said, "Listen, kid, leave her alone, wouldja? She's been through hell."

"I'm aware of that," Jacob said. "I'm trying to help her."

The man's lunch companion hunched behind amber sunglasses that reminded Jacob of his father's. He said, "She's heard that a million times."

"This is different."

"Different how?"

"I need to talk to her daughter," Jacob said.

"Her daughter's dead."

"Not that one. The other one."

The men exchanged a look. *Moron.*

"Kid," the first guy said, "they're both dead."

The manager's voice drifted from the lobby. *Ask him to leave, please.*

Jacob said, "Shit."

The second guy nodded. "She hung herself a couple years back."

"Shit . . ."

"Yeah," the first guy said. "Shit."

Footsteps.

"Excuse me," Jacob said.

He ducked out, jogging down a musty corridor that gave onto a breezeway. Signs pointed the way to the golf shop, fitness center, Founder's Lounge. Rhoda Stein was nowhere to be seen.

The smiling woman behind the fitness center desk handed him a sign-in sheet.

He wrote *Abe Teitelbaum*. "Sauna?"

"Basement level," she said. "Enjoy."

Jacob trod carefully on the slick tile, averting his gaze from furred potbellies and pendulous scrota. Nobody—no body—younger than seventy. What would happen to the roster when the Greatest Generation died out? They'd have to start running promotional discounts.

The sauna was deserted except for one man sitting motionless on the highest tier, head back, eyes closed, perspiration coursing down his torso while around him steam swirled and sank. He evoked some mountaintop Jewish Buddha.

"Mr. Stein?" Jacob said.

The guy didn't open his eyes. "Yeah?"

"Jacob Lev. I need to apologize to you."

"I forgive you."

"You haven't heard what I had to say yet."

Stein shrugged. "Life's too short for grudges."

Jacob's shirt, already glued to his front with piña colada, was beginning to stick to his back with sweat. "I upset your wife."

Now Stein peered at him through the mist. "Why'd you do that?"

"I didn't mean to. I—I made a serious mistake."

"What mistake."

Jacob hesitated, then told him.

Stein burst out laughing. "That's goddamned awful."

"I'm sorry."

"No, no, listen: that's more or less the worst thing I ever heard. And trust me, I've heard some winners. Did she take em?"

"Pardon me?"

"My wife. Your balls. Did she take em."

Jacob shook his head. "I guess I got lucky."

"You got that right, amigo," Stein said. "So? Why're you talking to me?"

"I—"

"Ahhhh *I* get it: you want to try and top yourself. Well, hunh. Dunno, I can't think of anything. Lessee. Okay, how about, how bout this: 'Hey, Eddie, Detective'—what is it, again?"

"Lev."

"'Detective Lev here. Good news, I got a lead on your daughters, turns out they're both alive. Denise's turning tricks at a truck stop in Barstow. And Janet, she works as a press secretary for Hezbollah. Just kidding, they're still dead as Christ.'" Stein smiled. "How'd I do?"

"Look—"

"Don't spare my feelings. Be honest. One to ten."

"Look, I'm sorry. I really am. I feel like an asshole—"

"Trust that feeling."

"—but your wife ran off before I could say anything, and I don't know where she went."

"That's easy," Stein said. "To get a refill."

Jacob said, "I just want to tell her I'm sorry."

Eddie Stein wiped his face and stood up. "Come on, let's go."

Standing before an open locker, Stein said, "Don't let me catch you ogling my manhood. Jealousy's a negative emotion."

"No, sir."

"People have been known to try. Its reputation precedes it. Although,"

Stein said, toweling his stomach, "come to think, I can't say anything precedes it. It's always the first one in the room."

Now Jacob really did want to look. Stein wasn't lying.

"Don't think I don't see you, Lev."

Jacob faced the opposite wall.

"Mind if I ask what you want with my dead kid?"

Jacob made a judgment call. "We found one of the guys."

Behind him, the whisk of terry cloth on flesh cut off. "Found who?"

"One of the guys who killed Janet. He's dead."

Silence. Jacob worried that he'd given Stein a coronary. "I'm going to turn around," he said. "You can cover up."

But Eddie didn't cover up. He was standing with the limp towel in his limp hand, his face streaming to match his still-streaming chest.

Jacob said, "Do you need a doctor?"

"No, you schmuck, I need a tissue."

Jacob pulled one from the dispenser. "I'm sorry to tell you like this."

"Sorry? What the fuck are you sorry for? That's the best news I heard since the little blue pill went generic." He looked at Jacob. "He's dead? What happened to him?"

"Somebody cut his head off," Jacob said.

Eddie barked a laugh. "Fantastic. Who?"

"I don't know."

Eddie nodded musingly. Then he seemed to recall that he was naked and pulled the towel around his waist. "I said no peeksies and I meant it. Go wait in the hall."

A few minutes later he emerged in fitted plaid slacks, a bright blue Izod shirt, and cream-colored calfskin loafers. His white hair was gelled back to his scalp.

"Tell me if I'm reading this correctly," he said, punching the elevator button. "You found this son of a bitch with his head chopped off and you got to thinking Denise did it."

"I wanted to talk to her," Jacob said feebly.

"And I'm Alfred, Lord Tennyson." Stein shook his head. "Well, based on my extensive experience with LAPD, you're par for the course. Par being retarded."

The elevator juddered, dinged, opened on the manager flanked by two security guards.

"Sir, you'll have to please come with us."

"Shut up," Eddie said, pushing through the men as through a bead curtain. "He's my guest."

THEY FOUND RHODA in the main building, at the second-floor bar, a new drink in front of her. Nearly empty.

"Do I know my wife or what," Eddie said.

She saw them approaching and flagged the bartender, pointing to her cocktail. "Another," she said. "Make it thick."

"Hang on, Arturo," Eddie said. To Jacob: "Tell her."

Jacob told her.

She didn't cry. She didn't react at all. She said, "Arturo. I'm getting thirsty."

"Yes, madame."

"I apologize," Jacob said. "From the bottom of my heart."

Rhoda nodded once.

"Who told you Denise was alive?" Eddie asked.

"I went to your house," Jacob said. "I talked to a woman."

"What'd she look like?"

"Big lips. Tracksuit. Dog on a pink leash."

"Nancy," Rhoda said.

"I thought she was your neighbor," Jacob said.

"She is," Eddie said. "She's also Queen of the Cunts."

Rhoda clucked her tongue. "She claims we blocked her view when we added on."

"View of what?"

"Exactly," Rhoda said.

A silence.

Eddie said, "I don't know what else we can tell you, Detective. But you find out who did it, you let me know. I want to send him a Rosh Hashana card."

Rounding the top of the stairs, Jacob saw the two of them huddled together, their arms around each other, two soft old bodies trembling. Laughing or crying, it was impossible to tell.

CHAPTER TWENTY-TWO

He texted Divya from the parking lot.

anything yet

Her reply came back quickly.

no prints

damn he wrote. *2nd offender?*

patience

not my strong suit

She responded with a smiley.

He dithered a moment, then typed *dinner?*

Her reply to that was far slower in coming.

busy

He rubbed his eyes, started the car, began to back out. The phone rattled in the cup holder.

sorry she had written. *maybe another time*

Something to work with. He started to type *hope springs eternal*; told himself not to be an idiot. He erased that and wrote asking her to be in touch.

THERE WAS STILL NO REPLY from 911 dispatch, not even an acknowledgement of his first two requests. He wrote directly to Mike Mallick, outlining the new developments at length and imploring him to intercede. Let Special Projects do some of the heavy lifting.

He ate his dinner, dogs and bourbon, sitting on the floor, a file open on his lap.

By eleven-thirty he had a tension headache and could no longer see straight. Trudging to his bedroom, he collapsed without brushing his teeth. To feel himself finally running out of steam brought palpable relief. For the present, at least, he was sane.

He itched.

Arm and back, neck and genitals.

It was a maddening sensation and he rubbed at himself and the itch regrouped elsewhere on his body, newly doubled in strength.

He looked down.

They were on him.

They were everywhere.

Beetles.

Swarming his body like a black coat of armor; twisting in his navel, the cracks of his toes, tiny feather feet whispering against him. He slapped at himself and they scattered in concentric circles, seeking refuge in his pubic hair, his armpits and buttocks, clogging his ears, tunneling up his nostrils then tumbling, wriggling, down to the back of his throat. The more he struggled, the worse it got. They were too fast, too numerous, sprung from an infinite source, burrowing into him, millions of tiny undulant bulges bubbling in the nonexistent space between skin and raw flesh.

He raked his fingers across his scalp, scraped in the crevices where they hid, screamed and screamed and screamed.

Then a sharp stone was in his hand, and he used it to flay himself, shins and elbows, the tops of his feet, peeling his stomach off in an unbroken sheet and still he *itched*, he would do anything to stop it and he turned the point of the stone on himself to stab and gouge; soon he wept from a hundred puckered mouths while the beetles continued to penetrate deep into his brain. He beat his forehead against a stony wall, yearning to crack his skull open.

He slit his own throat.

Reached his hand up between the ends of cleanly severed pipes, pushed his fingers through custardy matter to the very center of their squirming legions and closed his fist around them, knowing all the while that he was destroying himself in the process.

At four-thirty a.m. he lurched awake streaked red from clawing at himself in his sleep. Running down the hall, he plunged into a scalding shower until the nightmare burnt off, slumping cross-legged on the bath mat, heaving, slick, jittery with terrible epiphany.

He had missed something.

CRIME SCENE PHOTOGRAPHERS in the digital age could snap away without limit; their 1988 counterparts had the cost of film and development to contend with. There was no standard set of angles, and those in the Creeper file didn't correspond between cases.

Jacob did the best he could, ripping off his rank bedsheets, layering the mattress with 8×10s, lining them up in a grid, comparing, blood punching through his brain.

He swapped out some of the photos, juggled others around.

What was bothering him was Inez Delgado.

Why drag her back to the bedroom to cut her throat?

Why not leave her where she fell, like with the other women?

Now he suspected that was wrong. Now he suspected they'd *wanted* Inez in her bedroom, just as they'd wanted Helen and Cathy and Janet and Sherri in theirs, just as they'd wanted Christa in her living room and

Patty in her kitchen and Laura in her walk-in closet and Katherine Ann centered in her studio.

In some instances, they'd moved furniture.

In other instances not.

The constants: the legs were always spread, typical sexual assault positioning.

The backs were always bruised.

He projected himself into the killer's script, knelt, grabbed hair, yanked, reached around.

What did he see?

He ransacked the photos for mid-range shots oriented along the victim's body in the direction of the head. He found five that were perfect and four close enough.

Nine times, he looked at what the killer saw while drawing the knife.

Nine times, he was looking at a window.

BY SEVEN A.M. he could no longer contain himself. He picked up the phone.

Phil Ludwig said, "We need to establish some ground rules. I get to sleep in now."

"It's important. Listen," Jacob said.

The detective listened.

Then: "Huh."

"I reread the files," Jacob said. "I wondered if anyone else had noticed it."

A beat. "Obviously nobody did," Ludwig said.

"Nobody." Realizing how arrogant that must sound, Jacob added, "It's not obvious."

"Don't patronize me, Lev."

In the background, Grete Ludwig said *Take it outside.*

"So?" Ludwig said. "What's it mean?"

"I have no—"

Phil. I'm asleep.

"Hang on," Ludwig said.

Thwap of slippers, a door gently shut.

"I have no idea what it means," Jacob said. "But it had to be deliberate. Inez isn't running back into the bedroom. She's trying to get out of the apartment, they're trying to stop her. And something went wrong. For them. They stabbed her in the stomach—I'm thinking she managed to punch one of them, or kick him in the balls, and he just lost it and went off on her and gutted her. But that wasn't the plan, all along they meant to put her in front of the window—that's what they did with the rest of them, I can't tell you why they did it but they did. So with Inez, she's not dead yet, she's dy*ing*, they go, 'Fuck, let's get her in front of the window before she goes.' And it makes me wonder if some of the others were moved. I've been assuming any movement was due to an escape attempt but maybe that's why they tied them up, to get them into position while they were alive, at which point they sliced the bindings. As to why windows, I don't know. But Inez wasn't tied up, so it's worth thinking about."

Silence.

"Phil? You there?"

Barely audible reply: "I'm here."

"What do you think?"

"I think you've had too much coffee."

"I haven't had any coffee," Jacob said, annoyed.

"You're talking a hundred miles an hour."

"I feel like I might really have something here."

"Yeah. Maybe."

"You don't agree."

"It's not—look: good job, at least you're working it." Ludwig yawned, puncturing Jacob's enthusiasm. "What's your next step?"

"I don't know. I haven't had a chance to process."

"Okay, well, you do that. I'm going back to bed. Give a call if you need anything. After ten, preferably."

Jacob said, "Detective? You were right about Denise Stein."

A pause.

"Oh yeah?"

"She's definitely not the offender."

"Glad to hear it," Ludwig said. "Before I forget: I'm still working on that bug you showed me. Nothing yet."

"Thanks."

"Take care, Lev."

Jacob hung up, deflated. Ludwig's reaction was justifiably cautious.

The victims had been positioned toward the window. So what?

Jacob resolved to calm down, couldn't, resumed pacing his bedroom, rubbing the tips of his fingers together. He trotted to the kitchen, dumped out cold coffee, brewed a new pot, raised it to pour, noticed his hands vibrating, dumped out the new pot, too.

When in doubt, the computer. Nothing from 911, nothing from Mike Mallick.

His leg hopped and jigged as he typed out a lengthy e-mail to the Commander, detailing the conversation with Ludwig and restating his request.

A surfeit of nervous energy remained. He futzed around on the web for a while, then googled *Mai*.

Got a slew of hits about anime characters and recipes for mai tais.

Did you mean May?

He glanced out the window.

The white van was back.

He googled *Curtains and Beyond*.

Got an Australian company, its UK sub-branch.

Nothing Stateside.

He sat back, chewing his lower lip.

Glanced out his own window again.

Perhaps what mattered wasn't the victims' windows, but the view they gave.

He got dressed and wrote down the information he needed; grabbed the digital camera and went outside.

As BEFORE, the van was empty.

He took pictures of the interior, the license plate, the logo, noticing now that although the company name and motto were painted on the side, there was no contact information.

He fished out his card and scribbled on the back.

Hello, I would like to install some new curtains.

He trapped the note under the wiper blade.

CHAPTER TWENTY-THREE

Sherri Levesque's former residence was closest, a decaying ranch house west of the freeway and south of Washington Boulevard. Several of the homes on the block had been upgraded during the real estate boom. The eroded stucco and splintering porch rail of this one seemed more honest, making no promises.

Nobody answered, so Jacob ducked back under a low-hanging American flag baked to translucency and circled the property, attempting to extrapolate from the crime scene photos which of the windows belonged to her bedroom. Best guess was one overlooking the backyard. He flattened himself against the siding and waited for the scene to speak to him.

Clover and bluegrass and dew-jeweled dandelions.

Sprinkler heads.

A fence.

Beyond it, the rear neighbor, a dented play structure.

Above, electrical lines sagged under the weight of crows, black as the wires they sat on.

He waited and waited for inspiration to strike.

Wrong time of day?

Something once there, now missing?

As the thrill of revelation faded, he felt a pang for the prophets of old, their loneliness and disorientation when, touched by God or imagining they were, they ended up stumbling in the turbulence left by a deity's receding hand.

All at once, the crows raised up, shrieking and flapping and vanishing east.

Jacob took some photos, walked back to the Honda, and drove to Christa Knox's old place in Marina del Rey.

The unshaven man who came to the door refused to admit him without a warrant, loudly turning the deadbolt.

Quarter after ten a.m. He texted Divya.

She failed to answer and he sent her another text, immediately regretted it.

Katherine Ann Clayton's El Segundo studio apartment had been demolished to make way for a strip mall. On the corner where she'd lived and died, a Starbucks dispensed its wares. Jacob used the camera's panorama mode to stitch together a 270-degree view, bought a 470-calorie bran muffin and a decaf that tasted of charred cardboard, hopped back on the freeway to Santa Monica.

His luck improved: Cathy Wanzer's old condo was vacant, for sale. He phoned the listing agent and made an appointment to see it later that day.

As he was getting off the phone with her, call-waiting beeped: his father.

"Hey, Abba. What's up?"

"I wanted to see how you are," Sam said.

"Me? I'm okay."

"Good," Sam said. "Good. I'm glad to hear it."

"Yeah. Okay. Everything okay with you?"

"Oh, I'm fine."

"Well, good."

"Yes," Sam said. "Just terrific."

"That's great, Abba. You know what, though, I'm right in the middle of something, so—"

"What's that."

"What?"

"What are you in the middle of?"

"I'm working," Jacob said.

"Yes. Of course. On the case."

"Yeah."

"How's it coming?"

"Not bad. Slowly but surely. Look, can I call you back later?"

"Yes, of course . . . But—Jacob? I'm out of milk. Do you think you'd have time to pick some up for me?"

"Milk," Jacob said.

"I need it for breakfast," Sam said.

"Nigel can't do it?"

"I haven't asked him."

"Well. Can you ask him, then?"

"I could, but I don't know if he'll have time."

"Abba. It's noon."

"Tomorrow," Sam said. "Breakfast tomorrow."

"I'm sure he can get it to you before then. And if he doesn't I'll bring some by tonight, okay? I need to go."

"Yes. All right. Take care."

He hung up.

Bewildered, Jacob stared at the phone. His father had never been a nudge. He was an even more hopeless liar.

Milk? Really?

Why he would be pestering Jacob about the case was unclear, unless Sam truly was concerned about Jacob's stress level. It unsettled Jacob to realize that perhaps there *was* something to be concerned about. The nightmares; the boundless, electric zaps powering him through the day.

He wrote them off. Occupational hazard. He had a right to nightmares. He was staring down wickedness. He had a right to be excited. He was making progress.

He opened up the phone's settings and assigned his father a unique ringtone so he'd know which calls to ignore.

Laura Lesser, R.N., had lived in a Tudor-style cottage. The present owner, a middle-aged woman, listened to Jacob's pitch, wrote down his badge number, and asked him to wait on the porch.

He stood shifting his weight from foot to foot, thought about the last few days, and decided a three-day marathon work session, a crash, a smaller spike, and a gentler ebb was simply doing the job well. Mania didn't follow that pattern or cycle that rapidly. Right? Right.

The owner returned looking wary. LAPD had confirmed that Jacob was a cop, but not what department he was with or why he might want access to her house. Before allowing him in, she pelted him with questions, which he answered as evasively as possible. Even after she'd relented and let him in, she persisted.

"What sort of crime did you say it was again?"

He hadn't. "A break-in."

"Oh my God. Should I be worried?"

"Not at all," he said, coming to the end of the hall.

"How can you be sure?"

"It occurred several years ago."

"Then why are you here now?"

"It relates to some newer crimes, but nothing that'll ever connect to you." Smiling as he made a beeline through her house. "Promise."

He found what he was looking for: Laura Lesser's former walk-in closet.

It had been restored to a bedroom, a preteen girl's. Tufted fabric letters above the bed spelled ISABELLA.

Jacob superimposed Laura Lesser's savaged body on the purple rug.

Knelt on her back and gazed out the window at a stop sign.

He snapped a picture.

"What are you looking at?" the woman asked.

"Thanks, finished, sorry for the inconvenience." He made his way back to the front door. He was beginning to take grim satisfaction in finding nothing of interest. A negative pattern could be useful, in its own way.

The woman said, "We picked this neighborhood because it's safe."

"It is."

"My husband's been talking about getting a gun."

Thinking of the girlish accoutrements, Jacob said, "Tell him to keep it locked up."

AT CATHY WANZER'S CONDO, the real estate agent said, "It's been completely redone. Fabulous open-concept living-eating space."

"What about the master bedroom?"

"Also brand new," she said, striding off. "Right this way."

Quick-stepping up a corridor lit by shabby-chic sconces, the agent began to extol the virtues of wallpaper.

". . . really in right now . . ."

Jacob followed her into the master.

"Don't you adore these floors?" she said.

"They're nice," he said.

"Reclaimed teak. The previous owners got inspired by a trip to India and they found a school in Mumbai that was going to be knocked down, so they were able to—"

"Did they move any walls or windows?"

"In here? I don't think so. You can see they deepened the closet, perfect for a young . . . couple, or if you . . ." She watched him kneel and snap pictures. "We have a website, you know."

"Mm," he said.

"Do you want to see the master bath?"

He ignored her and walked to the window.

Across the street, a preschool.

"What can you tell me about that place?" he asked.

"The school? Oh, it's *fabulous*. It's less than four years old and the facilities are top-notch. There's a gifted track. Do you have children?"

"No."

"Oh . . . Well, from what I gather, they're very considerate neighbors. They confine the pickup to the opposite side, so you won't have traffic, and as far as noise goes . . . eh . . ."

He was taking more photos and could hear her brain screaming *pedophile alert!*

She endeavored to draw his attention to a different window by praising its lovely northern exposures.

He looked at her. "What was that?"

"I said, I know there's not much to look at on that side, but over here the light is *just fabulous*."

He turned back and stared at the school.

"Sir?"

He started to walk out.

"Did you—sir, did you want to take a brochure?"

He took one, to be polite.

HE SAID, "They all face east."

Phil Ludwig was silent.

"I still have no clue what it means," Jacob said. "And Katherine Ann's building is gone, so I can't be a hundred percent sure. But we're eight for eight on the others."

No clue was a white lie. He had a theory. Not one he felt happy with.

East was significant in the Jewish tradition. Praying to the twice-demolished Temple in Jerusalem.

Justice.

Why complicate matters, though, before he knew more?

For his part, Ludwig sounded content. "You did good."

"Thanks."

"I know I shouldn't be, but I'm kicking myself right now."

"You're right. You shouldn't be."

"Well, whatever. Not that it's worth a damned thing, but you have my blessing."

"I appreciate it."

"I e-mailed my scientist pal about your bug. He's gonna get back to me tonight or tomorrow."

"There's no rush."

"Screw you, no rush," Ludwig said. "Lemme solve something."

CHAPTER TWENTY-FOUR

On the TV above the sushi bar, the Los Angeles Lakers were employing their go-to strategy of blowing a double-digit lead late in the fourth quarter. Lawyers in open-necked shirts thumped their tables and shook their Rolexes at the screen.

Jacob had intended to celebrate his discovery by treating himself to a halfway decent dinner, consumed alone and in peace. That intention lasted as long as his miso soup, at which point the implications of his discovery began to sift down through his consciousness.

That he was, apparently, the first person to notice the east-west pattern was no knock on the previous Ds, regardless of what Ludwig said. Mystery novels were fun, sometimes even for cops, but real-life whodunits provoked dread and anxiety. In most homicides, you assembled facts, filtered out noise, pursued leads that were usually obvious because criminals were for the most part stupid. Case closed.

On whodunits, blind spots and biases were inevitable.

It was, in fact, just such a bias that had enabled Jacob to recognize the pattern. And even now, he couldn't help seeing everything through a Jewish lens.

Member-of-the-tribe Creepers?

His silent *God forbid* made him smile with self-derision.

You could forbid if I believed in You.

One Jewish Creeper taken out by another didn't make him feel any better.

The most palatable possibility was a new actor somehow rooting out the Creepers and engaging in felony cleansing. Better, but still repellent, because Jacob's gut response to freelance revenge was the old collective-guilt atavism born of pogroms and inquisitions and blood libels.

You did what? Oy vey, what will the gentiles think of us?

An uncomfortable relic of Judaism's tribal roots popped into his head: the *goel hadam*, the "redeemer of blood," partially entitled by biblical law to hunt down and slay anyone who'd ended the life of a kinsman. Partial, because of a strange restriction: the *goel hadam* retained his right of vigilantism only in cases of manslaughter or accidental death. Willful murderers were to be tried and executed by a court of twenty-three judges.

He raised his finger for another carafe of warm sake.

A Harvard sophomore who considered himself an expert on Japan had once informed Jacob that heating sake was a trick to mask the imperfections of a low-quality brew. Cold and expensive was the way to go. Jacob liked imperfections. Like the failing exterior of Sherri Levesque's house, crappy liquor was honest, reminding him he wasn't drinking for the taste.

He poured, swirled the lacquered box. In any other context he found sake cloying, but you couldn't beat it for chasing *tekka maki*. The fact that every culture had its own form of alcohol, tailored to pair with its cuisine, pointed to an obvious truth: eating was merely an excuse to get blitzed.

Banzai!

Groans rose as the Enforcer Formerly Known as Ron Artest clanged a three-pointer.

The day's breakthrough had earned him the right to dinner, at least. He handed the waitress his white Discover credit card. A minute later she came back shaking her head.

"Declined," she said.

Big surprise. Jacob tossed down four twenties and left.

THE SCENE AT 187 was the usual lukewarm mess, walls of sweaty bodies, what was probably music but sounded like a rhino stampede.

"Yo," Victor said, pouring him a bourbon. "I was just thinking about you."

"Do I owe you money?"

"Your friend's here."

Jacob looked around for his bug-bit mattress pal. Wouldn't be the first time he'd encountered a one-night partner here. If he was lucky, this one might not remember him.

It felt like you were stabbing me.

Don't count on it.

He didn't see her, mimed the universal sign for big breasts to Victor.

"Nuh-uh, bro, the chick you was asking about. The supermodel."

Jacob's chest tightened. "Where?"

"She came in like literally two minutes before you." Victor squinted. "I don't know where she went. Bathroom?"

Jacob left his bourbon untouched and shouldered his way through the crowd, overturning drinks and jostling pool cues and disrupting make-out sessions.

Watch it, asshole.

The line for the ladies' was four strong. Jacob cut to the front and, figuring he'd already seen everything she could conceivably care to hide, barged in.

A woman he didn't know squatted over the toilet with her jeans around her ankles. She was so busy texting that at first she didn't notice him. Then she looked up and shrieked, dropping her phone in the bowl.

"Sorry," Jacob said.

He left her scrambling for modesty and plunged back into the melee. He didn't find her there, either, and he headed for the exit.

Halfway across the dance floor, a meaty hand clamped around his biceps. He said, "Fuck off, pal," but the hand dragged him back and he felt a rush of frustration and a surge of adrenaline, his limbic system telegraphing *bar fight* as a meaty arm put him in a meaty embrace that morphed into a decidedly nonmeaty noogie.

"Lev, you skinny-ass son of a bitch."

Mel Subach grinned. "Didn't know you came here, Jake."

Jacob tried to free himself. It was like gator wrestling. Subach, still smiling, let go. "Let's have a drink. I'm buying."

"No, thanks."

"Come on, live a little."

Jacob pushed past him, toward the door.

"I thought we were friends," Subach yelled.

Outside in the alley, a shape hurried away into the night.

A woman—that much he could tell—but he couldn't fix her; she was fifty feet gone and walking fast, and as he began jogging after her, she seemed to come in and out of being, like a faint star, detectable at the periphery of his vision, winking out when he turned his gaze directly on her.

Behind him, music blared; the door opening. "Jake. Where you going, man?"

"Mai!" Jacob yelled.

She glanced back.

Saw him.

Started to run.

"Wait!" Jacob yelled, feet slipping drunkenly on gravel. The tread caught and he sprinted, Subach's lumbering steps close on his heels. The big guy could move.

So could Mai. The distance between them rapidly stretched.

"Mai. It's me, Ja . . ."—he was huffing—"Jacob. The—*wait*."

"Wait!" Subach yelled.

The alley was roughly the length of a football field. Jacob put on the jets, and he seemed to be gaining on her, and for a moment he thought he might get to her, but they reached the mouth of the alley and Mai streaked into the street toward a vacant lot surrounded by chain-link and filled with dark weeds and he stumbled after without pausing for traffic and from his left came an onrushing air pressure and the heat of headlights and a gnashing aluminum grille and his collar tightened and he flew backward like a hooked vaudevillian so that the side of a van passed inches in front of him, close enough for him to count paint scratches.

He landed hard, on his tailbone, on the concrete.

The van fishtailed, coming to a halt thirty feet up the road.

Panting, Jacob rose to his elbows.

Mai had vanished.

Subach knelt by his side. "You okay?"

Jacob stared.

In front of him: the vacant lot.

To the right: a plumbing supplier.

To the left: an unmarked warehouse.

"Where'd she go?" Jacob said.

He tried to stand but Subach restrained him gently. "Buddy. You got to relax."

The van gunned its engine and roared off, due south down La Cienega. Through the noxious orange of sodium vapor lamps, the weathered lettering was barely legible.

CURTAINS AND BEYOND—DISCOUNT WINDOW TREATMENTS

THE TOWER

Lying in a windowless chamber whose torchlight sustains an eternal dusk, Asham passes in and out of consciousness, fleetingly aware of a man's presence at the foot of the bed, blinking to find him replaced by a boy, the child's studious gaze identical to his father's.

Veiled, unspeaking maidservants regularly appear to feed her, clean her, tend to her wounds. They stoke the fire and massage her feet. When she musters the strength to ask questions, they ignore her, leaving her alone and bedridden, too weak to stand, too weak to do anything but fix on a point in the air and will her broken body to mend faster.

To occupy her mind, she maps cracks in the clay walls, counts freckles on the backs of her hands. She raises her limbs off the bed, one at a time, each day a few more, a bit higher.

The maidservants bring heaping food, strange cooked grains and soured milks that make her gag. Knowing she must eat to heal, Asham forces them down without appetite. It takes considerable willpower to refuse the first dish that appeals to her: a roasted haunch, cut in thumb-thick slices, oozing juice, pink to the center.

"Take it away," she says to the maidservant.

The girl stares blankly.

The aroma is making Asham's mouth water.

She seizes a pillow and hurls it at the maidservant. *"Leave."*

The girl hurries out, grease sloshing from the tray and splattering on the dirt.

If Asham had the strength, she would crawl over and lick it up. Instead she falls back, exhausted by her outburst, and drops into sleep.

A short while later, she feels the bed sag.

"I understand you're doing better. Well enough to be difficult."

Asham does not need to open her eyes to see the mocking smile on his face.

"Was something wrong with the mutton?" Cain asks.

"I don't want it."

"It's delicious."

"It's disgusting."

"There's no shame in eating meat," he says. "Everyone here does. It's considered a great luxury, excellent for health."

Asham doesn't answer.

"I'll bring you something else."

"You mean you'll have them bring it."

"Tell me what you'd like."

"Who are they?"

"My servants."

"Where do they come from?"

"Everywhere. They're wanderers, like me."

"Killers," she said. "Like you."

He shrugs. "There's more than one way to fall out of favor. You'd be amazed by how many, actually. Together, we've made a home for ourselves."

"They refuse to talk to me."

"I've instructed them not to bother you."

"Does that include not answering my questions?"

"You need to rest," he says. "It's not good to overextend yourself."

At last she opens her eyes. "The people in the city," she says. "They serve you, as well?"

Cain bursts out laughing, the way he did when she was a child and said something stupid.

"*What*," she says.

"No, the entire city doesn't cater to me. Only those who choose to."

"No one would willingly serve another."

"Again—you'd be amazed. And I seem to recall our father being a big proponent of service."

"To the Lord."

"That's different?"

"It absolutely is," she says. "There is no law except that of Heaven."

"You've become quite the zealot."

"It's not zealotry to do what's right."

"Is that why you're here? To do what's right?"

She does not reply.

"Well, whatever the reason," he says, taking her cold hand, "I'm glad you've come."

THE NEXT MORNING SHE WAKES to find the boy, Enoch, crouched in a corner, his head tilted, his tongue extended in concentration.

"I didn't hear you come in."

"I was quiet." He leaps up and begins to skip around the room, stopping to inspect minute variations in the walls. "You don't eat mutton. Why not?"

Because your father wants me to.

"I don't like it," she says.

"What do you like to eat?"

"Fruit. Nuts. Whatever grows from the ground."

"I like those, too."

"We have something in common," she says.

"You should see the market," he says. "It's full of growing things."

"When I'm well enough, you can show it to me."

"When will you be well enough?"

"Soon."

"How soon?"

"I don't know."

He plops down on the floor, elbows on knees, chin on fists. "I'll wait here."

She smiles. "It might take a while."

"Then I'll come back tomorrow."

"I don't know if I'll be ready tomorrow, either."

"Then I'll come back the day after that."

"You're very persistent," she says.

"What does that mean?"

"Ask your father."

"I will," he says. "He'll know. He's the wisest man in the valley. That's why everyone loves him. When I grow up, I'm going to be a builder like him. I'm going to have a son and name a city for him. Would you like to see my toys?"

"Not right now," she says, somehow fatigued by the thought of construction. "I think I need a nap. Hand me that blanket, please . . . ? Thank you."

"You're welcome."

True to his word, Enoch comes the next day, and every day thereafter. Affairs of state occupy Cain's time, and weeks go by in which the boy is the only person Asham talks to. It's less a conversation than an interrogation. What does she think about turtles? Has she ever seen a full moon? Does she know any good riddles? His chatter momentarily dispels the gloom; it distracts her from the pain of sitting up, or swinging her legs over the edge of the bed, or standing with quaking legs, supporting herself on the bedpost.

"Very good!" Enoch yells when she reaches some new milestone. "Very, very good!"

He dances around, the clanging bell summoning servants. They see who's calling them and grit their teeth and leave.

It is in part due to his unquenchable enthusiasm that she is soon hobbling back and forth across the chamber, leaning her weight on a wooden stick.

"Go faster," Enoch says.

"I'm trying."

"You can do it. Follow me."

"Enoch. *Slow down.*"

"You can't catch me! You can't catch me!"

"I can, and—"

"You can't!"

"I can, and I will, and when I do I'm going to clobber you."

"Ha ha ha ha ha!"

He fetches her sweets from the market, hot stones to ease her backache. Her hair has begun to grow; he combs it for her. The maidservants still won't speak directly to Asham, but they will answer Enoch, who acts as her intermediary.

"No more yogurt," Asham says. "Tell her that."

"No more yogurt," Enoch says.

"Master has said yogurt will give her strength."

"Tell her if she brings any more I'll dump it on master's head."

"But I like yogurt," Enoch says.

"Fine. Give it to him."

"Give it to him," Enoch says.

"No; you."

"You."

"Not *her*. *You*. You as in Enoch."

"Enoch." Wide-eyed: "You mean I can have your yogurt?"

"That's absolutely what I mean."

"Hooray! Give it to me!"

"Yes, master."

She reminds herself that she cannot permit herself to love him. Love is rich earth; regrets take root; and while she pulls them up as fast as she can, new ones break through every day.

She can see, for instance, how the boy shares Nava's features as well as Cain's. Although, considering the already strong resemblance between

Nava and Cain, any part of the boy could be any part of his parents—or any of Asham's own features, for that matter. She, too, leans toward the dark side of the family.

Which raises another question.

Where is Nava?

COME SPRING, Cain moves her to a roomier bedchamber on the second floor, with a balcony overlooking the city. Day begins at dawn with the birth of new cook fires and ends with the drums that signal the closing of the gates. The hours between pulse with activity, distant shouts and tantalizing colors mingling in the shimmery heat. The spectacle ignites Asham's curiosity and motivates her to work harder to recuperate. Enoch runs before her, taunting her, forcing her to extend her range day by day. First they go to the waste cistern down the corridor. Then to the courtyard. Then up to the ramparts, where he laughingly ducks between the archers' legs. Then back to the same places, swifter, without as many rest breaks. Then again, twice, three times, four. Finally, unaided by the stick.

"You can't catch me!"

"Here I come . . ."

When she does catch him, she gets to gather him up in her arms, to feel his tiny hot body quivering with terror and delight.

"Put me down!"

Unaided is not the same as unaccompanied. A pair of maidservants linger a few steps behind, ready to grab her if she falters. Asham has only to gesture and they rush forward to do her bidding.

The one command they won't obey is to leave her alone.

She complains to Cain.

"Am I a prisoner?"

"Of course not."

"Then don't treat me like one."

"Your door is unbarred. You're free to go wherever and whenever you want. Everyone here is free. That's the difference between us and them. We set our own boundaries."

"I'm not free with people following me every waking moment."

"They're there to help," he says.

"I don't want help."

"You might need it."

"I don't suppose I'm free to decide that for myself."

"Nobody's forcing you to do anything," he says. "And nobody's forcing them to follow you, either. I asked them to watch you and they agreed. Everybody's within his or her rights."

She'd forgotten how frustrating it is to argue with him. "Am I free to strangle you?"

He smiles. "We have laws against that."

"Laws you came up with."

"I had a hand in their creation, yes. It's for the public welfare. You can't have order if everyone's killing everyone else."

"You'd know."

He shrugs. "Never say I'm not a quick study."

"Tell me: what does your law say about murderers?"

"Justice shall be done."

She raises her eyebrows, and he shrugs again.

"The law didn't take effect until later," he says. "It would be unfair to punish people retroactively."

"Convenient for you."

"Reasonable for everyone."

"I'm having trouble differentiating the two," she says.

Cain laughs, long and hard.

THE HUMAN FRENZY she observed from her balcony is dizzying up close, a barrage of sights and sounds and smells that are individually offensive but oddly delicious when combined. Farmers who work the surrounding fields tug laden pack animals to the market square. Halved sheep carcasses sit out on stumps, lacquered thickly with flies that the butchers periodically shoo away. Dogs tussle with naked children. Cats chase rats twice their size. On one occasion Asham ventures inside a home, only to be greeted by perplexed stares and frostily asked to leave.

The idea that people can live so close together yet shut themselves behind doors seems nonsensical at first. It hinges on the confusing, enticing idea that space can be owned. Cain calls it property and says it is the cornerstone of a stable society.

To Asham it seems a vain division.

WITH ENOCH BY HER SIDE and the two maidservants never far behind, she explores stalls overflowing with produce brought from afar by refugees and recultivated in the valley's fertile soil. Vendors tout fresh limes and succulent oranges and dates and figs and pomegranates sweetly bleeding. Soon enough, people learn who Asham is, and they treat her with deference, kneeling to offer fistfuls of free samples.

"Do they have figs where you come from?" Enoch asks through a full mouth.

"Yes, lots."

"That's good. I like figs."

"Me, too."

"What else do you like?"

"I like you," she says.

He smiles and pops another fig in his mouth.

Along with foodstuffs, the people have imported the skills and customs of their native lands. They display handicrafts whose ingenuity rivals that of Cain's best inventions: stonework, metalwork, half a hundred types of weapon. Caged beasts snarl and snap at anyone foolish enough to stick his fingers through the bars. Caged birds sing elegies to freedom.

There are jugglers and healers, potters and barbers. Asham spends an afternoon spellbound by three men blowing into pipes to create twisting, haunting melodies.

So much to look at, so much to do.

She can all too easily see how one would come to make a life here.

Amid the hustle and bustle, they even make time for the Lord. At the center of the city stands a temple where, for a fee, a team of priests will slaughter a young lamb and sprinkle its blood on the altar while a choir sings incantations. She inquires about the origin of the ritual and learns that Cain has declared it binding on every man, to be performed three times a year.

She asks Cain why.

"It keeps them busy."

BY FAR, HER FAVORITE PLACE is a vast public garden fed by channels dug from the river. Enoch takes her by the hand, naming plants and demonstrating their special features.

"This one moves if you touch it," he says, grazing the tip of a leaf.

Asham stares in wonder as it folds in on itself. "Why does it do that?"

"Cause it doesn't like to be touched, so it hides."

"We shouldn't bother it."

"It's a plant," Enoch says. "Plants don't feel."

"How do you know that?"

"Father told me."

"Do you believe everything he tells you?"

"Of course."

The flowers grow in orderly rows, grouped by color. Asham feels compelled to point out to him that it is otherwise in the wild.

"You're very interesting," he says solemnly.

She laughs. "I am?"

"Oh, yes. You're the most interesting person I ever met."

"I don't know about that."

"You are. Father said so. Are you going to stay?"

"Stay . . . ?"

He nods. "You could be my mother."

Her stomach drops.

"I'd like that," he says.

"What about your real mother?" she asks. "Where is she?"

He does not reply.

"Enoch?"

"I don't know."

"You don't know where she is?"

"Look," he says, pointing to a blue dot weaving through the greenery. "A butterfly."

He runs ahead.

NEW IMMIGRANTS ARRIVE DAILY. The constant influx of refugees demands constant growth, and Cain toils long hours. Most mornings he leaves the palace before Asham is awake, although occasionally she will rise early enough to hurry to the window and catch a glimpse of his departing retinue: ten men stamping the dirt with the butts of their spears, calling ahead to clear the road.

It may be true, as Enoch claims, that the people love his father. If so, though, she has to wonder why he needs so many bodyguards. When she challenges Cain about it, he responds that respect is composed of equal parts fear and love.

His precise title remains vague, as do the duties it entails. He has described himself, variously, as chief architect, principal council member, treasurer, adjudicator. Whether the people love him or fear him, they certainly depend on him: he administers the law, collects taxes, suppresses dissent.

Without him, the valley would implode in disorder.

This realization, among others, holds her in check. Each time she looks at Enoch, fresh doubts break through. Every cold morning he climbs into bed to burrow against her, rubbing his soft cheek against hers; every silly gift he brings her; every clay edifice he builds and names in her honor; every lazy evening by the hearth, cracking walnuts and telling fantastic stories; every fever he sprouts that keeps her up, pacing a rut into the floor; every time he asks her, yet again, if she is going to stay; every time she asks him where his mother is and he has no answer.

THE NEW TEMPLE WILL DOMINATE the eastern edge of the valley—an enormous undertaking that will not be completed in Cain's lifetime. Indeed, in all likelihood, he says, they'll still be working on it when Enoch's grandchildren have grandchildren of their own.

"Then what's the point?" Asham asks.

"You build for the future," he says.

They are seated at the long wooden table where Cain holds council meetings. At present the two of them dine alone. Enoch is asleep; Asham tucked him in.

She's not sure what Cain means by building for the future. Is "the future" his heirs, for whom the temple will stand and function? Or does "the future" refer to the remembrance of Cain's own name?

In his mind, are those goals distinct?

She asks how he came to learn the secrets of building.

He cuts his mutton and piles it with lentils. "Trial and error."

She assumes he means his earliest clay huts.

He nods as he chews. "They weren't perfect, so I moved on."

"Nothing's perfect."

"This one will be."

"You believe that."

"You have to believe," he says. "Creativity is an act of faith."

"I thought you have no faith."

"Not in anyone else," he says.

His arrogance ought to fan the flames of her rage. Instead Asham feels a thrum of desire. She has drunk too much. She slides the goblet of wine away from her.

Cain notices. "You don't like it? I can bring something else."

"I'm not thirsty," she lies.

Cain shrugs, cuts meat. "Say the word . . . I promised Enoch I'd take him out to the building site next week. You can come along, if you'd like." He catches her eyeing his plate. "Take a taste?"

"No, thanks."

He grins, resumes cutting. "You can't hold out forever."

Asham relishes a flood of private thoughts. "I don't intend to."

"Aha," he says. "I knew it. I know you better than you know you. When's the happy day? I'll make sure to have them prepare something special."

"You'll just have to wait and see."

"Excellent, I don't mind suspense." He winks at her and slides a bloody triangle of flesh in his mouth, chews thoughtfully, swallows. "He's very fond of you. It's been hard on him, not having a woman around. A boy needs a mother."

"You never talk about her," Asham says.

"There's nothing to talk about. I told you already. She died in childbirth. I buried her in the grasslands. You saw the monument yourself."

She nods, remembering the smooth clay pillar.

"Please don't ask me about it again."

She nods, and he resumes eating. When he speaks next, his voice is bright.

"So? What do you say? Do you want to come with us and see the tower? Promise me, though, you'll use your imagination. It's not close to done."

She says, "I promise."

THE JOURNEY TAKES the better part of a day.

They march to the drone of insects, following a narrow track through the forest. Cain and his retinue go on foot, while the dog displays vestiges of his former occupation, scouting ahead and returning with a barked report. Enoch and Asham ride on a wooden palanquin borne by eight bare-chested manservants. Ever since learning that men in official service must submit to castration—it restrains them from excessive lust—she cannot look at them without feeling queasy.

"It's a good day," Cain says. "Nice and clear. Wait till you see the view."

Stone markers indicate the remaining distance; by mid-morning, they have reached the seventh of twenty, and Asham asks Cain if it wouldn't have made more sense to build closer to the edge of the city.

He sighs, explains that, again, he's thinking of the future: not where the city ends now, but where it might end in ten generations' time. By then, the tower will be centrally located.

She asks if growth is to continue forever?

He replies that forever is a long time.

She has noted that he refers to the building by different terms depending on whom he is talking to. When discussing its ritual function with the priests, or drumming up support with the masses, it's a temple, always a temple, a temple to replace the smaller, inadequate temple, the grandest of temples fit for showcasing the glory of the Lord.

But to her, when his excitement shows, it's a tower.

The distinction may go unnoticed by everyone else, but not by Asham. Her brother does not waste words. He divides and classifies, gives everything its proper name. Without precision, he is fond of saying, we cannot communicate.

He often says this before he's about to hedge or lie.

THEY PAUSE TO LUNCH on dried fish. The palanquin bearers wade into the river up to their knees to cool off, bending to quickly gulp great handfuls of water which just as quickly reappear beaded on their brows and arms and hairless, coppery chests. Enoch climbs a tree and pelts them with pinecones. Asham satisfies herself with a millet cake.

"Not long now," Cain says.

Enoch claps his hands. "Not long!"

The sun is falling on their arrival, and as the tower comes into view, she mistakes it for a new city, so sprawling is its footprint.

Cain helps her down from the palanquin. He sees her astonished gape and laughs. "This is nothing yet."

They tour the perimeter so that he may review progress with his foremen. Half the city seems to be here. Temporary housing has been erected for the host of workers who labor under a hot sun in daytime and by torchlight at night. The racket never ceases. There are woodchoppers and mule drivers, carvers and smiths. Twenty dozen red-faced men take shifts, doing nothing but stomping mud, molding bricks, firing them.

Thus far, seven levels have been completed, each one slightly smaller than the one below. A ramp spirals around the exterior, wide enough for foot traffic to pass in both directions. Eventually it will wind up to the top, so that pilgrims who want to reach Heaven may do so, purchasing access for a nominal fee.

Asham looks at him. "Heaven?"

"Come on, I want you to see the inside."

The bottom floor is a grand hall devoted to works of art. Enoch runs in sloppy circles, hollering at the top of his lungs and basking in his echo, while Cain shows off a series of delicate floral friezes. Coming to a prominent niche, she stops, struck dumb by a life-sized granite statue of a man.

"Do you like it?" Cain asks. "I hired the valley's most gifted sculptor."

She doesn't know what to say.

"He was working from my design, though."

"It's an idol."

"Oh, please. Nobody's worshipping it. It's for decoration."

She stares at him. "It's *you*."

"And? People ought to know whose idea this was. It'll encourage them to dream."

Slowly, she walks around the statue. It is a good likeness: she can admit that. Still, her father's oft-repeated warnings against forming the image of man ring in her ears with the force of a natural law. She feels as though she's committing a grave sin simply by standing there.

The sculptor has placed a torch in one hand and a knife in the other.

"Light and power," Cain says. "Tools of the trade. You want to know what I've learned, I can sum it up for you like this: one capable man working alone can build a house. One capable man commanding thousands can build a world."

"The world is already built," she says.

He laughs. "We'd better go if you want to catch the sunset."

To Enoch's immense displeasure, he is ordered to wait at the bottom.

"But I want to see."

"It's not safe," Cain says. "Keep the dog company."

"Why do you get to go?"

"We're adults."

"I'm an adult."

"No, you're not."

"Yes, I am."

"I'm not going to argue about this." He motions to one of the guards, who lifts Enoch and carries him, squealing, back to the palanquin.

Watching them go, Cain sighs. "I hate it when he defies me."

"What did you expect?" she says. "He's your son."

He smiles wistfully. "Let's go."

They haven't climbed far before Asham decides that he was right not to let the boy come along. She herself has half a mind to turn back. The tower's height funnels the wind into upward gusts that whip her robes, and she edges along the inside of the ramp, leery of the incomplete outer wall. Cain strides on, unconcerned. Not wanting to look weak in front of him, she screws up her courage and follows.

The seventh floor has no walls at all, making for a magnificent vantage. In every direction the sky drips honey. The distant city could be mistaken for a natural feature, its buildings running together, like a clay plain. Cain unfastens his cloak and offers it to her for warmth. She draws it tight around her, watching with a knotted throat as he saunters out to within an arm's length of the edge.

"Beautiful, isn't it? Imagine what it'll look like from the top. You'll be able to see the entire valley and beyond."

"And Heaven, apparently."

"And Heaven."

"You used to argue with Father about Heaven."

"So I did."

"You didn't believe in it."

"I still don't."

Asham approaches the edge, daring to lean out and peer down a seven-story clay cliff. Her head spins; she steps back. "You're building a ramp to a place that doesn't exist."

"Anything to keep the people interested."

"They're going to demand a refund if they climb all that way and there's nothing to see."

"Well, I won't *rule out* the possibility that Heaven exists. But I won't know unless I see it for myself, and since I never will, I'll trust my intuition."

"And if you're wrong?"

"Then I'm wrong."

"What I don't understand is why you need to know."

"One can't choose freely without knowledge."

"And that's more important than angering the Lord?"

"Who said anything about angering him?"

"I have a feeling He's not going to be happy with people showing up at His door, demanding entrance."

"He's the Lord," Cain says. "I'm sure he can handle it."

The sun squashes against the horizon. Down below, the workers scurry like beetles. The wind carries shouts, whipcracks, whinnies, groans.

"We're not going to make it back before dark," she says.

"I thought we could spend the night. There's a room I use when I have to stay over."

"Where will I stay?"

He turns to her. "With me."

She feels the blood beat in her ears.

"Say something," Cain says.

"What should I say?"

"Yes. Or no."

A silence.

She says, "Your son keeps asking me to be his mother."

A silence.

Cain says, "It's your decision, not his or mine. I learned that a long time ago, and I told him so."

"He's not listening."

Cain pauses. "He wants to help."

"I know."

A silence.

He says, "I did love her. Nava."

She nods.

"I may have failed to convey how hard it's been on me."

"I can imagine," she says.

"You can't. I had someone and I lost her. You can't possibly know what that's like."

She says, "I know."

For a moment, he sags. Regret, or fear. Either would be a first. Either would soften her heart.

She says, "Do you ever think about him?"

He disappoints her then: he straightens up and his green eyes shine and he speaks with confidence. "I only think about what I can control."

"That's impressive," she says. "I remember whether I want to or not."

"I used to see him, in my dreams." The wind makes snakes of his hair. "But it's been so long. Now, when I try to remember . . ."

He starts to laugh.

"What," she says.

He shakes his head, laughing. "I see a sheep."

Asham stares at him.

"I'm sorry. That was unkind. I've changed. Everything has changed. That things turned out the way they did is unfortunate. But it's past, and I can only act in the present. I've tried to atone. You've seen how I give everything I have to my people."

"They're not your family."

"But they are. All men are. That's what Father was so afraid of, you see. That's why he wouldn't let us leave the valley. I didn't give him enough credit. I admit that now. He knew. He knew others were out there, that we'd find them, that we'd understand: all men are equal. He knew that if we understood that, we would refuse to submit to him."

"We submitted to the Lord, not to Father."

"And who told us what the Lord wanted? Father. Who told us what to do, when to do it; how we'd be punished if we didn't? Who changed the rules when he saw fit? He did."

"Why would he lie?"

"To control us. That's what men want. Power."

"What makes you special?"

"Nothing," he says. "I'm like any man. *I* am no different. But *we* are. An assemblage of men. What makes *us* special is that there are many voices speaking at once. Some speak for each other. Some against. It's that loud mass of voices that produces a unity. Look at what we've been able to build. Not because of any one person. I've taken the greatest burden on my shoulders, yes, but I rely on people to help me. Do you see what I'm saying? Man survives together. It isn't right to be alone. Not for anyone."

He pauses. "Not me. Not my son. He needs a mother. He needs you. We both do. I brought you here to show you what we're building. I'm building this for you. It's a monument to togetherness. We've both wandered, we've both been alone, we are all that we have. Don't you think I've had offers of marriage? Every man in the city wants to give his daughter to me. I refused them all. I waited for you. Every day I watched the horizon. I put sentries by the gates and I told them to watch for you. I sent the dog out to hunt for your scent. I still have your robe. I carried it with me, over mountains and through the plain. When I felt I could not go on, I raised it to my face and I remembered you. It still smells like you. I told the dog to find you and he did. Because I knew you would come, and I knew that by the time you arrived here you'd be coming in love, not anger. I have loved you forever and I will love you forever still."

A silence.

Asham says, "Forever is a long time."

Cain laughs: a high, frightened sound. "You see? That's what I love you for. I love you for saying that. I live in a world of flatterers and liars. You speak the truth. I need truth to come home to. I need you to come home to. Enoch does. Do it for him. No. No. Do it for me. Because you love me, I know you love me. You can't deny that. You wouldn't."

He kneels by the edge of the tower. "If you say you don't love me, I will fling myself off."

A silence.

Asham says, "I do love you."

"So it's yes," he says. "You will be my wife, as you have always meant to be."

The wind slices through Asham's cloak, and she shivers.

Cain says, "Don't stand there like a statue."

She kneels to be level with him.

"My love," he says, "my love."

She presses her mouth to his. His tongue pushes back, and their bodies kiss from chest to groin.

His skin smells of dust and oil; with demanding hands he urges her toward the ground, as he has done once before, and she breaks away, and he says, "What? What is it?"

She brushes his hair from his eyes, kisses the crown of his head, embraces him again, staring over his shoulder at a dark sky speckled with dark crows.

She holds him tightly, so as to never let him go, and—fixing the balls of her feet against the rough surface of the clay—says, "Forever."

With the strength and conviction of vengeance long deferred, she pushes them both over the edge.

CHAPTER TWENTY-FIVE

Roughly twenty-seven thousand white Ford Econolines were registered in the state of California, not one of which bore the license plate number Jacob copied from his photograph. He ran it several times, each successive search taking longer to return the same verdict.

Not found.

Head spinning, back smarting, he rechecked that he'd entered the number correctly.

Not found.

Forged plate?

He tried his own license plate number. It came back as expected.

He plugged the van's plate in for a fifth time. The progress bar slowed, froze. He waved the mouse, whaled on the space bar, cursed. He was reaching around to do a hard reset when the system crashed entirely, a wisp of smoke wafting from the front panel vent.

To stop himself from bashing the screen in, he escaped to the kitchen. Nothing to eat; he didn't dare take a drink. It was two in the morning. He put on a fresh pot of coffee.

Mindful of his bruised tailbone, he eased down to the floor in front of his sofa, slumping against his disconnected TV, and wondered what terrible thing was happening to him.

He flashed back: the van, speeding past. Screaming tires, stench of burnt rubber. No normal person could grab on without dislocating a shoulder. So either Mai was a stuntwoman, or he hadn't really seen her.

But he had. Clear as his own reflection.

And Victor—Victor had seen her, too.

And if Victor hadn't?

Would he trust his own perception?

Subach, cradling him in his linebacker's arms.

Where'd she go.

Who?

Mai. The girl.

What girl?

The girl.

Jake—

Don't fuck with me. Don't you fucking fuck with me.

Jake. Buddy. Calm down.

Did it—did she get hit?

You sound funny, man.

I'm—

Maybe I hurt your neck. You should go to the ER. You might have whip-lash.

I need to go.

What's—hey—wait a second.

I need to get out of here.

Wait. Jake. Wait. You're not good to drive. Jake.

Breaking free, standing. *Tell Mallick to call me.*

You need to chill out, lemme buy you a drink—c'mon, give you a ride, at least . . .

ASAP.

The computer panel was no longer smoking, and the desktop booted up normally, but the moment Jacob opened up the DMV database and retried his search string, the screen froze again.

He left the coffee untouched, the progress bar grinding away in futility, staggered to his bedroom, swept aside the crime scene photos still blanketing his duvet, and fell into a blessedly dreamless sleep.

———

Divya Das said, "Good news first or bad?"

"Good."

"I found your second offender."

"That's great news."

"Well, but the bad part is he doesn't bring up any additional hits. All I can tell you is he's male and probably Caucasian."

"Thanks for trying."

"My pleasure," she said. "What next?"

"I'm going to start poking around seriously for other cases that match the Creeper MO. Maybe L.A. got too hot and they moved on to someplace else."

"Sounds like fun."

It sounded like grunt work, and it was: once he restarted the still-churning computer and sat down at the desk, he didn't get up for another ten hours except to refill his glass, go to the bathroom, or stretch the muscles bunching in his lower back. Grunt work, and he needed it, because if he allowed himself a second to think freely, his mind brought him to the events of the previous evening, and his guts began to roil.

He had seen her.

He'd seen the letters, too.

He was seeing things, and they were disappearing. Blame Sam and his eyes. Blame Bina and her mind. Sooner or later, he thought, he'd have to get himself to a doctor. An ophthalmologist. A shrink. For now, he wrote his own prescription: facts and liquor, maximum strength.

By eleven-thirty p.m., four Post-its fluttered on the wall over the desk.

Lucinda Gaspard, New Orleans, July 2011.

Casey Klute, Miami, July 2010.

Evgeniya Shevchuk, New York, August 2008.
Dani Forrester, Las Vegas, October 2005.

The information Jacob had access to online didn't indicate what direction the vics had been facing when they died.

Put that aside and the cases matched up.

Four women, mid-twenties to late thirties, living alone. Fresh-faced and smiling, the new quartet was right at home alongside his nine.

Four first-floor residences, four doors with no forced entry.

Sixteen rope burns, two for each of eight ankles and eight wrists. No ropes found.

Eight rapes, four vaginal, four anal.

Four facedown bodies.

Four cut throats.

Four cold cases.

Zero offender DNA recovered, except in New York, where traces of vaginal semen had turned up. In the last case, Vegas PD noted that their vic's fingernails had been closely trimmed, far down enough to draw blood, maybe to eliminate skin cells. No mention of that in the other files.

Maybe the evil twins had grown more careful over twenty years. In the New York case—Shevchuk—he guessed broken condoms.

If the sample taken from Shevchuk was filed in CODIS, why hadn't Divya gotten a match to Mr. Head?

Jacob wondered if he was reading too much into the similarities, desire deepening shallow footholds. He needed to speak to the other Ds, find out more about body positioning. Midnight. Too late to call.

Perfect hour for building speculative castles, though.

NONE OF THE INVESTIGATORS had linked their murders to the Creeper—understandable, given the lack of proximity and the fact that the story had been out of the news for two decades.

Nor had they linked any one of them to any other. He couldn't fault them for that, either.

What jumped out at Jacob were the dates. If even one of the four murders belonged to his bad guys, the duo had been active within the last seven years, possibly as recently as last year.

Increasing the likelihood that the remaining guy, Mr. Head's partner and possible slayer, was alive.

Out there.

The first killing had gone down in 2005. Bad guys checked the paper like anyone else. More often, and more carefully, if they were looking for information about themselves. Could be they'd read the 2004 *Times* article about Ludwig retiring and decided it was safe to resume operations—just not in L.A.

New Orleans, Miami, New York, Las Vegas.

Each of those cities had its fair share of action and distraction. They were places you could go and be anonymous.

Find a cheap weekend fare, carve up a girl, come home?

Open-ended searches for the cities and dates yielded too many hits. Putting quotes around each city and year created the opposite problem.

The months of the murders clustered, somewhat: July through October. At this point, anything remotely patternlike was tempting. Human nature to see faces in the clouds or Jesus in oatmeal.

NCIC had only listed one sample found on Shevchuk, raising another possibility: one of the bad guys had gone solo. Or found another partner who hadn't left semen.

The latter seemed a big risk to take. Three can keep a secret if two are dead. And one or both of the Creepers had been careful enough to evade capture for this long. So if one bad guy had found a new buddy, he'd have to be persuasive.

I'll cut off your head persuasive?

Jacob checked his e-mail yet again, hoping for an answer from Mallick about the 911 recording. Instead, a message from Phil Ludwig caught his eye.

The subject heading: *Your bug.*

From my friend the entomologist, best I could do, sorry.

Below it, a forwarded e-mail.

Dear Phil,

We're good thanks, Rosie sends regards. Exciting news, we booked Costa Rica.

Jacob skipped down several paragraphs of chitchat.

So anyhow about your friend's beetle. I agree w/ you, v. hard to tell from low-res images. Head shape and size (if he is remembering it correctly, that seems pretty big to me, people get spooked, he probably overestimated)

Jacob frowned. He knew how big the beetle was; he'd held it, and it had easily stretched the length of his palm.

He kept reading.

put me in mind of rhinos but none that I know a lot about, I'm no expert, maybe O. nasicornis (see below) but coloration is wrong and never seen one in Southern California. Could be someone's pet that got out? Too bad you don't have it, you could name your own species lol.

Take care

Jim

The attached photo showed top and bottom views of a beetle. The head was spadelike, with a prominent central horn. Jim was right, though: the color was off, a shiny reddish brown instead of jet black.

Jacob typed *O. nasicornis* into Wikipedia and read about the European rhinoceros beetle, a member of the subfamily Dynastinae (rhinoceros beetles), of the family Scarabaeidae (scarabs). It ranged in size from about three-quarters of an inch to an inch and a half, and its maximum of two and a half inches appeared too small. Where his beetle's underside shone like onyx, *O. nasicornis* sprouted long red hair.

A pet?

He started clicking through links, hoping he'd luck onto a match, but it swiftly became clear that Ludwig's estimate of a hundred jillion species was conservative. He did learn that large horned beetles were indeed kept as pets in parts of Asia, and that they were pitted against each other for money, like pit bulls or gamecocks or tiny exoskeletal MMA fighters.

At least he knew what to get Bar Lady for Valentine's Day.

He closed out the browser and went around the apartment, checking his roach motels. They didn't seem to be doing much business, so he tossed them out and determined not to think about it anymore. He had enough on his hands without worrying about an infestation that, for all appearances, had cleared up on its own.

CHAPTER TWENTY-SIX

The first detective he reached was Tyler Volpe, from Brooklyn's 60th Precinct. He sounded friendly enough, if somewhat guarded. His interest jumped when Jacob mentioned the Creeper.

"That was what, eighty-five? Eighty-six?"

"Eighty-eight. You were around then?"

"Me?" Volpe laughed. "Shit. I was *nine*."

"It made an impression on you," Jacob said, thinking of himself at that age.

"My dad was on the job, and I remember him discussing it with my mom, like, 'Thank God it ain't mine.'"

"It's mine now."

"Huh. All this time, still nothing?"

"For the most part. You mind telling me about your vic?"

"I mean, it was like my second homicide. I almost shit my pants."

"That sounds about right."

"The brutality read like a mob thing, which made sense, cause she danced at one of those nightclubs in Brighton Beach where the Russian guys in leather jackets hang out. Also did some stripping on the side. She was studying to be a dental hygienist. Nice girl, but a cocaine vacuum, so we figured she ran up a bill she couldn't pay, or jilted the wrong guy."

"Makes sense."

"We looked at that, dead end, ex-boyfriends, dead end. We always had it as an isolated incident. Still is, far as I'm concerned, until proven otherwise."

"What about the semen?"

"CODIS came back negative to prior offenders. Why? You have DNA?"

"Yeah. It didn't hit yours, though."

"Well, that should be the end of it," Volpe said. "Yours ain't ours."

"Did you ever consider more than two offenders?"

There was a pause. "Why?"

"That's what I'm dealing with."

"Nothing we saw said it was anything more than a single guy." Volpe sounded irritated. "Two guys?"

"Lemme ask you something else," Jacob said. "How well do you remember the scene?"

"Pretty freakin well. You see something like that, you don't forget it."

"She was on her stomach, throat cut from behind."

"Uh-huh."

"Facing . . . ?"

"What?"

"Did it look like she was facing anything?"

"The floor."

Jacob said, "Anything interesting about the way she was laid out?"

"Well, she had rope burns, but her hands and feet were loose. I remember thinking that was pretty weird. We never recovered the rope, but we matched fibers to a national brand."

"Meaning, useless."

"Pretty much."

"Okay," Jacob said, "but what I'm asking is, if you're the bad guy, kneeling on her back, and you look up, what are *you* looking at?"

A silence; Jacob heard Volpe's breathing slow.

"I got no fuckin idea," he finally admitted.

"Can you do me a favor and check the photos for me?"

"Yeah, fine. Why's it matter, though?"

"My vics were arranged with their heads pointing to an east-facing window."

"What's that about?"

"Wish I knew."

"Look, tell you what. I'll go past the building, next couple of days."

"I appreciate it."

"Sure thing. How'd you get stuck with this, anyway? You piss someone off?"

Jacob told him about the head.

"Holy shit," Volpe said. "And you think this guy is one of your killers?"

"I know so. He was at seven of the nine scenes."

"That is *bananas*."

"I'll send you a picture of him, if you want. Maybe you'll know him."

"Yeah, do that. Sorry I don't have more for you. A partial or something."

"The direction'll help."

"I don't see how, but sure," Volpe said. "I always thought of mine as a one-off, but talking to you kind of makes me wonder if my perp got around."

"I can save you some work there. New Orleans last year, Miami the year before that, Vegas oh-five."

Volpe whistled. "For real?"

"No samples, but the same trademarks. Gonna call the other Ds to see if anything else turns up. It does, you're the first I tell."

"Appreciate it."

"Sure. One more thing. Vegas said their vic's fingernails were cut extremely short, like bloody short. Does that match?"

"I can check the autopsy report."

"Thanks again."

"Yeah, no problem. You know what, Lev, you're not bad for LAPD."

"The hell's that supposed to mean?"

"Here I was thinking you guys were all about beating the shit out of innocent folks."

"Yeah, and you guys shove a broomstick up everybody's asses."

Volpe laughed. "Send me that picture, all right?"

"Don't look at it before you eat, unless you want to lose your appetite. Or after, unless you want to lose your lunch."

"The fuck'm I supposed to look at it, then?"

"Have a drink first," Jacob said. "I find that helps."

LESTER HOLTZ, the New Orleans D, was AWOL. Nobody had heard from him in months, and the bulk of his caseload had been dumped on a rookie named Matt Grandmaison who began to stutter when Jacob asked about body positioning.

"Uh, I b'lieve," Grandmaison said, his accent nearly identical to Volpe's Brooklyn honk, "whad I b'lieve is dat, uh . . ."

What Jacob believed is that Grandmaison's cubicle looked like a hoarder's basement. He could hear papers shuffling; could hear the poor guy accidentally knocking crap off his desk and grunting as he bent to retrieve it. Jacob managed to extract a promise to revisit the crime scene, although he assumed Grandmaison would forget as soon as he'd hung up.

Vegas PD was used to calls from L.A., and vice versa: bad guys from one city often fled to the other. Jacob phoned a contact from a previous case. Reintroductions were made, and he ended up on the phone with a D named Aaron Flores, who corroborated the particulars of Volpe's account and was remarkably quick to confirm that his own vic, a thirty-year-old casino hostess at the Venetian, had been found with her head pointing east.

"You're sure," Jacob said.

"Sure I'm sure," Flores said. "I walked in there at five a.m. and the goddamned sun punched me in the face."

He went on to explain that Dani Forrester had had money problems.

"She's making thirty grand and she's got four mortgages, one condo for herself and three she can't rent out cause of the slump. Her sister told us she'd also run up her credit cards, and turned out she'd been making visits to a loan shark. We picked him up, worked him over good, never got anything we could pin on him."

He agreed to send Jacob a copy of the file by the end of the week.

Miami PD put him on hold, midway through a Muzak version of "Smells Like Teen Spirit." Jacob thought Kurt Cobain would kill himself all over again if he heard it.

The doorbell rang.

Through the peephole, Subach and Schott.

He put the chain on before cracking the door.

"Morning," Subach said. "How's your neck?"

Schott said, "Mel told me about your mishap."

"We wanted to make sure you're okay," Subach said. "Can we come in?"

"I'm fine."

"Come on, Jake," Subach said. "We come in peace."

The hold music had switched to a jazzy "Born to Be Wild."

Jacob hung up the call, took the chain off, and let them in.

"Thanks," Schott said. He strolled around the living room, stopped before the disconnected television. "You didn't hook it back up."

"I've been busy," Jacob said.

"You want us to do it for you?" Subach said.

"What's the deal? You're not here cause you care about my neck."

"Hey now," Schott said. "Always there for a brother in blue."

"You sounded pretty upset the other night," Subach said.

"So?" Schott said. "How are you?"

"Fine," Jacob said.

"What the heck happened, anyway?" Schott said.

"Ask him," Jacob said, chinning at Subach. "He was there."

"All right, Mel," Schott said. "What the heck happened?"

"I don't know," Subach said. "There I am, trying to buy a buddy a drink, and all of a sudden he's running away, yodeling his head off."

Jacob said, "That's not what happened."

They looked at him.

"That's not what happened," he said again, "and you know it."

Schott said, "Tell us what happened, then."

"You saw her," Jacob said. "The girl."

He was talking to Subach, but Schott responded: "That's what you saw? A girl?"

"I told you," Subach said.

"You saw a girl," Schott said.

"Yeah, I saw a girl. Mel saw her, too, unless he's blind."

A silence.

"The important thing's you're okay," Schott said.

"Sleeping well?" Subach asked. "Eating?"

Jacob said, "Last time I'm gonna ask: what do you want from me?"

"We want you to do your job," Schott said. "Best way you can."

"Then get me a new computer," Jacob said.

"The one we gave you's brand-new," Schott said.

"It keeps freezing."

"They all do that, eventually," Subach said. "You probably got a virus or spyware."

"It only happens when I try to search for certain things."

"What things," Schott asked.

"A tag. Some other stuff."

"Other stuff, like?"

"Can you run it for me?"

"Sure," Subach said. "Give it to me, I'll give you a ring back."

"Why don't you run it on your MDC?" Jacob said. "I can wait."

Schott said, "You know, funniest thing, we're having problems with ours, too."

A silence.

Jacob said, "Must be a department-wide issue."

"Yeah," Subach said. "These days, everything's connected."

"I've left Mallick three voicemails and he hasn't called back."

"Try e-mailing him," Schott said.

"I did. Like ten times. I need to get hold of a copy of the 911 call."

"We'll pass it along," Subach said.

"Will you?"

"Of course we will," Schott said

Subach said, "We're on your side, Jake."

Jacob remained silent.

Subach wished him a good day and the men exited, shutting the door without a sound.

CHAPTER TWENTY-SEVEN

Tyler Volpe said, "How awesome am I?"

Any detective coped with a certain amount of tedium; just the same, after spinning his wheels for several days, Jacob felt especially grateful for the interruption. Grandmaison from New Orleans had neglected to get back to him, Flores's file from Vegas hadn't yet arrived, and the Miami PD kept putting him on hold, subjecting him to a thousand different pop songs rendered in cheesy saxophone and synth bass.

Meanwhile, Subach and Schott had gone dark, Divya Das was buried in bodies, and Mallick continued to ignore him. Jacob didn't know who they were shielding by giving him the runaround, but it pissed him off, in part because it implied that they expected him to give up at the first sign of pushback.

Let's not kid ourselves, okay?

I talked to your superiors.

I know who you are.

No, you don't.

Fed up, he'd dialed Marcia, his old pal from Valley Traffic.

"The prodigal son returns," she said.

"I need you to have someone run a plate for me, please."

"What's the matter, you're stationed on the moon? Thought you left us for bigger and better things."

"Smaller and worse," he said. "I also need a recording of a 911 call."

She took down the information. "I'll see what I can do."

"Last thing: check an address for me?"

She sighed.

"Pretty please," he said. "I need a physical location for a division called Special Projects. Mailing address, PO box, anything."

"Special Projects? What is that?"

"My new home."

"You don't know where you are?"

"I'm not there. I'm here."

"Where's here?"

"My apartment."

Marcia said, "This is getting a wee bit abstract for a simple Valley girl like me."

He returned to tracking down the people on Ludwig's interview list, eliminating those Ludwig had starred because they turned out to be deceased. He'd covered around a quarter of the list, no one warranting further investigation, when Volpe phoned back, sounding revved up.

"How awesome am I?"

"I'll tell you in a minute," Jacob said.

"Okay. First thing, you were right on about the body. Her head was definitely facing the east, toward the bathroom window."

"Killed there or moved?"

"Originally, I thought she was trying to climb out the window when he took her down. But now I'm thinking he—or they, if it was two guys—jumped her while she was sleeping. The bedroom was a fuckin mess, so she probably struggled there. Whatever, she faced east. I went back to the apartment and checked it myself."

"Excellent," Jacob said.

"So?"

"You're awesome."

"Yeah, I know."

"You said the first thing," Jacob said. "What's the second?"

"I showed your head around," Volpe said. "You were right about that, too: nasty shit."

"Tell me someone recognized him."

"Not him. The MO."

"You're kidding."

"Head, no body, sealed neck, puke." Volpe paused. "Stop me if I'm getting it wrong."

"No, that's it. That's it, exactly. Who's the D? What's his number?"

"Well, here's the kicker," Volpe said. "I have this buddy, Dougie Freeman, I was telling him about your thing, and he's like, 'Holy shit, that sounds like this other thing that guy told me about.' And I'm like, 'What guy?' And he tells me back in May last year, he goes upstate for a seminar on human trafficking, and they got this group of cops flown in from around the globe, some sort of DOJ initiative, establish goodwill, mutual trust, cooperation, blah blah . . . Anyhow, one night they're hanging out, getting shitfaced—universal language—and this one guy starts going on about this crazy case he's caught, head but no body. So when I mentioned to Dougie about your guy, he's like, 'Show me the picture.' I showed it to him. He's like, 'That's what the guy described to me, with the neck and the puke and everything.' And so I'm like, 'Great, I'll tell Lev, what's the guy's name?' And Dougie's like, 'I don't know, I don't remember.' And I'm like, 'You remember the case but you can't remember his name?' And he's like, 'Course I remember, it was a fuckin cut-off head.' And I'm like, 'Well, *think*, motherfucker.' And he's like, 'I dunno, it had a lot of consonants.'" Volpe made a sad noise. "I love Dougie, but for the betterment of the species I oughta disengage his nutsack."

"He say where the guy's from?"

"Prague," Volpe said. "Anyway, he and Dougie swapped badges. I got the guy's right here. You want me read it to you?"

Jacob didn't answer him. He was thinking: Prague.

Eastern Europe.

East.

"Lev? You there?"

"Yeah," Jacob said, picking up a pen. "Go ahead."

"Policy . . . che—cesk . . . Fuck me. I'm gonna spell it out."

Jacob copied down *Policie Ceske Republiky.*

"The *c* in *ceske*'s got a thing on it, like a upside-down hat. And the second *e*'s got an accent mark."

"Number, department?"

"That's what I have. Badge isn't his, just a souvenir he brought to swap. You want to talk to Dougie, I can give you his cell." Volpe read it to him. "Talk slow. No big words."

"Thanks, man. I really appreciate it."

"Yeah, sure thing. You know, since I talked to you, I'm thinkin about having another crack at Shevchuk, see if I missed something else."

"Good luck. I'll let you know what I come up with."

"Same here. Take it easy, Lev."

Clicking on the link for the Policie České Republiky home page brought up an imposing wall of Czech. Jacob pasted the URL into Google Translate and it rebooted in pseudo-English, allowing him to locate the main switchboard number.

As soon as the operator grasped that he was American, she transferred him to another woman, who began by asking where Jacob had been walking when his wallet was stolen.

"No," Jacob said, "I'm looking for a homicide detective. Can you please—"

A series of beeps; a blast of Czech.

"Hello?" Jacob said. "English?"

"Emergency?"

"No emergency. Homicide department. Murder."

"Where, please?"

"No, not—I need—"

"Ambulance?"

"No. No. No. I—"

More beeps.

"Ahoj," a man said.

Jacob's mind instantly conjured a sea captain on the other end of the line. "Ahoy. Is this Homicide?" He nearly added *matey*.

"Yes, no."

"Uh. Yes, this is Homicide, or no, it's not?"

"Who is calling, please."

"Detective Jacob Lev. Los Angeles Police Department. In America."

"Ah," the man said. "Rodney King!"

THE GUY'S NAME WAS RADEK. A junior lieutenant, he didn't know who'd gone to New York last year, but cheerily offered to make inquiries.

"Thanks. I have to ask, of all things, how is it you know about Rodney King?"

"Okay. Snowproblem. After Revolution I am watch American television programs. *A-Team. Silver Spoons.* Sometimes news. So I see videotape. Pah, pah, pah! Black guy down."

"We've improved our customer relations since then."

"Yes? Good!" Radek laughed heartily. "Is okay for me to visit? Don't kick my ass?"

"Not if you behave."

"I have a cousin, he's go to Dallas. Marek. You know him, I think?"

"I live in California," Jacob said. "It's kind of far."

"Ah, yes?"

"It's a big country," Jacob said.

"Snowproblem. Marek, he marries American lady. Wanda. They have a restaurant for Czech food."

"Sounds good," Jacob said.

"You know this food? *Knedlíky?* My favorite, you should try."

"Next time I'm in Dallas I'll be sure to check it out."

"Okay, snowproblem, I call you soon."

He did, early the following morning, his voice tight and low.

"Yes, Jacob, hello."

"Radek? Why are you whispering?"

"Jacob, this is not good thing for talking about."

"What? Did you find out whose case it is?"

"One moment, please."

A hand over the receiver, muffled voices, then Radek blurted a string of numbers that Jacob hastily scribbled on his arm.

"Who am I calling?"

"Jan."

"Is he the detective?"

"Jacob, thank you, good luck to you, I must go."

Dial tone. Jacob stood puzzling, then punched in the number.

The phone rang eleven times before a tired-sounding woman answered.

"Ahoy," Jacob said. "Can I please speak to Jan?"

Kids fighting in the background, bright commercial jingles. The woman shouted for Jan, and a phlegmy cough drew near.

"Ahoj."

"Jan."

"Yes?"

"My name is Jacob Lev. I'm a detective with the Los Angeles Police Department. Do you understand me? English?"

Screaming silence.

"A little," Jan said.

"Okay. Okay, great. I got your number from a colleague of yours, Radek—"

"Radek who."

"I don't know his name. His last name."

"Hn."

"I understand you were in New York last year, and a police officer who met you told me about a homicide where you found a head, the neck sealed up, and as it happens—"

"Who told you this? Radek?"

"No, an NYPD cop. Dougie. He—or, his colleague, actually—"

"What do you want?"

"I'm working a similar case. I was hoping to compare notes."

"Notes?"

"To see if there's anything worth exploring."

The chaos in the background had reached a fever pitch, and Jan turned away to bark in Czech. There was a very brief reprieve, then the battle resumed. He came back on, coughing and swallowing audibly. "I apologize. I cannot talk about this."

"Is there like a gag order, cause—"

"Yes," Jan said. "I am sorry."

"Okay, but look. Maybe you can send me some crime scene photos, or—"

"No, no, no photos."

"At least let me send you mine, so you can have a look, and if you—"

"No, I apologize, there is nothing to discuss."

"There is to me," Jacob said. "I've got thirteen dead women."

A pause.

Jan said, "If you come here, we can talk."

"We can't just talk on the phone? Is there a better number?"

Jan said, "Call when you are here."

And he hung up, too.

CHAPTER TWENTY-EIGHT

No such tag," Marcia said. "Anthony reran it three times to make sure."

"What about the 911 tape?"

"They haven't gotten back to him."

Figures. "Special Projects?"

"Nothing. What kind of top secret stuff are you into these days, Lev?"

"I'd tell you if I knew."

"Keep safe."

"I'll try."

The soonest affordable flight to Prague was a Wednesday-night red-eye on Swiss, connecting through Zurich and costing eleven hundred dollars. While leaving Mallick a voicemail explaining his intentions, he fiddled with the white credit card, then tossed it aside disgustedly, girding himself to cough up a grand of his own money with no hope of reimbursement. Maybe the interest on the $97,000 advance on his salary would bring him back up to even in due time.

The sat phone rang before he could finish typing in his own credit card number.

"Lev, Mike Mallick."

"Commander. Nice to finally hear from you."

"We need to talk. Face-to-face."

"You want me to swing by the garage?"

"That location's no longer active," Mallick said. "Stay there. I'll come to you."

HE CAME ALONE, pressed and slender, towering and tidy.

Standard eight-foot ceilings emphasized his height: he ducked his head as he entered, remained warily hunched, the habitual stance of a man living in a world not designed for him.

Jacob pulled out two kitchen chairs and offered coffee.

"No, thanks. But help yourself." Mallick sat, smoothing down the white tufts of hair above his ears. "Getting along here?"

"That's one of the things I was hoping to talk to you about, sir. I've been having a few technical issues."

"Is that so."

"I keep trying to run a tag and my system crashes."

"Mm."

"I asked a friend in Traffic to run it for me, and she said it doesn't come up."

"Then I'd assume it's bogus."

"Yeah, maybe. But I also encounter the same problem when I look for the division address."

"Special Projects?"

Jacob nodded.

"That's because there is none. This isn't an official detail. You want to know the address," Mallick said, tapping his chest, "you're looking at it."

"I sent you an e-mail," Jacob said. "You never wrote back."

"When was that?"

"A few days ago. I've sent several, actually. About a 911 recording, too."

"Did you, now? I must have missed it."

"All of them?"

Mallick smiled. "I'm bad with technology."

"I asked Subach and Schott to tell you."

Mallick didn't answer.

Jacob said, "You came here when I told you I was going to Prague."

"Well, that's a significant expense."

"No kidding," Jacob said. "I'm the one paying."

"You have a card for operational expenses."

"It doesn't work."

"Have you tried it?"

"Several times. It won't go through."

"It'll go through," Mallick said placidly. "At any rate, given the expanding scope of this investigation, I thought it would be best to discuss it."

"Face-to-face."

"I'm a people person, Lev."

Jacob said nothing.

Mallick said, "You're making progress on the case."

"I'd be doing better if I had the 911 tape or even the slightest sense why you're stonewalling me."

"Don't be melodramatic."

"You have a better word, sir?"

"I told you. It's sensitive."

"Then I don't get the point of working from home. Or having a secure line. The idea was to avoid attracting attention. Not to put me in a box so small I can't function."

Mallick didn't respond.

"Pardon my language, sir," Jacob said, "but what the fuck is going on?"

"I've given you a very important task and I need you to carry it out."

"What task is that, sir?"

"Exactly what you're doing," Mallick said. "That's what I need you to do."

"Tread water?"

"From what you've told me, you've done a good deal more than that."

"So you did read my e-mails."

"I read them."

"Then you know there's crucial information that I'm not getting access to."

"We're on top of it."

"Who's we? On top of what?"

"That's all you need to know at the moment."

"With respect, sir, fuck that."

Mallick chuckled. "Everything they said about you is true."

"Who said? Mendoza?"

"Are you asking me to take you off the case?"

"I'm asking to not feel like everybody's running around behind my back."

"Everybody being?"

"Subach. Schott. Divya Das. Even the guy I talked to in Prague sounded spooked."

"What's in Prague?"

"Another head."

Mallick's brow creased, and his eyes grew unfocused. He remained that way for some time, nodding slowly.

At last he said, "I think you should go to Prague."

"So that's a yes, sir?"

"That's a yes."

The bout of permissiveness bewildered Jacob. "Thank you, sir. But can I ask why you're okay with me leaving the country but you won't help me obtain a simple 911 recording?"

Mallick rubbed his forehead and contemplated for another long stretch. He seemed to consider several alternatives before settling on taking out his phone, placing it on the coffee table, tapping the screen a few times.

Recording hiss.

Nine-one-one, what is your emergency?

Hello. A woman's voice. *I'd like to report a death.*

Sorry, ma'am, can you repeat that? A death?

The woman recited the address of the house on Castle Court.

Are you—ma'am, are you in danger? Can you tell me if you—do you need assistance?

Thank you.

Ma'am? Hello? Ma'am? Are you there?

The hiss cut off as Mallick leaned over and touched the screen.

"Did that help?" he asked softly.

Jacob looked at him.

"Do you want to hear it again?"

Jacob nodded.

Mallick touched PLAY.

Nine-one-one, what is your emergency?

By the end of the second listen-through, Jacob's mouth was dry and he was gripping the edge of the table hard enough to feel his pulse.

Thank you.

Mallick reached over and pressed PAUSE. "Do you understand now?"

Jacob looked at him. "No."

"I can e-mail you a copy, if you'd like."

Jacob nodded.

"Regardless of whether you understand," Mallick said, "it's vital that you keep doing what you're doing. Vital."

"Sir?"

"Yes, Lev?"

"Are you sure I should go to Prague?"

"Why not?"

"I should probably stay here to try and . . . chase that down."

The Commander gazed at him with strange tenderness.

"Go," he said. "I think you'll find it educational."

Long after he'd left, Jacob was sitting, motionless. The apartment got dark. He rose to shut and bolt the front door.

His computer seemed to be working fine now. As promised, Mike Mallick had e-mailed him the audio file. Jacob listened to it five, six, seven times, many more times than he needed to be absolutely certain that he'd heard right, that the voice on the recording belonged to Mai.

CHAPTER TWENTY-NINE

He called his father to tell him about the trip.

Sam said, "No."

Jacob stuttered laughter. "Excuse me?"

"You can't go. I can't allow it. I, I—*forbid* it."

Jacob had never heard his father like this before. "Abba. Seriously."

"I am serious," Sam said. "Do I not sound serious?"

"I've got a job to do."

"In Prague."

"What, you think I'm lying to you?"

"I think there's no reason for you to have to travel halfway around the world."

"I'm pretty sure that's my call to make, not yours."

"Wrong," Sam said. "Wrong. Wrong."

"I'm not asking for permission."

"That's good," Sam said, "because I'm not giving it to you."

"What's gotten into you?"

"You can't do this to me."

"What are you talking about? I'm not doing any—"

"You're leaving me."

"You'll be fine. I spoke to Nigel. He'll be by every day."

"I don't need him," Sam said. "I need *you*, here."

"What aren't you telling me? Are you sick?"

"I'm speaking, as your father—"

"And I'm telling you, as a grown man, that this is not a negotiation."

A wounded silence.

"I thought you'd be excited," Jacob said. "Home of the Maharal."

Sam did not reply.

"Look," Jacob said, "I'll drop by later, all right? Right now I've got to go."

"Jacob—"

"I have a ton of stuff I need to do. I'll see you later."

He hung up before Sam could object.

HIS PASSPORT WAS a few months shy of expiration and bore two stamps from the previous decade: a winter jaunt to Baja, a last-ditch attempt to repair things with Renee; another to Paris, same deal with Stacy, more expensive, equally unsuccessful.

Per Mallick's instructions, he used the white credit card to book his flight and hostel.

It went through.

Maybe they had a list of preapproved purchase categories—travel, for instance, but not food. Long as he wasn't paying.

He went off to pack, delaying going to Sam's until the late afternoon. He wasn't in the mood for an argument, and the abrupt shift in his father's personality had him worrying about the possibility that Sam might be losing it, too.

He found a spot on the street behind Nigel's red Taurus, a broken-down bundle of nonmoving violations.

"Consider yourself warned," he said, stepping onto the patio, where Nigel stood holding a full trash bag. "Again."

Nigel grinned. "The Lord is my shepherd."

"Fine if you drive a sheep."

Nigel's smile widened until nothing remained of his cheeks; he began to laugh, a gold cross bouncing on the trampoline of T-shirt stretched between massive pectoral muscles.

"I'm not kidding," Jacob said. "Each of those infractions is like a two-hundred-dollar ticket."

"Which one should I handle first?"

"The taillight, and the windshield, and the bumper, and—"

Nigel clucked his tongue.

Jacob said, "The taillight. That's what's going to get you pulled over."

"Yakov," Nigel said, enunciating the Hebrew name with his usual glee, "I don't need anything extra to get pulled over."

Driving while black. End of debate. Jacob glanced at the trash bag. "You need a hand?"

"Taking this out and I'll be on my way."

"I'll walk you to your car."

As soon as they were out of earshot of the apartment, Jacob said, "How's he doing?"

Nigel seemed confused by the question. "Could use a haircut."

"You haven't noticed anything weird, though."

"Like what?"

"Anything. Mood changes."

Nigel shook his head.

"And you'd let me know if you did."

"Most definitely."

"I'll be back in a week, tops," Jacob said. "Promise me you'll keep a close eye on him. I know you will, but I need to say it again so I can feel better about leaving."

"Don't you worry. He's a strong one."

Jacob felt it unnecessary to point out that Sam didn't buy his own groceries; Nigel did, as well as take in Sam's laundry and shuttle him to any destination beyond a half-mile radius of the apartment. A deeply religious Evangelical, Nigel held Sam in awe, and he took his assignments seriously, although how they had come to be his remained a trifle unclear. For a man who worked at a lumberyard, he had extremely soft hands. That made a great deal more sense when you learned the lumberyard was owned by none other than Abe Teitelbaum.

Nigel put the trash bag in the curbside can. "He has that light within him."

"Too bad I didn't get any."

Nigel smiled. "Take care of yourself, Yakov."

"Thanks. Since we're on the subject of light?"

"Yes?"

"Taillight."

SAM HAD HIS MAGNIFYING SPECTACLES ON, the ones that made him look like a mad scientist. Books smothered the dining room table.

"I still can't see why it's necessary to go all the way there."

"This guy wouldn't talk to me otherwise."

"What makes you think he'll talk to you in person?"

"He implied as much."

"But what if I need to get in touch with you?"

"Call my cell."

"It's too expensive."

"Call collect."

"Too expensive for you."

"I'm not paying. Give it up, Abba."

"I do not approve."

"I understand."

"Does that mean you're not going?"

"What do you think?"

Sam sighed. He plucked two softcovers from the nearest pile and slid them to Jacob. "I took the liberty of pulling these for you."

Jacob picked up a guidebook to Prague. "I didn't know you'd been."

"I haven't. But where you can't go, you can read."

The guidebook had to be a quarter century old, minimum. Jacob scanned the table of contents and saw a chapter devoted to traveling in Soviet bloc countries, including a subsection titled "Bribes: When and How Much?"

"I'm not sure this is current."

"The important stuff stays the same. Don't take it if you don't want. The other one I know you'll like."

Jacob recognized the cover art immediately: the lurching ogre that had sent him fleeing into his mother's arms. He'd forgotten the title, if he ever knew it.

Prague: City of Secrets, City of Legends
Classic Tales from the Jewish Ghetto
TRANSLATED FROM THE CZECH BY
V. GANS

"Thanks, Abba. Not sure how much pleasure reading I'll do." He was thinking of the file from Aaron Flores, arrived that morning, occupying the front pocket of his carry-on.

"There's the plane ride."

"I was hoping to sleep," Jacob said. Sam's evident dismay led him to add, "I'm sure I'll appreciate it when I'm jet-lagged and up at two in the morning."

Sam said, "That was your favorite book, when you were little."

Mine, Jacob thought, *or yours?* He nodded, though.

"I was thinking about how we used to read together, when you were very small. Most babies, they come out smushed. They barely look human. That wasn't you. You . . . you had a face, a—a substance, to you. Fully formed, from the womb. I looked at you and I thought I could see the future, read all the days, even the ones that hadn't been written yet." He paused. "And I would read to you, and you would listen. I would read the words and you would look up at me, like a wise old man, and you wouldn't stop looking until I said, 'The End.' I must've read that book to you five hundred times. You didn't like to sleep, so I would tie you inside my bathrobe and read to you till the sun came up and we said *Shema*."

He paused again. Cleared his throat. "Those were good mornings."

Sam abruptly removed his spectacles and tapped the book twice. "Anyway, I thought you might enjoy it."

"Thanks," Jacob said. He was picturing himself as a grown man, tied inside his father's robe, pressed to his bony chest. It was both creepy and comforting, as was the revelation that Sam had been reading him the tales since before he could remember. "You want me to bring anything back for you?"

Sam shook his head. Then: "As long as you're there, though."

"Yes?"

"Visit the Maharal's grave. Place a stone for me. Not if you're too busy, of course."

"I'll find the time."

"Thank you. One more thing," Sam said, reaching into his pocket. He pressed some money into Jacob's hand. "For *tzedakah*."

It was an old custom: giving a traveler charity money to ensure his safe passage. When one was engaged in a good deed, no harm could befall him, and charity, in particular, preserved one from death.

Allegedly.

Jacob ironed out the bills, expecting a couple of dollars, seeing instead two hundreds.

"Abba. This is way too much."

"How often are you in Prague?"

"I don't need two hundred. One's fine."

"One for the way there, one for the way back. Remember: you're my messenger. That's what protects you. The kindness, not the money." He reached for Jacob's neck, pulled him in for a scratchy kiss. "Go in peace."

THE BEGINNING OF FOREVER

Father always said that souls passed from the earth and returned to the garden, to reside for eternity in closeness to the Lord.

Asham, falling, sees the ground screaming toward her and hears Cain screaming betrayal in her ear and her chief thought is a peaceful one: soon she'll be with Abel, forever. As her tumbling body picks up speed, and the stones of the tower streak past like clay comets, Cain with a wounded shriek spirals away into oblivion, and it occurs to her that—if what she was told was true—he'll be there, too, forever.

She hadn't considered that part of it.

She does not have time to decide what she'll say to him before she dies.

Nothing she was told is true.

No garden.

No Abel.

No Cain, either. That's a relief.

She's right where she landed, standing on the ground.

All around her is chaos, a terrifying din that drives her to crouch and cover her ears.

She has no hands to cover them with.

She has no ears to cover.

She is not crouching.

She has no feet.

She has no legs, either. She's not actually standing but—

What?

She's existing.

She tries to cry, has no lungs, no throat, no lips, no tongue, no mouth.

The chaos is men, hordes of them. They've dropped their axes and are running; they pour off the tower, sprinting past her, carrying torches, cloth, jugs of water. Their voices are louder than a pack of beasts and Asham fails and fails to cry.

A sweet voice: Don't be frightened.

Before her stands a woman on fire, beautiful face smoldering with compassion and wrath.

Asham screams; nothing comes out.

You're confused, the woman says. It's understandable.

The woman puts out a fiery hand. Here.

I don't understand.

The woman smiles. There. Nicely done.

Asham has said nothing yet the woman heard her.

You're trying too hard, the woman says. You have to let it come naturally.

What?

That.

This?

Excellent. You'll get better with practice. The woman smiles. My name is Gabriella.

Your clothes, Asham says. Your hair.

I know. It takes me forever to get ready in the morning.

Asham doesn't know what to say.

A joke, Gabriella says.

Oh. Asham feels calmer, now that she can communicate. She looks around. Where am I?

Technically, you're right where you were a moment ago.

I—I am?

Yes.

Where?

See for yourself?

How?

Gabriella says, See.

For Asham to see requires that she exert herself. Like standing on her head or balancing on one foot. It isn't a matter of moving her body or her eyes but of projecting her will. Her perspective waddles here and there like a newborn chick, alighting on the smoke rising from the kilns, the outline of the unfinished tower, the mules with their besmirched hind-quarters.

Good, Gabriella says. That's very good.

Asham beholds the focal point of the commotion, a stand of collapsed scaffolding.

Is that me? My body?

No. Cain's.

How'd he get way over there?

He hit a beam on the way down.

Asham winces. Where am I?

Gabriella smiles sadly. Right there.

Asham shifts below.

Beneath her hovering presence, her body lies in pieces.

Her limbs are split, her bowels strewn, her head obliterated.

She emits a cry of grief.

It's hard, Gabriella says. I know.

I was so beautiful.

Yes, you were.

Why are they there, with him? Why does no one come to care for me?

He was their leader. You killed him.

Asham weeps without weeping.

FOR SEVEN DAYS, Gabriella sings to her.

> As painful as needles to the flesh of the living,
> so is the destruction of the body to the spirit to which it once cleaved.

It is
the shattering of a fine vessel;
the collapse of blown glass;
the casting off of an anchor;
the razing of a temple.

Gabriella stops singing.

All right, she says. That's enough of that.

And she spirits Asham away on a warm western wind, raising her over the world, a shifting patchwork of color. Boastful yellows, living greens, the steady marine of peace.

What is this? Asham asks.

Mankind, Gabriella says. Look.

Where?

Come with me, Gabriella says, taking her hand.

Their perspective shrinks.

In the city that bears his name, Enoch stands before his father's funeral pyre.

A gray aura surrounds him.

Perched at his side, the dog sticks out its tongue, licks his hand.

Enoch glares at it.

A priest is chanting the funerary rites.

The dog again licks Enoch's fingers.

Stop it, he says.

It whimpers. Sticks out its tongue.

Enoch lashes out, striking it across the muzzle.

The dog yelps and flees.

What's the matter with him? Asham says. Why would he do that?

He's angry, Gabriella says. Look.

They shift again, and Enoch, a young man of fifteen, crowned in gold, sits upon the throne. The gray around him has thickened, a mucoid mass that pulses and oozes and drips. His face is a stone as he listens to the pleas of his advisers. There are not enough men to complete the tower, they tell him. There is not enough money. The treasurer rises to speak and Enoch takes a gray sword from his belt and drives it through the man's heart, which spurts.

He always was his father's son, Gabriella says. What was good in him has been extinguished.

I didn't mean for this to happen, Asham says.

Nobody ever does.

Please. I don't want to see any more.

I'm sorry to have to show this to you. Look.

Enoch, a young man of twenty-two, rides out of the valley amid a rumbling gray cloud, leading his army to war. They return with a caravan of captives and treasure. The prisoners are brought to the marketplace where once Asham walked with the boy, laughing and eating fruit. Ten of the vanquished are tied to posts, whipped until their skin hangs in strips before being beheaded as examples. Of the rest, the women and children are sold for private use and the men strung together with gray chains and sent to work on the tower, where they all die eventually, their skulls staved in by falling bricks, their chests crushed under timber piles, diseased and hacking up blood.

Please, Asham moans. Stop it.

But Gabriella gently insists. It's the way of this world. Look.

A vengeful tribe arrives at the valley to make war upon Enoch.

Blood flows in the gray streets.

What have I done. What have I done.

Look.

Enoch, an old man of forty, encased in a hard gray shell, dies at the hand of his own son, who kills his brothers and ascends to the throne.

All right, Gabriella says. I think you get the point.

Aloft, they leap eons. The gray mucus continues to spread. It overflows the valley; it washes across the plains and mountains; between the reds of lust and the golds of joy it fills the gaps, overruns them, hardening like mortar along the borders of nations, its advance mindless and ravenous and inevitable.

Gabriella says, We begged Him not to allow this. We said, What is man, that You are mindful of him?

I wanted justice, Asham says.

And yet you wrought more death.

In a gray alley of a distant gray city, gray men hold down a woman. Her screams, purple and fungal, catch the attention of a passerby, who watches what is happening for a moment and then walks on, leaving gray footprints.

Make it stop, Asham says. Please.

One thing at a time.

How can you say that? Look what they're doing to her.

No, Gabriella says. I mean: I can only do one thing at a time. I'm here with you, so I can't help her.

Then *go*.

Gabriella shakes her head, trailing flame. It's not my charter.

A gray fog cloaks the woman, and she is gone, and silence prevails.

Call it a question of jurisdiction, Gabriella says. The world was not given to us, but to men.

She pauses. They're doing a terrible job, mind you.

They rise, watching the gray as it smothers the surface of the earth.

It's really a mess down there. It's gotten so bad He's thinking of starting over.

I'm a monster, Asham says.

No. It only seems that way to you, because you see the consequences of your deeds. Go forward. Learn from your mistakes. Turn a negative into a positive. Right? Gabriella puts a burning arm around her, squeezes. That's where you come in.

Me?

Gabriella nods. If you want. I can't get involved, but you can.

Anything, Asham says. Anything to make it right.

You're sure? If you agree, you will be committed to this pursuit.

I agree. I'm committed.

Gabriella opens the ledger. Sign here.

Asham looks at the book. Its pages are white fire, and for a moment she hesitates.

What's wrong? Gabriella asks.

Nothing. I just—what am I signing?

Gabriella's expression grows fearsome. You want to help, don't you?

Yes. Yes. Of course.

Then sign.

Asham thinks of the gray world and thinks of her ravaged self. What else remains, if not to correct the wrong she has done? She commits herself, and when she looks at the book again, her name has appeared in letters of black fire, tremulous against the white fire of the page.

אשם

Other figures appear on the fringes of her perception, arrayed in ghostly semicircles, their tall forms nodding at her; they come from all directions, borne in on waves of earth and crests of wind, their faces numbered one and two and three and four, reflecting an eternal light. Prominent among them stands the man Michael, who smiles his sad smile and says, You have chosen. You can't go back.

The tall figures around him nod. Something in their eyes frightens Asham: their single-minded stares.

The planet has gone chillingly gray, from one end to the next.

Asham says, When do I begin?

It's not time yet, Gabriella says.

Asham looks down at the world, up at eternity. Until then? Where do I go? What do I do?

Gabriella smiles at her. Touches her cheek.

Sleep.

CHAPTER THIRTY

Jacob shuffled off the jetway in Prague having slept two hours of eighteen. Much of those 120 minutes had been occupied by muddled green dreams: Mai, old tools, his mother babbling manically to his father, his father pretending to understand.

The endings of every dream identical: butchered women, facing east.

Bringing up the rear for a zombie-squad of backpackers and business-men, he advanced down the terminal amid piped-in Lady Gaga, lining up to confront a beagle-faced bureaucrat who scanned and stamped and waved him on into the City of Legends without a second glance.

Some quick math revealed that the spring breakers sharing his bus to town had been born after the Velvet Revolution. Jacob could therefore excuse their enthusiasm on grounds of naïveté. They had, absurdly, dressed the part of early-nineties pioneers, arrived to prospect among the cultural rubble of the Berlin Wall: carrying rolled copies of *The Meta-morphosis* and sporting vintage Nirvana T-shirts, inherited from uncles who "were there."

Feeling ancient, he squinted through scratched plexi at flat polygons of gold and green, periodically relieved by wooded breaks and farm-houses. A quaint countryside diorama that curdled into the present day, one billboard at a time.

Piebald Communist-era apartment blocks appeared, arrayed without logic, like partygoers milling around after the stereo cuts out. At the outskirts of the city, he noted a lot of construction, much of it halted midway, offering itself up as a canvas for graffiti.

So far, the only legend he'd seen was the one on the complimentary map he'd swiped at the airport, and its only secret was the location of TGI Fridays.

The road rose, then dipped into a shallow valley. An uneven mosaic of burnt-orange roofs rimmed a glaucous coil of river, sun-dappled and sluggish.

The bus lumbered down over a bridge, depositing him at the central station.

He bought a bottle of mineral water and took a tram schedule; changed his mind and set out on foot, trying to stave off jet lag, his carry-on rumbling over sidewalks patterned from black and white stone and grouted with cigarette butts. It was a glorious bath of an afternoon, mellow and dreamy and warm. High, narrow streets snuck up behind him, jackknifing, warping, fracturing into ghostly echoes the whine of a motor scooter, the disco ringtones of cheap phones.

There was something disconcerting about foreign signage, and Czech, with its sibilants, its unexpected letter combinations barbed with diacriticals, read like the words of a madman hissing condemnation.

Yawning, blinking, he walked Hybernská Street beneath the scowl of roofline gargoyles, encountering living faces just as hard, faces not quite Western, not quite Eastern. Proud mouths, slit eyes, young people with rooty, aged hands. They looked mistrustfully at Jacob; looked through him, as though he did not exist, and he found himself crunching his toes in his shoes in an effort to prove that he did, smiling and failing to have it reciprocated.

He gave up on people and turned to architecture, gazing up at a gorgeous, mischievous rogue's gallery of styles. Baroque, Art Nouveau, and rococo shouldered together like strangers on an overcrowded bus. Plaster façades were black with soot or so fresh they appeared wet.

In Republic Square, he paused to wipe his sticky neck and admire the verdigris cap of the Municipal House before turning north, toward the portion of Old Town squashed by the river's jutting thumb.

The Hostel Nozdra lived up to its one-star rating. As a concession to dignity, he'd sprung for a private room rather than the dormitory. He dragged his bag up four flights and unlocked the door to a linoleum cell equipped with chipped wood laminates and a gimpy chair half turned, as though caught red-handed in some shameful act.

He'd wanted to be judicious with his use of department funds, but not this judicious.

Someone had etched a frowny face in the wall, along with an inscription.

Sarah u broke my heart.

Get used to it, dude.

He stripped to the waist and flopped down, drawing weak protest from the mattress.

His phone had picked up a local carrier. He dialed Jan's number, let it ring ten times. Next he tried the main Prague PD switchboard and got tangled up in a confusing exchange with the wrong guy.

How many Prague cops named Jan?

Roughly as many Johns or Mikes on LAPD.

He called back and asked for Radek.

The switchboard operator began scolding him in Czech.

Jacob ended the call, yawning into the crook of his elbow. If he meant to beat jet lag, a nap was the wrong strategy.

Nobody had ever accused him of excessive discipline. He set an alarm, sank back into a pillowcase redolent of patchouli, and passed out.

NEON ORANGE FILTERED THROUGH window grime.

He pried his phone out from between the bedframe and the wall.

The alarm had gone off hours ago. He'd slept through it.

And he'd just missed a call.

"Shit."

Mercifully, Jan picked up.

"Ahoj."

"Hey. Sorry. I couldn't get to the phone."

In the background, the kids were screaming, as though the tantrum had been ongoing for a week. "Who is this, please?"

"Jacob Lev, LAPD. I called you recently, about a case?"

"Ah-hah. Yes, okay. I remember."

"You said to get in touch when I came to Prague."

"Yes, okay."

"Well, here I am."

An interlude of slaps and crying.

Jan coughed, cleared his throat. "You are here?"

"Yeah."

"In Prague?"

"I got in a couple hours ago. This conversation's costing me two bucks a minute, so how bout we finish it in person? Tomorrow work for you?"

"Tomorrrrrrow," Jan said. "No, I'm sorry, it's very busy. I have many things to do."

"Saturday, then."

"This is not good, either."

"All right, why don't you pick a day?"

"How long do you plan to remain in Czech Republic?"

"Four days."

"Four days . . . I don't know if it will be possible to meet."

"Are you kidding me? I flew here to talk to you."

"This decision was yours, not mine."

"*You* said—look, man, please, come on. I know a cop's schedule. Nothing's in stone."

"Perhaps for you this is true."

"I brought the photos," Jacob said.

"I don't know any photos."

"Yes, you do, I told you. Give me your office address. I'll drop them off. You can look and then decide."

"I apologize," Jan said, sounding genuinely rueful. "This case is private, there is nothing to discuss."

Jacob said, "Did someone tell you not to speak to me?"

The phone clattered down, and Jan could be heard yelling at the kids. When he returned he was coughing mightily. "I apologize for your inconvenience," he said. "There are many things to do in Prague. You will enjoy yourself."

"Hang on—"

The line went dead.

Jacob stared at the phone in astonishment.

He called back. Ring ring ring ring ring. "Pick up, asshole."

Hanging up, he gazed out the window, blotting his chest with a handful of rough muslin sheet. It was six p.m. and he was alone in a strange city.

What now?

He hadn't yet made up his mind when the phone shook with a text from an unfamiliar number.

pivnice u rudolfina
křižovnická 10
30 min

CHAPTER THIRTY-ONE

The Czechs knew their beer. The pub met and exceeded Jacob's standards: a cavernous, low-ceilinged, centuries-old room with mahogany accents and stone walls. Fried meat and quality pilsner were brought by a poker-faced waiter who materialized with a fresh glass whenever the one on the table dipped below fifteen percent. While it was still too early for serious partiers, a raucous atmosphere prevailed.

The only thing missing was Jan.

The hacking cough and the feral brood had led Jacob to picture a man in his late forties. Loose jowls, yellow teeth, bad skin. Nobody fit that description, so he began making eye contact with every male who walked in, receiving in return a series of irritated *not gay* stares.

He drummed his fingers on the manila envelope containing the crime scene photos from Castle Court. He called Jan's number, then the second number. He sent texts to both. He checked with the waiter that there wasn't another establishment that went by the same name.

"Hello!"

The girl didn't wait for an invitation, sliding in next to him. "British? American?"

"American," he said. "I'm waiting for a friend."

She laughed. "Yes, me too! You are my friend. My name is Tatjana."

He stifled a smile. "Jacob."

"Nice to meet you, friend Jacob." Sweet and blond and plump, she put out a dimpled hand. "How is your beer?"

"Killer," he said.

"Hah?"

"It's very good."

"One for me?"

"You don't look old enough to drink."

Tatjana socked him in the shoulder. "I am nineteen."

"In America it's twenty-one."

"Then I will stay here." She raised her thumb to a passing waiter. "Jacob America, where do you come from?"

"Los Angeles."

"Hollywood? Movie stars?"

"Drug dealers. Prostitutes."

No reaction; he decided she probably wasn't a hooker.

"We have these, too," she said.

"So I hear." He consulted his phone. Nothing from Jan, now a full forty minutes late.

"You have been before in Prague?"

"First time."

"Yes? And how do you like?"

"I haven't seen much yet. But so far it seems very pretty."

Tatjana grinned broadly.

Whoops.

"The architecture is amazing," he added.

"Hah?"

"The buildings."

"I think you must go to see the castle. This is the most beautiful place in Prague."

He checked his phone. Sent another text. "I'm on a tight schedule."

"You are a businessman?"

"Of a sort."

The waiter brought her beer.

She raised her glass. *"Na zdraví."*

"Back atcha." They clinked and drank.

"What business?"

Jacob wiped foam from his upper lip. "I'm a cop."

"Hah?"

"A policeman."

Tatjana blinked. "Ah, yes?"

Maybe a hooker, after all.

Still, she didn't leave, yammering in his ear as he sent text after text. Neighboring tables emptied and were wiped down and filled up again. At one point she broke off her monologue, and Jacob followed her stare to a group of simian toughs sporting chunky gold chains.

"Friends of yours?" he asked.

She snorted. "Russians."

"How can you tell?"

"These ugly necklaces."

One of the men smiled sourly and raised his glass at Jacob.

"This makes me angry," Tatjana said. "We get rid of them, they come back, they are shit on everything."

"You can't possibly remember those days," he said.

"No. I was not born. But my father was dissident." Then, sensing that she had steered the mood awry, she smiled. "Everyone was dissident."

"I'm Jewish," he said. "Far be it from me to tell you not to hold a grudge."

"Ah, I understand. This is why you come to Prague."

"How's that?"

"There are many Jewish tourists. They come to see the synagogue. You will go?"

"It's a big business," he said. "Jewish tourism."

"Yes," Tatjana said. "This and Kafka."

"And what do you make of it?"

"Tourism? I think is very nice. Czechs are friendly people."

"Just not to Russians."

She laughed. "No."

"You like Kafka?"

"I have not read."

"Come on."

She shook her head. "Under Communism this was not allowed. Kafka wrote in German, so there is Czech translation only one year ago, two. I will read it soon, I think."

"You should read 'A Hunger Artist.'"

"Yes?"

"It's one of my favorite stories. That and 'The Village Schoolmaster.'"

"Please," she said, handing him her phone so he could type in the titles. "Your friend, I don't think he is coming."

"Yeah, me neither." He typed, returned the phone to her, threw back the rest of his beer, put down enough money to cover them both. "Nice talking to you, Tatjana. Have a good night."

She didn't get up to follow him.

Not a hooker.

OLD TOWN WAS IN FULL RIOT. Buzzed, Jacob threaded along, catching snatches of expat English, Spanish, French. Chesty bass drum, rubbery guitar, off-key vocals. Squeals of delight presaged tomorrow's regret. Pizza parlors and Internet cafés abounded, the ubiquitous Pilsner Urquell shield swinging in the sweet, foul breeze. Urine. Marijuana. Grilled onions dripping with sausage fat.

His umpteenth call to Jan went unanswered. Eurotrash. Chinese version of Eurotrash. A woman in a fraying corset attempted to entice him into a strip club. A woman in an evening gown attempted to entice him into a casino.

Back in his room, he opened up his bag and fished out the Dani Forrester file. He'd read most of it on the plane, and so far it consisted of stuff Flores had told him over the phone. A casino hostess dealt with a range of unsavory types. They'd gone through her BlackBerry, running down everyone she'd met with in the weeks leading up to the murder: bachelor party organizers, low-rent gamblers, hard-luck cases *hondling* for cheap rooms, conventioneers.

He came to the last page. Nine-fifteen p.m. Lunchtime in L.A.

He reached for the remote control.

No remote.

No TV.

Twenty bucks a night, you get what you pay for.

For the next hour, he read the obsolete guidebook from cover to cover.

Learned what to say if he was detained by customs.

Learned how to avoid having his film confiscated.

Wide awake, he shut off the light and stretched out, free-associating through the Castle Court chronology.

Eleven p.m., the call first comes in.

Hello.

Who greeted 911? People calling 911 forgot their own names. They stammered. They repeated themselves.

I'd like to report a death.

Not *a head* or *a dead body* or *oh my God please help*.

A death.

As though the victim had departed the earth peacefully, doing what he loved best. In the bathtub. On the golf course.

The woman's tone was grotesquely at odds with the content of her words.

She'd *like* to report it.

She *enjoyed* reporting it.

It would *be my pleasure* to report a death.

Ms. Mai with an i *Whoknowswhat, of Whoknowswhere, kindly requests your presence at the discovery of a corpse. Dinner and dancing to follow. RSVP to LAPD. Black tie suggested.*

Giving the address, she enunciates, so as not to be misheard. It's the dispatcher who's tripping over her own words.

Thank you.

Again: who does that?

Per Divya, the murder hadn't taken place long before the call. *Hours, not days.* But no body, no blood, no spatter. Off-site.

Where?

I'm just a nice young lady who came down for some fun.

Down from?

Up. That's where you come down from.

An especially nasty in-joke? A reference to the fact that the house was in the hills?

An hour passes between the call and Hammett's arrival.

During that time, what does Mai do?

Hunker down, waiting to see if they take her seriously?

Does she watch the patrolman go inside? Snap pictures with her cell phone?

Post them to Facebook? Tweet?

w/cops @ murder scene

#justice

lol!!

Or has she already split? She might have phoned it in from another location. The lack of background noise on the recording made it difficult to tell.

Meanwhile, Hammett radios in. The information gets punted around.

Not for very long, though. Divya Das arrives at the house around ten to two. She lives over an hour away, and that's assuming she goes straight to the right address, without getting lost. Meaning she's called out no later than twelve-forty-ish. Meaning the news hits Mallick's radar in under an hour.

Making for a level of efficiency Jacob had never encountered at LAPD.

Unless they're already on the move.

Meaning, they know about the head *before* the call comes in.

Nonsense.

Unless they're with Mai at the scene.

Maybe *they* cut the guy's head off.

Maybe Divya's there, too.

Maybe they all are.

A grand conspiracy! The whole goddamned department!

He indulged himself, wallowing in paranoia. LAPD death cabal, put that Jew Lev on the case, then obstruct him. The bizarro work-at-home arrangement, the fritzy computer system. The unresponsiveness when he requested the recording, Mallick's attitude when he finally played it for Jacob.

Did that help?

The Commander *expected* him to recognize her voice? Meaning, Mallick knows Jacob met Mai?

But Mallick can't know that.

Go. I think you'll find it educational.

Go fuck yourself, Confucius.

Neither O'Connor nor Ludwig had mentioned anybody named Mai with an *i*. Not that that meant a thing. Her real name could be Sue or Helena or Jezebel.

Whoever she is, at some point after making the call, she heads over to 187.

For some fun.

Fun with Mr. Sunshine, so drunk he can't even remember the color of her hair. His inability to perform self-evident. What's she doing, talking to him?

Why drive him home?

Why spend the night and get him stoked for sex, only to disappear?

Minutes later, Subach and Schott show up.

The timing made his stomach ache.

He played the recording through several more times, pressing the speaker up to his ear. It sounded like Mai—his memory of Mai. But what, really, was that memory grounded in? Ten hungover minutes. The wilder his thoughts wanted to be, the tighter he leashed them, and eventually he was able to listen to the recording and decide that it wasn't her, after all. He'd been dreaming about her and thinking about her, far more than he ought to, and that was making him hear her specific voice when in fact it was a generic female voice, a voice that could belong to any woman. He listened again, noting the sound's diminished quality, considering the route it had taken to get to him, the signal filtering through a phone and a satellite and a computer, emerging through a tiny crappy built-in speaker. He should get some high-quality headphones. He listened again and concluded that he'd been wrong, dead wrong. The voice wasn't Mai's. And his earlier conviction that it *was* her voice now discomfited him profoundly, as it implied his critical apparatus wasn't functioning too well.

Restless, he turned on the bedside light and leaned over to root through his bag.

Prague: City of Secrets, City of Legends
Classic Tales from the Jewish Ghetto
TRANSLATED FROM THE CZECH BY
V. GANS

The crude cover art: the golem, forever pursuing someone beyond the edge.

Read him a normal book, like a normal child.

A book of ghoulish tales probably wasn't the right choice to induce sleep. But he had a vague recollection of the golem as a benevolent being, fearsome appearance notwithstanding, and right now, a take-care-of-business pile of super-sludge vanquishing evil sounded terrific.

He opened up and started to read.

The Jews of Prague, unlike their brethren in other kingdoms, oftimes dwelt in harmony with their gentile neighbors.

However, it did so happen that there once was a gentile man, a tanner of leather, who employed a certain Jewish maid, an orphan, a girl of great beauty, and also very pious and chaste, which qualities the tanner did not fail to notice. Day by day he observed her kindness and modesty, and soon he came to love the maid, and to desire her for his wife.

But when he professed this wish to her, the maid refused, citing the laws of her fathers, and although the tanner continued to petition her with amorous declarations, she continued to spurn him, her obstinacy serving to inflame his wrath, until at last there came a day when, catching her unawares, he sought to take her by force.

Valiantly the maid fought to free herself by any means necessary, and this she did, seizing upon a pair of heavy iron shears, made to cut animal hide, and blinding the tanner in one eye, so that he cried out and released her, and she fled.

The tanner's convalescence lasted many weeks, but more painful than the healing of his wounds was the humiliation boiling inside him. Thus he schemed to enact a wicked revenge. He charged the local priest to investigate the disappearance of a Christian child, a boy, also an orphan, and said further that he had seen this boy in the company of a certain Jewish man, named Schemayah Hillel, who was in plain fact the aforementioned maid's uncle.

Accompanied by the royal guard, the priest arrived at Schemayah Hillel's house and demanded admittance on the grounds that a crime had taken place therein. And Schemayah Hillel, knowing himself to be innocent of any crime, permitted the priest to enter. This proved a grave error, for the tanner had some days earlier stolen into the courtyard behind Schemayah Hillel's home and placed the murdered body of the boy, killed at his own hand, beneath a pile of burlap sacks.

Upon discovery of the corpse, the priest charged Schemayah Hillel with having taken the boy's life for the purpose of extracting blood for the Passover ritual.

Now, it was clear to all that Schemayah Hillel was a respected elder, not to mention feeble-bodied and therefore incapable of committing such a foul deed. Nevertheless, he was hanged in the street, and as ever men hate and fear what is different from them, many innocent souls, women and children alike, perished at the hands of the mob. And the distraught maid, seeing the misfortune that had come about, stood on the edge of the Charles Bridge and, filling her apron with stones, cast herself down into the waters of the Vltava to be drowned.

In those days, the holy and revered Rabbi Judah son of Bezalel, sometimes called MaHaRaL by his initials, presided over the community. After meditating upon these matters for thirty days, he summoned two of his most trustworthy disciples to the banks of the river. There they gathered mud and clay and, moving quickly in the dead of night, they ascended to the garret of the Old-New Synagogue.

In accordance with his Heavenly vision, Rabbi Judah instructed his disciples to fashion the clay into the shape of a man of towering height. Then, placing a piece of parchment containing sacred names of God in the creature's mouth, he inscribed a mark in its forehead, letters to form the word EMETH (truth), from which the world is built.

Seventy times seven they circled the creature, reciting incanta-

tions that caused the creature's body to glow red-hot with life. At the third hour of morning, when the Holy One roars like a lion, Rabbi Judah spoke and said, "Arise!" And at once the creature sprang up, landing on his feet with a mighty crash. The disciples swooned with fear, but Rabbi Judah came forward and spoke to the giant in a powerful voice.

"You shall be called Joseph. You shall do as I command, just as I command it, and you will never disobey me, for I have created you to serve."

The disciples saw that Joseph had comprehended the Rabbi's words, for he nodded. However, he did not answer, lacking the power of speech, which is not man's to give.

They dressed him in simple peasant's clothes, and Rabbi Judah set him to work in the synagogue as a sexton, explaining to any-one who questioned the giant's sudden appearance that the man was a mute, found wandering in the streets, unable to pronounce his own name.

To discourage inquiries, the Rabbi established for him a bed in the corner of his very own home. This bed was never used, though, for every night, Joseph would leave the Rabbi's home and walk the ghetto, protecting its inhabitants and driving out evil.

CHAPTER THIRTY-TWO

Loud pounding dissolved the gold-green of Jacob's dream, bringing his cheap room to the fore.

He sat up, the splayed paperback sliding from his stomach as he knuckled the crust from his eye. His phone, charging on the bureau, said 6:08 a.m.

"Come back later, please," he yelled.

But the knocker kept knocking, and Jacob angrily pulled on jeans and a shirt. He put on the chain and squinted out at a man with a shaved head and a lean but soft body. Early twenties, at most. Red-eyed, wheezy, he wore shin-length denim shorts and a brown DKNY shirt. His thin goatee looked like mascara, and as he twiddled it, Jacob half expected it to smear.

"Can I help you?"

"Jacob," the man said.

"Yeah?"

"I am Jan."

The mismatch between Jacob's mental image and the man-boy before him spurred rapid revisions. Screaming kids became kid brothers. Smoker's hack became asthma.

"Can I come in, please?"

"ID first."

Jan grimaced. "You also, please."

They traded cards through the gap, each of them pretending to verify the other.

"All right." Jacob undid the chain, and Jan sidled inside, taking stock of the room before settling on the edge of the chair.

"I waited for you for two hours," Jacob said.

"I apologize."

"What happened?"

"I wanted to see you."

Jacob held out his arms. "Happy?"

"Yes, okay."

"Look, forget it. Let me buy you a cup of coffee."

But Jan had fixed on the manila envelope nosing from Jacob's bag. "Your photos?"

Jacob nodded.

"Can I see, please?"

"Knock yourself out."

Jacob watched Jan's fingers struggle with the clasp, watched the evolution of understanding in his face: horror to disbelief to resignation.

"Look familiar?"

Jan nodded.

"The neck."

"The neck, and the vomit."

"The arrangement? The Hebrew?"

"It's the same."

"You never found a body."

Jan said, "I am not supposed to discuss this with anyone."

"Why not?"

Jan did not answer.

"Who said you couldn't discuss it?"

Jan said, "I don't know."

"You don't *know*?"

Jan shook his head.

"What's that mean, you don't know."

"I never saw them before."

"Who's they? Your boss?"

"Him also."

"Did he say why?"

"This was like a very unusual occurrence."

"I'm sure."

"No," Jan said, regaining some spine, "you don't understand what I'm saying to you. In Czech Republic we don't have murders. We have, okay, people get drunk, they fight, sometimes there can be like a bad accident. But this? Never. My boss, he said, 'Jan, this could cause very big problems. People will feel scared.'"

"He told you to bury it? A homicide?"

"Not to bury. To be quiet."

"But some other guys came to talk to you, too."

Jan hesitated, then nodded.

"Before your boss spoke to you, or after?"

"After. I went to United States, and when I came back men were at the airport."

"They were tall," Jacob said.

Jan started.

"Like, really tall."

Jan stared, egg-eyed.

"They claimed to be from some department you'd never heard of. Friendly enough, but there was something weird about them, and they made you promise you'd never discuss what you'd seen, or else you'd be transferred out, or some other bullshit."

Jan said, "I can lose my job."

"That's what they told you?"

Jan nodded.

"The same guys came to see me," Jacob said. "They didn't threaten me. The opposite: they claimed to be helping me. But actually, they've been cockblocking me left and right. Then when I said I wanted to come here, they approved, so I don't know what the hell's going on. Maybe they're happy to get me out of town. The whole thing's weirder than shit."

A silence.

"What is 'cockblocking'?" Jan asked.

Jacob broke up laughing, and for the first time, Jan grinned, and then they were two cops laughing together, bound by resentment of superiors.

"In this—in this context, uh—like, stalling. Like, they're blocking my, uh. Cock." Jacob pointed.

"Yes, okay. I like this word. I, also, am cockblocked."

Jacob said, "That's why you wanted to see me. To see how tall I was."

Jan nodded.

"You were at the bar last night."

"My sister."

Jacob smiled. "Tatjana."

"This is what she told you? Her name is Lenka."

"Well, whatever. She found me."

"She said, 'Jan, don't worry, he is like a nice guy, he bought for me a beer.' She wants to be a policewoman, too. I told her it's not a good job for her. I said, 'You are young, be happy.'"

"Says you. What are you, twelve?"

"Twenty-six."

"How in the hell are you a lieutenant?"

"After the Revolution . . ." Jan whistled and made a wiping motion. "We begin again." He sighed. It turned to a cough.

"Lenka," he said. "Lenka, Lenka."

He slapped his thighs. Stood up.

"Okay, let's go."

CHAPTER THIRTY-THREE

Dlouhá veered southward to Old Town Square, silent but for the purr of pigeons foraging between the legs of café tables.

Jan laid a hand on a park bench, one of many ringing a sprawling bronze monument.

"The girl was here," he said. "She was crying, like very upset. She says there is a man, he tried to rape me outside the synagogue. The patrolman calls for the ambulance to take her to hospital, then he goes to look for the man. Follow me, please."

They walked over damp cobblestones and onto Pařížská, toward Josefov.

Jacob should've known better than to trust his father's guidebook. The former Jewish quarter was no longer run-down, but leafy and posh. Designer clothing draped mannequins posed behind boutique windows. A man in a chef's jacket emerged from a basement door to tip a bucket of sudsy water into the gutter.

Jan said, "The *městská policie* cannot investigate murder, they must call us. Usually there are several detectives, crime technics. But when I came, I didn't find this, only one patrolman. Very soon a technic I don't know arrived to collect the remains."

"Was he tall, too?"

Jan had to think. ". . . yes. I didn't pay attention to this. I was not investigating him, I was investigating the scene. This is what you experienced?"

"Basically."

"The technic was making me crazy, because I wanted to look carefully, and he says, 'Hurry, please, we must go quickly.' I thought he wants to clean up before the tourists arrived."

He paused his account to snap a picture of a metallic gold Ferrari with Russian plates.

"Lenka wouldn't approve," Jacob said.

"She is too angry. I told her, this time is over."

"Not for her."

"This is because she was not there. I told her, you can't be angry, you need to be practical. It's the same with the police. These guys who were working for—do you know what is ehs-teh-beh?"

Jacob shook his head.

"Státní Bezpečnost. Czechoslovak secret police. Most of them, they left after the Revolution. Some were very bad guys, okay, it's true. But some of them, we said, 'Stay,' because they have experience, knowledge."

"You don't find that uncomfortable? Working with them?"

Jan shrugged. "The policeman, he's the hand of the law. Before, our laws were bad, so . . ." He mimed slapping a face. "Now, we have good laws. So it's okay. Okay, we are here."

Jacob recognized the shape of the Alt-Neu Shul from the grainy black-and-white guidebook photograph. In real life, it was waist down the color of parchment, its upper half layered in brown, scabby brick, as though the orange roof tiles had bled downhill and clotted. Ten steps led to a cobbled area inset with a central drain, given onto by an embossed metal door.

Trash cans were stacked nearby: this was the service entrance. A cloudy stained-glass rosette cut into the building's exterior wall revealed its considerable thickness.

A stack of metal rungs rose to a smaller wooden door, three stories up.

Weighty with soot, sunken into the earth, the entire structure seemed nevertheless to hover, its contours uncertain.

Jan paused halfway down the steps. "You are coming?"

"Yeah," Jacob said. He followed. "Yeah."

"THE HEAD WAS HERE." Jan was crouched near the drain, indicating with his finger.

He pointed two feet to the left. "There, the vomit."

Standing, he arched his back and coughed. "This was like difficult for me to understand. There is no blood, so it must be they washed it to the drain. But the head and the vomit they left."

"Same thing with me. I figured the murder took place somewhere else."

Jan shook his head. "The girl, when she goes, the man is standing here. The patrolman comes, the body is here. The killer takes him away, cuts his head, and brings it back? This is not logical. There is not enough time. Where can he do this? I search the neighborhood. There is no blood. There is no weapon. Nobody hears nothing. Nobody sees nothing."

Despite himself, Jacob felt his own theories starting to slip. He had come seeking the certainty of common ground. "We're in the middle of the city. No witnesses?"

"At that time, it is quiet." Jan pointed across Pařížská, to the luxe apartments set over a brasserie. "These flats, the bedrooms are away from the street. The jewelry store has a camera, but the angle is not right. Here, it's like invisible."

Jacob's gaze traveled up to the small wooden door.

. . . moving quickly in the dead of night, they ascended to the garret . . .

Jan said, "It was open."

"That door?"

"Yes."

For a moment, Jacob's field of vision pinched. When the world returned, Jan was staring at him, brows knit. "Jacob? You are okay?"

"Fine." Jacob swallowed, smiled. "Jet lag."

He turned to study the undersized door. At that height, it appeared to serve no purpose, as though a child had gotten hold of the blueprint and scribbled it in, builders following the instructions unthinkingly before anyone noticed the absurdity.

"Any idea how it got open?"

"The man in charge of security for the synagogue said a wind."

"Was it windy that night?"

Jan shook his head: *I don't know.*

Distantly, unwillingly, the city stirred: arthritic trams, gaseous hiss of street sweepers.

"Tell me about the girl. What brought her here?"

"She works in the synagogue, cleaning at night. She is standing here, there is a noise behind. She turns and sees a man with a knife. He grabs her, she is fighting, boom, he lets her go, and she runs away."

"Did she see what happened to him?"

"She was scared, she's not staying there to wait."

"She could positively ID the head as the same guy who jumped her, though."

"I came to hospital to show her a picture. She started to scream again."

"I assume that she denied having anything to do with killing him."

"Yes, of course."

"And you believe her."

"She was not strong enough to do this."

"She was strong enough to fight him off."

"Yes, okay, but this is not the same. She had no blood on her clothes."

"She could have changed."

"I'm telling you, it is not possible."

"The reason I ask, it was a woman who called in my case."

Jan raised his eyebrows.

Jacob got out his phone, and together they listened to the audio file. It disturbed him to realize that he was still hearing the voice as Mai's. He thought he'd worked through that possibility, and dismissed it.

If Jan noticed anything amiss with the woman's words, he didn't mention it.

"This cannot be the same person," he said. "She was Czech girl."

Jacob believed him—believed that he believed it, at any rate.

On the sidewalk above, a man with a briefcase hurried past, barking into his headset, paying the detectives no heed.

"Where'd you find the Hebrew?" Jacob asked.

Jan pointed out a blank cobblestone, less foot-worn than those around it. "When I came back from United States, it was replaced."

"What happened to the original?"

"The case was not mine, so I was not able to ask questions."

"Do you have a picture of it?"

"On my computer. I can send it to you."

"Thanks."

Jan said, "The man in charge of security for the synagogue, I showed him this word. It means, 'Justice.' This made me think of the girl's boyfriend or brother or father. But she has no boyfriend or brother or father. She has a sister. It cannot make sense. The killer, where did he come from? I look for footprints, for fingerprints. There is nothing. It's like a bird came down, *shhhhp*."

He paced a bit. "You cannot say he heard the girl screaming and came to save her and had a big knife and cut off a head and closed it up. It's like not possible. There was a plan to do this, you must agree. So what, he's hiding in the bushes, waiting for someone to rape a girl, with special tools? It isn't logical. I conclude, the man who tried to rape the girl, somebody else was following him. But this is not logical, either. How does the killer know what this guy will do?"

"It's not logical, unless they already knew each other."

"Hah?"

Jacob elaborated on the Creeper killings.

Jan paled by shades, until he said, *"Ach jo."*

"Yup."

"This is sick."

"Yup."

"You think your guy, he killed my guy? And then someone kills him?"

"I don't know," Jacob said. "Right now it's all I got."

Jan nodded politely, but his expression said: *Tell me another fairy tale.*

"Please tell me you got DNA."

"This requires special permission."

"Which you couldn't obtain."

"No."

"We could sample the remains."

"If nobody claims after one month, they are going to the crematorium."

"Shit. Shit. Fuck."

"I am sorry, Jacob."

"Not your fault."

Jan made a sorrowful face that suggested that everything was his fault.

"You don't remember anything similar, either in Prague or another city?"

"No, no, I told you, we don't have this in Czech Republic."

"Now you sound like the Board of Tourism."

"We have solution rate of ninety percent. Always when we come, the guy is still there. He is too drunk to leave."

"Better than drive-bys."

"Drive-by?"

"Gangs," Jacob said. "They shoot out of cars."

"Ah, we have gangs, too. They are not so bad like American gangs.

They steal bicycles, to sell over the border, in Poland. They make *pervitin.*"

"I don't know what that is."

Jan searched for the word. "You know the show, *Breaking Bad.*"

"Meth."

"Yes, meth." Jan paused. "I enjoy this show very much."

They made a circuit of the building, stepping through a thicket littered with cigarette butts and crushed cans, and ending at Maiselova Street. Jacob spied CCTV cameras mounted at the main entrance. Jan shook his head.

"They are not real. I asked the security man for the tape. 'There is no tape, we don't have money for this.'"

The synagogue didn't open for well over an hour. A number of tourists were already out front snapping away.

Jan said, "I had one idea. The security man told me on Friday night before the murder, a British man came to prayers. They didn't let him in, because he's acting suspicious. I started to investigate. The same week, there is a hotel manager complaining to the police about a British tourist who didn't pay his bill. It's not unusual, people do this, but the manager was like very upset, calling very often, because the man stayed for a month."

"What makes you think it could be the same guy?"

"I talked to the manager, he said this man, Heap, left all his clothing."

"Heap."

"This is like his name."

"Uh-huh. Did you show him the picture of the head? The manager, I mean."

"Of course not. This would create a big sensation. I am supposed to be quiet."

"I take it you didn't contact the British embassy, either."

"If they come to us to say, 'Our citizen is missing,' okay. But this never happened. Two weeks, I'm starting to make phone calls, my boss brings me to his office. 'You have a new job, sex trafficking.' Boom. I am on airplane to U.S."

"And that's that."

"Yes," Jan said. "Cockblock."

"So what's the official story?"

"The tall men gave me a paper to sign. The man tried to rape the girl. She escaped, the man became scared and tried to climb up the ladder to hide in the synagogue."

"Hence the open door."

"Yes. Then he fell down."

"Severing his head?"

"Yes, I know."

"And sealing it? And writing Hebrew letters on the ground?"

"I know. I said I wouldn't sign this. Then they told me I am going to lose my job. I feel like a criminal, but what can I do? I have my family. I sign."

Jacob nodded to show he would've felt the same—and done the same.

He looked up at the *shul*'s saw-toothed façade, a frozen flame reaching against the burnished blue morning.

"Can I ask you a personal question? Are you Jewish?"

"I am atheist. Why?"

"I don't know," Jacob said. But he was remembering Mallick's words. *It's your background I'm interested in.* Were Jewish cops so rare in Prague? Or perhaps they—whoever *they* were—had gone with the young lieutenant, expecting him to be compliant.

He took out his notepad. "Do me a favor? Contact information for the security guy and the girl? The hotel, too."

Jan hesitated.

"I'll keep your name out of it. I promise."

While Jan took the pad and wrote, Jacob consulted the black-and-gold clockface on an adjacent building and saw that it was, impossibly, four p.m.

Then he realized his error: the characters were Hebrew letters, the clock hands reversed, making it eight a.m.

Jan returned the pad. He'd printed three names: Peter Wichs, Havel (Pension Karlova), Klaudia Navrátilová. Beside the latter two were addresses.

"The guard, I'll send you his number, it is on my computer. The hotel is close, you can walk there. The manager, I don't know his family name. The girl, she quit the synagogue, now she's working at this place, a café."

"How's her English?"

"Maybe you will need a translator."

Jacob looked at him hopefully.

"I apologize," Jan said. "I must go to work."

Jacob cut him some slack. As it stood, he'd put the guy in a tight spot. "I get it. Thanks. And—any crime scene pictures you can text me? I need something to show these people."

Jan cracked his knuckles, flicked his flimsy beard. Finally: "Yes, okay. This case is not mine. I am finished, but you . . . good luck, Jacob."

They shook hands, and Jan left him watching the clock, time running backward.

GILGUL

Spirit of Vengeance who wanders like a pilgrim between the gates knocking for eternity be born of the Mothers Aleph-Shin-Mem descend and fill this imperfect vessel so that the will of the One Without End may be done on earth amen amen amen

Crushed by an unimaginable pressure, consciousness quilting together.

"Arise."

The command is gentle and loving and irresistible.

She rises.

Sensations run together like children playing a game without rules. She grabs at their elbows, forces them apart. *Behave.*

A drippy canopy, scrawly claws, forlorn screech and howl. In dazzling firelight, darkness engraves shapes: a giant's grave, a pile of mud, shovels, bootprints ringing a patch of forest floor baked bone-dry, crackling as it cools.

Before her stands a regal man, old and splendid, elongated like an iris, his shoulders broad beneath a sashed black robe, a tight round cap of black velvet on his polished scalp. Moonlight glazes kind brown eyes and shines a beard of filigreed silver. The awed set of his mouth cannot hide the delight pushing up at its corners.

"David," he calls. "Isaac. You can come back."

Long moments later, two younger men approach, stop a ways off, crouch in the foliage.

"He won't hurt you. Will you . . ." The kind-eyed man gives in to his smile. "Yankele."

That's not my name.

"Yes," he says. "I think that will be fine. Yankele."

I have a name.

"You won't hurt them, will you?"

She shakes her head.

The two men come timidly forth. Their beards are black, their garments humble and limp with rain. One of them has lost his hat. The other tremblingly clutches a shovel and mouths silent prayers.

The hatless man says, "Rebbe is all right?"

"Yes, yes," the kind-eyed man says. "Come. We have much to do and far to go."

The two men swarm over her, grunting as they stuff her, sausage-sleeved, into a blouse far too small. But the indignity of being dressed in doll's clothing is as nothing compared to the wave of sick surprise that rises when she beholds herself.

Gnarled chair hands.

A cabinet for a chest.

Blood-starved flesh lumpily thumbed.

She is monstrous.

And the pinnacle of this comic insult, dangling between wine-cask thighs like a dead rodent, foreign and grotesque, a man's organ.

She would shriek. She would tear it off.

She cannot. She remains dumb, pliant, deboned by confusion, tongue knotted, throat hollow, while the men force her misshapen feet into boots.

David squats, raises Isaac on his shoulders; Isaac pulls a hood over her face.

"Ah, yes," Rebbe says. "I'm sure nobody'll notice a thing, now."

When they are done with her, they stand back, perspiring, to await a verdict.

Before Rebbe can speak, her left sleeve splits loudly.

He shrugs. "We'll have something more suitable made."

Out of the woods, they tramp across boggy fields. Chill mist hovers over the surface of waist-high grass, the tips of which kiss her knees. To avoid dirtying their robes, the men walk with their hems raised; Isaac the Hatless has drawn his own collar up over his bare head.

Farmhouses break the monotony of the countryside until they come to a muddy highway, hissing dung piles beneath dreary cloud pack.

Rebbe talks in a soothing voice. He speaks of the confusion *Yankele* is experiencing. It's natural, he reassures her, a misalignment between body and soul. It will pass. Soon he will feel good as new. They have called him down to discharge an important duty.

Down from where? Up, she supposes. But really she hasn't the faintest idea what he's talking about. Nor can she understand why he keeps referring to her as him, and she as he, or who is Yankele, or where this body has come from, or why it moves the way it does.

She cannot say where she was before; cannot speak to ask; cannot do anything but obey.

The road rises slightly and breaks open onto a valley. There, along the banks of a scaly river, lies a sleeping town, a black curtain embroidered with firelight.

Rebbe says, "Welcome to Prague."

HER FIRST NIGHT she spends standing in a box, silent, unmoving, wondering, wounded.

Dawn wedges raw fingers between the planks and the door swings open on a woman. A tight wimple frames a pure pale face, luminous green eyes that flash disbelief.

"Yudl," she sighs.

Yudl?

Who's Yudl?

What about Yankele?

What happened to him?

Make up your mind.

"Come on," the woman says, beckoning her out. "Let me have a look at you."

She stands in the center of a courtyard, while the woman walks around her, clucking her tongue. "What are these rags? Oy. Yudl. You've really done it this time, haven't you? What were you *thinking* . . . Hang on, I'll be back in a minute."

She waits. She has, it seems, no choice.

The woman returns carrying a stool and a length of string, hitches up her skirts.

"Hold out your arm, please. The left one."

She obeys automatically.

"No, to the side. Yes. Thank you. Other arm, please . . ."

The woman scurries around her, using the string to measure her, re-tucking coils of black hair that sneak free. "He certainly didn't skimp on you, did he? He's a saint, of course, my husband, but a head in Heaven pulls a man's feet off the ground. He might've warned me. Stand up straight, please. You gave me quite a fright, you know. Although I suppose that's the point, isn't it . . . Oh look at this, *look* at what he's done. Your legs don't line up."

I am a freak. I am an abomination.

"Something like this, I can't tell if he's done it on purpose or because he's rushing, or . . . I don't know. It doesn't make it hard for you to walk, I hope."

A crime. A pillar of disgrace.

"This is going to take me a few hours. Let's get you covered properly. The rest we can worry about later. In the meantime you don't have to go back in that terrible box. Is that all right? What am I saying, of course it's all right. I'm Perel, by the way. Wait here, please."

Hours later, sun high overhead, Perel returns with a blanket folded over her shoulder.

"What are you still doing there? I didn't mean you had to stand in one spot all day . . . All right, never mind, let's try this on."

The cloak is coarse burlap, several dozen motley pieces hastily sewn together.

"I'm sorry. It's the best I could manage on short notice. I'll see if Gershom has something nicer in stock, a nice piece of wool. He gives a discount if he knows it's for me. We'll have to pick a color. Something dark, it's slimming—"

A man's voice: "Perel?"

"Back here."

Rebbe appears at the back of the house.

Beholds the scene.

Pales.

"Eh. Perele. I can explain—"

"You're going to explain why there's a giant in my woodshed?"

"This—eh . . ." Rebbe hurries forward. "This is Yankele."

"Is that his name?" Perel says. "He didn't mention it."

"Well, eh," Rebbe says. "Yes."

No.

"Yankele."

That's not my name.

Rebbe says, "He's an orphan."

"An orphan."

"Yes. I was—David came across him wandering in the forest, you see, and, and, it seems he can't speak." Rebbe pauses. "I'm afraid he's simpleminded."

I am not.

"A simpleminded orphan," Perel says.

"Yes, and I thought it can't be safe for him, wandering alone like that."

Perel stares up at her immense head. "Yes, I can see he'd be vulnerable to attack."

"Well, at least I thought it would be inhospitable to abandon him. I have to set an example for the community."

"So you locked him in the shed."

"I didn't want to disturb you," Rebbe says. "It was late."

"Let me see if I've got this right, Yudl. David Ganz, who leaves the house of study so infrequently that his mother has to bring him fresh socks, happened to be out in the forest at night, alone, and he happened to come across a simpleminded mute giant wandering, alone, and he happened to bring him here to you, and you decided to have him spend the night outside, in the courtyard, in a shed."

A pause.

"I suppose that's more or less the size of it, yes."

"If he's mute," Perel says, "how do you know his name?"

"Well . . . that's what I've been calling him. But I suppose it could be something else—"

It is.

"How do you know he's an orphan?"

Another pause.

"Did you make this cloak?" Rebbe says. "What a marvelous piece of work. Yankele, look at you, you're a regular gentleman."

"Don't change the subject, please," Perel says.

"Darling. I was going to tell you as soon as I got home. I was held up, I had to adjudicate a case, extremely complex, you see—"

Perel waves a shapely hand. "Never mind. It's all right."

"It is?"

"But he can't stay in the shed. To begin with, that's my space. I need it. More important, it's not right. It's worse than inhospitable. It's inhuman. I wouldn't put a dog in there. Would you put a person there?"

"But, you see, Perel—"

"Yudl. Listen to me. To my words. Carefully. *Would you put a human being in the shed?*"

". . . no."

"Of course not. Be sensible, Yudl. People will ask questions. Who lives in a shed? Nobody. Especially nobody that size. They'll say, 'That's no man, living there. Who lives in a shed?'" She clucks her tongue. "Besides, it's shameful. 'This is where the Rebbe puts his guests?' I won't allow it. He can have Bezalel's room."

"Eh. Do you really think that's the best place for—wouldn't it be better, I mean to say, if he were to—Yankele, I apologize that I'm speaking about you like you're not here."

That's not my name.

"He can help around the house," Perel says.

"I'm not sure he has the . . . the intelligence."

I do.

"He does. You can see it in his eyes. You understand me, don't you, Yankele?"

She nods.

"See? That was the light of comprehension, Yudl. I could use the extra hands. Do me a favor, Yankele," Perel says, pointing to the well in the corner of the courtyard. "Draw water."

"Perele . . ."

While they continue to argue about where to house her, and what to tell people, she lumbers dumbly to the well. The rapture of being able to move is dulled by the knowledge that she isn't moving of her own volition. Draw water.

"It's not that it's a bad story," Perel is saying.

Draw water: she pulls up the rope, takes the sloshing bucket in hand.

"It's just that you're a bad liar, Yudl."

Tips it out on the ground.

Wait a minute. Wait. That's not what she meant.

Draw water: her body begins lowering the bucket again.

"Truth shall sprout from the earth," Rebbe declares.

"And righteousness shall be reflected from the heavens," Perel replies. "Wonderful. Until then, let me do the talking, please."

The second bucket she also dumps out.

Fool. That's not what she meant.

But her body keeps going, heedless of the howling objections of her mind; it has one directive—draw water—and it fulfills it with perfect obedience, bucket after bucket, and each time she bends to lower the rope, the reflection that greets her repels her. It is a face like the knot of an oak tree—lumpy and lopsided, furred unevenly like lichen; a huge, cruel, stupid face, devoid of emotion. Is this how she is to exist? She would rather drown herself in the well. She cannot choose to do that any more than she can choose to stop, and she raises the bucket and pours it out and raises the bucket and pours it out until Perel yelps: the courtyard has flooded, ankle-deep.

"Yankele, stop!" Rebbe shouts.

She stops. She cannot understand why she has done something so plainly absurd, and she burns with hatred for her own idiocy.

"You have to be very careful how you phrase things," Rebbe says.

"Apparently," Perel says. Then she bursts into helpless laughter.

Rebbe smiles. "It's all right, Yankele. It's only water. It'll dry."

She appreciates their attempts to console her.

But that's not her name. She has a name.

She cannot remember what it is.

CHAPTER THIRTY-FOUR

The café was near the Charles Bridge. Jacob breakfasted with hung-over backpackers on tasteless coffee and oily pastry, sizing up each of the waitresses against the archetypal Creeper victim—wispy, vulnerable—and waiting for a lull in service to flag down a petite, delicately featured redhead.

"Klaudia?" he said.

She pointed to the outdoor tables, attended by a homely brunette he'd ruled out right off the bat.

Big-shot detective. He reseated himself, smiling as the brunette brought him a new menu.

"Klaudia," he said.

She reacted to his use of her name. *"Prosím?"*

"English?" he asked.

She showed him the translated menu options.

"You, I mean. Do you speak English?"

She pinched her fingers together to show how little.

"Can I talk to you? Can you sit down for a second?" He opened his badge. "I'm a policeman. *Policie? Americký?*"

She said, "Moment, please."

She left and came back with a manager in tow.

"Sir, there is a problem?"

"Not at all. I was hoping to talk to Klaudia."

Klaudia's face slackened, and she craned up to whisper into the manager's ear. His mouth corkscrewed in annoyance. He flashed Jacob a hand. "Five minutes."

He directed them to the back of the kitchen, and they stood on watery rubber mats, conducting a largely one-way conversation, her responses limited to sign language and head movements. Engulfed in clouds of dishwasher humidity, she seemed dissociative, threatening to liquefy before his eyes—a not uncommon response to sexual trauma. He felt bad badgering her; he admired that she was putting on a good show; he wanted nothing more than to let her go, so she could run home to hide, rechecking the locks ten times before balling up under the covers.

Could she remember that night? (Yes.) Was it okay to talk about it? (Yes, okay.) She'd seen the man's face? (Yes.) Was she sure it was the same man the lieutenant had shown her in the hospital? (Yes.) Did she see what had caused the man to let her go? (No.) Did she hit him? Elbow him? Kick him? (Yes, yes, yes.) Was she aware of the presence of another person? (. . . no.) Had she heard anything, seen anything, while she was running away? (No.)

"I understand you've been through a lot," he said. "I need you, please, to really try and think back. A voice, a hair color."

She said, "Blotto."

For a moment he thought she was mocking him—booze on his breath, left over from last night. He didn't feel drunk. He didn't think he was acting drunk. He'd never been the kind to leave the house with TP trailing from the seat of his pants.

She repeated, "Blotto."

"Would you mind writing that down?"

She obliged.

Bláto.

"What is that?" he asked.

She started to sign an answer, but the manager then appeared, clapping his hands. "Okay, okay." He thumbed out at the dining room.

Klaudia bent her head and vanished through the steam.

"Excuse me," Jacob said. "Can you tell me what this means?"

The manager put on his reading glasses. *"Bláto.* Is . . . nnnnmm." He took Jacob's notepad and pen and sketched a half-inch tube, filling it in hazily with wavy lines—water.

"Vltava," he said.

"The river."

The manager added an arrow beside the tube, pointed. *"Bláto."*

"Riverbank? Boat? Shore?"

"Nnn." The manager made a squelching noise, then waved Jacob out back to the alleyway. From behind a reeking mound of trash bags he hauled out a plastic planter plugged with dry soil. He signed for Jacob to stay put.

"It's okay," Jacob said. "I can look it up on the Internet."

But the manager was on a mission. He fetched a glass of water from the kitchen and poured it into the planter, kneading it into the soil. He scooped a dark, oozy handful and presented it to Jacob's nose, giving him a whiff of cat piss and pesticides.

"Bláto," the manager said.

Mud.

THE GHETTO WAS OPEN for business.

Fanny-packed tourists orbited tour guides waving plastic paddles and shouting in a half-dozen different languages. Tchotchke vendors flogged golem T-shirts, golem water bottles, miniature ceramic golems. The chalkboard outside the U Synagogy restaurant advertised two daily specials: a Golem Tenderloin and the ill-conceived Leg of Turkey à la Rabbi Loew—said limb stuffed with bacon.

He bought a ticket for the Alt-Neu, along with an updated guidebook to Jewish Prague, skimming it as he joined the queue.

There are several explanations for the synagogue's remarkable name. Some say that the Jews of Prague, while digging the foundation for a new house of worship, discovered the remnants of a much older structure. Others suggest that the building was erected on the condition that it would exist only until such time as the Messiah arrived. In this account, the name "Alt-Neu" is a pun on the Hebrew words "Al-Tenai"—"on condition."

Regardless of its origins, the Alt-Neu has become forever associated with Rabbi Judah ben Bezalel Loew (c. 1520–c. 1609), spiritual leader and mystic, who according to legend created the golem in the synagogue garret. When the creature proved unmanageable, the Rabbi was forced to destroy it, sealing its remains in the garret and forbidding anyone to enter on pain of excommunication. Some have cited the golem legend as the origin for Mary Shelley's classic novel Frankenstein, *as well as Czech playwright Karel Čapek's science-fiction play* R.U.R., *which introduced to the world the word "robot" . . .*

Three steps down into a gloomy, dogleg antechamber scented of groundwater. The temperature plummeted. Street-level windows revealed bare shins and double-knotted sneakers. To his right ran a corridor that ended at an arched iron door, the verso of the one outside. In front of him lay the entrance to the synagogue sanctuary. A rope forbade access to the women's section.

He asked the ticket taker where the garret was.

Her expression implied that she had answered this question roughly a hundred billion times. She pointed beyond the barrier rope. "Closed."

"Is it ever open?"

"No."

"What about the women's section? Does that open?"

She gave him the stink-eye. "On Sabbath," she said. "For women."

The pressure of the line was mounting behind him, so he stepped toward the sanctuary, where a bulletin board outside the entrance listed the upcoming service, that evening's *Kabbalat Shabbat*, scheduled to commence at six-thirty.

For the moment, it was guidebooks and baseball caps, not prayer books and yarmulkes. Jacob joined the current of humanity making a circuit around the dais. The northern wall had viewing portals at eye height, allowing him to peer into the women's section on the other side. Not the most egalitarian setup: a stark hallway and folding chairs. At the far end, a tatty purple curtain, drawn. The entrance to the garret, he assumed.

He trailed his fingers along soft stone walls, waiting for the significance of the place to kick in. This was the Maharal's *shul*; that was *his chair*. Yet the scene was too familiar—familial—to evoke anything but weariness. The Holy Ark. The curtain, velvet and brocade. The Eternal Flame. *Know before Whom you stand.*

Jacob loved it and hated it, needed it and rejected it, for the same reasons.

What did it say about him, he wondered, that he couldn't stir himself to awe? An aversion to commercialism?

Or a symptom of his own numbness?

Was he a cop, examining a crime scene? A Jew in a house of worship?

His soul caught in a tug-of-war, he squeezed into a cramped wooden pew, its seat scalloped by thousands of backsides.

A young woman in a Hollister T-shirt passed, arm in arm with her boyfriend. Jacob overheard her say, "They totally filmed *The Bachelorette* here."

Unable to stand the tension, he leapt up like a man on the verge of vomiting, hurrying to the exit, pausing to fish out his wallet and tug free one of the hundred-dollar bills. He folded it in quarters and reached to poke it in the slot of the communal donations box, olive wood engraved with a single word.

צדק

Tzedek.
Justice.
And he stared and stared, because that wasn't right, and then his mind snickered at him and he looked again and it read, as it should—

צדקה

Tzedakah.
Charity.
He'd seen it wrong, because the final letter, *heh*, was rubbed smooth.
Because the lighting was bad.
Because he was hungover.
His eyesight—that could be starting to go, too.
"Excuse me, please."
"Sorry," Jacob mumbled. He crammed the money in the *pushke* and backed away. He'd fulfilled half of his *mitzvah* obligation to his father. Now all he had to do was get back to L.A. safely.

AT ELEVEN O'CLOCK, with still no word from Jan, Jacob decided to make good on another of Sam's requests.

The old Jewish cemetery ran twelve layers deep. Whenever the community had run out of space, they'd simply piled on more dirt. Snaggle-toothed stones rose from a lumpy swamp of leaves. A sagging chain restricted visitors to a perimeter path that wound past the major highlights. It was packed. Three times in twenty feet he stopped to answer *kaddish.*

Death tourism—a reliable boom industry.

The resting place of the Maharal had caused a snarl in the foot traffic. Jacob paddled to the middle of a group of Hasidic men and rose up on his toes for a better look. The tomb was carved from pink sandstone, its peaked shape faintly evocative of the Alt-Neu Shul.

Fitting; centuries later, place and man defined each other.

Pebbles and coins lined a ridge jutting below a carved lion, the Loew family crest. *Loew* shared a root with *Leo*. It was one of those things his father had told him again and again, which Jacob had absorbed without realizing. The guidebook added that the figure was also a reference to the coat of arms of Bohemia, which featured a two-tailed lion. Another Fun Sam Fact: the Maharal had been an acquaintance of the Emperor Rudolf II, who had invited the rabbi to court to discuss Kabbalah and mysticism.

Several misguided souls had stuck notes in the tombstone's crevices: the gravely ill petitioning for health, the barren for children, and no doubt lots of folks seeking material wealth.

Jacob could hear his father's admonishing voice.

You don't pray to a man—any man.

Elbowing his way closer, he saw that the tomb was in fact double-width. On the left, the Maharal himself, whose epitaph declared him *the great genius of Israel*; on the right, his wife, lying at his side for eternity.

The righteous woman who contented.

Perel, the daughter of Reb Shmuel.

A woman of valor, the crown of her husband.

Strange form of praise. Content with what? Her lot in life? Her husband? A rabbinic dictum had it that the rich man is one who is happy with his portion, so perhaps Perel had been famously pleased.

For all the stories he'd heard about the Maharal, none mentioned anything about a wife. But of course she'd existed. Jewish scholars were encouraged to settle down early. That Perel shared a name with his mother—middle name; but still—made him smile and shake his head.

Maybe that was what had attracted Sam to Bina in the first place. They were both women of valor. Standing before the tomb, it seemed less absurd to Jacob that his father continued to sing the Shabbat song. To love a dead woman was Sam's right as much as it was his failure. The same could be said of Jacob's unwillingness to forgive.

He crouched to pluck a pebble from the ground.

A beetle darted across his hand.

A startled shout burst from his throat, and he sprang back, crashing into one of the Hasidim and sending his camera flying. The Hasid began to scream at him in French, and Jacob apologized and snatched up his own camera from the dirt.

The beetle had meantime scampered back along the path; he spotted it in a bed of dry leaves, standing up on its hind legs, waving its black arms smugly.

Seized with rage, Jacob lunged for it, coming up with a handful of moist earth. He tried again, and again it danced back, and he began hobble-hopping after it, swimming upstream, worming his way through stocking legs and flip-flops and sensible shoes, raising screeches of disapproval.

The beetle flitted from stone to stone, its wings unfurling for one luminous instant and then vanishing into its black casing while it waited for him to catch up, its legs bent, poised to take flight.

He coiled to lunge again and hands grabbed hold of him, eight arms and four heads like some crazy Hasidic Vishnu, dragging him toward the exit, yelling curses in his ear in Yiddish and French. Jacob didn't understand a word of it except for *beheimah*—animal.

Shoved through the cemetery gates, he found himself in the narrow road facing the Alt-Neu, where he had only just left, as though he was pinned to some monstrous creaking wheel.

He stumbled away, making turns at random, coming to a side street. In the privacy of a doorway he collapsed, trembling like a wet dog.

Bugs were in cemeteries. Bugs were everywhere.

The Creator had an inordinate fondness for beetles.

The worst part was realizing that he'd failed: he'd forgotten to place the stone.

His pocket buzzed and he jumped.

Incoming texts filled the screen: the severed head, shot at multiple angles. A phone number for the *shul*'s director of security, Peter Wichs.

The defaced, long-gone cobblestone.

צדק

Peter Wichs answered in Czech, but upon hearing Jacob's voice he switched to a fluid, idiomatic English. They arranged to meet at the Alt-Neu at five-thirty, allowing an hour before services.

Jacob bought himself a Coke, drained it in four desperate gulps, and set out for the Pension Karlova.

HAVEL THE HOTEL MANAGER regarded the photos of the severed head with the resignation of a man who's not only seen worse but has also scrubbed it out of carpeting. While he couldn't definitively identify the head as belonging to the Brit who'd skipped out on his bill, he did agree to retrieve the guest registry, playing out his tale of woe with tragic brio.

"Who can do this? I am a good man, honest man, I pay taxes, I don't cheat."

The registration form listed a UK passport number, issued to one Reginald Heap; a London address; a credit card number.

"Decline," Havel said. "I call police."

Heap's birthdate was given as 19 April 1966.

Right in the zone for the Creeper killings.

Hoping for hair or skin cells, Jacob asked Havel what he'd done with Heap's belongings.

"Throw away."

Crap. "Can I get a copy of his information?"

Havel pointed to Jacob's phone. "Picture."

"You want a picture."

Havel nodded.

"With me?"

Havel frowned at him. *"Head."*

"A picture—of the head?"

Havel nodded.

"I'm not sure I can do that."

Havel slammed the registry shut.

"Come on," Jacob said. He opened his wallet. "Let's work this out another way."

"Picture," Havel insisted.

"You're serious."

Havel set his jaw and looked past Jacob.

"Fine, what's your e-mail address?"

Once Havel had received the photo, he disappeared into a back room, gone for a solid fifteen minutes. Jacob dinged the bell, to no avail.

At last Havel returned. He handed Jacob a copy of the registration form and proudly displayed a black-and-white printout of the head, upon which he'd scrawled, in red marker, ten or so words in Czech.

Waving the gruesome photo, he taped it to the wall beside the key rack.

"Please don't do that," Jacob said.

Havel proudly translated the caption: "This is happen for people who don't pay."

WITH A TALL GLASS of beer in front of him, Jacob commandeered a booth at an Internet café.

A Miami detective named Maria Band had e-mailed him, inviting him to call her cell.

He dialed her.

"This is Band."

"Jacob Lev. LAPD."

"Oh, yeah. Sorry about taking forever to get back to you. I'm getting crushed here."

"Understood. Talk to me."

Having reviewed the Casey Klute file, Band could confirm that the murder matched the pattern of the others: bound and unbound, throat slit, east-facing corpse.

"Nice gal, lots of friends, drove a pink Corvette, ran her own party-planning business, a talent for consistently picking the shittiest guys imaginable. Ex-boyfriend doing five to ten for possession with intent. Ex-husband with four priors, including one for armed robbery. I thought for sure he was our man but he was out of the country when it happened. After that we kinda ran out of air. Still bugs the hell out of me. I'm glad someone's on it. Just not me."

He thanked her and promised he'd be in touch.

Next, a note from Divya Das.

> *Hey—*
>
> *A little birdie told me you had to take a trip. I hope it's going well. Do keep me informed.*
>
> *I wanted to reiterate my regrets that we had to part on an awkward note. I hope you can appreciate that it was never my intention to mislead you. Believe you me, if I had any say in the matter, I would relish the chance to get to know you better. But in the words of a great philosopher, you can't always get what you want.*
>
> *Warmly,*
>
> *D*

He reread it twice, prying for meaning.

Why didn't she have any say in the matter?

Hey Divya,

Greetings from Prague. Interesting developments, though I'm not sure where it's all leading. I promise to keep you looped in.

About the rest of it, no problem. Like I said, I'm a big boy. It's been fun working with you and I wish you nothing but the best.

Anyhow, don't count me out yet. I've been known to wear a girl down.

Hope to see you soon.

Jacob

Pruning the rest of his inbox took him to the bottom of a second beer. He swirled his finger at the waitress: *Keep it coming.*

The address Reginald Heap had given turned out to be Waterloo Station, and after further searches yielded nil, Jacob began to worry that the name was bullshit, as well.

He tried *Reggie Heap*, and up came an archived page with an Oxford University domain name.

In 1986, when Reggie Heap had won the Undergraduate Art Society's award for a work on paper, the prize money was a modest two hundred pounds, a fifth of the present-day sum.

The other hit was a newspaper article, seven years old, concerning proposed legislation to ban fox hunting. The writer quoted one Edwyn Heap, of Clegchurch.

They ought to mind their own damned business.

To create ironic contrast, Heap's son, Reggie, was also quoted.

I can't conceive of anything more barbaric.

Jacob could.

He mapped the village along the M40, halfway between Oxford and London, then called the airline to price out a ticket, placing a hold on a short haul from Prague to Gatwick, leaving tomorrow mid-morning;

ditto a Monday morning reroute, Heathrow to LAX. He'd talk to the guys at the *shul* first, see if they could help him justify a $450 detour.

Five o'clock. He took a long draught, considered calling his father to wish him a *Shabbat shalom*, but balked. Doubtless Sam would want to know if he'd visited the grave.

I tried.

There were bugs.

The waitress approached with the sloshing pitcher. He covered his glass with his hand. "I'm good, thanks."

The bill—six bucks for five beers—sparked a momentary fantasy about selling his worldly possessions and moving to Prague.

If he got past the case and looked at the city as any tourist would, it was lovely and vibrant. A place for new beginnings. Buildings built atop buildings. A police force wanting elder statesmen.

He could meet a nice Czech girl, convince her to lay off the eye shadow . . .

Remembering something, he flipped through the guidebook.

STATUE OF RABBI JUDAH BEN BEZALEL LOEW (1910)
NEW TOWN HALL, MARIÁNSKÉ NÁMĚSTÍ

This work, commissioned by the municipal authority and exe-cuted by famed Art Nouveau sculptor Ladislav Šaloun, imagines Rabbi Loew moments before his death. That it was chosen to adorn a public building stands as testament to the reverence with which all Czechs, Jew and gentile alike, regard Loew, and his importance to Czech culture as a whole.

The map showed the statue on his way to the *shul*. It wasn't the same as putting a stone on the grave, but a photo of the great man might soften Sam's disappointment.

He left a generous tip and got going.

CARVED FROM BLACK STONE, standing well over six feet tall, atop a five-foot pedestal, the Maharal cast a surreally long shadow in the late afternoon light.

> *For his subject matter, Šaloun makes use of a popular legend. It is said that, having achieved an unprecedented spiritual level, the Rabbi could foresee the coming of the Angel of Death. As the day drew near, he embarked upon a program of round-the-clock study, heeding a Kabbalistic tradition which states that any man so engaged cannot die.*
>
> *One afternoon, the Rabbi's granddaughter entered his chambers to present him a freshly picked rose. Seizing the opportunity, the Angel stole into the center of the flower, and as the Rabbi paused to inhale its sweet scent, he expired.*

The figure twining around the Maharal's legs looked more imp than granddaughter. Notably, she was naked—pretty unseemly for a member of the rabbi's household.

> *The statue's impressive height is in keeping with a tradition that describes Loew as extremely tall. No portrait of him is known to exist, however, so Šaloun's rendering should be regarded as a work of pure imagination.*

The sculptor might've been admired in his day, but his take on Loew's face revealed a certain laziness: grotesquely large nose; dour pout; eyes filled with Pharisaic scorn.

Obeyest thou the Law!

Still, Jacob didn't want to come home empty-handed, so he got the camera out, zooming in and out on the statue's face, wondering what Loew had really looked like.

He finished and slid the camera back in his pocket. He stooped to the sidewalk and snatched a nugget of asphalt, placing it at the foot of the statue. He stared at it for a few moments, then changed his mind and brushed it away.

CHAPTER THIRTY-FIVE

Grand title notwithstanding, Chief of Synagogue Security Peter Wichs stood all of five-foot-four in polyester pants and a short-sleeved shirt with a chewed-up collar. Black eyes floating in black pools snapped from point to point on Jacob's face, committing him to memory—a veteran security man's practice.

"You are the detective Jacob Lev," Peter said.

Jacob laughed. "Heard of me?"

Wichs's smile resembled a badly broken bone: jagged and white and protruding unnaturally through split flesh.

The handshake went on a bit too long for Jacob's taste; his palm felt moist when he offered it to Wichs's assistant, Ya'ir, a rangy blond man no older than Jan, with an Israeli accent.

They went inside the *shul*, ducking under the barrier rope and heading down the hall, past the rabbi's study and various offices labeled in flaking gilt, to a door marked BEZPEČÍ/SECURITY.

The log was kept in English, the guards' common language. The entry for the night of April 15, 2011, described a white male, 1.75 to 1.8 meters tall, approximately 70 to 80 kilos. He had light eyes and brown hair and wore metal eyeglasses, brown overcoat, gray suit, black necktie with silver or light blue stripes. He'd kept his hand in his coat pocket and appeared to be making a fist, raising the possibility of a concealed weapon. He sweated visibly and sounded nervous. He stated that he came from the UK, but declined to supply a passport or ID. He could not correctly name the last Jewish holiday, and when asked to wait, he had run away.

"This guy," Ya'ir said, "if I sawed him at the airport, I would pull to the alarm."

"Did you call the cops?"

Peter gestured to the well-used logbook. "This is Prague. We can't report every unusual character. They'd stop taking us seriously."

"Then the lieutenant contacted you."

"For the tapes. Unfortunately, as I told him, the cameras are merely a visual deterrent."

"Did he ask you to take a look at the victim?"

Ya'ir shook his head. Peter said, "I wasn't notified until later that afternoon. The body had already been removed."

Jacob said, "What I'm about to show you isn't pretty."

He handed his phone to Ya'ir, who recoiled from the gory image.

"Bear in mind, a lot of things change after death. Skin color, muscle tone."

"He is not wearing glasses," Ya'ir said. "But for me, I think yes, he's the same."

He passed the phone to Peter.

The Czech guard's reaction was rather different: he glanced briefly at the screen, turned it facedown on the desk. There was none of the visceral horror that even now had Ya'ir chewing his tongue.

Peter Wichs simply stared off into nowhere, the epitome of indifference.

Jacob shifted, unnerved. As a rule of thumb, the more excitably someone acted in the interrogation room, the less likely he was to be guilty. Conversely, the worst guys put their heads down and took a nap. They had nothing to discuss.

"What do you think?" Jacob asked. "Same guy?"

Peter shrugged. "It's hard to say."

"You want to take another look?"

"That's not necessary."

"Or I can show you a different—"

"It's not necessary."

"Uh-huh," Jacob said. "Okay, well . . . I talked to Klaudia Navrátilová this morning. She seemed unclear on what had happened."

"Naturally. She experienced a terrible trauma."

"Did you discuss it with her?"

"Me? No. Our interactions were professional and infrequent."

"Still, you must've been upset when you heard what happened to her."

"Naturally," Peter said.

"She's nice girl," Ya'ir said.

"You were friendly," Jacob said, more to Peter than Ya'ir.

The Czech guard shrugged again. "As I said, professional. And infrequent."

"Did she give a reason for quitting?"

"I imagine she found the memories too painful."

"She told me something I'm having trouble understanding." Jacob opened his notepad to the page where Klaudia had written *bláto*. "Do you know why she'd say that?"

"I don't know what is this," Ya'ir said.

"It means 'mud,'" Jacob said. "Is that right?"

Peter nodded once.

"What do you think she meant by that?" Jacob said.

"She's maid," Ya'ir said. "She is all the time think about dirt."

"Mud. Not dirt."

"Put water, it's the same."

Jacob waited for Peter to say more. Peter continued to gaze away. "Can either of you think of anyone who might've been in or around the building on the night of the attack?"

"Who would be here?" Peter asked.

"Somebody who has a key, say, and wants to come in early to get ready for davening."

"We have enough difficulty getting a *minyan*, let alone at four in the morning."

"Members of the community who take an especially protective view of the *shul*?"

"We all do," Peter said. "It's our heritage."

"You're chief of security, though. It must mean more to you than most."

"Everyone respects the *shul*."

Silence.

Jacob said, "There was a message left on one of the cobblestones."

"We have graffiti," Ya'ir said.

"This wasn't done by a run-of-the-mill vandal," Jacob said. He lifted the phone off the desk, found the picture of the defaced stone, displayed it.

"You can understand," he said, "why I think it's not entirely out of line to wonder about an offender with a Jewish background."

The guards remained silent. Ya'ir shot a glance at Peter.

Jacob said, "Someone replaced the stone."

"Naturally," Peter said. "It wouldn't be appropriate to leave a hole in the ground."

"Do you know what happened to the old one?"

"I assumed the police had taken it away as evidence."

"Lieutenant Chrpa said he came back to look at it and it was missing."

"I can't tell you anything about that."

"Can't tell me?"

"I don't know," Peter said.

Jacob looked at Ya'ir, who made a helpless face.

"Perhaps the lieutenant misplaced it," Peter said.

"He didn't seem like the kind of guy who would," Jacob said.

Peter tapped his chin. "Anything is possible."

"I've also been told that the garret door was found open," Jacob said.

"Occasionally someone tries to climb up the exterior ladder," Peter said. "Tourists who've read the stories and had too many beers."

"What do they do, once they're up there?"

"Come down. There is no access. The door is locked from the inside."

"You're not concerned someone might fall?"

"We can't be expected to account for everyone's foolishness," Peter said.

"Sure. Sure. But you told the lieutenant that a wind had blown it open."

"Did I?"

"You did."

"Well," Peter said, "I imagine that's possible, too."

"Not if the door's locked from the inside," Jacob said.

Ya'ir looked intrigued.

Peter, harder to say.

He said, "Ordinarily, it's locked."

"But?"

"I would have to imagine that it wasn't, that night."

"You imagine," Jacob said.

Peter smiled wanly. "It's a bad habit."

"All right, then. Who do you imagine unlocked the door?"

Another silence, longer.

Peter said, "Go take the first shift, please, Ya'ir."

"There is time still," Ya'ir said.

Peter didn't reply, and the Israeli sighed and got up.

When he was gone, Jacob said, "What's wrong?"

"It's him," Peter said. "Your head. It's the same man, the Englishman. I have no doubt."

"You didn't want to say so in front of Ya'ir."

"I didn't want to upset him."

"He seems like a pretty tough guy."

"On the outside. There's a program, young Israelis fresh from army service. We fly them out for a couple of years, then they go back." Peter studied him. "How old are you, Jacob Lev?"

"Thirty-two."

"This is your first visit to Prague."

Jacob nodded.

"You never wanted to come before."

"I never had the chance. Or the money."

"How do you like it so far?"

"Honestly? It kind of creeps me out."

"You're not the first to think so."

"You never answered my question. How'd the garret door get unlocked?"

"It's possible that I left it open by accident."

"You've been inside."

"Often."

"I thought it was forbidden."

"Somebody has to tend it."

"The chief of security doesn't have better things to do?"

Peter smiled. "A big title, for a small job."

"Who else goes up there?"

"It's not open to the public."

"Besides you, who has access?"

"No one."

"What about the rabbi?"

"Rabbi Zissman has only been with us three years. He knows better than to ask."

"How long does someone have to work here before they can go up?"

"Longer than three years."

"And how often are you up there?"

"Every Friday."

"Before Shabbat."

Peter nodded.

"And do you typically unlock the door?"

"Not typically."

"So, then."

"It's merely one hypothesis," Peter said.

"The other being?"

"Tourists."

"You can't blame everything on them," Jacob said.

"I don't see why not," Peter said. He shifted. "I suppose I must've left it open, that day."

"That's your final answer."

"Yes, Jacob Lev," Peter said. "I imagine it is."

Jacob asked, "What's up there, anyway?"

He expected Peter to laugh, or to rebuff him with a cluck of the tongue.

Instead the guard stood, jangling his keys. He withdrew a small flashlight from a drawer and rapped its butt end against the desk.

"Come."

CHAPTER THIRTY-SIX

Peter hung a right out of the office, stopping to unlock an unmarked door. He flicked a switch, and blue fluorescent tubes limned a stone staircase that wound down and out of sight.

"After you," he said.

"That's the garret?"

"The *mikveh*," Peter said. "Anyone who goes up must immerse first."

"No, thanks."

"It's not a choice," Peter said.

Jacob hesitated, then started down the rough-hewn steps through soggy air. The odor of groundwater detectable everywhere in the *shul* grew stronger and developed a spiky, chemical overtone: chlorine. He was hyperconscious of the guard following close behind—close enough to raise the hairs on the back of his neck, close enough to give Jacob a good hard shove and send him tumbling, broken legs, broken neck, broken back.

The stairs ended at a tiled basement equipped with a fiberglass stall shower and a raw pine vanity. A basket of mismatched towels sat on the floor beside a rice paper screen.

Through an archway Jacob saw the *mikveh*, a six-foot cube hewn into the floor, filled with shimmering water.

"You don't think we're cutting it a little close to Shabbat?"

"All the more reason not to delay," Peter said.

He took a towel and went behind the screen. His backlit shape contorted as he stripped. Reemerging bare-chested, lower body wrapped in the towel, he turned on the shower. While the water warmed, he stepped to the vanity to clip his nails, brush his teeth with a disposable brush, and gargle with mouthwash from a paper cup. Once steam had begun to billow from the shower, he put the towel on a hook and stepped into the stall, soaping himself from a wall-mount dispenser. Naked, he looked vulnerable, with smooth shins and collapsed buttocks.

At least now Jacob knew Peter wasn't carrying a concealed weapon of his own.

The guard stepped out, dripping, and presented himself for inspection. "Okay?"

"Good to go."

In the adjoining room, Peter climbed into the *mikveh* and waded to the center. He glanced at Jacob, held his breath, and dropped down, his pale shape rippling and distorting beneath the surface.

While Jacob watched, it occurred to him that at no point had Peter said *This is a ritual bath* or *Check me for stray hairs* or *Make sure I'm completely submerged*. These were ceremonial fine points known only to someone with a fair amount of religious instruction. So far as Peter was concerned, Jacob wasn't even Jewish. *Jacob* was the most popular male name in America. He could be Episcopalian or Zen Buddhist or Scientologist or what he really was, agnostic.

Peter stayed under for a solid twenty count, surfacing with red eyes. "Your turn."

Jacob hurried through the prep, covering himself with a towel whenever possible. Approaching the *mikveh*, he toed the water and winced: it was freezing.

He tossed his towel aside and in he went, gasping, his testicles scrambling for cover, his chest constricting as he forced his knees to bend.

The cold surrounded him, a cell of ice carved to his exact dimensions.

Unable to tolerate it any longer, he burst upward, newborn; tingling, red, irate.

"How do you stand it," he said, clambering out.

"The water comes directly from the river," Peter said.

"Doesn't make it any warmer."

Peter smiled and handed him a fresh towel.

JACOB HAD LOGGED countless hours in synagogues. Few in women's sections. None in one so depressing. More fluorescent tubing cast a sepulchral glow. Rust swallowed the hinges of the folding chairs, ensuring that they would never be folded up again. He could hardly make out the sanctuary through the skimpy viewing portals. He asked Peter if women actually came to pray.

"Mostly tourists."

"Can't say I blame them. It's like a prison back here."

"You're very cynical, Detective Lev."

"Part of the job description."

"It won't help you here," Peter said.

He drew back the purple curtain on a second door. Behind it lay a cramped, low-ceilinged room roughly the size of a phone booth.

"You don't lock it?"

"Nobody can enter without permission," Peter said.

"People must be tempted."

"That's why the entrance is through the women's section." Peter clicked on the flashlight, and they stepped in.

"Some might say women are more prone to temptation than men," Jacob said. He could feel the heat of the guard's body; he breathed in the man's river-damp scent. "Adam and Eve?"

"Maybe it was that way originally," Peter said. He shut the curtain, shut the door, and trained the flashlight on a loop of rope hanging from the ceiling. "Step aside, please."

Jacob had time enough to press himself against the wall before the guard reached up and tugged on the rope.

A trapdoor opened, and a ladder slid out, showering them with dust that plastered their wet heads. Jacob coughed and waved his hand in front of his face, peering up through stinging eyes. Above him stretched a dust-choked shaft, like the inside of a grain silo but far narrower. The ladder extended at least another ten feet; beyond that, the flashlight surrendered to darkness.

Peter put his foot on the bottom rung. "Up we go."

The ladder creaked and vibrated and rained grime as they climbed. Within moments, Jacob was panting, sweat feathering his lower back. He couldn't remember the last time he'd had to do anything this demanding. The academy, probably. Since then: too much liquor. Too many hot dogs. He was a desk jockey.

Still, he'd always considered himself sound of body, if not of mind, and he couldn't recall losing wind this quickly.

The flashlight bobbed above him, disclosing cobwebs and stray nails and a thickening firmament of dust. Occasionally the beam swung back down, blinding him momentarily, leaving him groping without confidence for the next rung. He pictured the exterior door, gauged its height in his mind. Three stories. They should have reached the garret by now, but Peter went on, dogged as faith, humming a one-note drone, the slap of his shoes setting an increasingly demanding pace, the flashlight guttering.

Gasping for air, Jacob called for him to slow down.

"You're doing fine, Detective."

He didn't feel fine. His thighs ached and his forearms bubbled, as though he'd climbed a high-altitude mile. Heat flashed over him; he was having a heart attack, a panic attack, or both.

"How much farther is it?" he yelled hoarsely.

The answer came from a great distance. "Not far."

The flashlight winked out, immersing Jacob in a black as total as death.

Panting, he hooked one arm over a rung, tugged out his phone, clutching it in one sweaty hand as he resumed his ascent. Its blue glow penetrated less than a foot into the dust; it shut off every ten seconds. He kept reviving it, glancing at the screen. He was getting no service.

It was 6:13 p.m. They were never going to make it down before Shabbat.

And still Peter kept climbing.

To keep his anxiety at bay, Jacob began counting rungs: thirty, fifty, a hundred. He couldn't see the flashlight but he could hear the humming, chased after it, his heart straining, every step a torment. When he next checked the time, he saw that it had not changed, and he told himself that the lack of reception was affecting the operation of the clock, although he knew very well that the clock ran on its own internal circuit; so maybe the problem was the dust, a special dust, a toxic dust, maybe it had clogged up the phone and caused it to freeze, an explanation he accepted because that alone could account for the fact that it remained 6:13 after he'd counted sixty more rungs, and again, and again, until the phone refused to light up, either out of juice or else the dust was so enveloping that he couldn't see the screen, even with it pressed right up against his face. He had lost count of the rungs, hand over hand without end. The humming had died, too. He called out and the close echo told him that, as he could not hear Peter, Peter could not hear him; nobody could; he faltered, knowing that he would never reach the top. Nor could he go back down. He was alone. There was nothing to do but let his fingers uncurl and his toes unbend and release himself into the abyss.

Weeping, he grasped the next rung.

A glowing gap opened in the cosmos. Syrupy orange light sang to him.

The dust knitted itself into cloth; folded over itself, forming a warm moist pumping canal that sucked him upward, and as he drew nearer, the gap widened and the light streamed down, carrying voices. He stretched and strove toward the sound, suffocating, skull unknitting and segmenting and deforming, and the voices multiplied: forty-five, seventy-one, two hundred thirty-one, six hundred thirteen, eighteen thousand, a thousand by a thousand voices, every one of them unique and discernible and strange, the light spreading oceanically, a terrible buzzing chorus, and the voices swelled to twelve by thirty by thirty by thirty by thirty by thirty by thirty by three hundred sixty-five thousand myriads, the thrum of innumerable wings.

CHAPTER THIRTY-SEVEN

Y ou are here, Jacob Lev."
    Jacob lay on his back, body stunned and numb, chest thudding.
Through fuzzy infant eyes he saw Peter kneeling over him. Not a hair
out of place. His shirt unwrinkled.

"How do you feel?"

"I ffff . . ." Tangle-tongued. "I feel . . . I can prowuh, proll, prolly . . .
skippa gym . . . today."

Peter smiled and patted him on the shoulder. "You did well."

The guard hoisted him to a sitting position.

Blood stormed into his temples, and his vision went gold-green, and
for less than a second he peered through a green filter at a lush garden,
green grass insisting through the floorboards, spore-engorged ferns exploding greenly from the rafters, vines climbing through mist, dripping
orchids, acres of lichen, an ecosystem thriving and sultry, sexual in its
zeal, real enough to fill his nostrils with the heady vapors of rot and re-
generation.

Then his mind clenched like an overused muscle and the green band
lifted and the garden withered and petrified, curvaceous tendrils stiffening to woodwormed structural beams.

"Can you stand?"

"Think so."

"Okay, up up up."

A brief, awkward dance, Jacob leaning on the smaller, older man.

"I'm going to let you go. All right? Yes? Okay? Here we go . . . Very good. Very good."

They were at one end of a sprawling, windowless, unfinished attic, amok with a truly awesome amount of junk.

Lingering vertigo yanked the horizon back and forth. A kerosene lantern hanging from a wall bracket made a meager and uncertain buffer against the darkness that slunk through the crevices, expanded in the open air, obscured the peak of the sloped ceiling.

"How are you now? Better?"

"Uh-huh."

"Do you need to sit down?"

"I'm okay."

Peter regarded him skeptically. With good reason: it was taking every ounce of focus for Jacob to keep himself upright. His neck and face felt flushed with fever, his damp shirtfront swaying in a sourceless breeze. Clearly he was in lousier aerobic shape than he'd imagined. Or maybe he was sick. Physically sick. The dust. An allergy attack from hell.

Could allergies tweak your visual field? Make you hallucinate?

He was probably dehydrated, too; in mini-withdrawal and jet-lagged, and preoccupied. Any of these explanations he greatly preferred over the onset of psychosis.

"As you say," Peter said. "Now, listen carefully, please. If you have any unusual thoughts, you must tell me, at once."

"Unusual?"

"Anything at all. A strong urge to do something, for instance." Peter unhooked the lantern. "Please stay close; it's easy to get lost."

They waded into the maze, the lantern swinging, carving shapes in the gloom, throwing weird shadows that evolved from moment to moment, so that blank space lurched forth as solid and vice versa. The darkness had a tangible, oily quality, contracting at the touch of light like a drop of soap in grease, alerting Jacob at the last second to shifting floor depths, sagging planking, masonry remnants, and flaccid, chin-high ductwork.

More dust. Not as bad as in the shaft. It stuck to his skin, mixed with the sweat, formed a kind of clayey paste that dried and crackled as he moved. But his lungs weren't rebelling.

He was, in fact, breathing easily. Better than usual.

"Must be tough getting a vacuum up that ladder."

"Pardon?"

"To clean it. Every Friday."

"I said I tend it," Peter said.

"There's a difference?"

"Naturally. That's why there are two separate words."

A vacuum would have been beside the point, a blowtorch the right tool for the job. Much of the mess was bookcases, stacked deep with water-stained parchment scrolls, moth-eaten *talleisim*, crates of prayer-book confetti—the components of a *genizah*, a community depository for disused ritual objects too holy to destroy. There were other items, too: peeling steamer trunks and wrecked furniture and piles of shoes filled with rodent droppings.

Eight centuries, he supposed stuff added up.

His equilibrium was returning, and with it, his detachment.

He said, "Have you ever considered a garage sale?"

Peter chuckled. "Most items of value have already been sold off. Almost nothing here predates the war."

"Mind if I take a couple of pictures? My father's a big fan of the Maharal."

The guard glanced back to arch an eyebrow. "Is he."

"It's kind of an obsession, actually."

"I wasn't aware that rabbis had fans."

"They do among other rabbis."

"Ah. Please."

They paused so Jacob could dig out his camera. He wasn't sure what he hoped to achieve, other than to prove to Sam that he'd been here—not that you could prove anything from pictures of garbage. "What was here before that was so valuable?"

"Old books, manuscripts. There was also a letter, the only one surviving in the Maharal's own hand."

Jacob whistled. "No kidding."

Peter nodded. "You'd do better to bring your father photographs of that, Jacob Lev."

"I assume it's in the state museum or something."

"Unfortunately not. The Bodleian has it."

Jacob's heart kicked. "The Bodleian Library."

"Yes."

"In Oxford."

"Unless there's another I don't know about. Is something wrong, Jacob Lev?"

". . . no. No."

They resumed bushwhacking in silence. Jacob was wondering whether to share with the guard that Oxford was Reggie Heap's alma mater—simultaneously wondering whether there was any significance to that fact—when Peter spoke.

"The Nazis leveled many of the cities they came through. The Communists, too. But they left Prague intact. Do you know why?"

"Hitler wanted to convert the ghetto to a museum of a dead culture. The Communists didn't have the money for demolition."

"That's what historians say. There's another reason, though. They were afraid to overturn the earth. Even men such as they, evil men, understood that things are buried here that one should not disturb."

"Mm."

"You don't believe me," Peter said. "It's all right. Ya'ir is the same way."

"I'm not sure what you're asking me to believe."

Peter didn't reply.

Jacob said, "How'd the letter end up in England?"

"A later chief rabbi sent it away with the manuscripts for safekeeping. It was a prophetic decision; soon afterward, there was a pogrom, and everything in the *shul* not nailed down was dragged out into the street and burned." Sidling past a crippled lectern. "This rabbi, Dovid Oppenheimer, was a German, a great lover of books. Accepting the position in Prague meant leaving behind a huge library in Hanover in the care of his father-in-law. After both men had passed, the entire collection, including the Maharal's letter, was bundled together. It changed hands several times before the Bodleian bought it."

"Kind of a shame it's so far from home."

"Frankly, it's better this way, Jacob Lev. They are precious pieces of history. We couldn't care for them properly. The insurance alone would eat up our annual budget ten times over. Though I will admit that it would be nice to see them."

"Cheap flight to Gatwick. Thirty pounds. I just booked it."

"Yes, well, I've never left Prague."

"Really?"

"When I was a boy, travel was restricted, and then I took over at the *shul*."

"They don't give you a day off once in a while? I'm sure Ya'ir can hold down the fort."

Peter swiveled aside a freestanding mirror, de-silvered to flat pewter. "Here we are."

Along the length of the eastern wall ran a three-foot-wide path cleared of detritus, providing access to the exterior door, its arched shape outlined in sunlight, an iron bar holding it firmly in place.

"May I?"

Peter hesitated. "If you must."

Jacob worked to pry free the bar, which was heavy and rusty to boot. The door swung in with an ovine croak. Light dazzled him; instantly he felt tugged toward the cool evening air. He braced his hands on the doorframe and thrust his head out.

"Careful, please," Peter said.

Jacob peered down.

Below, the rungs.

The cobbled area.

The drain.

Foot traffic coursed along Pařížská Street, backlit by a pinkening sky, shoppers and lovers and sunburnt vacationers oblivious to the eye observing them from above. It put Jacob in mind of that morning, standing with Jan at the scene, the man on the cell phone rushing along, taking no notice of them.

Here, it's like invisible.

He swooned, drunk on fresh air.

"Detective," Peter said. "Careful."

"How high's the drop?"

"Thirty-nine feet."

"And there's no way to open the door from the outside."

"None. That's enough, now, step back."

But Jacob craned further, gulping sweet air, so wonderful, inviting him to dive into it . . .

He wouldn't fall.

He would float.

He let go.

With shocking strength, Peter grabbed him by his shirt and hauled him back inside, slamming him against the wall, pinning him there. The guard said, "Don't move, Jacob, please," and released him, hurrying to slam and bolt the door.

Jacob wasn't moving. He had slumped docilely and he remained that way as the drop in brightness caused his eyes to ache. With the door shut, the urge to hurl himself out had begun to dwindle, and in its stead came the horror, humiliation, and confusion of realizing how close he had been to obeying it. He shuddered violently, chewing the edge of a thumbnail, while in his mind he saw the cobblestones rising up to meet him.

Peter crouched down in front of him. "What happened."

What do you think, motherfucker? I'm going off the deep end.

Jacob shook his head.

"Jacob. You must please tell me what you were thinking."

"I don't know. I don't know what came over me. I just—I don't know."

"What were you thinking?"

"I wasn't." He commanded his body to stop shaking. "I'm fine. I mean, obviously, I'm—tired, and I was just standing there, and . . ."

"And . . ."

"And nothing. I slipped, okay? My hands—they're sweaty. I'm all right now, thank you. I'm sorry. Thank you. I really don't know what came over me."

Peter smiled sadly. "It's not your fault. This place affects people in unpredictable ways. Now we know how it affects you."

Jacob bit off another spasm. He would not allow this to happen to him. He waved off Peter's offer of help, struggling to his feet, resting against a splintery beam.

"I trust you've seen what you wanted to see," Peter said.

"Unless you're going to show me where you keep the golem."

The smile he received was a dry reflection of his own.

Peter said, "Prepare for disappointment."

THEY FOLLOWED THE CLEARED path around the corner to the end, coming up against a hulking rectangular shape standing inert in shadow.

Ten feet tall, broad as two normal men, it slumbered beneath a moldering shroud held tight by ropes—a coffin for a giant.

Peter set down the lantern and began untying the ropes. One by one they fell to the ground, until he whipped the shroud away and the tension whooshed out of Jacob's chest, and he realized he'd been holding his breath, brain coiled up in expectation of a monster crashing forth with crushing hands.

He began to laugh.

"Not what you were expecting."

"Not really, no."

Rudely built, unvarnished, the cabinet squatted on warped legs—a flea market leftover. One door was missing; inside were deep shelves, riddled with scores of peculiar, quarter-inch holes. The back and sides were similarly perforated.

For the most part, the cabinet appeared empty. Drawing closer in the low light, however, Jacob saw a number of pottery shards scattered on the center shelf—wafer-thin husks of clay. It was then that he understood what he was looking at: a drying rack, an old-fashioned version of the one his mother had kept in the garage. Before he could ask what such a thing would be doing in the attic of a synagogue, Peter pointed to one of the shards and said, "There."

Jacob looked at him. "What."

Peter's answer was to lightly pluck one of the shards and place it in Jacob's palm. It felt insubstantial; it grew translucent as Jacob held it up to the lantern.

The guard said, "I told you to prepare for disappointment."

Jacob stared at the shard, uncomprehending.

"You may find this of greater interest," Peter said.

The guard dragged over a crate to stand on, reaching elbow-deep into the topmost shelf, withdrawing an object the size of a pomegranate, wrapped in black woolen cloth and fastened with twine. He traded it to Jacob for the clay shard.

The bundle was heavier than its size predicted, as though it contained a miniature cannonball. Jacob picked loose the knot, let the cloth fall open. Inside lay a matte ceramic spheroid, gray mottled with black and green. Its cool surface warmed rapidly as he turned it in his fingers.

A head; a human head, modeled by hand, finely wrought. Of special delicacy were the needle-like fronds of a beard. The same precision had been applied to the sharp jaw; the brow nobly swollen; the parentheses around the mouth; the eyes clenched against a blinding light.

Peter said, "It's the Maharal."

"Really?" Jacob said, fighting to keep his voice even.

In his mind, the truth: assaultive, clangorous.

My mother's work.

My father's face.

THE GARRET

Blanketed in night, she patrols a warren of alleyways bent sinister.

Even at that lonely hour, quiet fails to gain a foothold in the ghetto. Snatches of song undermine midnight lamentation. Shutters snap. Glass breaks. Opposing rooflines teeter forward, chins dripping, like drunks coming in for a kiss. Rain falls upward and downward and slantward, filling her boots; rain drums every surface, producing a spectrum of characteristic sounds; rotting timber and corroding tin; quicklime and leather; excrement and feathers and trash.

Prague.

Her home.

There are no secrets here, grubby swaybacked houses stacked close enough for neighbors to answer each other's questions. A day after being awakened, the worst of her disorientation had passed, and everyone from the biggest *macher* to the humblest kitchen maid knew about the simpleminded mute found wandering in the forest.

At first she resented this description, but as weeks went by, she realized the protection it afforded her. She has taken her place in the ghetto's tender pantheon of the grotesque, alongside Hindel, the junk dealer's daughter, with her shriveled left arm; Sender, who repeats back whatever one says to him; Aaron, the cobbler's apprentice, whose hair grows red on one side and black on the other.

Nowadays, if people remark at all, it is to praise the generosity of Rebbe and Rebbetzin, taking in an orphan at their age.

With his unchanging face, his treadling gait, Yankele the Giant has become something of a local mascot, popular especially with the children, who run before him in teasing circles.

Can't catch me! Can't catch me!

She feigns sluggishness, swiping at them with her tree stump fists while they giggle and scream; pretending to lose her balance and land on her rear; then springing up like a jack-in-the-box to show her true agility, snatching, gingerly, so gingerly, one child in each hand, their tiny hot bodies quivering with terror and delight.

Put me down!

At such moments the curtain around her memory draws back, triggered by a voice or a face or by an idle moment, teasing her with a shining fragment. In those brief intervals she recognizes that this is not the first turn of the wheel. There have been other times, other people, other places.

Names drift up, haunting her with their meaninglessness. *Dalal. Leucos. Wangdue. Philippus. Bēi-Niántŭ.* Names no better or worse than *Yankele.*

Men's names, to match her man's body.

More telling than any one memory is the negative impression it leaves. She knows that she is hideous, abased, and helpless. Which means that once she must have been beautiful, and proud, and free.

While much about her present existence dissatisfies her, she knows she could do far worse than to live with Rebbe and Perel. They have made her a fixture of their lives, and indeed, it sometimes seems that the house on Heligasse would cease to function without her. But of course this isn't true. They got along fine before she arrived, and if she were to leave, they would get along fine once more. They allow themselves to depend on her as a kindness to her; everyone needs to feel needed.

Very different people, they relate to her differently. Perel is a maker of things: clothing, challah, you name it. The demands of a rebbetzin are myriad, and her demands on Yankele are practical. A heavy load of laundry. A basket out of reach. Draw water—one bucket only, please.

Whereas Rebbe has been known to have trouble cutting up his food. On several occasions he has sent her to the house of study to fetch a book already sitting open on his lap.

It is the interchange between the couple that elevates them both, their marriage an embodiment of one of Rebbe's favorite themes: erasing the barrier between the material universe and the spiritual one.

Every afternoon they convene in Rebbe's study to pore over the Talmud together. This time is sacrosanct, and they have assigned Yankele the duty of ensuring their privacy for thirty minutes. She stands outside the house, guarding the door, listening to them spar with Godly words. The love they share overflows the threshold, spreading out along Heligasse to lap warmly at her deadened feet.

A jangle of keys; an off-key whistle; Chayim Wichs, the sexton, hurries home from locking up the *shul.*

"*Shalom aleichem*, Yankele."

Expecting no answer, he ducks into the wind and carries on, keen to get himself in front of a fire. She likewise pulls her cloak close in imitation of a man feeling cold. To let him know that his discomfort is reasonable.

Such gestures require constant practice. She has become a collector of mannerisms, wrapping her fringes around the ends of her pinkies to signal preoccupation; cultivating the asymmetry of exhausted shoulders. It is of course the Loews' habits she knows best: the sentimental vibrato beneath Rebbe's beard when he refers to her as *my son*, the green slant of Perel's eyes at the mention of her dead daughter, Leah.

A repertoire performed for her own benefit, it makes her feel something like human. Perhaps in time, her heart—if she has one, if inside the cabinet of her chest there is more than empty space—will follow upon the actions. For her own body remains a fearsome thing, and despite having regained partial control over it, she still suffers maddening spasms of literalism.

Just the other day, Perel asked her to go to the riverbank and bring back some clay, and instead of taking a bucket or a box, as a sensible creature would, she ferried as much as she could in her bare arms, depositing it in the middle of the courtyard, a colossal heap bristling with wet roots. Black-shelled beetles wriggled up to the surface and, confronted with an abyss of open air, frantically burrowed back down.

Oy gevalt. Yankele. I said clay from the riverbank, not the entire river-bank. I'll have enough to last me a year . . . Never mind. Put it in the shed, please.

Lately, she's noticed something disturbing. She has ceased to correct people in her mind. On occasion she has even caught herself thinking of herself as *Yankele*, and upon realizing it she has felt a mixture of disgust and relief.

What a pleasure it would be—what a burden lifted—to have a self. To relinquish her threadbare memory, agonizingly transient hints of beauty, and accept that she is in fact what others perceive.

Then she reminds herself of her previous selves. They didn't last. Why should this one be any different?

ONE NIGHT LAST SPRING, the week before Passover, she spotted a gummy gray glow spilling from the mouth of the alley behind Zschyk's bakery. She assumed the baker was forgoing sleep, toiling overtime to make enough *matzah* to serve the community all holiday long.

Then she heard the mumble of gutter language, and a stirring, and mice began to pour from the alley, as well.

The light had a cold quality to it: rather than illuminate, it smothered. The fleeing mice avoided it, skirting its edges.

Mesmerized, she came forward until she stood just beyond the light, leaning in to behold its source.

A man.

Dressed in peasant's garb, he was crouched down, carefully arranging the body of a dead infant—its tiny belly slit—in the trash heap.

Gray leaked from his margins, a watery, shaky ribbon that moved with him, eroding whatever it touched.

He did not notice her, watching him. Odd but true: her size helps her disappear. She becomes part of the architecture, a lie too brazen to see through.

Besides, he was hard at work, tucking the infant's legs under a shard of broken crockery, reconsidering and covering the face instead. Throughout this process of perfecting the scene, the aura changed. He grabbed the child's body roughly and the color deepened, a flood of sludge. When he let go, it reverted to the pale ribbon that seemed to be its natural state.

He propped one tiny dimpled arm so that it stood up like a candle. No doubt by sunrise the flesh would be chewed to strings. No doubt it would appear that someone had attempted to hide the body, but that it had been dragged free by rats. No doubt a passerby would spot it, and no doubt that passerby would happen to be a gentile; no doubt the baker would be questioned—what did he do in there, all night long?—and no doubt his answers would not matter to the authorities, who would have found him guilty well in advance.

Within her, an ancient rage began to gather.

Pleased at last, the man stood up, using the collar of his shirt to mop the sweat from his neck. He turned to go and walked smack into her, emitting a choked scream as he flattened himself against the wall of the alley like a jagged vein in marble.

She waited, unmoving as a pillar of stone.

The man goggled up at her; swiveled to look at the infant's body, as though hopeful that it had disappeared. But the tiny arm was still jutting up.

It wanted to be found.

He had seen to that.

He said, "They made me do it."

She believed him. He was not the true villain. The aura wasn't strong enough.

Who were *they*?

She couldn't ask, of course.

Of course, he ran.

Her hands closed around the soft lower half of his midsection. She lifted him so their faces were nearly touching, and squeezed gently, forcing the blood out of his midsection. He vomited and made a broken-bellows wheeze; his limbs shot out rigid as broomsticks; his hands inflated like the stomach of a diseased animal; his forehead glowed scarlet except for a jagged scar at his hairline, the sight of which triggered a cascade of images running in reverse.

A patch of burning sand, flying away from her;

a rush of demon wind;

a tower a city a boy a dog

faster still:

valley earth ice garden

The man had by then turned a deep purple, his neck swollen wider than his head, his eyeballs distending, the blood vessels in them bursting open like thousands of poppies. He wept blood. Blood streamed from his ears and from his nostrils. His midsection charred and smoked where she gripped it.

Joyously the rage flowed through her.

Her lips split and cracked.

She was smiling.

She smiled wider and gave a last, lazy squeeze, separating his upper and lower halves, which tumbled into the muck, each half pinched shut like a wineskin.

The aura around him died, and with it went the pictures in her mind.

She fumbled for the halves of the corpse, squeezing at them, desperate to revive the warm rush of life-giving hatred.

But it was too late. He was dead, and she succeeded only in making a mess of him, innards oozing through her fingers.

She bundled both bodies in her cloak and walked down to the river. The child she buried in a clean patch of bank, reciting in her head the *kaddish* prayer she has heard Rebbe intone. The pieces of the murderer she hurled into the water. They bobbed and floated away, leaving her alone to contemplate a truth as piercing as it was vague, as exhilarating as it was terrifying.

For one glorious instant she had hovered close to revelation, her real name on the tip of her useless tongue.

For one moment she became marvelous, essential, natural.

She was, for that moment, herself—what she was and always had been.

A savior.

A killer.

THAT WAS ONE YEAR AGO, almost to the day.

Now, standing in the doorway to Petschek's butcher shop, she observes with interest the hooded figure rushing down Langegasse, a bundle under its arm.

She allows a comfortable gap, then sets out to follow.

It is an art, following someone through the ghetto. Passageways appear from nowhere. Stairwells plunge. Distractions abound. She steps over handcarts mounded with moldy potatoes. The storm heaves, eliciting from the loose roofing a slow, sarcastic round of applause. Long after the ghetto's human residents have grown accustomed to and then fond of her, their animals continue to herald her appearance with panic. Even before she has rounded the corner, the horses are stamping and snorting in their stalls; the chickens hysterical; the dogs puling; cats and rats in exodus, hostilities momentarily suspended.

They see her. They know her.

Whoever the figure is, he's moving fast, taking turns without a second thought. Someone from the neighborhood? Not in this weather. Not at midnight. In the interest of public safety, Rebbe has decreed that everyone except the sexton, the doctor, and Yankele must remain indoors after dark. Wichs she already saw, repairing to his quarters. The doctor it cannot be. He goes nowhere without his satchel, and he wears a bell around his neck to warn her of his approach.

Just because the figure is dressed as a Jew does not mean anything, either.

So was the man with the dead infant.

Down Ziegengasse, across the Grosse Ring, riverbound.

Someone else wishing to dispose of a dirty secret?

The bundle is the right size to hide a child's corpse.

Or, more charitably, a loaf of bread—a householder getting a jump on cleaning out the pantry for Passover.

In the dead of night?

A northward turn at double-wide Rabinergasse forces her to hang back. Thirty seconds later she steps out, and the figure has vanished.

Bootprints dwindle in the pounding rain. They arc toward the Alt-Neu and culminate in a series of muddy smears on the stone: feet wiped before entry.

The door to the synagogue remains closed, no violence done to it, although she supposes any competent thief could make short work of it. Before she arrived, vandalism was a perpetual plague. Torah scrolls shredded, ritual objects looted or destroyed.

She tries the handle.

The door swings open, unlocked.

Only Rebbe and the sexton have a key, and they are both in bed, or ought to be. Perhaps Rebbe has come seeking an hour or two alone? No. The figure she saw was too short. Besides, he wouldn't disregard his own edict. He leads by example.

She shakes the rain off her cloak and steps inside.

In the sanctuary proper, Wichs has pursued his duties with especial vigor, not a tassel astray. The holiday of Passover, Rebbe says, stands for cleansing and rebirth. Every craftsman in the ghetto has come through in recent days, sawing and sanding and polishing. The Ark has been inspected for mouse holes, its curtain laundered free of smoke. Perel took it upon herself to re-embroider the fraying *bimah* cover, adding a personal touch, decorative floral motifs.

There's another aspect to Passover. It is also the time of year when those who hate the Jews come seeking revenge for imaginary crimes.

She stands, listening to the storm beat down.

The stone walls smolder with the light of the Eternal Flame, filled to burn all night.

Then: a gray throb bulges through the viewing portals to the women's section.

It sickens and excites her.

She knows that color.

She squats down to look through the portals. The light is coming from the far eastern end of the room, radiating through the crack beneath a wooden door. She feels slightly foolish to realize that she has never noticed that door and does not know where it leads. Although she attends services three times a day—standing with inert lips, her arms and head wrapped in specially made *tefillin*, the work of Yosie the Scribe, who complained to Rebbe that he would need a whole calfskin to make them—she's never been inside the women's section.

Why would she? She's a man. She belongs with the other men.

If they knew who she really was—

There's a sound, too, a distant grinding drone, punctuated by a chunk, like a lame wagon.

Its rhythm matches the pulse of the light.

SHE LEAVES THE SANCTUARY and rounds the corridor, entering the women's section and pausing to watch the light. Each peak shines brighter than its predecessor, each trough correspondingly vacant. She can see now that it possesses its own unique shade, more silver than gray, cool and annihilating and beautiful.

sssssssTHUMPsssssssTHUMPsssssssTHUMPsssssssTHUMP

She can't remember the last time she felt afraid.

It's strangely satisfying.

She crosses to the unknown door and pulls it open.

Silver swells out, clinging to her like wet wool.

An antechamber, no bigger than four cubits on a side and swirling with dust. It is half her size and yet it yawns to admit her, and she places her foot on the bottom rung of the ladder that stretches up through a hole in the ceiling.

sssssssTHUMPsssssssTHUMPsssssssTHUMPsssssssTHUMP

She lays partial weight on the rung, expecting it to splinter. It holds, as does the next, and she commences to climb, covering the distance to the top in three reaches.

She surfaces through a trapdoor into a sloped room awash in silver light: a human figure, bent over with busy hands, barely visible at the center of a raging gray inferno, burning cold and glossy and charging the air so that it snaps and seethes.

sssssssTHUMPsssssssTHUMPsssssssTHUMPsssssssTHUMP

The rhythm stokes her desire to kill, her need building to a full-body thrum.

Whoever it is—whatever is happening—she must stop it.

She takes a step forward.

Tries to.

The light pushes her back.

She is unused to this. She has not known any physical limitations. She gathers her strength and steps forward again, and the light warps, groaning, shoving her into the wall with a heavy crash.

Startled, the figure looks up, and its aura immediately dims, revealing surroundings previously drowned out: a low, three-legged stool; the undone bundle, consisting of a piece of burlap and its dirty secret, a small pile of riverbank mud.

Lastly, the source of the noise, a spinning wooden wheel set atop a table, a half-formed lump at its center.

The wheel begins to slow.

The aura to fade further.

Her bloodlust subsides.

In half a minute all is still, and the only light is that of a small lantern, and the figure is fully visible.

She wears a long woolen skirt. Her wimple pulled free, a corona of frizzy black hair. The sleeves of her cloak are rolled up to her elbows. Muddy water streaks smooth, slender forearms. Delicate hands are gloved in clay, swollen to twice normal size. Wry green eyes regard her with resignation.

Perel says, "It's a good thing you can't talk."

CHAPTER THIRTY-EIGHT

The likeness of the face in Jacob's hands to Samuel Lev was close to perfect. It was a face he loved, the face of a man who had kissed him, blessed him. The face of a man who had died four hundred years ago.

He said, "How did you get this?"

Peter Wichs said, "It's always been here."

"Where did it come from? Who made it?"

"Nobody knows, Jacob Lev."

"Then how do you know it's the Maharal?"

"How do we know anything? We tell our children, who tell their children. My father worked at the *shul*, his father before him. I grew up hearing their stories, passed down from generation to generation."

"A myth."

"You may call it that, if you prefer."

Jacob's arm began to cramp, and he looked down to see the muscles in his forearm quivering; he had the object in a split-fingered grip, as though to pulverize it. He relaxed his hand, leaving red dents in the flesh of his palm.

"Do me a favor," Jacob said. "Stand back."

Peter obliged.

He appeared as short as Jacob remembered.

Not much faith in his memory, though. "Are you one of them?"

"One of whom?"

JONATHAN KELLERMAN AND JESSE KELLERMAN

"Special Projects."

"I don't know what that is," Peter said.

"A police division."

"I'm not a policeman, Jacob Lev," Peter said. "I have one job, and that is to stand guard."

Jacob looked again at the face. It was so vivid that he expected it to open its mouth and speak in Sam's voice.

You can't go. I can't allow it. I forbid it.

You can't do this to me.

You're leaving me.

Jacob said, "Why did you let me up here?"

"You asked."

"I'm sure a lot of people ask."

"Not a lot of policemen."

"Who else?"

Peter smiled. "Tourists."

"Did you let Lieutenant Chrpa up?"

The guard shook his head.

"Then who."

"I'm not sure what you mean, Detective."

"You said this place affects everyone differently. Who else has it affected?"

"This is an ancient place, Jacob Lev. I can't claim to know everything that has gone on here. I know that, of those who come, some find happiness, and peace. Others leave bitter. For a few it can be too much to handle, enough to drive them mad. All leave changed."

"What about me," Jacob said. "What's happening to me."

"I can't read your mind, Detective."

A wild laugh. "That's good to know."

"I think it's time for us to leave now, Jacob Lev," Peter said.

He plucked the clay head from Jacob's limp hand, began to rewrap it.

"Why do you keep calling me that."

"What?"

"Jacob Lev."

"It's your name, isn't it?" Peter got on the stool and put the bundle back on the top shelf. "Your name, it means 'heart' in Hebrew, I think. Lev."

"I know what it means," Jacob said.

"Ah," Peter said. "Then I think perhaps I have nothing more to offer you."

THEIR DESCENT WAS QUICK, no different from climbing down any moderate flight of stairs. Jacob's limbs worked smoothly, his chest felt open. His mind? Another matter.

Moments after they'd reemerged through the purple curtain, a woman in her forties, modestly clad in dark knits, entered, a prayer book tucked under her arm.

"*Gut Shabbos*, Rebbetzin Zissman," Peter said.

"*Gut Shabbos*, Peter."

"*Gut Shabbos,*" Jacob said.

The woman took in Jacob's dusty, uncovered head. "Mm," she said.

A bearded man in a fur hat and a black satin caftan waited expectantly by the sanctuary entrance. Peter greeted him in Czech, and Jacob heard his own name spoken.

"Rabbi Zissman apologizes for his poor English and invites you to join us for services."

"Maybe another time. Thanks, though. *Gut Shabbos.*"

The rabbi sighed, shook his head, and disappeared into the sanctuary.

"You were smart to say no," Peter said. "He speaks forever."

Outside, Ya'ir sat on the curb, reading *Forbes*. He stood up to shake Jacob's hand.

"I hope you luck finding this person."

"Thanks," Jacob said.

"Go take a break," Peter said.

Ya'ir shrugged. "Okay, boss."

He tossed Peter the magazine and trotted down the block to light a cigarette.

When they were alone, Peter said, "What's next for you, Detective Lev?"

"Go to England. Find out more about Reggie Heap."

"As I said, I'm no policeman. But if that's your instinct, I'd say you should heed it."

"My instincts made me want to throw myself out a window."

Peter smiled. "You're down here, now."

He patted Jacob on the shoulder and went to take up his watch.

Jacob glanced at the Hebrew clock tower. Once again, he needed a moment to be certain he wasn't reading it wrong. But his phone agreed. It was 6:16 p.m.

CHAPTER THIRTY-NINE

The flight to London lasted two brutish hours. He spent the first downing airline booze and the second eating peanuts to mask his breath—successfully, because the fellow behind the Gatwick rental counter handed him the keys to a bare-bones English Ford.

Driving on the left side of the road, sheeting rain, and a pervasive sense of dread that made every other vehicle appear hell-bent on a head-on turned the ride to Clegchurch into a nerve-corroding ordeal.

The outskirts of town had been given over to sad blocks of council housing, and while the high street retained its architectural charm, plastic bottles and Mylar snack wrappers lined the rushing gutters. The two establishments doing a midday trade were the off-track-betting facility and the adjacent pub, called the Dog's Neck.

He pulled over, cut the engine. Rain thumped the roof.

Perhaps the adrenaline had cleansed his system, because his days in Prague had already begun to acquire the quality of a dream, the smooth flow of time calving into chunks that drifted away from each other, softening at the edges, so that no event or sensation bore any causal relationship to any other.

He listed off the reasons not to trust himself.

Stress.

Jet lag.

Genetics.

The poison he'd pumped into himself for the last twelve years.

The city of Prague itself, a four-dimensional fever dream.

Happened every day; you saw someone who looked like someone else. Function of statistics: seven billion–plus people in the world. Had to happen. *Not* happening would be more remarkable. Why else would the idea of a doppelgänger exist?

Atop that argument he piled a layer of generalized language. *Stuff* had happened to him; *weird stuff*, but not impossible *stuff*. *Stuff* he would process at a more convenient later date, long after it had begun to break itself down and digest itself into a warm heap of forgetfulness. Cross your eyes hard enough, you could always find a rational explanation.

And on some level, he had been waiting for this moment—looking forward to it, even—his unconscious counting down, clicking away like prayer beads. He had gotten away too long with simple depression. He felt he should send himself a bouquet of flowers. *Congratulations on finally losing your mind!* It was something of a relief to realize that he no longer had to pretend he was the master of his own fate. He would go home, surrender to expertise, find himself a doctor, tell the story, have a cry, climb the wagon.

Start jogging. Eat organic. Take pills. Get right.

For the moment, he had a job to do. A blessedly concrete job, in drab, sensible England.

And if that job entailed going into a bar, he wasn't about to argue.

THE DOG'S NECK SHARED some of the Czech beer hall's decorative features. It did not, however, share its convivial vibe. A group of mouth-breathing layabouts watched a televised soccer match, their apathy thrown into high relief by the histrionics of the play-by-play man. A woman with teased hair mashed the smeared screen of a video poker machine. The air reeked of bleach and burnt cooking oil.

Jacob shook the water off his sleeves, sat at the bar, and ordered a pint of stout.

The bartender vacillated between several glasses before selecting one of average filth.

Jacob slid him a ten-pound note. "Keep it."

"Cheers."

He drank it quickly and ordered a second, again paying with a ten and telling the bartender to keep the change. The injection of alcohol diminished his road jitters but exposed a deeper, rawer current of anxiety. The clock above the bar read eleven a.m. Three a.m. in California. He was tempted to call his father. Ordinarily Sam wouldn't answer the phone on Shabbat, but the late hour might lead him to assume an emergency, justifying desecration of the holy day.

Jacob wasn't sure what he'd say.

You know that dead rabbi you admire so much?

Well, he's you.

By the way, before I forget: I'm being pursued by a beetle.

The bartender came to collect his empty glass.

"One more," Jacob said.

"Commin right oop."

It came right oop.

Jacob dropped a third ten and said, "I'm looking for someone."

The bartender grinned. He had enormous teeth. "Are you, now?"

"Edwyn Heap."

The grin disappeared.

"You know him?"

The bartender developed an interest in polishing a spot at the other end of the bar.

The soccer commentator was saying *I can't believe it, I simply can't.*

Jacob addressed the room. "Anyone?"

No one looked at him.

"I've got a twenty for whoever can tell me where Edwyn Heap is."

No answer.

"Thirty," he said.

The poker machine blooped a downward-spirally losing noise.

"Or his son," Jacob said. "Reggie."

One of the TV watchers told him to fuck off.

"Nice," Jacob said. "That's the way to welcome a tourist."

The man stood up, as did another, and they began making their way toward him.

A fantastic shot!

They were drunk and unshaven, badly but abundantly fed. The guy on the left wore a yellow Oxford United jersey; the guy on the right, a shabby crewneck.

They flanked him at the bar.

Jersey said, "So it's the Heaps you're wanting?"

"Yeah."

"And why's that?"

"I'm trying to get in touch with them," Jacob said.

"That's a bit of circular reasoning, that," Jersey said. "Wanting to see them because you want to get in touch with them."

The woman at the poker machine had upended her purse in search of money.

"I heard they lived around here."

"Did you?"

Jacob nodded.

"Hate to break it to you, mate, but you heard wrong. Ages since Reggie Heap's been seen in these parts."

"Ages," Crewneck confirmed.

Ooooooh, that's a vicious maneuver.

"What about his father?"

"He's not like to show his face."

"Why's that?"

"What's it you want with him, aside from to see him?"

"I want to talk to him."

"He'd be a friend of yours, then." Jersey spoke to the bartender. "Imagine that, Ray. Here's a friend of old Ed's."

"Imagine that," the bartender said.

"Imagine that, Vic."

"Can't," Crewneck said.

"I didn't know Ed had any friends left," Jersey said. "Reggie neither."

The remaining men had begun to approach the bar.

The woman at the machine tied on a rain bonnet, gathered her possessions, and exited.

"It's just a question," Jacob said.

"You got your answer, mate," Jersey said. "Shove off."

"I'm not finished with my beer," Jacob said.

Crewneck took Jacob's glass and handed it to the bartender, who diligently poured it out.

"You're finished," Jersey said.

Jacob eyed the three other men. They were the same as Jersey and Crewneck, except bigger and drunker. One of them actually had a streamer of drool resting on his chin.

"Can I get my change, please?" Jacob said to the bartender.

"What?" the bartender said.

"My change."

"You said to keep it."

"That was before you revoked my drink. Five'll do."

After a beat, the bartender put a wadded note on the bar and flicked it toward Jacob.

"Thanks," Jacob said. "Have a great day."

Jersey followed him to the door, stood there watching as he hustled through the downpour and climbed into his pathetic little rental car. He felt like a schmuck, doubly so as he stalled out. Finally he got the car in gear, driving half a block and glancing in the rearview.

A blue car was behind him.

He tried and failed to make out the driver, taking his eyes off the road long enough to nearly run down an old man in a plastic poncho, creeping along the muddy shoulder on a bicycle.

Jacob laid on as much speed as he dared, taking turns without signaling. At each, the blue car stayed behind. He tried to work the GPS on his phone but it was impossible to do while steering and shifting.

Fuck it, he thought, and pulled over.

The blue car followed suit.

The road he was on cut like piano wire through two vast muddy fields. A farmhouse on the horizon. An idle tractor. No people.

The driver of the blue car got out.

It was the poker-playing woman. Wind billowed her rain bonnet. She pinched it tight and hurried to Jacob's passenger-side window and began tapping.

"Open the bloody door."

He leaned over and pried up the lock.

She heaved herself into the passenger seat, flecking him with droplets. He smelled lipstick, tobacco, PVC.

"Some manners, leaving a lady in the rain."

"Can I help you?"

"No, but I can help you."

"Okay."

Her mouth twitched. "I'll have that forty first."

"It was thirty."

Fault lines appeared in her makeup as she smiled. "Inflation, what."

He gave her half. "The rest when you're done."

"Right," she said, tucking the money in her brassiere, "you're not like to make anyone happy, mentioning the Heaps."

"I noticed."

"Reggie, he kilt that girl."

Jacob said, "What girl?"

"They found her in the wood, back behind old Heap's."

"When was this?"

"Twenty-five years ago, like. Poor girl. Bloody awful. The animals had gotten to her."

"Reggie Heap murdered a girl," Jacob said.

"Hit her with a shovel. She worked for the family. Everyone knows. But old Ed's old Ed, and they never could prove nothing, so la-dee-da-dee. Danny, the bloke what was back at the pub, it was his cousin, Peg."

Twenty-five years ago was 1986, the year Reggie had won his drawing prize.

"Poor Mrs. Heap, her heart gave out. She was a nice lady. I don't think she could stand living with those two bad ones."

She gave him directions to Edwyn Heap's house, using landmarks rather than street names.

"Any suggestions on how to approach him?"

The woman was pleased at being consulted. "I've heard it said he likes toffee."

Jacob handed her another twenty. "Good luck at the table."

"No need, love," she said, tucking the money in her bra. "Britain's got talent."

CHAPTER FORTY

The decrepit fence surrounding the Heap estate told the story: land-rich, cash-poor. Jacob squeezed through a gap in the chain-link, carrying a package of Tesco brand toffee.

In the hour since the rain had let up, the pools in the pitted asphalt had been colonized by insects. If he hadn't known any better, he might've looked at the teeming life and thought it the product of spontaneous generation. He couldn't blame the ancients for making that assumption.

No beetles.

Still, he hurried up the driveway.

The door knocker came off in his hand. Jacob reinserted it on loose screws and circled around the house. Someone had carelessly left several upper-story windows open. Wet, ragged curtains ballooned and snapped in the wind.

Out back, he mounted a buckling terrace, surveying a wide, unkempt lawn, bounded by treeline.

He cupped his mouth and bellowed *hello*.

Silence.

He called again, received no answer, turned to knock on the French doors.

A clap and a whine and the concrete planter fifteen feet to his left cleaved in two.

The second shot removed the stump. Jacob had by then dropped behind the balustrade, balled up, his head between his knees, his arms around his shins.

A third shot shattered the planter to his right.

The gunfire was coming from the trees. Run and he'd be open season for the minute it would take to cover the lawn.

Option two was scrambling for the French doors. Kick in a panel, dive for safety. He'd cut himself. He'd probably still get shot. Obvious break and enter, no charges filed.

Frantically he keyed his phone. It loaded one agonizing byte at a time.

The fourth shot went wide, chunking the house's brick exterior.

The number for emergency services in the United Kingdom was 999. You could also use 112 or, charmingly, 911.

He dialed.

The voice that answered was American.

Two more shots; two more exploding bricks.

He tried the other emergency numbers, without success; either his phone beeped at him or he ended up speaking to someone in West Virginia. He added a 1, then a 1-1, a 0-1-1. Futile; he returned to Google.

He was going to die while incurring massive data roaming charges.

The shots stopped, replaced by the sound of boots on grass.

"You're trespassing."

Without moving, Jacob called, "I knocked."

"And therefore?"

Jacob dared to poke the box of candy over the balustrade. When his hand wasn't blown off at the wrist, he rose, showing his badge. "I'm sorry. Really."

The human bulldozer before him wore baggy flannel trousers. Seventyish, with snow-white streamers whipping from a sun-splotched scalp, he carried a string of hares slung over one shoulder, a hunting rifle propped on the other.

"Those were warning shots. Fifty yards. From this distance, I reckon I could shave you blindfolded."

"I'm sure you could, sir."

"So. Move along."

Feeling like the butler, Jacob opened the box and held it out.

"What is that? Is that toffee?" The man clomped up the steps and selected a piece, pink cheeks reddening as he chewed. He grunted and grimaced, as if he were having his teeth torn out and enjoying every moment of it.

He swallowed. "This is revolting," he said, reaching for another piece.

"Edwyn Heap?"

"Mm."

"Jacob Lev. I'm a detective with the Los Angeles Police Department."

"How marvelous for you."

"I'm here about your son, Reggie."

"A term best used loosely."

"Pardon?"

"I told Helen from the outset: I don't fancy squandering my life and treasure on a stranger's mistakes."

Jacob said, "He was adopted."

"Of course he bloody was. No natural son of mine would've turned out that way. What's he done in Los Angeles?"

Jacob noted the syntax: not *what's he doing* but *what's he done.* "I'm not sure."

"Rather a long way to come in a state of doubt."

"Was he in Prague last April?"

"Prague?"

"In the Czech Republic."

"I know where Prague is, you prat."

Heap swallowed wetly and plucked another piece of toffee, leaving seventeen in the box.

"Absolutely, perfectly revolting," he muttered.

Jacob had an idea that the conversation would last as long as the candy. "Do you know if he's been there?"

"I do not, nor do I care. He's a grown man, or so says the law. He may go where he pleases. Nor can I see what an American police officer's got to do with any of it."

Jacob glanced at the gun. Close enough that he could get to it if necessary, wrest it away. "I'm afraid I have some bad news. Prague police found a body that appears to be his."

Heap stopped chewing.

"I'm sorry," Jacob said.

Heap leaned against the balustrade, his eyes bulging as he gulped the half-chewed toffee.

The rifle clunked down, and he clutched his chest. Jacob reached for him, but Heap swatted his hand away, breathing savagely. "What happened."

"Are you okay, sir?"

"What happened."

Jacob said, "It's not entirely clear. It appears that he was murdered—"

"'Appears'? What the bloody hell's the matter with you? Murdered by whom?"

"We're still working on that—"

"Well *work on it*, you idiot. Don't stand there asking *me* questions."

"I'm so sorry to have to tell you this."

"I don't give a toss how sorry you are. I want to know what happened."

"It appears—"

Heap snatched up the gun and leveled it at Jacob's midsection. "You dare tell me one more time what it *appears* to be and I'll paint my house with your guts."

A beat.

Jacob said, "He tried to rape a woman."

Heap said nothing; nor did he react.

"She fought him off and fled the scene," Jacob said. "When the police returned to look for him, they found him dead. Murdered."

"How."

". . . how?"

"How was he murdered?"

"He was . . ." Jacob cleared his throat. "He was decapitated."

The rifle wavered in Heap's hands.

Jacob said, "I know it's hard."

Heap smiled sourly. "Do you have a son?"

"No, sir, I don't."

"Then you don't know what it's like to find out he's been murdered, do you?"

"No, sir."

"And, consequently, you don't have the faintest notion of how hard it is."

Jacob said, "None."

A silence.

"If you could show me a photo," Jacob said. "I need to confirm that it was him."

The gun swung loosely at Heap's side. He went in through the French doors. Jacob followed.

CHAPTER FORTY-ONE

I suppose you'll be wanting money for the funeral."

In the minutes it had taken Heap to stow his rifle and confiscate the remaining toffee, he had recovered his cool, along with his contempt.

"You won't be having it from me, I can assure you of that."

A burled walnut gun cabinet dominated the ground floor library. Discolored patches of flooring and wallpaper spoke of rolled-up rugs, bygone art. There was an aluminum frame cot, surplus woolen blanket, and tousled linens. Cans of baked beans and tinned asparagus were stacked, incongruously, atop a baroque demilune table. Between its carved feet sat an electric hot plate and a crusty frying pan.

Heap dropped the string of hares, their dead bodies reviving a giddy crop of dust bunnies.

He headed for the stairs. "Don't gawk."

Jacob had been wrong about the upper-story windows. They hadn't been left open. They'd been shot out, as had portions of the banister. The whole house, in fact, had been given over to target practice. Bullet holes pockmarked the walls and ceiling, ranging in size from small-caliber puncture wounds to catastrophic shotgun blasts that laid bare the plumbing. While the damage didn't follow a consistent pattern—some rooms were untouched, others hardly existed at all—the effort behind it spoke to a certain perverse dedication.

In a strange way, the place reminded him of Fred Pernath's house in Hancock Park. Both suggested the same hermetic impulse, the masculine will to power gone haywire, reveling in its inhospitality.

A house was a body; to kill it, pick your method. Fred Pernath had chosen strangulation, clogging out light and life, like a heart bursting with fat. Edwyn Heap, the inverse, a gradual erosion of the boundary between inside and out.

There was also the shared lack of family photos, although Jacob supposed that, in Heap's case, that could be construed as a kindness. Anything hung on the wall was subject to be being blown to smithereens.

"Did Reggie come home often?" he asked.

"Helen would let him stay when he was hard up," Heap said. He was wheezing as they climbed. "Once she died, I put my foot down."

"When was that?"

"Four years, September. The woman had a spine of gravy."

"Has he been back since?"

"Not long after the funeral he turned up looking for something to pinch and sell. I chased him off and that's the last time I laid eyes on him."

On the second floor, they came to a door so long shut that the paint around the frame had adhered to itself. Heap shouldered it open and it swung wide, wobbling on its hinges.

"The chamber of the little prince."

The little prince, who would've been in his mid-forties had he not died, had once been a boy, and Jacob felt a chill as he regarded an otherwise ordinary boy's room. Tight duvet, race-car pattern, as though the occupant had not progressed beyond age nine. Textbooks, gooseneck desk lamp, CD player–tape deck combo.

No DIY taxidermy.

No knife collection.

That there was nothing sinister about it made it somehow more sinister.

What had gone wrong?

When had it happened? How?

A handful of items hinted at maturity. A reclining female nude—poster for an Egon Schiele retrospective at the Tate—affixed to the walls with yellowing tape. A framed certificate from the Oxford Undergraduate Art Society, acknowledging Heap's first prize for his drawing titled *To Be Brasher.*

Edwyn Heap plucked a school photo off the desk.

"And the prince himself."

Aswim in a sea of starchy white and somber black, the young Reggie Heap had a hunted look, sweat flashing on his forehead, his eyes seeking an escape route.

"It was a mistake to send him up," Edwyn Heap said. "He didn't stand a chance." He tossed the photo on the desk. "Well. What do you intend to do about it?"

Jacob used his camera to take a picture of the picture. It came out blurry; he tried again. Better. "I was hoping you could give me a starting point. A last address, maybe."

"He didn't have one."

"He must've lived somewhere."

"Not to my knowledge. He went here, he went there."

"Was he employed?"

"Not respectably. Most often he went hand-to-mouth. My hand, his mouth. I believe he played office boy whenever the direness of his circumstances grew particularly pronounced. It's turned out just as I warned. He went up to read law. Not halfway through Hilary, he rang to announce his intention to change to fine art. It goes without saying that I forbade this caprice. 'We'll be underwriting him for the rest of our lives,' I told Helen, and so it has been. Ah, but you should have seen how she defended him. It was a splendid performance, tugging all the right strings. 'Teddy, he's lost.' 'Then let him get a bloody map,' I said. He rang again a week later, saying he had reconsidered; it was *history* of art he wanted to do—and Helen said, 'What a smashing idea, he can be a professor, it's very prestigious.' You see how they tricked me. I was made to consider it a compromise."

Heap shook his head. "I suppose they had plotted together all along. Bloody history of bloody art . . . Nor could he see that through to the end. Off it was, soon enough, to broaden his horizons. Exorbitant course fees, supplies. Six months in Spain, six in Rome. 'To what end?' 'He's in search of inspiration.' A hopeless Neanderthal, I was to them. But a bowl of fruit is a bowl of fruit whether in Paris or Berlin or New York."

"He was in New York?"

"Don't ask me. I don't bloody know. Timbuktu. I don't know."

"He did travel in the United States, though."

"I'm sure he did. If it cost money, he wanted to do it."

"He didn't tell you where he was going?"

"I long ago ceased to ask. Hearing about it gave me indigestion."

"When I mentioned that I was from Los Angeles, you said, 'What's he done there?'"

"Yes, all right."

"That's an interesting choice of words."

Instantly, Heap's guard was up. "Why."

"Has he been in trouble before? Run-ins with the law?"

"I can't say I know anything about that."

"The girl in Prague said he tried to rape her."

"Naturally she'd claim that, now that he's not around to prove other-wise."

Jacob said, "There was another girl, Peg. She worked for you."

"I've had too many employees to remember them by name."

"Some folks around here seem to think that Reggie was involved in her death."

"Only a fool believes everything he's told."

"That's a no, then."

"I don't reckon I like the way you're talking to me," Heap said. "You inform me my son has been murdered, and in the next breath you're regurgitating slander for which not a single shred of evidence has ever been produced."

Now he wanted to claim him as his son? "I apologize. I didn't mean to upset you."

"You upset me insofar as your willingness to accept the conjectures of imbeciles as fact demonstrates you to be easily misled. You said he was found in Prague. Why are you here? Why am I talking to an American? Was there nobody else available? Has it truly come to this?"

"Help set me straight," Jacob said.

"Pearls before swine," Heap said.

"You don't know where he was traveling."

"I told you, no."

"But he was traveling a lot."

"I suppose," Heap said.

"With what money?"

"Helen laid aside a sum for him to collect on the first of every month. Mind you, that didn't stop him from ringing me up on the fifteenth, groveling for more."

"Did the money go into his bank account?"

"I suppose."

"Which bank?"

"Barclay's. What business is it of yours?"

"I could contact them and find out where the withdrawals were made."

"Why are you so concerned with where he's been? You know where he was murdered. Go there."

"You mentioned a job—"

"I don't believe I did. As a matter of fact, I was quite clear that there was none."

"You said he played office boy."

"I refuse to dignify that as more than it was: a cheap stalling tactic."

"Be that as it may, I'd like to know who he worked for, and where."

"An architect," Heap said. "A former tutor of his at school."

"Name?"

"James, George, something royal. The selfsame worthless poofter who had years earlier convinced him to lay aside his studies and take up doodling."

"It was my impression that Reggie had some talent as an artist."

A glimmer of pride; it rapidly curdled. "So said my wife."

Jacob indicated the framed certificate. "At least a couple others must've agreed."

"Ah yes, achievement of a lifetime, as he'd have you believe. And never let her forget it, whenever he ran short of dosh."

"Do you have any of his work?"

"Connoisseur of the finer things, are we?"

"Humor me."

"That's all I've bloody done for the last half hour," Heap said. He nosed at the bed. "Under there."

Jacob knelt and drew out a pair of portfolio boxes, along with a bag of stubby charcoals, some fine-tipped artist's pens, a sketch pad.

He opened the first box on the bed.

Heavy, creamy paper carried ink beautifully, maintaining the surgical crispness of Reggie Heap's vision.

He could draw. No doubt about that. There were the aforementioned bowls of fruit; stark countryside landscapes. They had a mechanical quality, like photographic tracings.

"Hung them all over the house, she did," Heap said. "I took them down, I couldn't stand to look at them."

Most of the drawings were signed and dated; they had been thrown together without regard for chronology. Jacob saw work as recent as 2006 and as old as 1983.

"You kept them," he said.

"To get rid of them would have required effort."

"More effort than taking them down and putting them in boxes?"

"What's your damned point."

That you were prouder of him than you want to admit. Which is both endearing and disturbing. "Which one did he win the prize for?"

"None of these. The bloody Art Society kept it. Helen offered them a thousand pounds but they said it was the terms of the competition."

The art got more interesting with the second box, which contained nude studies and facial portraits. The women were arrestingly frenzied, Reggie's id outstripping his hand. Jacob could virtually hear the panting that had accompanied their creation.

By contrast, the men were controlled, heroic, formidable.

"Recognize any of these people?" Jacob said. "Anyone I could talk to?"

"I presume they were his friends."

"From?"

"I don't bloody know. Doodlers. Reprobates."

"Did he mention anyone by name?"

"If he had, I would have labored to forget them."

"Girlfriends?"

Heap snorted.

"I ask because I'm trying to find out what kind of people he was associating with."

"Not the kind who'd kill him," Heap said.

You'd be surprised.

Two-thirds of the way through, Jacob stopped and flipped back several pages.

He'd nearly missed it.

He wasn't paying attention. He was thinking about the nudes and what they said about Reggie's relationship to women.

He was thinking about his own father's visage in clay, his mother's hands working.

The intervening years had also done their part: the drawing was dated December 1986.

He was trying to avoid concocting imaginary connections. Above all, he was trying to stay clearheaded and do his job.

Yes. The job.

And here was the payoff.

Jacob flipped slowly to the next page. There it was again. And again. What he had mistaken for a careless mark repeated itself on five consecutive pages—a scar on the chin.

Five angles.

The same man.

Mr. Head.

Through static, he heard Heap say, "That's one of them."

"Who."

"The doodlers. He came to stay a Christmas. Helen's idea."

"Who is he?"

"A school friend. Buggered if I can remember his name."

Jacob said, "Can I borrow these?"

Heap stared at him. "He's the one that you're after."

"I don't know," Jacob said. "But it'd be helpful if I could find out."

Heap snatched up a few of the drawings, flung them at Jacob. "The rest of them you can put back where you found." He turned to go. "Ten minutes. Then off with you, or I'll summon the police and have you arrested for trespassing."

Jacob carefully rolled up the drawings of Mr. Head, securing them with a rubber band he found in the desk. He cleared the rest of the mess off the bed, then poked his head into the hallway.

Hearing movement from a lower floor, he hurried to search the bureau, looking for old socks or underwear, anything that might cough up a piece of DNA.

Zip.

Downstairs, a gigantic boom, followed by crumbling plaster.

Exit music.

CHAPTER FORTY-TWO

He arrived in Oxford too late for anything but a chip shop dinner. Outside, roving packs of townies warbled football anthems and amiably chucked bottles at undergraduates.

The Black Swan hostel had no private rooms. Jacob opted to share a triple, taking care not to wake his roommates, a pair of backpackers, asleep with their arms around their bags, proxy lovers made of ripstop nylon.

He stashed his own bag under his bed, removing first his passport and the drawings of Mr. Head.

Downstairs in the common room, smelly, dented beanbag chairs surrounded an abandoned game of Scrabble. A German neo-hippie covered "Touch of Grey" on a pawnshop guitar while his inamorata attempted to retighten her electric-blue cornrows, a hand mirror clamped between her knees.

In an act of divine benevolence, the front desk adjoined a fully stocked bar.

Armed with his seventh pint of the day and an Internet passcode, Jacob swung by the wire rack to take a street map, then sat down at the computer kiosk.

There were fewer than a dozen local architects. Of those, four were women. Of the men, two had vaguely kingly names: Charles Mac-Ildowney and John Russell Nance. He clicked on Nance's CV first, assuming *John* was more readily confused with *James*. But it was Mac-Ildowney—BArch (Manc.), DPhil (Oxon.), RIBA—who had lectured in the history of architecture at Oxford. Jacob marked the location of his office on the map.

The song ended.

Jacob applauded.

The hippie smiled drowsily and raised a V.

After mapping a few more stops, Jacob set aside the mouse pad and spread out the drawings.

Mr. Head, in the prime of life. A fellow artist. A fellow traveler.

Meeting Reggie Heap.

Discovering a common interest.

Really. You don't say.

Okay, okay, but:

Tell me:

Rape.

Front?

Back?

Which do you prefer?

Back?

Really.

How convenient.

Because it just so happens that I am, one hundred percent, a front man.

Heap and Head!

World's worst buddy sitcom. He could picture the logo, the *p* and *d* spinning, a delirious visual pun.

The timeline fit. Reggie, born in 1966, would've graduated in 1987 or 1988.

What brought a pair of Englishmen to L.A.?

Had they been all around this great big world and seen all kinds of girls?

Did they wish they all could be California girls?

Or: Mr. Head wasn't English. A visiting student; an exchange program.

Cream of our crop in return for yours. Reinforce the Special Relationship.

Inviting Reggie back to the States to continue their collaboration.

You're gonna love the weather.

Reggie, appealing to his generous mother for a graduation present.

There's this amazing program . . .

The unique synergy of two lesser malignancies—each man validating and goading the other, twisting him into something exponentially worse.

The Lennon and McCartney of evil.

The long hiatus—what accounted for it? Jacob could not connect either man, either directly or implicitly, to any crimes between 1988 and 2005, when Dani Forrester bled out in her overfinanced condo.

And there was a wider world to wonder about. What mischief had Heap the Younger wrought while out broadening his horizons?

What about New York? Miami? New Orleans?

How long had they been at it?

Like artists, psychopaths were temperamental.

Collaborations of either kind rarely lasted a lifetime or spanned the globe.

Heap and Head could've started out as partners before venturing into side projects.

Side projects that had blossomed into full-fledged solo careers?

Then: once a year, a hop across the pond, get the band back together?

Heap and Head: the U.S. Reunion Tour!

The Las Vegas Strip . . . Bourbon Street . . .

And coming soon to a ground-floor apartment near you!

He shuddered to think of the shower of red tape triggered by requesting a copy of Reggie's passport.

It felt wonderful to have facts, however few, at his disposal. He quashed his excitement, as concerned with controlling the fluctuations in his mood as he was with making a mistake.

Let's not get a Head of ourselves, mmmmmmmm?

Even if he did definitively ID H&H as the Creeper, that still left open the question of who'd killed them. They couldn't very well have decapitated each other, separated by twelve months and six thousand miles.

Psychopath vs. Psychopath was out.

Vengeful party looking better by the minute.

But: how did VP know?

How did he (she) find them?

Whose voice on the tape?

How did it fit with Special Projects?

It was 2:13 a.m. The hippies had passed out and were sawing wood. Jacob went upstairs. For the first time in a long time, his dreams were in full color.

CHAPTER FORTY-THREE

With a decent night's sleep under his belt, he had gained some mental traction. In the hostel's cafeteria he loaded up a tray with meats 'n' grease and sequestered himself at the end of the communal table, away from a gaggle of Canadians chirping over their idealized itinerary: punting on the Thames, followed by lunch at an authentic pub, Blackwell's Literary Walking Tour, a visit to the Bodleian . . .

Jacob's own itinerary was themed Rational Cop. First stop: the Thames Valley Police's St. Aldates station.

He meandered along the river path under the caress of willow trees. Waterfowl busy in the marsh grass rose up at his approach to demand bread in shrill addict's tones. He spotted a narrow red streak across gray water: a boat, eight oarsmen, a coxswain politely urging them toward the bridge.

The station was decidedly inconspicuous, three tan stories that played down the possibility of crime in a town so picturesque. If not for a modest white sign and two glass cases containing bulletin boards with information about community watch, he could have been walking into the registrar's office.

The constable on duty jotted down Jacob's badge number and led him to a cheerless conference room.

In five minutes, he'd finished his tea; after twenty, he stood up to wait in the hallway. He assumed the locals were establishing his bona fides with LAPD. He could speed up the process by giving them a direct number.

Mallick? Or his ex-boss at Traffic, Captain Chen?

Who was less likely to make Jacob sound like an imposter?

He hadn't yet decided when a woman with a pert blond bob appeared.

"Good morning, Detective. Inspector Norton."

"Good morning. Everything check out?"

A flicker of a smile. "To what do we owe the privilege of your visit?"

He showed her the photos he'd taken of young Reggie Heap; showed her the drawing of Mr. Head; told her, in general terms, what he wanted: local homicides, unsolved, 1983ish to 1988. Bonus points if they fit the Creeper MO.

"It doesn't have to match up in every respect. The method could have evolved."

"That's well before my time, sir."

"Of course," he said. "You're far, far too young to have firsthand knowledge."

"Of course I am. In 1983, I was a mere child."

"I can't imagine you were even born then."

"It's possible I was. Not much before, of course."

"Of course not. Might there be someone else? A wise elder?"

She said, "Let's try Branch."

Branch was about fifty, with a shaven scalp and a toothbrush mustache. He recognized neither the drawing nor the name Reggie Heap.

"He was a student," Jacob said.

"Those days, the university had their own force," Branch said. "The Bulldogs."

"Not anymore?"

"They were disbanded for budgetary reasons," Norton said. "Ten years ago, roughly."

"Any of them still around?"

"Sure," Branch said. "Good luck getting em to talk to you."

"What you'd expect," Norton said, "given the university's standing as an incubator of only the nation's finest young men and women."

Jacob said, "I'd expect a tendency to keep problems in-house."

"You'd expect correctly, sir."

"Still, is there someone you could contact on my behalf?"

Branch shook his head. "Won't matter."

"What you'd expect in a locality such as ours," Norton said, "notorious for its lengthy history of town-gown conflict."

"Departmental bad blood," Jacob said.

"Once again, Detective, your expectations prove exceedingly reasonable."

"I'll put my brain to it," Branch said. "Whatever that's worth."

That sounded like lip service, but Jacob thanked him anyway.

Norton accompanied him to the street.

"Sorry we couldn't be more helpful."

"Not a problem."

"Shame," she said. "I'd have thought Branch would be more enthusiastic. It's not every day we get someone dropping round about a murder." She paused. "Though I will say, we're quite good at breaking up raves."

He smiled.

She said, "May I ask how you plan to proceed?"

"Identify the architect. Go to his college. Maybe someone remembers him."

"And if that line of inquiry fails to bear fruit?"

"There's always punting on the Thames," he said. "Inspector Norton?"

"Yes, Detective Lev?"

"I expect that you, with local policing authority, would command more respect than I would, and furthermore, since I don't see any raves in progress, I expect that you might be interested in accompanying me on my rounds, after which I expect that you'd enjoy lunch, gratis, courtesy of LAPD."

She hooked her hair behind her ears. "Detective Lev, your expectations grow more lofty by the moment."

"Inspector Norton, that's the American way."

IT WAS A BRIEF STROLL down St. Aldates to Christ Church. Spring rain had brought a lively resurgence of the meadows. At mid-morning, the joggers were mostly gone and the picnickers not yet arrived.

Norton's first name was Priscilla. She asked where he was staying.

"YHA, near the train station."

"How delightful."

"Don't knock it. Fifteen pounds includes a full English breakfast."

"Good God, what a nightmare."

Nearing the entrance at Tom Tower, he observed that not much had changed since his college days: a girl with a smeary face hobbled out in men's sweatpants, a large Kaiser Chiefs T-shirt, and perilously high heels, a gauzy black dress slung over her head to shield her eyes from the sun.

The college's imposing sandstone walls evoked a fortress. Jacob felt like a marauding barbarian, come to breach the ivory tower and put its inhabitants to the torch, more so as they approached the gate, patrolled by a gin blossom in a bowler hat and a dark coat. His name tag identified him as J. Smiley, Porter, Christ Church.

"Hello, Jimmy," Norton said. "All right?"

"Hallo, Pippi. My lucky day. What brings you by?"

"Touch o' local color for my American friend," she said.

Smiley stiffened as Jacob described what he was after.

"Regular visiting hours start at one," the porter said.

"Be nice, Jimmy," Norton said.

The porter sighed.

"There's a good lad," she said.

He waved at her in annoyance and picked up an extension.

"Like magic," Jacob said.

She shrugged. "A little leg goes a long way."

The dark tunnel of the gate framed emerald lawns, a leaping fountain daring the onlooker to dash forward in defiance of the signs: KEEP OFF THE GRASS.

"They like their privacy," Jacob said.

"In-group, out-group."

"And you, doing your part to repair the rift."

"Heal the world," Norton said.

Jimmy Smiley hung up. "Mr. Mitchell's on his way."

"Cheers," Norton said.

Deputy Head Porter Graeham Mitchell bore Jacob's spiel with a tolerant smile. "Is this an official police enquiry, Inspector?"

"Not as such."

"Then I'm afraid I can recommend no course other than to return at one o'clock. There is a guided tour which most people find highly informative."

Jacob said, "I was hoping to speak with people who would've been around then."

"You are welcome to register your request, in writing, with the steward."

"Any chance you might remember him?" Norton said. "What was it again, Detective?"

"Reggie Heap," Jacob said. He displayed the photo. "His father, Edwyn Heap."

"My sincerest apologies," Mitchell said, "but I cannot recall anyone by that name."

"If you could take a look at—"

"I regret that I cannot be of further assistance, sir."

"What about this one," Jacob said, starting to unroll the drawing of Head.

"I hope you'll excuse me? The sermon will have begun. Best of luck to you both." Mitchell marched off, his shoes tapping on the cobblestones.

Norton turned to Smiley. "Thanks anyway, Jim."

The porter, writing in the logbook, tore off a corner of a page and handed it to her. Norton put it in her pocket. "Ta," she said.

The porter touched his hat, clasped his hands behind his back, and resumed his pacing.

Jacob waited until they had gone ten yards to ask, "What was that about?"

Norton showed him the scrap of paper. On it Smiley had scrawled *Friar & Maiden 20:00.*

CHAPTER FORTY-FOUR

Charles MacIldowney's address belonged to a converted row house opposite the river.

The shingle warned that the architect was available Tuesday through Friday, by appointment only; a handwritten note, taped and fluttering in the breeze, instructed deliverymen to ring next door, at number 15.

They did, and an elegant, aquiline man answered. He was around Edwyn Heap's age, but tan and trim in chinos and a blue twill button-down.

He said, "Please bring it—oh, sorry. I was expecting someone else."

Norton badged him. "Charles MacIldowney?"

"Yes?"

"May we come in, sir?"

"Is something wrong?"

"Not at all, sir. A few questions."

"It's not the best time."

Jacob said, "We'll be brief."

MacIldowney started at Jacob's accent. He ran his fingers through his coiffure, once and then again. "Yes, all right, please."

A blizzard of pastels softened the living area's industrial character, tubular steel and vaulted ceilings and exposed ducting. MacIldowney apologized for the mess, shifted straw baskets and packages of tissue paper to allow them to sit.

"We're hosting our annual garden party this afternoon. I thought you were the florist."

A voice from above said, "Charles? Is that them? Are they here?"

"Not yet."

"Who are you talking to?"

"Nobody."

A man two decades MacIldowney's junior appeared barefoot at the top of the floating staircase. "It doesn't look like nobody to me."

He came down. "I'm Des," he said.

Norton introduced them, and Jacob explained the purpose of their visit. Both men reacted to news of the murder with genuine shock.

"I'm sorry to break it to you like this. Were you close?"

"Close?" MacIldowney said. "Not—I mean, I don't think so. I never knew Reggie to be close with—I suppose—well, he was—"

"An odd duck," Des said.

"Without question, but—to be honest, I don't know what I'm saying. This is awful, just . . . awful."

A silence.

"Can I offer anyone some tea?" Des said.

"I'd love that," Jacob said.

"No, thanks," Norton said.

Des clapped his hands and strode off to the kitchen, separated by twenty feet of bleached flooring and a stainless-steel peninsula.

"Would you prefer privacy?" MacIldowney asked. "We can go to my office."

"It's all right," Jacob said. "You both knew him?"

Des, filling a speed kettle, nodded.

"He worked for us on occasion," MacIldowney said. "Though I haven't seen him in some time."

"At least a year, I reckon," Des said.

"His father said you were his tutor at one point," Jacob said.

"You spoke to his father?"

Jacob nodded.

"Is he—I mean, does he know . . ."

"He knows."

"Well—yes. Obviously he would. I apologize. It's all rather—I've never known anyone—it's a dreadful . . . yes. I was Reggie's tutor. Years ago."

"What was he like in those days?" Jacob asked.

"Painfully shy. He hardly spoke to anyone. I have—well, it's going to sound callous, out of context, but—I have a distinct memory of thinking he resembled a turtle." MacIldowney paused. "Is that horrible? I'm sorry. He had this coat he wore every day, regardless of the weather. I don't think I ever saw him out of it, I reckon it could've stood up on its own. It was this hideous murky color, and he would sort of shrink back into the collar, like so . . . It gave one the impression that he was short, although I don't believe he was, or no more than average."

"Edwyn Heap told me he was supposed to study law, but you convinced him to change."

"Well, that's—thank you," MacIldowney said, accepting a cup from Des, who set down a tray with more cups, sugar, and a plate of digestives.

"Thanks," Jacob said, adding three lumps in an effort to pacify his stomach. His full English breakfast had morphed into a bellowing South American revolutionary. "He—Edwyn—he seemed pretty angry about it."

"I'm sorry for him, I am, but that's simply untrue. Reggie had decided to change courses well before I met him. The university doesn't have a program devoted to practical architecture, per se. I came for my doctorate, after which I lectured in history of design for a brief period. I might've attempted to bolster his confidence, but I never told him to *do* anything. He was quite . . . needy, I suppose, is the right word. He would bring these massive batches of drawings up to me and thrust them in my face. The moment I showed the slightest approval he cottoned on to me and began asking for help transferring into Ruskin."

"The drawing school," Des said.

MacIldowney nodded. "Apparently he had applied there once already and they'd turned him down. He wanted me to throw my weight around."

"Did you?"

"I had none to throw. But when I tried to explain that to him, he got extremely cross."

"And then?"

"I left to open my practice, and he drifted out of my life. I didn't see him for fifteen years or so."

"He turned up on our doorstep, begging for a job," Des said.

"He wasn't *begging*, Desmond."

"You must've been surprised," Norton said.

"Oh, I was astonished," MacIldowney said. "I only just caught myself before shutting the door in his face. I didn't recognize him—it'd been so long, and he'd lost the coat. Nor did he say hello, introduce himself, ask how I'd been. He said, 'I need a job,' as though I would hand him the keys straightaway."

"Fifteen years is a long time to be out of touch and think that," Jacob said.

"Yes, well," MacIldowney said, blowing on his tea, "I gathered from the way he talked that he was hard up."

"Did he say what he'd done in the meantime?"

"He had a portfolio with him, so I suppose he must have taken some courses or worked elsewhere."

"His father described him as an office boy."

"That's rather uncharitable. He was quite a capable draftsman, especially with pen and ink. I never would have hired him otherwise."

"We can't run a business based on pity," Des said, "though Charles makes every effort to do so."

"Nowadays everyone uses computers," MacIldowney said. "We're no different. But I often prefer to work by hand, as I was taught, and it gratified me to meet a like mind."

"He was an odd duck," Des said.

"I'm not going to dispute that he had . . . tendencies."

"The house connects to the office via the second floor," Des said. "I used to come down to the kitchen for a drink of water at midnight and hear him in there, listening to the radio while he worked."

"He got his assignments done on time," MacIldowney said.

"You can't deny it's out of order, Charles."

"Did he get along with people?" Jacob asked.

"Well, that was the crux of it," MacIldowney said. "I always thought that his reason for keeping late hours was to avoid interacting with the rest of the staff, which he couldn't have done at a larger firm. Aside from Des and me, we employ two architects and an office manager. Reggie would turn up to lend a hand for a few months, around Christmastime. Under any other circumstances I would have insisted on a more stable arrangement, but it so happened he fit the bill precisely. It helped to have someone picking up the slack for the rest of us."

Des said, "Tell the truth, darling. You felt bad for him."

"I suppose I did. I couldn't help it. I looked at him and saw the same confused little boy."

"He wasn't a boy when you knew him," Norton said.

"Yes, but he had a certain quality to him," MacIldowney said.

"You liked him," Jacob said.

"I didn't like him or dislike him," MacIldowney said. "I thought, 'Well, this is what fate has ordained.' He showed up in my life again and it seemed wrong to disregard that."

"What about when he wasn't with you? What kind of company did he keep?"

"I haven't the faintest idea."

"Relationships?"

"He was guarded about his personal affairs. I recall something about traveling for continuing education."

"Did he say where?"

MacIldowney shook his head.

"That didn't strike you as strange?" Jacob asked. "He works a few months max, but he's pursuing continuing education?"

"Odd duck," Des said.

"None of us is without his foibles," MacIldowney said. "And no, it's not strange. It can take eons to become certified, and if you're attempting to do it part-time, all the longer."

"You let him stay," Des said.

"Here?" Norton said.

MacIldowney hesitated. "He had no place else to go."

"It was like having a giant lizard in the house," Des said.

"Stop it," MacIldowney said.

Jacob said, "How long was he here?"

"Not long, perhaps—"

"Ten weeks," Des said.

"It wasn't that long."

"I assure you it was. I counted every day."

"Did he leave clothes?" Jacob asked.

"He lived out of a suitcase," MacIldowney said. "It was temporary."

"Allegedly," Des said.

MacIldowney shook his head. "I asked you to stop, please."

The architect's voice had begun to hitch, the burgeoning intuition that he had picked the wrong horse. Jacob unrolled the drawings. "Any idea who this is?"

Des shook his head. MacIldowney studied the page at greater length, but appeared equally at a loss.

"Is he—that's not the person who, who harmed him?"

"I don't know. I found it in a bunch of Reggie's old drawings. It's dated around the time you knew him. I thought possibly a friend."

"I don't remember him having very many friends," MacIldowney said.

"He wasn't what you'd call a social butterfly," Des said.

"Come to think of it," MacIldowney said, "there was this one fellow, about the only person I remember ever seeing him in the company of. What was his . . ." He picked up the drawing. "I—no. I mean . . . I don't think it's the same person."

He frowned. "No. But—well, no, I don't think it is, though." He paused. "This fellow, Reggie's friend—he was American. What was he called? Perry? Bernie? Something like that."

"Not the person in the drawing."

"I'm fairly certain it's not. What was his name." MacIldowney began raking his scalp.

Des put a hand on MacIldowney's back. "It's all right, Charles. It's been thirty years."

Jacob said, "Do you remember where in America he was from?"

MacIldowney shook his head.

"But you remember that he was American."

"Well, I saw them around together—it's a small town, you know—and I have this idea that I bumped into them in a . . . restaurant, or—no. It was at the library."

"Which library?"

"The Bod, I reckon. I suppose I must have exchanged pleasantries with them. I wish to God I could remember his name. I'm sorry. I'm so sorry. Is it important?"

"Not necessarily," Jacob said.

At his side, Norton nodded faintly, appreciative of the courtesy.

"I'll tell you what I do remember: this other chap was quite good-looking. He and Reggie made a rather curious pair."

"Reggie wasn't one for the ladies," Norton said.

"No, but—I mean, he might have had a friend, I suppose. As I said, I saw very little of him after that first year."

Jacob said, "Let me ask you something else. Was Reggie ever in any sort of trouble?"

"Trouble?"

"Legally," Norton said.

"Not that I know of," MacIldowney said.

"Has he done something wrong?" Des asked.

Norton and Jacob looked at him.

Des shrugged. "I don't otherwise reckon you'd be telling us he's murdered and showing us pictures and asking questions about him being in trouble with the law."

A silence.

"Before he was killed, he tried to rape a woman," Jacob said.

He watched then as MacIldowney's composure began to flake away; the architect tilted his head back as if to keep bits of it from getting into his eyes. "My God," he said.

"You sound surprised," Norton said.

"Well, wouldn't you be?"

"It depends," Norton said. "Some people, when you find out they've done something horrid, it's no surprise at all."

"I never knew him to be involved with anything like . . . that."

"Do I get an opinion?" Des asked.

"Sure," Norton said.

"I wouldn't think it impossible."

MacIldowney made a sharply irritated noise. "It's one thing to resent him because he was a bad houseguest. Quite another to accuse him of rape."

"I didn't accuse him of anything. I said it wouldn't be beyond imagining."

The doorbell rang.

"That'll be the florist," Des said. "Excuse me."

MacIldowney said, "He really did that?"

"Afraid so," said Jacob.

There was a silence.

At the door, Des was saying, "We asked for orchids. Those are calla lilies."

"If you remember anything else," Jacob said, writing down his number, "you'll be sure to contact me."

MacIldowney nodded. "Certainly."

"Or if you think of someone who might know. I can send you a copy of the drawings. Maybe it'll come back to you."

"They are not *remotely* similar," Des said.

MacIldowney said, "You don't suppose there's anything I could have done differently?"

Jacob shook his head. "Not a thing. Don't waste time worrying about it."

"Charles. My love. Do you mind."

MacIldowney rose. He looked frailer than when he had greeted them. He smiled queasily.

"Well," he said. "Party time."

THEY'D GONE HALF A BLOCK when they heard Des calling for them to wait.

"Sorry," he said, jogging up. "I was dealing with idiots."

"What's up?" Jacob asked.

"I thought of something," Des said. "It slipped my mind before. When Reggie stayed with us, it began with him ringing us from the train station, asking us to come collect him. He'd just returned from Edinburgh and he'd had an accident."

"What sort of accident?" Norton asked.

"He said a motorcyclist ran over his foot. He was limping and bloody. I told Charles, 'Don't bring him here, take him to hospital,' which I think you'll agree is the logical response, but Reggie was adamant about not wanting to go. He spent the whole night moaning like a zombie. It was three or four days before he would agree to see a doctor. Charles went with him, and on the way back, they went shopping for a new pair of shoes for when the cast came off. I was furious."

"I don't blame you," Jacob said.

"I wanted him out immediately, but Charles said we couldn't put him out on the street. Anyway, after he'd finally gone, I went down to the cellar—I drew the line at his sleeping upstairs—I went down there to clean up, and I saw the old pair of shoes. I think he tried to scrub the blood out, but it didn't work, so he left them behind. I intended to chuck them, but I couldn't bring myself to touch them. As far as I know, they're still there."

An arriving caravan of rental chairs blockaded the front walk. Des led them around to the side of the house via a brick path lined with peonies. Though MacIldowney was out of view, his voice could be heard, cajoling the florist.

Stone steps led down to the cellar, a space as crowded as the house was spare—though Jacob noted that his threshold for clutter had been raised considerably in Prague. Here they met the relatively benign resistance of wine racks and plastic storage bins. A shelf above the basin sink displayed bright bottles containing an array of poisons, from lye to metal polish.

"I kicked them," Des said.

They looked at him.

"The shoes. I know it's childish, but I was so cross."

"Where'd they land?" Norton asked.

Des waved vaguely. "Thereabouts."

Jacob found them behind the furnace. Crepe-soled loafers, brown suede uppers furred with dust, the right one mottled with stains one shade darker. Norton spitted each on a pen while Des rooted around for a spare bag.

"Can I ask you something without offending you?" Jacob said. "I'd be remiss if I didn't."

"I'm not easily offended," Des said, "but you're welcome to try."

"Was there anything between them, ever?"

"Charles and . . . Reggie?" Des laughed. "No. I asked Charles myself. Reggie wasn't the comeliest lad, but Charles took such an interest in him, and I wanted to know before I let him in our home. Anyway, Charles swore nothing had ever happened. He's a hopeless liar, so I tend to believe that's the truth."

He came up with a plastic shopping bag from Boots.

"Fitting," he said, holding it open for Norton. As she placed the shoes inside, he wrinkled his nose at the blood. "You don't reckon it's someone else's, do you?"

CHAPTER FORTY-FIVE

One wonders," Norton said, dabbing soup from her lips, "how a personality as sterling as Reggie's was lost on a man of MacIldowney's intelligence."

"I don't think intelligence has anything to do with it."

"It so rarely does."

"You think he was being honest about not recognizing Mr. Head?"

"Des said he's a bad liar. They appeared candid enough."

"I agree. Too bad he didn't recognize my guy."

"Cheer up. He gave you a name: Perry-Bernie."

"That's a third guy."

"The mysterious American." Her smile made a sweet little bulge under her chin. Her eyes were blue, on the cusp of purple—what the crayon makers called *cornflower*.

"How about this," he said. "Mr. Head and Reggie travel to L.A. For whatever reason."

"Sunshine and self-reinvention," Norton said. "Or Perry-Bernie invites them."

He nodded. "They do their thing. Twenty-month reign of terror, then the band breaks up, and Reggie, at least, leaves town. Mr. Head decides he likes it in L.A., and stays. That accounts for the fact that someone, the same person, takes them both out: Perry-Bernie."

"You're pinning a lot on this fellow," she said. "For all we know he's simply another Charles MacIldowney, a nice chap trying to help out the hapless Reggie Heap."

He brooded, stirring his cold peanut noodles. He had no appetite; he felt like he could go without food for several days, and he was anxious to get back to work. He was also dimly aware of Norton watching him curiously. It wasn't right, the way he felt.

She said, "Do you want to go somewhere else? Aren't you hungry?"

"I'm okay."

"Of the three bites taken of your lunch, all have been taken by me. Can I offer you some tom yum? It's gorgeous."

"No, thanks. I don't like cilantro. It tastes like soap to me. Lemongrass, either."

"Who doesn't like lemongrass?"

"Be a lemon," Jacob said. "Be grass. Choose."

"If you don't like lemongrass, and you don't like cilantro, then why are we having Thai?"

"You wanted it."

"Gallant of you."

He raised his beer to her.

She said, "There can't have been that many Americans enrolled in a given year. You could check with Student Records. Although they won't be open today."

"What about a yearbook?" Jacob said. "They have those?"

"I'm sure they do, or something like it. I can ask Jimmy."

"What's the deal with him?"

"Friend of my father's. I've known him since I was a girl."

"You grew up around here."

She nodded.

"What's that like?"

"Loads of fun. Get pissed and beat up students. Huzzah."

Jacob smiled. "Was your dad a cop?"

"Schoolteacher," she said. "He taught Latin. A real grammarian, you know, the kind who's singing along to the radio and Eric Clapton comes on, and he starts to yell, '*Lie* down Sally, *lie* down.' My mother would say, 'That's all very well and good, John, but can we state with certainty that he's not in fact pleading with her to smother him in goose feathers?' And he would say, 'Well, Emmaline, that's hardly the point,' and she would say, 'Indeed,' and then she would turn the volume up." She smiled. "There you have it, my childhood in a nutshell. You?"

Her pleasant memories brought home what he hadn't been privileged to know.

"Los Angeles. Born and raised. My mom's dead. She was an artist. My dad's a rabbi, although he wouldn't call himself that."

"Ooh, that's a rather fancy pedigree."

For a moment he came close to spilling everything to her. She was the first normal person he'd spoken to in weeks. In her presence, he'd managed to focus. She was smart and pretty and she wasn't tall.

She was sitting back, happy to listen.

He said, "I was taught from an early age to chase the money."

"Joke if you must, but we don't get a travel stipend."

"My boss is good at twisting arms."

"Is there a special fund for wooing the local constabulary?"

He raised his beer again. "To international relations."

THEY RETURNED TO HER OFFICE to use the computer.

According to its website, the Oxford Undergraduate Art Society served those students not majoring in fine art but who wished nonetheless for opportunities to exhibit their work.

Jacob read between the lines: art school being the cliquey affair that it was, the club functioned as a cocoon within the larger cocoon of the university, a venue for second-string aesthetes to gather and feel a sense of belonging.

"Heap's father told me Reggie wanted to transfer to fine art, then backed off."

"He couldn't hack it," Norton said.

"I saw his stuff. He could draw."

"I was under the impression that that was no longer relevant to obtaining an art degree."

He laughed. "Either way, the club would be the wrong place for someone with serious artistic aspirations. Maybe Reggie was hanging out there for social reasons. Do they have a roster of past members?"

She scrolled down. "Not online."

"A headquarters?"

"They meet once a month in the Christ Church junior common room."

"When's the next meeting?"

"Three weeks."

"Shit."

"Hang on, though, there's an archive of past competition winners in the Bod. Should we have a look?"

THE GUARD AT THE ENTRANCE to the Bodleian's main stacks referred them to the admissions office in the Clarendon Building. There, a clerk made photocopies of Norton's badge, along with Jacob's passport.

"Fill these out, please."

Please tell us why you need to use our resources.

Norton said, "Oooh, let me."

She wrote *To solve a murder.*

Jacob sighed and asked for another form, writing *Dissertation research.*

"You're deadly boring, you know that?"

Ninety minutes and three bureaucrats later, they stepped out of an ancient elevator, a temporary access card and a call number tucked in Jacob's shirt pocket.

Since the award categories included sculpture and painting, they expected a storage room or a cage and crates. Instead they found themselves crabbing down a tight aisle, matching the call number to four oversized archival albums.

They carried them to an abandoned carrel and squeezed in, shoulders touching. Norton wasn't wearing perfume, but the aroma of soap and water was pleasant at close range.

Oxford Undergraduate Art Society
Awardees, 1974–1984

Polaroids tucked into cloudy plastic sleeves featured the winning entries in each category. Most were unlovely in the extreme. A turgid statement of purpose accompanied each.

"Edwyn Heap said Reggie had to forfeit his piece," Jacob said. "No one else seems to have."

"Maybe he lied. He's got it hidden away somewhere."

"He showed me Reggie's other drawings. Why would he care if I saw that one?"

He shut the first album and opened the second, *Awardees 1985–1995*, flipping ahead to the 1986 competition.

"That's why," Norton said.

To Be Brasher was a female nude. That wasn't remarkable in itself. Jacob knew from examining the portfolio boxes at the Heap house that Reggie had drawn his fair share of nudes. Every artist did. There was a long and proud tradition of becoming an artist simply for the excuse.

Every artist had his favorite body part. Reggie's were breasts: heavy, and detailed, every crease and birthmark lovingly rendered. No alarm bells, there. Breasts symbolized motherhood, nourishment, comfort.

She was spread-eagled. But the Schiele poster in Reggie's boyhood room showed a woman similarly posed and that was considered a masterpiece. Jacob wondered if in fact Reggie had been making reference to that image.

Whereas Schiele's hand was erratic and jagged, Reggie's was direct to the point of being clinical. An abundance of ornamentation was rendered in strong, swooping lines, a marked contrast with his previous nudes. The Reggie Heap who had drawn *To Be Brasher* was a realist, masquerading as a sensualist.

Here, he had found his muse.

Sinuously curved, the woman lay among undulant vines. They twined her limbs, bound her wrists and ankles. A draftsman more technically skilled or more imaginative might've left room for interpretive ambiguity. Reggie was both accurate and limited: he knew just what he wanted to draw, and he'd drawn it.

His muse was headless.

Energy radiated from her open neck, wavy lines that fanned out toward a rising sun.

They stared at the drawing for a long time. Finally, Jacob turned the page over, revealing Reggie's artistic statement of purpose.

To examine the causes of life, we must first have recourse to death.

CHAPTER FORTY-SIX

Norton's phone broke the silence.

"It's Branch," she said. "He's going to have my head." Then, coloring: "Sorry. Poor choice of words, that."

She answered. "Yes, right away, sir. Sorry." Hanging up. "I've got to get back."

Before they left, Jacob copied down the statement of purpose, then took a picture of the drawing, checking to ensure that it had come out in the low light.

Norton punched the lift button. "I'll stop by the college and ask Jimmy about yearbooks."

"Thanks. See you tonight?"

"Eight o'clock. I trust you'll be able to entertain yourself till then."

"Do my best," said Jacob.

"What's it to be till then? Punting on the Thames?"

"Not quite."

THE LIBRARIAN IN CHARGE of the Bodleian's Special Collections was a surly ostrich of a woman named R. Waters. The regular reading room was undergoing renovation and her interim domain was the basement of Radcliffe Science Library, an ill-lit concrete catacomb blockaded by portable humidifiers and dehumidifiers waging a war of attrition.

Unable to find fault with Jacob's temporary access card, she begrudgingly showed him to the computer kiosk. A search of the electronic catalog for the Maharal, limited to documents prior to 1650, yielded a single entry, the Prague letter.

Jacob asked if there was any way to tell who had examined it previously.

Waters sniffed. "That information is privileged."

The document request slip she thrust at him required a signature guaranteeing that he would not eat, drink, chew gum, write in ink, take photographs, or use a mobile phone. As a temporary user, he was also forbidden from requesting more than one item at a time or more than four items per day, although, as R. Waters added, that would be unlikely, given that it was nearing half-three, and the collection closed at five.

Jacob traded away his rights for a pair of white cotton gloves and an eraserless golf pencil. He waited, sitting at a padded-leathertop table while the document came up from storage.

At four o'clock sharp, it arrived, suspended in an archival board folder borne on the librarian's palms. She opened the flaps with a snide flourish, withdrawing to a nearby workstation so she could spy on him.

He stared at the letter anxiously without reading it, aware of precious minutes ticking by. It measured about five inches square, three of its corners eaten away, its edges mottled, its center water-stained and shot through with wormholes, so fragile that he held his breath, afraid to exhale and scatter it into dust.

He held his gloved hand over the ink, millimeters from the paper that had touched the skin of the great genius of Israel.

R. Waters didn't miss her opportunity. "I must ask that you please refrain from touching the material excessively, sir."

"Sorry." He tucked his hand in his lap. The great genius of Israel had atrocious penmanship, careless about keeping his lines straight. Letters thinned where his quill had run dry, blotched after he'd redipped it.

These imperfections made Jacob feel like a trespasser, a peeping Tom;

they also helped restore his equilibrium. The great genius of Israel had been a man, a real man—not a character, scissored from history. He'd eaten, belched, used the bathroom. Had good days and bad days, found himself subject to the push and pull of right and wrong.

You're very cynical, Detective Lev.

Jacob switched on the magnifying lamp and bent over the lens.

The going was excruciatingly slow. The letter was a couple of hundred words at most, but the script was hurried, the gaps numerous, the Hebrew poetic and obscure. The idea of Reggie Heap plumbing this material for inspiration was outlandish. Jacob, with a yeshiva education, would need hours, if not days, to fully decipher it. He'd gotten through the date, the salutation, and half of the first line before deciding that his time was better spent transcribing, allowing him to work later, at his own pace.

He opened his notepad and began to copy, his attention wholly on the shape of the words and not on their meaning. That was challenge enough.

R. Waters checked her wristwatch and clucked her tongue.

At last he came to the signature.

יהודה ליווא ב״ר בצלאל

Judah Loew ben Bezalel.

Jacob was about to put his hands up—done!—when his breath caught.

ליווא

It meant *lion*. The English rendering, *Loew*, was little more than convention, German processed into Hebrew, reprocessed into English, shedding its vowels along the way.

It could easily be read as *Lowe*, or *Leyva*, or *Levai*.

Your name, it means "heart" in Hebrew, I think. Lev.

By his own admission, Peter Wichs spoke hardly any Hebrew. That was why he kept the security log in English, the better for him to communicate with his Israeli subordinates.

Yet he'd felt the need to tutor Jacob.

I know what it means.

Ah. Then I think perhaps I have nothing more to offer you.

Jacob picked up the golf pencil and wrote the word for heart in his notepad—

לֵב

The simplicity of Hebrew reduced it to two letters: *lamed* and *bet*. *Bet* was the first letter of the Five Books of Moses—the initial letter of *Bereshit*, Genesis. In the beginning. And *lamed* was the last letter of its last word—*Yisrael*. Israel.

Two letters that completed a cycle. Encasing the heart of the matter.

It made for a nice metaphor. Jacob Lev was a man of heart.

Except, he wasn't.

That wasn't the way *he'd* been taught to spell his surname.

Two distinct Hebrew letters made a *v* sound. What he had learned— what Sam had taught him, what Jacob now wrote—was not *lamed bet*, but *lamed vav*—

לוֹ

And, in turn, the letter *vav* had two pronunciations: *v*, as a consonant, and *o*, as a vowel.

Which gave his name, as it was spelled, two pronunciations.

Lev.

Or *Loew.*

The German *w*, the slurred *oe*. *Lev.* Classic Ellis Island Special. The wonder was that it had taken him two days to figure it out.

Make that thirty-two years.

There, in the middle of the temporary home of Special Collections, Jacob burst into giddy, hysterical laughter.

He didn't know his own name.

"Kindly lower your voice."

He quieted down, his stomach muscles twitching.

He craved alcohol.

So he shared a name with a famous rabbi. So what? There were plenty of Loews in the world. And even if he really was a great-great-great-great-whatever, who cared? Families grew exponentially. He'd once read that there were something like a thousand Rockefellers alive, no more than four generations removed from the original wealth, most of them ordinary middle-class Americans—a few of them poor. People reverted to the mean.

The Maharal had died in the early 1600s. Figure twenty-five years to a generation—maybe less, because people got married early and died young in those days.

Sixteen generations, eighteen. At best he was one of *tens* of thousands of descendants.

Even so, his father's obsession with the Maharal took on new meaning. Much more than academic curiosity.

Then why say nothing about it? You'd think it would be a point of pride.

He shut his eyes and Sam appeared before him, interchanging rapidly with the clay model Peter Wichs had shown him.

The image shifted to Wichs, studying him. Processing him. Recognizing him?

But Jacob didn't look like Sam.

He took after Bina.

You are the detective, Jacob Lev.

He had taken the guard's use of his full name as a quirk of speech or an affectation. *It's your name, isn't it?* Now it began to feel like a rote lesson, a drill, the sounds scratched over and over again into the clay of Jacob's mind, until they took.

Jacoblevjacoblevjacoblev.

Why did you let me up here?

You asked.

I'm sure a lot of people ask.

Not a lot of policemen.

לו

Every Hebrew letter corresponded to a number. *Lamed* was thirty. *Vav* was six.

A durable legend had attached to that number: in every generation, thirty-six hidden righteous people sustained the world.

Your father the lamed-vavnik.

Anyone who thinks he's a lamed-vavnik *is by definition not a* lamed-vavnik.

I don't think. I know.

Grandiose thinking: another sign of incipient madness.

The pencil snapped between his fingers. He could no longer restrain himself; he burst into laughter.

"Sir."

He turned to the librarian to apologize and she recoiled, as if she perceived in him something unspeakable. He stood up and she scurried behind the desk; he asked her to return his possessions and she held the basket at arm's length. When he thanked her, she didn't reply, and as he tripped toward the stairwell, he heard the door to Special Collections slam and bolt.

THE WHEEL

Looking back, Yankele, I can hardly believe it, how young we were. What does a six-year-old girl know? Nothing. A ten-year-old-boy, even less."

The topic of tonight's monologue is love, inspired by the recent betrothal of the Loews' youngest daughter, Feigele. In honor of the couple, Perel is fashioning a spice jar, for use in the *havdalah* ceremony marking the end of the Sabbath. She builds up speed on the pottery wheel, her wet hands beginning to glow silver.

"Even at that age, Yudl was known as a scholar. Our parents agreed we'd marry when he returned from the yeshiva. I felt like the luckiest girl in the world."

Perel smiles. "Also, he was tall and handsome." She touches her fingers to the clay, and it shivers like a lover's body.

The aura erupts around her.

"No road runs straight, Yankele. When I was sixteen, my father made a bad investment. His entire fortune disappeared overnight. Our Sages say the rich person is the one who is contented with his portion. They also say a poor man is like a dead man. Before the catastrophe, everyone had taken to calling my father Reich, not Schmelkes, which was his real name. You can imagine what that felt like, being called rich, then losing everything. Father was so ashamed, he could barely face us."

She can imagine. She knows well the mockery of a misnomer.

Perel works the clay. The aura does not drape her body evenly, shining brightest at her hands, head, heart; beneath her skirts, between her legs.

"Everyone expected Yudl to break the engagement. My father wrote to him, stating that he could no longer afford the dowry. I was heartsick, of course, but what could I do?"

The vessel achieves symmetry, taking on shape and dignity, the aura growing to an unbearable brightness, engulfing Perel in a rainstorm of grays: quicksilver, tin, and fog, but also silence and boredom and ambiguity and patience and wisdom and that terrible, terrifying sludge that is pure wickedness.

The coexistence of these elements mystifies her. What does it say about the Rebbetzin?

"I was a teenager. I felt my life was over. I sank into melancholy, I couldn't get out of bed for weeks. My mother worried I had plague. She moved me out of the room I shared with my four sisters and had me sleep in the attic." A soft smile. "Maybe that's why I like it up here so much."

She wonders if she has an aura, too. If she does, she can't see it. Perhaps that's what the animals are responding to when they snarl and cower. While it saddens her to think that she will never know herself as well as a dog does, she has decided that this experience is universal. People perceive the nature and texture of others more easily than their own. It is evident, for example, that Perel's own aura is invisible to her. If she could see it—bubbling like molten silver—she wouldn't be chatting so blithely.

"Being alone didn't help me, it made it so much worse. But when I was with people I was miserable, too, and nobody wanted to be with me because I would try to draw them into my misery. So they avoided me, and consequently I felt more alone than before. A dreadful pattern. I was in the depths, Yankele, the absolute pit of despair."

The memory clouds Perel's lovely face, and she works for some time in silence, fashioning an interior lip. She lets the wheel slow. The aura dissipates. When both motion and light have died away, she inspects the jar. Finding it satisfactory, she removes it to the side.

"That's the easy part. It's the lid that takes practice."

Perel picks up the gut string cutter, and slices off a hunk from the mound of riverbank clay. For several minutes she wedges it against the floor to force out air pockets; then she kneads, pressing down with the heels of her hands, forming a face that she folds over on itself.

"Two things saved me, Yankele. The Holy One, Blessed Be He, and clay. From out of the depths I cried out to Him, and He bent his ear to the voice of my plea, for His mercy is eternal. One afternoon I was walking along the river, lost in unhappiness, and I sat down to rest. Without thinking, I gathered up a handful of mud and began to squeeze it, so that it oozed between my fingers, as if I was forcing out black feelings, and I realized that I had stopped weeping. Well, I thought, 'That's good, but it won't last, I'll be miserable again soon.' And I forgot all about it until a few days later. I was walking in the same spot. And wouldn't you know it? The shape of my palm—I found it lying there, just as I had left it. It had dried. My fingers fit into it perfectly."

The Rebbetzin pulls away a chunk of clay and begins to form the lid, rekindling the aura.

"It's special stuff, you know, Vltava mud. Strong and elastic. It dries hard, even without firing. I began to go to the river whenever I felt sad, and I would make shapes. Animals and flowers. I made a *kiddush* cup for my father. He was pleased. It was the first time I had seen him smile since he learned of the loss of his cargo ships. He thanked me for bringing beauty back into his life. Little by little, I began to get better."

Perel gauges the size of the lid against the bowl, resumes shaping.

"In those days the mail was slow, Yankele. There was a war going on, too, and that caused lengthy delays. When a letter came from Lublin, we saw that Yudl had sent it seven or eight months before, in response to my father's offer to end our engagement. You know what he wrote, Yankele? I will remember it word for word until the day I am exempted from this world. 'Reb Shmuel, I will delay marriage only until such time as I can locate sufficient funds to give your daughter the home she deserves.'"

Perel smiles.

"The Sages say that arranging a match is harder than splitting the Red Sea. The Holy One, Blessed Be He—it was His doing, Yankele, that I should find a husband so well suited for me. I can find no other explanation."

Perel falls silent again, working the lid smooth. "The top and bottom will both shrink, but not at the same rate. Normally I'd let the bowl dry first and then make the lid, but Chanukkah is less than a month away. Soon it'll be too cold. The clay becomes impossible. It's like trying to knead a stone. I suppose I could have you do it for me, eh? No, I'm only joking . . . I hope Isaac and Feigie will be happy together. I trust they will."

She nods agreement.

"Thank you," Perel says. "That's kind of you to say. He's a fine young man. Yudl considers him like his own son." She laughs. "Which, in a sense, he is."

That Rebbe has chosen a Torah scholar for his youngest daughter is appropriate and expected. What has the ghetto buzzing is *which* young Torah scholar: Isaac Katz, Isaac the Hatless, Rebbe's foremost disciple.

More to the point: the widowed husband of his older daughter, Leah.

Except for Rebbe, all interested parties have reservations about the new match. Including the betrothed couple. Long accustomed to averting his eyes in the presence of his sister-in-law, Isaac now looks as though he might faint. Feigie paces, reciting psalms for hours on end, like a woman praying for a stay of execution.

Perel says, "I'll miss being up here in the winter. It's so peaceful. It's like I'm a girl again, dressed in finery, my desires attended to. Funny, because look at me: I'm filthy. It's a feeling of belonging, a wonderful feeling."

I don't know what that feels like.

"I gave up working with clay after I got married. Yudl didn't like it. He said it was the dust of idolatry. He was very zealous in his younger days, you know. He still won't let me put my name to the pieces, or tell anyone where they came from. But he loves me, and there's no greater leniency than love, mm? Anyhow, he knows he can't stop me, and he knows better than to try. When Leah died, it was the only thing that allowed me to forget my sorrow. Every woman loses children. I lost three before her, all of them less than a month old. But Leah was a woman. Modest, and elegant. Too frail for this world. I was always afraid for her, and—I was right."

The Rebbetzin wipes her upper arm against her eye, laughs hoarsely. She holds out the lid. "What do you think, Yankele? Too plain? I think a flower would be nice. Feigie's that kind of girl."

Perel's hand hovers over her tools. There are knives; wooden combs; paddles of varying sizes with soft, scalloped edges. Things of beauty in themselves, the smooth handles glowing from within. She picks up a roller and begins to flatten out a piece of clay.

"Leah would have preferred it plain. She was good at clay herself, you know. I don't know why I keep talking about her. It's Feigie I should be thinking about. I keep telling myself Leah can't have been as lovely as I remember, as witty, as kind. We remember only the best parts of those who are no longer with us. But what does that mean for my other daughters? How do you mourn the dead child and celebrate the living one? That's what I struggle with, Yankele."

Perel raises the sheet of rolled clay. It is thin enough for lamplight to pass through. She drapes it carefully atop a plank. Moistening a whetstone, she draws the smallest knife against it with a pleasant, methodical rasp. She plucks out a single strand of silky black hair and draws it floatingly down upon the blade. It splits with ease, and she tugs gently at the sheet of rolled clay to free it of lumps and bubbles, commences cutting out tiny ovals.

"I don't see why one ought to conceal one's talents, especially if they bring good into the world. There's enough suffering as it is. There's nothing wrong as long as your intentions are correct. Isaac and Feige, they'll make the blessing over the spices, and smell the sweetness, and I'll be participating in their joy. Don't you agree? Of course you do. You know, Yankele, that's why I like having you around: you never argue."

She coils one of the ovals around itself, moistens it with a droplet so that it adheres to the top of the lid. The aura flickers back to life: rippling, tentative.

More ovals, pressed together, form a minuscule rosebud.

"The key, Yankele, is proportion."

She thinks of her monstrous self, the mismatch of body and soul.

Perel begins a second rose. "It must get very lonely, not being able to speak."

You will never know.

Perel stops. "Have I offended you? If I have, I beg forgiveness. I didn't mean to mock you."

She shakes her head: *no offense taken.*

"Thank you, Yankele. You're a mensch . . ." The Rebbetzin glances at her hesitantly, then says: "Your mind is sound. It's your tongue that's the problem, you know."

She tilts her head. She did not know she had a tongue; she assumed she didn't. No point in giving a tongue to a mute.

Perel drags the bucket of water between them. "Here. Open your mouth."

Open her mouth? She cannot open her mouth.

It then occurs to her that she has never tried.

"Open your mouth," Perel says, "and stick out your tongue."

Clumsy lips part, and in the black glossy surface of the water, she beholds stumpy teeth forming the bars of a cage. She pries them open and gazes down her nose at a runty piece of flesh, lolling in the cavity of her mouth like a deep-sea creature mistakenly hauled to the surface.

A tongue, sure enough, though it hardly deserves the name. It fascinates and repels her. It's been inside her this whole time and she never knew.

She squeezes her cheeks together, forcing it out farther, and receives another shock.

Her tongue has a waist.

A string, tied so tightly that it causes the gray flesh on either side to bulge out. There's a knot, too, with a big floppy bow, ends sticking out, begging to be tugged free.

Or—she squeezes her cheeks harder—not a string, but a thin strip of—

Paper?

No wonder she can't talk.

How exhilarating to finally grasp that the problem is so simple. Simple problem; simple solution.

She reaches up to untie the strip.

Perel shrieks. *"No."*

She pauses.

"You must never, ever do that," Perel says. "Do you understand? Never."

She nods.

"Tell me: you will never touch that."

What kind of absurd, cruel demand is that? She can't *tell* her anything, not with her tongue tied up like a dog.

"It's the Divine Name. Written on parchment. If you take it out . . ." Perel pauses. "Don't touch it, please."

She stares sadly at her reflection for a few moments more. The stupid little organ, the pathetic little scrap. They—not her misshapen body, not her glutinous mask of a face—are what make her a monster.

"I'm sorry, Yankele. I shouldn't have shown it to you. I just didn't want you to think there was anything wrong with you."

But there is. And there always will be.

She knows that, now.

And now that she knows the knot is there, she can't stop feeling it. She scrapes it against the roof of her mouth as the Rebbetzin completes the final two roses in silence.

After cleaning her tools and rinsing her arms in the bucket, Perel dries her forearms and rolls down her sleeves.

"Pour this out for me, please, Yankele?"

Obedient, as always, she carries the bucket to the small arched door set into the garret wall, lifts the iron bar, and dumps the water out onto the cobblestones below.

Perel dries her tools, bundles them in leather, and stores them in the drying cabinet, along with the new spice jar.

"I'm sorry for showing you that. I truly am."

She nods. She's already forgiven her.

"I'm going to show you something else. Hopefully it will lighten your heart." Perel stands on her stool, reaching to the back of a shelf. She removes an object wrapped in wool and tied in twine, begins undoing the knots.

"Yudl must never know," she says. "He'd be furious."

Unfurling the wool, she holds up an astonishingly lifelike model of Rebbe's head.

"It was an experiment, to see how realistic I could make it. You can't use a wheel for something like this, you have to trust your fingers. I don't know about you, but I think it's very good. Is that vain? I meant to destroy it after I was done, but couldn't bring myself to do it. More vanity. I want my creations to live on. I also think—maybe I'm being self-serving—but I think it would be a shame if no one were ever to know what he looked like." The Rebbetzin grins nervously. "*Nu?* What do you think?"

I think it's perfect.

Perel contemplates the sculpture. "I don't know. Perhaps I've done a sinful thing. But it can't be good, to keep everything buried." A hand flutters toward the ceiling. "Yudl says God is best reached in a state of joy. I try, Yankele, but then I think about Leah, the sadness of the world overtakes me. I feel sometimes that I am standing in a river of tears. What does one do with that? Me, I have to keep my hands busy."

Perel rewraps the sculpture, replacing it at the back of the shelf, pinning the cabinet doors shut with a wooden peg.

"I'm glad I showed you, Yankele. I think that you understand what I'm feeling, whether I tell you or not." The Rebbetzin pauses. She looks abashed. "And I know you're unhappy with the way you are, and that makes my heart ache. You don't have to speak for me to know."

She nods again.

"I wish I could hear what you're thinking. Being with you is wonderful but it's sometimes like listening to someone chewing in another room and guessing what they're eating."

Perel shakes her head, looks at her, green glowing eyes. "I'd give much to know what is in your mind—the exact words."

I love you.

CHAPTER FORTY-SEVEN

Sam's voice over the phone was subdued and remote. "It would be better to have this conversation in person."

Jacob said, "Did you hear me, Abba?"

"You need to come home, Jacob."

"I'm flying out tomorrow."

"There's no sooner flight?"

Jacob paced the sidewalk outside Radcliffe Science Library. Exiting students gave him a wide berth. "I'm in the middle of an investigation."

"You had enough time to call me."

"Yeah, well, *sorry*, but I'm kind of pretty freaked out."

"Getting upset is not good for you."

"I wouldn't be upset if you'd just give me a straight answer."

"What's the question?"

"Did you know?"

"Every family has stories. Who can say?"

A Talmudic dodge; Jacob wanted to scream. "Why didn't you want me to come to Prague?"

"I explained to you. I'm an old man, I didn't want to be left alone—"

"You told me to visit the cemetery. You didn't tell me to visit the *shul*. Why?"

Sam, softer, sadder, tinged by fear: "Please come home."

"I'll tell you why: because you *knew* I would see it."

"How in the world would I know that? Jacob. Listen to yourself. You sound—"

"What. What do I sound. You can say it. Say it."

"I'm concerned about you," Sam said.

Jacob laughed, flailing his arm up, nearly whacking a girl wearing a bicycle helmet. "You know what, Abba? *I'm* concerned about me, too."

"Then come home."

"Don't, don't, don't do that."

"Do what?"

"Condescend to me."

"I'm not—"

"You *are*, when my brain is, like, *throwing up*, and you're sitting there telling me that the remedy is to come home and have a cup of tea with you. I'm *busy*. Okay? I *work*. I have a *job*, all right, and as far as jobs go, it's kind of fucking important, so will you please, *please* stop talking to me like I'm six."

The tirade left his mouth feeling coppery. He'd never sworn at his father, and the silence stretched, and Jacob felt their relationship splitting open, giving birth to something ugly and muck-covered and irreversible.

Sam said, "Do your job."

Then it was his turn to do the unprecedented.

He hung up on his only child.

OVERCOME WITH REMORSE, Jacob phoned back to apologize. Sam didn't pick up. Second and third attempts were similarly futile.

Jacob bought a four-pack of Newcastle and sat outside the gate to Balliol to drink them, notepad resting on his knees, finger wedged into the pages, marking the spot where he'd copied the text of the Maharal's letter. Several times he began to read it. He got no further than that first line before slamming the covers shut, pinching the tip of his finger, feeling that the pain was appropriate.

He arrived at the Friar and Maiden in a state of disarray, worsened by the pub's overhot, overloud atmosphere. Chicago blues roared from an antique PA. Among a sea of blotchy middle-aged faces, Priscilla Norton glowed coolly lunar, canted forward over a pint, talking animatedly to the porter, Jimmy Smiley.

Jacob worked his way toward their booth. "Sorry I'm late. I got caught up."

"No problem," Norton said.

Smiley gave a neutral nod. He wore a grandfatherly sweater vest over a ratty T-shirt. His black coat was folded on the bench. A horseshoe-shaped dent in his hair memorialized his missing bowler.

Norton slid a brimming glass at Jacob. "Hope you like Murphy's."

He liked anything.

The brew was rich and dark, like running through a barley field with an open mouth; he chugged half of it and set it down to impressed stares.

"Thirsty," he said.

"Evidently," Norton said. "Well, shall we get started? Jimmy, tell him what you told me."

Smiley licked his thin lips. "Mr. Mitchell, he wasn't pulling your leg. He wouldn't know them boys, he wasn't around when they was."

"You were."

"Sure, I knew 'em. The whole rotten lot. There was a scout, see. No older'n you, Pip. We were friendly, and one time—eighty-five, I believe it was, because I was three years a full porter—this scout, Wendy was her name, she was on her hands and knees, scrubbing a toilet or some such, when he sneaks up behind and lifts her skirt."

"We're talking about Reggie Heap," Jacob said.

"Not him, no, his friend, the one in your picture."

Jacob tugged out the drawing of Head. "Him."

"That's the one. Now, she—"

"What's his name?"

"Hold your bloody horses, I'm not done." Smiley licked his lips again, settling back into raconteur mode. "Where was I? Right, so, Wendy, she feels a hand on her arse and up she jumps—'What's that now, what you doing.' He grabbed her, you know what he meant to do, but she was a spirited lass, Wendy was. She bit him"—he tapped himself on the chin—"and he let go. Thank her lucky stars he slipped on the tile or else who knows what he might've done."

Jacob held up a finger to pause him, pointing to Mr. Head's identifying scar.

Smiley nodded. "Could be. Could be."

Under the table, Norton squeezed Jacob's thigh. "Go on, Jim."

"Well, after it happened, she came to see me all ajumble. Cause Wendy and me was a bit friendly, you see. Nothing out of order, but I liked her. I says, 'Don't wrinkle your pretty little brow,' and up I went to speak with Mr. Dwight. He was the head porter in those days, good man, God rest him. He says, 'Okay, Jimmy boy, we'll sort it out.'

"The next day I go looking for Wendy, to find out how she's getting on, and I hear the other ladies gossiping about she quit. Back again I went to Mr. Dwight, to get the skinny.

"I never seen him so rattled. He didn't want to talk to me. 'There's nothing can be done, Jim. Do us a favor and shut your mouth.' He did his best, I know that now, but I didn't like it, see? 'What's Wendy done to deserve that? She didn't do nothing.' I kept on him about it until he said, 'Jimmy, you don't shut it, I'll punt you out my own self.' Well, I told him—"

Abruptly he devolved into a goofy grin. "Hallo, Ned," he said. "All right?"

A tubby man with a five-o'clock shadow saluted as he stumbled past, en route to the restroom. Smiley waited for the man to move out of earshot to continue.

"I went round the place where Wendy lived with her nan. I was feeling bad about it, see, because I was thinking about how I promised to help her out, and now she's out of a job.

"She was none too happy to see me. 'They sacked me,' she says. 'What you mean sacked you, they said you quit.' 'They had me say I was leaving of my own free will. Tell me how it's my own free will when they're the ones made me do it?'

"I told her I couldn't believe Mr. Dwight would stoop so low. Wendy said it wasn't Mr. Dwight, it was Dr. Partridge, the junior censor. He had her up to his office and who should be sitting there but the little bastard himself, plasters stuck all over his precious boat like he been in a bloody knife fight, along with your lad Heap, who swears he saw Wendy grab this other bloke and try to kiss him, which's pure rubbish. Dr. Partridge won't hear her side of it. He delivers her a talking-to about he's disappointed in her, the way she threw herself at that young man. 'Can't tolerate that type of behavior, you understand.' Wendy being Wendy, she says, 'I ain't going to apologize to him, he's a bleeding liar, they both are.' Dr. Partridge says, 'That's a shame, I'm afraid I won't be able to recommend you to a future employer.' Wendy, she didn't even know she was being sacked until then. She thought maybe they'd dock her or assign her a crap duty. Not send her packing. She begun to apologize, but the boys, they was having none of it. 'She called me a liar. My father this, my father that.' Dr. Partridge, he said, 'Come on, now, Wendy, let's be dignified about it.'

"Now, that had me ripe to bang down the censor's door. But my wife said, 'It's terrible what happened to that poor girl. But Jimmy, use your loaf, you're not going to get her her job back. And say somehow you do, what's to stop the young fellow from putting his hands on her again, and this time maybe she won't be so lucky. A blessing in disguise, is what it is. Let her find someplace else where nobody's going to bother her.' See, I hadn't thought of it that way. The last thing I wanted was to bring more trouble on her. On me neither. I had three mouths of my own to feed."

He tugged his lower lip ruefully.

"Most of the kids I've known are decent, mind. I wouldn't've stayed if I didn't think so. Most of them are good. But, you're eating peanuts and you bite down on a rock, it's that you're liable to remember, not the rest of the bowl."

Norton asked what had become of Wendy.

Smiley shook his head. "Can't rightly say."

Jacob said, "What was the name of the guy who assaulted her?"

The porter hesitated.

"It's all right," Norton said. "You can tell us."

"Not you I'm worried about, love."

Smiley inclined his head toward the dartboards, and Jacob saw the man who had earlier passed their table. He was laughing with a group of drinkers cut from similar cloth—fellow porters, Jacob assumed.

He said, "We can go elsewhere." Impatience strained his voice.

Smiley said, "They'll clear out soon enough. Ned's wife skins him if he's late, and them geezers follow him like ducklings. Make yourself useful and stand us a round."

When Jacob returned, the mood in the booth had lightened a degree, Smiley chortling while Norton said, "Not if I can help it, y'poncy bastard."

The porter beamed. "She's a gem, this one."

"A diamond," Jacob said.

"I think of her as my own."

"Aw, you're sweet, Jim."

"Sweet nothing," Smiley said, corralling his pint. He jabbed a finger at Jacob. "You be polite to her."

Priscilla said, "I can take care of myself, thank you, Mr. Smiley."

"I know you can, I want him to know it, too." Smiley winked. "She might hurt you otherwise."

As PREDICTED, NED WAS the first to depart; the other three wandered out a few minutes later, each one in turn stopping by the booth to clap Smiley on the shoulder.

"Good night, boys."

"G'night, Jimmy."

Once they were gone, Smiley reached under his folded coat and brought out a weighty leather-bound book with an elaborate coat of arms stamped into the cover.

Ædes Christi

Anno MCMLXXXV

"Had to smuggle it out, I did," he said, propping the book against the wall. "Mr. Mitchell wouldn't be pleased."

The frontispiece clarified, somewhat: *being the annual pictorial chronicle of The Dean, Chapter and Students of the Cathedral Church of Christ in Oxford of the Foundation of King Henry the Eighth.*

Smiley ran his finger down the table of contents, pausing twice, then flipped to page 134.

Rows of students.

The photo of Heap was the same one Jacob had seen at the house.

Reginald Heap

History of Art

"Him you know." The porter paged ahead to the third-year students. "And *that's* the git who grabbed Wendy."

Having referred to Mr. Head as Mr. Head for so long, Jacob wasn't sure he'd be able to start using his real name.

Terrence Florack

Fine Art

Snub nose. Beetle brows. Scarred chin.

Perry-Bernie.

Terry? Could MacIldowney have been mistaken?

Jacob said, "Was he American, this Florack?"

"No, that was the other one," Smiley said.

"What other one?" Norton said.

Smiley turned more pages, his palsied hands fumbling. "Quite a threesome, they made." Finally, he reached his goal, a section headed CLUBS AND ACTIVITIES.

Yearly summaries, assorted group portraits: the Music Society, the Boat Club, the Chess Club, and, not last and certainly not least—

The Christ Church chapter of the Undergraduate Art Society had an exciting year. Two exhibitions of new work were put forth. It would not be inaccurate to call these unqualified successes. Here's to more! Ladies, from left: Misses L Bird, K Standard, V Ghosh, S Knight (sec), H Yarmouth, J Rowland. Gentlemen, from left: Messrs D Bowdoin, E Thompson III (pres), R Heap, T Florack, T Foster.

"That's him, that's the one," Smiley said, placing his finger on a sinewy man with a penetrating stare, set off from the students. "Like a big brother, he was."

Graduate student advisor: Mr R Pernath.

"Quite the charmer," said Smiley. "You can see why all the lasses fancied him."

It wasn't so much that Pernath was handsome. His smile was a touch lopsided, his nose too small for his face. A well-moussed shelf of hair, drastically cantilevered over his brow, cast a shadow over his eyes. They were the eyes of Rasputin, or Charles Manson, or the Reverend Jim Jones. Hard dark gems in a polished preppy setting. Even in grainy black-and-white, a quarter century later, they exerted a queer hypnotic power, and Jacob had to force himself to look away.

He said, "I need to make a copy of this."

Without hesitation Smiley folded the page at the binding and tore it out.

Norton said, "You're not going to get in trouble for that?"

Smiley slid the page to Jacob. "Good riddance to bad rubbish."

CHAPTER FORTY-EIGHT

Back at the station, Jacob said, "I'm an idiot."

"Now, now," Norton said. "Let's love ourselves."

"Rule number one. Value the crime scene. I didn't."

"The evidence said he was killed elsewhere. Strictly speaking, it wasn't the crime scene."

"The *head* was there," Jacob said. "That's scene enough."

Norton whacked the side of her laboring desktop. "Come on, you. Load."

"I had his name at the outset. I met with his father."

"You're being a mite hard on yourself, don't you think?"

"No. I don't. Because it was his family's house. I met the father. The father was a weirdo. I should have at least *talked* to the son."

"I said *load* . . . Bloody BT." Norton glanced at him, pacing behind her cubicle, grinding his fist into his temple. "Fancy a soda?"

"I'm fine."

"Well, then fetch me one, please."

He found the squalid nook that served as the station's snack bar, selected a minimally chilled cola. When he brought it to Norton, she was grinning and pointing at the screen.

Richard Pernath's curriculum vitae, a neat capsule bio.

Combined BArch/MArch, UCLA, 1982.

MSt History of Design, University of Oxford, 1987.

Jacob said, "He's an L.A. native. He met the other two here and brought them back. Now he's cleaning house. What MacIldowney told us, Perry-Bernie—it's a nickname. For Pernath. Perry, Pernie, or something like that. Look up Florack."

"I'm typing."

"Type faster."

"You know what," she said, abandoning the chair to him, "you take over, you're going to shout my ear off."

Jacob could feel his eyeballs vibrating in their sockets while the page loaded. "This is so fucking slow I want to put my head through the wall."

"Don't do that, please. Here we are."

Terrence Florack: Freelance Draughting Services.

After graduating from Oxford with a second in fine art in 1988, Florack had worked for three years in the Los Angeles office of Richard Pernath, AIA.

"*Yes,*" Jacob said, punching the air. Then he looked at Norton, her mouth puckered.

"*What,*" he said.

It came out a challenge, far harsher than he'd intended.

"Not to tinkle on your parade," she said. "But. Who's the woman who phoned in your emergency?"

"Another partner. Pernath—he's a delegator. These other people are disposable. For all we know he never touched the vics, just stood there directing."

"Or your revenge theory applies to him, as well, and he's lying somewhere with his head cut off."

"A hundred bucks says he's just fine. A hundred more says he, or someone he knows, was in Prague last spring, right when Reggie Heap was."

"That's two hundred dollars. Should I be writing this down or is your word good?"

Jacob hunched over, rubbing his head. "The period between 1989 and 2005 is an awfully big blank for a bunch of sexual psychopaths. I can't see them just taking a vacation."

"Agreed."

"Be nice to know their whereabouts."

Norton reclaimed the mouse, squinted at the screen. "London, in Florack's case. His page still lists an address in Edgware."

"What brought him to L.A. recently?"

"An airplane, I presume."

"What's the CV say?"

"For God's sake, please, chill out. It doesn't detail his every movement for the last twenty years," she said. Then her expression turned grave. "I should contact Scotland Yard."

As she reached for her desk phone, Jacob called Charles MacIldowney.

Des answered. "Hello, Detective. What can I do for you?"

"Do you have Reggie's CV on file?"

"I'm sure we don't."

"Would you mind double-checking?"

Des sighed. "Well, only because you took away those hideous shoes. I'll ring you back."

"Thanks."

From the sound of it, Norton was being shunted from department to department. Jacob knelt, took the mouse, clicked back to Pernath's page. He opened up the LINKS tab.

Keynote address, North American Architectural Design and Drafting Society annual conference, 2010 (full text).

Priscilla was saying, "Quite so, sir."

Jacob combed through Pernath's speech, titled "To Bravely Face a New Dawn."

Priscilla hung up. "They promise to get back to me in the morning."

"Check this out," Jacob said.

"Yes?"

"'To Bravely Face'?" he said. "Sounds a little like *To Be Brasher*."

"You think?"

"Fine, then this part: 'A New Dawn,'" he said. "Every one of my vics faced east."

"Mm. Could be."

Detective's reserve. A virtue, but at that moment it annoyed him, because he did not doubt: he knew, he could see the universe peeling back, see its warp and weft, his brain a gyroscope. He didn't expect her to understand how amazing he felt. He could chew through steel.

Taking pains to appear casual, he found the architectural society's website, moused over the mission statement ("to serve and promote the interests of the growing community of graphics professionals") and the tally of membership data (fifty-seven thousand and counting, Manitoba to Mexico City and points between).

The 2012 conference was scheduled for August 10–12, at the Sheraton in Columbus, OH—three jam-packed days of educational workshops, networking, and vendors offering the latest technologies. Register before July 15 to receive the early-bird discount, plus a complimentary insulated travel mug.

There was a list of past conferences. He ran his finger down to the previous year's and felt his spine light up.

2011: New Orleans, LA.

Tearing open his notepad, he found the page, thrust it out in triumph.

Lucinda Gaspard, New Orleans, July 2011.

Norton said, "Bloody hell."

The webpage listed the location of the 2010 conference as Miami, FL.

Casey Klute, Miami, July 2010.

"Bloody. Fucking. Hell."

The lack of a 2009 murder made more sense when he saw that the conference had taken place in Calgary, Ontario. He hadn't looked outside the U.S.

"Where's Rye in 2008?" Priscilla asked.

"Forty minutes north of Manhattan," Jacob said.

Evgeniya Shevchuk, New York, August 2008.

The 2007 and 2006 conferences—in Evanston, IL, and Sacramento, CA, respectively—made him sit up and take notice. Again the thought haunted him that he had missed other murders that fit the pattern. In due time, he would have to ping the local PDs.

2005: Las Vegas, NV.

Dani Forrester, Las Vegas, October 2005.

"That's the beauty of it," Jacob said. "The three of them were there legitimately. Professional development, they're in the same industry. They were also old school chums. Nobody would think twice if they were hanging out."

"Reliving the bad old days."

Jacob copied all the dates going back to 1988. *Akron, 2004; Orlando, 2003; Providence, 2002* . . . Every one of them would have to be checked and rechecked.

Los Angeles hadn't played host to a conference since 1991. The nearest was Orange County, three consecutive years between 1996 and 1998. No matching murders. Maybe he was right about Southern California being too close to home, the memory of the Creepers' victims fresh enough to warrant caution.

His phone rang. Priscilla grabbed it before he could. She listened, said, "Thank you," and hung up. "That was Des. He can't find the CV."

A setback; Jacob barely noticed; he was on to the next thing, dialing Detective Maria Band in Miami.

"Favor to ask you," he said. "Your vic, Casey Klute. Party planner, right?"

"Uh—I—"

"I know she was, it said so in the file."

"Okay."

"Okay, so what was she up to, work-wise, in the couple weeks before her death? What was she planning?"

"It might be in the file," Band said.

"I don't have it with me. I need your help here."

In the background, a man's voice murmured impatiently. Band said, "I'm kind of tied up at the mom—"

"Please," Jacob said. He was trashing Maria Band's social life and he couldn't care less. "I'm getting close."

"How close is close?"

"Like, contact lens close."

Band sighed. "All right, what?"

He told her to look for the names Richard Pernath, Terrence Florack, and Reggie Heap, or any mention of the drafting society.

"Who are they?"

"The A-Team," Jacob said. "As in Asshole."

"I don't have the files with me," Band said. "I have to go back to the office."

"Call me as soon as you find out. Doesn't matter what time it is."

He made the same request of Volpe and Flores. Grandmaison in New Orleans didn't pick up. Jacob left him a message.

"Hey there, friendo. I've been trying you for three weeks. I have your killer. You're welcome."

He clicked off. Norton was eyeing him.

"What?" he said.

"You've nothing to do but wait," she said. "I think we should clear out of here."

He allowed her to take him by the arm and lead him out into the street.

"Where are we going?" he asked.

"My place."

SHE LIVED A FEW BLOCKS from the station, on the uppermost floor of a brick-faced row house, not dissimilar in style from MacIldowney's house but a fraction its size.

Five feet past the front door they were clenched together on the thinly carpeted living room floor, her left leg curled around the back of his right thigh, a knuckle-bruising four-hand pile-up as they went for the same buttons, zippers, seams.

"I need to fuck you right now," he said.

"Well, that's the general idea."

Proof of his newfound strength: he bench-pressed her, lifting her bodily from atop him, placing her on the sofa and then pouncing atop her while she shrieked and laughed and slapped at his naked back. She was hot and soft and intensely present, filling his hands and his mouth, her body perfectly imperfect that way that he always liked, a kind of pardon for his own shortcomings, helping rid him of thoughts of Mai and Divya Das. He tugged at her lip with his teeth, tasting blood; it was delicious and filling.

She took him in one hand, stroking urgently. Fixed his chin with the other so that he was looking straight into her cornflower eyes. "Go slow," she said.

He meant to obey her. But as soon as he pushed in, her head snapped back and her torso went rigid and then melted beneath him, her eyes rolling backward to blank white, her open mouth taking no air.

Not ecstasy. Pain.

He shoved himself up and off her.

As soon as he had, her eyes dropped back into view, scared and confused, flicking across his face without recognition. Then her fear rose to terror and he heard it behind him, ten thousand demons howling, and turned and saw a black buzzing fist rocketing toward him.

He dove, rolling across the carpet and hitting his head on the leg of the coffee table as Norton began to scream.

He righted himself, groaning, and he saw it in high definition, a black beetle, without question the same one he'd seen again and again but now grown to an incredible size, and he did not move, could not move, dumbstruck by the immensity of the thing, watching as it attacked Norton, using its horn to ram repeatedly into her arms and chest and neck while she shrieked and flailed and tried to protect her face from the violence of the assault.

Get it off she screamed.

Her voice slammed Jacob into gear: he lunged, swinging at the beetle with an open palm, and it dodged and then focused its attention on him, buzzing his head. He could feel the downdraft from its wings. It flew around and around him in deafening circles, and he spun after it, his still-erect penis swinging and flapping like a carousel horse come unscrewed.

The beetle raced to the far side of the room and plopped down on the carpet, its forelimbs darning the air.

Jacob launched himself toward it.

Its shell parted and its wings shot out and it ripped away, dive-bombing Priscilla, hounding her around the apartment while she screamed and clawed at her hair.

Get it off. Get it off.

Jacob seized a paperback from the coffee table and hurled it at the beetle, which arced back, chittering and buzzing, a noise sickeningly akin to laughter. Enraged, he threw a second book, knocking over the floor lamp, leaving him and Norton stumbling around in semidarkness, forcing him to track the beetle by sound alone as it zoomed and raced and buzzed and giggled, hovering in one spot long enough for him to get a bead on it and swing a woolen throw blanket like a whip, then darting through his legs, grazing his scrotum.

Norton had begun to fumble with the window latch, saying *God, oh God, come on.*

The beetle rose up directly before Jacob, suspended in midair, louder than life, its wingbeat blowing his hair back as it floated, now smaller, nearly invisible but for enormous bottle-green eyes. He knew he should reach up and crush it in his palm, but he saw the oil-slick shimmer of its armor, the gossamer of its wings, and he knew that he would never, could never, destroy something so beautiful.

Norton had managed the latch but the sash was stuck. *Come on.*

The beetle drifted closer to Jacob, bobbing gracefully on a sea of air.

He felt warmth as it pressed itself to his lips.

Jaws opening and closing, a whisper of hard exoskeleton.

Breathing hot sweet breath into his mouth.

Then it backed away, regretfully, never taking its eyes off him until it turned and roared off, heading straight for Norton.

She heard it coming, screamed and ducked. The beetle cleared her by several feet, hitting the window and punching a hole clean through, disappearing into the night, one more black star among many.

UNION

The marriage of Isaac Katz and Feigele Loew takes place in the Alt-Neu on a Wednesday afternoon, so that the union will be consummated that night and into the next morning, capturing Thursday's inherent blessing of fruitfulness.

On the platform, beneath the canopy, stands the core of the wedding party, the couple and their fathers and the witnesses, splendid Mordecai Meisel and retiring David Ganz, surrounded by male siblings and in-laws. Benefactors, intimates, and intellectual lights grace the pews, Chayim Wichs the sexton and Jacob Bassevi the financier, delegations of scholars from Krakow and Ostrog and Lvov. The Emperor has sent a letter of congratulations, gilt-bordered, calligraphed beautifully. The roll of parchment has been given its own seat of honor, on a red silk pillow, in the front row.

In the cramped women's section, the mothers and female relatives take turns at the viewing portals. The synagogue is packed so densely the mortar holding the building together seems to extrude.

And in the doorway, Yankele the Giant keeps the masses at bay.

From near and far they have come, decked in their finest to show their love and respect. Dozens upon dozens swarm up to the roof and hang over the edge in hope of catching a glimpse of the action through the rosette. Hundreds upon hundreds wait outside, ears pressed to stone walls. Thousands upon thousands more clog the streets around the Alt-Neu, old and young, sick and well, bitter enemies pressed chest to back, straining with cupped ears for the tinkle of broken glass that will signal the completion of the ceremony.

When it comes, the melody can be heard as far away as Sattelgasse, and countless voices roar their approval.

Mazal tov!

Nine separate bands of musicians, temporarily freed from the ban on public performance, strike up nine separate songs. People stamp their feet and whistle and clap and sing, a raucous, delirious explosion that redoubles as Yankele steps forth to clear the way so that the couple may stand in the threshold to wave at their adoring public before being ushered back inside to be sequestered in the chamber of privacy.

Food, drink, smiles: for once, nothing is in short supply. Meisel and Bassevi have seen to that. The ghetto has been transformed into an enormous outdoor reception hall, tables stretching the length of Rabinergasse. Everyone is invited to partake, and they do, emptying platters of spiced carrots and stuffed derma, jellied calves' legs, and potato dumplings. Whole stuffed river pikes sparkle atop pungent snow-heaps of horseradish. The feast replenishes itself like a spring. Children gobble honeyed *koláče* and tear off chunks of rosewater marzipan and sneak dripping handfuls of cherries stewed in beer.

Following their fifteen minutes of solitude, the couple emerge once more, and the crowd roars again and wipes its mouth on its sleeve and the dancing begins.

Golden chairs are placed on a platform. The consolidated army of musicians, having somehow managed to agree on a single song, begins to play furiously, whipping up a vortex of flying beards, black coats, shoes kicked off, and feet flung skyward. Chazkiel the Jester marshals his troupe of clowns; acrobats somersault and build human towers four levels high, juggle fruit and fire and glass.

Enthroned at the eye of the melee, Feigele and Isaac applaud each feat, grinning like fools, grinning at each other.

More? More!

It is holy revelry, for there is no good deed more prized than cavorting before the bride and bringing her joy. Hidden talents blossom. Everyone knows Yomtov Gluck can fix a wagon. Who knew he could walk on his hands, too? Who knew Gershom Samsa could do the bottle dance?

Leading the way is Rebbe himself, who repeatedly leaps to the front of the pack to do a funny little hopping maneuver that gives Feigele squealing fits. Heaving, red-faced, the great man returns to his chair long enough to catch his breath, and then he's up again, swinging his arms with abandon, late into the night.

More!

Doors unlocked and bonfires raging and everyone drunk, the ghetto is at its most vulnerable. Yet Rebbe has decided that there will be no patrol tonight. It would ruin the mood. To prove his point, he cited Scripture.

God protects the simple, Yankele.

Old habits die hard. While the party rages, she stalks the fringes of the crowd, rubbing the knot of her tongue against the roof of her mouth—as has become her habit—parsing the many unfamiliar faces. Most ignore her, caught up in the celebration. A few stare fixedly at the ground as she draws near, whispering once she has passed.

Look at the size of him.

They think she can't hear them. The clamor is tremendous. But her senses, once dull as soap, have grown powerfully acute. She can stand in the courtyard behind Rebbe's house and focus her attention on the windows of the house of study and eavesdrop on Talmudic debates. She can track an insect across the sky on a foggy night.

And other, unexpected changes have begun to come about.

Auras: she sees them everywhere now, on everyone, a little brighter each day. It comforts her to know that other colors exist besides gray—rose and sapphire and cream and earth, desire in all its infinite, subtle divisions.

Who loves, and who loves unrequited. Who hates, and whose hatred is ingrown.

Envious neighbors and jealous spouses and fickle children. The naughty pleasure of innovation. The bottomless misery that fuels braggadocio.

Every individual glows uniquely, and now, as humanity floods the streets, she sates herself with its dazzling, unimaginable spectacle.

Reaching the northern end of Rabinergasse, she cranes over the partition that divides the men's party from that of the women. For any other man, this would constitute an intolerable breach of modesty, but everyone knows that Yankele the Giant is simpleminded. Never in a million years would they imagine him subject to carnal lust.

Dry-eyed, the Rebbetzin sits, clapping her hands in time to the distant music. She appears to have made her peace with the match. Still, it can't be easy, watching one child replace another. She is flanked by her daughters and daughter-in-law. A chair has been left open in Leah's memory.

She catches Perel's eye, and they communicate silently through the smoke and noise.

"Yankele!"

Chayim Wichs is tugging at the hem of her coat.

"Rebbe is asking for you!"

The Rebbetzin smiles and raises a hand. *Go. I'm all right.*

She allows Wichs to drag her to the center of the dancing circle, where Rebbe waits with his arms out. She clasps his hands, taking great care to be gentle, and they turn in a circle of their own. He's huffing and puffing, perspiration streaming down his long, lean face, but when she tries to slow down, he pulls her closer, presses his body to hers, rocking against her, murmuring into her shirt, "Don't let me go. Don't ever let me go," and she hears the weakness in his voice and realizes that he's not sweating. He's crying.

And it pains her to know that she cannot reflect his love back to him. She raises her head and stares out, hating herself, and that is when she sees the men.

There are three of them.

Three variations on tall, the middle one enormous, towering above his companions, above everyone—rising nearly to her level. Gaunt as a reed, long-eyed in the firelight, he sports tufts of white hair above his ears. Wind ripples a rough-spun robe more suited to a cave-dwelling hermit than to a man of urban Prague.

The men with him are like two burlap sacks stuffed with potatoes. The dark one grimaces and shifts. The mottled red cheeks of his counterpart bunch in a secretive smile.

You'd think that three strange giants would attract a certain amount of attention, but nobody else appears to notice them. Standing near the rear of the crowd, they resemble a kind of human orchard. Yet they are not human. They cannot be. They have no auras. Amid the riot of color created by the partygoers, they hover in a chill vacuum, pitiless and tranquil, and the sight of them fills her with horror, drawing the binding around her tongue tighter, and tighter, threatening to cut the flesh in two pieces, like a wire through clay.

They're watching her.

"That's enough, now, Yankele, enough, please." Rebbe's voice calls her back to herself. He releases her from his embrace and beckons her to kneel. She does so reluctantly. Her back is to the men, and she feels their long invisible shadows on her.

Rebbe places his hands on her head. For barely a moment his gaze flicks over her shoulder and his face tautens with apprehension.

He sees them, too.

He smiles. "It's all right, my child."

The blessing streams from his lips.

May God make you as Ephraim and Menasheh.

May God bless you and guard you.

May God light up His face to you and be gracious to you.

May God lift His face to you and establish for you peace.

He kisses her on the forehead. "Good boy."

Warmth permeates her, cradling the space where her heart ought to be.

The musicians strike up the *mezinke*. Chazkiel elbows forth wielding a broom, which he thrusts into Rebbe's hands. She rises to clear out of the way, searching the crowd for the tall men. They're nowhere.

"I WON'T LIE," PEREL SAYS. "I'm glad it's over."

A week and a half after the wedding, life has returned to normal. In the wake of the frenzy, the streets feel eerily vacant, the filth more pronounced than usual. Residual heat raises a scummy fog off the river; it oozes in the twilight as she and the Rebbetzin return from the riverbank bearing a fresh load of clay.

"Don't get me wrong. I'm happy for her. You know that."

She nods.

"I woke up this morning and the house was so quiet. Yudl was already gone, and I lay there, waiting for Feigie's footsteps. The silliest thing is that I wasn't longing for her as she is. I was thinking about the sound her feet made when she was a baby. It's ridiculous, it's weak, I can't help it. I think that's my right, don't you? I raised her. Twenty-nine years I've been raising children. I think I deserve a little time to pity myself."

She nods, careful not to spill the mud. *I know.*

"I know," Perel says, "it's not as if she moved to another city." She laughs. "Well, enough of that. We've got work to do. I promised Feigie I'd finish making her new dishes. No reason to panic yet, we'll get it done. Here's what we'll do: we'll go in shifts. Every circuit, you stop in and collect what I've done and bring it to the blacksmith for baking. We'll work through the night if we have to. Does that sound good? We'll stop at the house first to refill the shed."

They turn the corner, onto Heligasse. Among the murmurs of the evening, the familiar sounds of the Loew household filter through. The slap of a wet rag as Gittel, the maid, yawns and scrubs the kitchen floor. The scurry of the mice that live under the stairs. The sough of a fire.

And from the open window of the study, Rebbe's voice, strained and urgent.

I understand. I understand. But—

The voice that interrupts him is a tired whistle, and it stops her dead in her tracks.

There is nothing more to discuss. At your request, we gave you the week of celebration.

Plus a few days extra adds a second voice, gravel in a jar.

"Yankele?" Perel says. "What's wrong?"

I'm well aware of that Rebbe says. *I appreciate it, more than I can express. But you must believe me. It is not yet time. We still have need of him.*

Her the gravelly voice says.

Your sisters and brothers are highly displeased the whistling voice says.

I beseech you Rebbe says. *We are in need. An extension—*

There are no more extensions.

Perel's fingers clutch at her arm.

A new voice—round and sympathetic but no more inclined to bend— says *It has been two years.*

And for two years we have had peace Rebbe says. *Take him away—*

Her the gravelly voice snaps.

—and it will not last. I guarantee you that.

Every evil shall be dealt with in its own time and place the whistling voice says.

But if we can prevent it from happening to begin with—

I knew this would happen the gravelly voice says. *I said it, didn't I?*

We are not in the business of prevention the whistling voice says. *It is not granted to us, nor to you.*

I said he'd get attached, and I was right.

It'll only get harder if you wait the round voice says.

The balance of justice the whistling voice says *demands a correction.*

Beside her, Perel has grown still. She is listening, as well.

Forlornly, Rebbe says *Where will he go?*

She the gravelly voice corrects. *And that's not your concern.*

Somewhere the need is greater the round voice says.

The need to flee is sickeningly primal, a kind of nauseous gravity. But she cannot move: Perel's fingers lightly clasping her wrist are like an anchor.

Rebbe says *It will be done.*

She looks down, wishing her blank face could show the sorrow she feels, now that their time together has come to an end. The Rebbetzin is staring at the house, in the direction of the voices, and her green eyes are fixed and calculating.

Perel says, "Come with me."

CHAPTER FORTY-NINE

Don't tell me that," Priscilla Norton said, gesticulating like an auctioneer as she shouted into the phone at her landlord. "Don't tell me I need to hire a housekeeper, I keep it quite clean, thank you."

Cross-legged on the floor, an ice pack pressed to his head, Jacob watched her stomp around, glad and guilty that she had chosen to vent her distress at someone other than him.

"I resent the suggest—excuse me. Excuse me. I resent the—don't you tell me that. Don't tell *me* it's *my* fault. I've never had bugs in my life, not a fly."

She was naked save the woolen throw carelessly draped over one shoulder, and he could see bruises splotching her milk-white skin: shins, arms, collarbone, wherever the beetle had hit her.

She jabbed the cordless with a thumb and hurled it to the sofa. "Bloody bastard. Accuse me of poor housekeeping."

"Asshole," he said.

"It had a horn, for God's sake. You don't get things with a *horn* from not taking out the bloody *rubbish*."

Jacob began to stand to offer her comfort, but she shook her head and backed away. "I need to take a shower."

She hurried into the bathroom and shut the door.

He sank down, listening to the water run, examining his own body for marks. In addition to the soft lump at the side of his head, he had a rug burn on his stomach and another on his flank. No bruises.

It had reserved its true wrath for her.

His lips still tingled where it had touched him.

The water cut off, and minutes later Priscilla appeared in pajama bottoms and a hoodie, her hair tied back severely.

"Do you need more ice?" she asked.

"I'm okay," he said. "Thanks. How're you?"

"I'll live. Time for bed." She paused. "Are you coming?"

"Mind if I stay up a bit?"

She looked relieved. "Can I get you anything? Hungry?"

"No, thanks."

She retreated without an argument.

Jacob sat on the couch, staring at the jagged hole blown in the window.

Behind her bedroom door, Priscilla tossed and turned and mumbled.

His jeans, puddled near the door, began to vibrate. He crawled over to them, turned them right side out, and dug out his phone.

Maria Band said, "I'm keeping track of the favors you owe me." She sounded noticeably friendlier, though.

Among the events Casey Klute had worked on in the weeks prior to her murder was a cocktail reception for the annual conference of the North American Architectural Design and Drafting Society.

"That help?" Band asked.

"A lot. A whole hell of a lot. Thanks."

He put down the phone. He got up, went to Norton's bedroom, opened the door softly. He stood there for a while, watching her small form rise and fall, the duvet pulled up to her neck.

She said, "Who was that?"

"Sorry," he said. "Go back to sleep."

"I wasn't sleeping."

He sat on the edge of the bed. "Miami PD."

"What did they have to say?"

He told her.

"That's good news," she said.

He nodded.

"Are you coming to bed at some point?"

"I'm not really tired."

She pushed herself up against the headboard. "Should we talk about what happened."

"What part of it?" he said.

He tried a smile. It felt artificial, and she didn't return it.

"It hurt," she said. "When you went inside me, it felt like—"

"I was stabbing you."

She grimaced. "You haven't got some horrible disease or something, have you?"

Not a physical one. "No."

"Then . . . ?"

He said, "I don't know."

She emitted a strange, hiccupping laugh. "I'll tell you what I know. I know we've both had far too much to drink on an empty stomach, followed by far, far too much excitement."

"Agreed."

A silence. He reached for her hand but she withdrew, hugging herself, rubbing her upper arms. She wasn't looking at him, so he couldn't tell if she was angry or cold or what.

She said, "I want to tell you something, but I'm worried you're going to think I'm mad."

"I won't think that."

"You will."

"I promise," he said.

A silence.

She said, "I saw . . . I mean, it wasn't like normal seeing. More like, I felt it. I don't know how else to describe it." She paused. "I can't say it out loud without feeling like I *am* mad."

Now when he reached for her hand, she was ready to give it to him. He waited.

"I saw a woman," she said. "Behind you. Standing behind you. For half an instant, if that. Like lightning, sort of, in the shape of a person."

"What did she look like?"

"Please don't mock me."

"I'm not," he said.

"I feel crazy enough already without you—"

"Pippi. I swear to you. I am not mocking you."

She fell silent.

"Tell me what she looked like," Jacob said.

"Why?"

"You saw her," Jacob said. "Tell me what you saw."

"Yes, but . . . I mean, she wasn't real."

"Tell me what you saw."

"She—are you really asking me this?"

"I really am."

"Well . . . She was beautiful, I suppose."

"How?"

"How beautiful?"

"What made her beautiful?"

"Everything. Just—I don't know. I know a beautiful person when I see one. She . . . She was perfect, I reckon. But I really don't see what—"

"Hair color? Eye color?"

She made a frustrated noise. "Why are we discussing this?"

"You told me—"

"I told you because I can never tell anyone else, can I, or they'll cart me away, and to be honest I should never have said a thing to you, either. It's over and done with and I don't want to talk about it anymore."

"Pippi—"

"I've nothing else to say, Jacob."

"She was beautiful," he said. "That's it."

"She looked angry," she said.

Pippi Norton, smart cop, clever girl, began to cry. "She looked jealous."

SHE LAY ON HER SIDE, curled away from him while he rubbed her back, talking softly to her. She was right: the whole thing was best forgotten. He spoke as much for his own benefit as for hers. He steered her back to the case, emphasizing how much they'd discovered together, shoring up her bravado. She promised she'd follow up with Scotland Yard. He promised he'd send DNA profiles. They were not coauthors of a shared delusion; they were not failed lovers; they were two cops, absorbed by details, and their parting was cordial, hinged on a tacit agreement to never again discuss the matter.

"It certainly has been a terrific adventure knowing you," she said.

"You, too."

"Should you chance through these parts again, please don't hesitate to get in touch."

"Long as you call an exterminator."

"Believe you me," she said, "it's top of my list."

BACK AT THE HOSTEL, he packed his belongings by the light of his phone while his roommates grumbled and clamped their pillows over their heads.

The lobby was deserted. He sat at a computer kiosk and unfolded his transcription of the Prague letter on the table. As before, it was a slog. He frequently stopped to consult the Internet for definitions. No solution for missing words, so he guessed.

The Maharal's fondness for allusion made it difficult to determine where his personal voice ended and Scripture began. Jacob kept a running list of sources. The clacking of the keyboard made a lonely sound.

It was nearing five a.m. by the time he'd finished.

With the support of Heaven
20 Sivan 5342
My dear son Isaac
   And God blessed Isaac so may He bless you.
   As a bridegroom rejoices over his bride, so may God rejoice over you. For the sounds of joy and gladness yet ring in the streets of Judah. Therefore this time I, Judah, will praise Him.
   And I say to you now, what man is there that has married a woman but not yet taken her? Let him go and return to his wife.
   But now let us remember that our eyes have seen all the great deeds He has done. For the vessel of clay we have made was spoiled in our hands, and the potter has gone to make another, more fit in her eyes. Shall the potter be the equal of the clay? Shall what is made say to its maker, you did not make me? Shall what is formed say to the one who formed it, you know nothing?
   But let your heart not grow weak; do not fear, do not tremble.
   For in truth we have desired grace; it is a disgrace to us from God.
   In blessing
   Judah Loew ben Bezalel

Shivering, he folded the note up and put it in his pocket and went to check out.

The clerk asked if he had enjoyed his stay in Oxford.

"Yes and no," Jacob said.

"More yes than no, I hope."

Jacob handed over the white credit card. "I wouldn't go that far."

CHAPTER FIFTY

They were waiting for him beyond customs.

Subach grasped the handle of Jacob's bag. "Allow me."

Beneath a loud L.A. sun, they rafted pockets of exhaust toward the short-term parking lot.

"Nice of you guys to pick me up."

"Beats the SuperShuttle," Schott said.

"America greets you with open arms," Subach said. "How was your flight? Watch the movie?"

"*Kung Fu Panda 2.*"

"Any good?" Schott said.

"Not like the first."

"They never are," Subach said, punching the elevator button.

Schott said, "I hope you brought a book."

Jacob shrugged. He'd spent the majority of the journey reviewing his notes and studying the page torn from the yearbook, inoculating himself to Pernath's stare. He'd read the in-flight magazine cover to cover, done the crossword and the sudoku, browsed *SkyMall*. Even after he'd run out of reading material, he had not looked at the letter, nor at his translation.

A smooth crossing, devoid of turbulence, everyone else serene, while around him the tube of the cabin spun, endlessly contracting.

Sucking thin recycled air, he'd loosened his seatbelt as far as it would go, watching the dot of the plane as it skipped across the Atlantic Ocean, touching the tingly strip of skin where the beetle had pressed itself to his lips, raising his finger at every approach of the drink cart, grateful for the lack of judgment in the flight attendants' faces as they sold him his nth eight-dollar mini-bottle of Absolut.

Must be a nervous flier.

Now he stepped from the elevator, and they crossed oil-slickened concrete toward a bank of livery cars. Schott raised a remote, popping the locks on an extra-long white Crown Vic with unmarked plates and mirrored windows.

Jacob flinched at his own reflection: a wild-eyed prophet with a five-day beard.

He reached for the door but it swung open on its own, and he saw Commander Mike Mallick, his bamboo body stretched across the bench seat.

Mallick patted the leather. "Hop in, Detective."

IT WAS CHILLY AND DARK inside, the air-conditioning cranked to the max. Schott rammed the car into four p.m. traffic.

"What happened to your lip?"

"Sir?"

"Did you burn yourself?"

Reflexively, Jacob ran his tongue over the spot in the middle of his lip. It no longer tingled, but a coin of dead, dry skin remained.

"Pizza," he said. "Fools rush in, sir."

"Mm. Heck of a trip you took."

"I tried to be frugal, sir."

Mallick waved. "I'm not concerned with that."

"Duly noted," Jacob said. "Next time I'll stay at the Ritz."

"Next time?"

"Should the need arise, sir."

In the front seat, Subach snickered.

Mallick said, "You found it fruitful, though."

"You were right on, sir. Highly educational."

"Good. Good. Tell me what you learned."

The sanitized-for-sanity version omitted any mention of Jacob's experience in the garret; his hour and a half in the basement of Radcliffe Science Library; the botched coupling with Norton; his new six-legged friend.

She was beautiful.

She looked angry.

She looked jealous.

When the recital was over, the Commander looked vaguely disappointed, although that might've simply been his default world-weariness.

"You've done a fine job, Lev."

"Thank you, sir."

"Anything else you want to share?"

"Sir?"

"I recall that when we last saw each other I played a tape for you."

"Yes, sir."

Mallick weighed his words. "What's your thinking on her."

"How so?"

"Have you made any headway, figuring out who she is?"

"My plan, sir, was to gather intel on Pernath, seeing as he's a strong suspect. If the woman's involved, and I'm not sure she is, she may very well show up with him."

"And if she doesn't?"

"I'll continue to focus on Pernath, hope he screws up and I can grab him, swab him, and squeeze him for info."

"And if he turns out to be a law-abiding citizen?"

"He is. He's gone twenty-five years without getting caught. But he's also a psychopath."

"So you leave him running around but keep an eye on him."

"Yes, sir."

"A psychopath."

"I don't see what choice I have, sir. Everything I've got on him is circumstantial. Move too soon and I guarantee you he'll never so much as make a rolling stop for the rest of his life."

"Meantime she's also running around out there."

"For now, yes."

"I don't like it."

"Me neither, sir. But I don't see how else to locate her."

Mallick didn't reply.

"Sir? Is there something I need to know?"

"Such as?"

"Do you have an idea who she might be?"

The mood in the car shifted as Mallick drew up, smiling thinly. "Is that a joke, Detective?"

"You seem more concerned about her than Pernath, is what I mean."

"Certainly I'm focused on her. She calls in Florack and disappears? Far as I'm concerned, that's probative."

"True, sir, but even if she did do Florack, I think Pernath's running the show, just as he was with Florack and Heap. Get him, kill the cancer."

"This investigation is about the murder at Castle Court," Mallick said. He leaned forward, his head grazing the felt of the ceiling, and Jacob could feel his breath, cold and odorless. "That was your assignment. That makes her the priority. I appreciate your creative thinking, and I'm willing to adopt your strategy and wait it out. Lest there be any confusion, though, let me reiterate: she is our primary target. Not Pernath. Do you understand?"

Jacob said, "Ten-four, sir."

"Another thing. I want updates."

"A hundred percent, sir. I'm giving you one right now."

Mallick shook his head. "I want more. And I want it more often.

From this point on, you're going to inform me on an hourly basis where you are and what you're doing."

Jacob chuffed. "Come on."

"You're really that close?"

"I think I am, but—"

"Then loop me in."

"Sir. It's tough to operate like that."

"You'll figure it out. Text me. E-mail me. Call. Set an alarm, if you need to. I don't care. I certainly don't want you moving on either of them, Pernath or the woman, without us there to support you. Understood?"

Jacob turned to look out the window at nudie bars and off-site airport parking. They'd gone no more than a mile down Century. He felt angry and jumpy; eager to throw open the door and walk.

Mallick said, "You haven't told me about Prague."

"I thought I covered everything, sir."

"Not the case," Mallick said. "The city."

"What about it, sir?"

"Anything. General impressions."

Jacob said, "It was pretty good, I guess, sir."

"We send you on an all-expense-paid European vacation and that's it? 'Pretty good'?"

"I'm very grateful for the opportunity, sir."

"I hope you had a chance to do some sightseeing."

"Some," Jacob said.

"How did you find that?"

"Pretty good, sir. Thank you, once again."

A silence.

"I haven't been to Prague in years," Mallick said.

Jacob looked at him. "I wasn't aware that you'd been at all, sir."

Mallick nodded.

The rest of the trip dragged on in tight silence. Finally, Schott pulled over outside Jacob's building, leaving the motor running.

"Keep me apprised," Mallick said.

Subach carried Jacob's bag, setting it down outside the door to the apartment.

"Do I tip you now, or when the case is closed?" Jacob asked.

Subach smiled. "Don't worry about the Commander. Times like these, he gets nervous."

"Times like what," Jacob said.

"You need help with this Pernath guy, let us know. We'll get you what you need."

"Mel? Can I ask you something? You ever been to Prague?"

Subach chuckled. "As it so happens, I have."

"What about Schott?"

"I think he might've said something about that once or twice."

"I never knew cops to be such a well-traveled bunch," Jacob said. "We should start a club. Get together. Do slide shows."

Subach patted him on the shoulder and lumbered back down to the idling car.

CHAPTER FIFTY-ONE

Jacob's apartment was dusty but otherwise exactly as he'd left it. He'd entertained the foolish thought that his physical world would reflect the changes in him, and now he didn't know whether to be grateful or disappointed.

He dumped his bag and showered and shaved. It was clear why Mallick had commented on his lip: the affected area was one shade darker than the surrounding flesh. It looked like a strong vein, or a faint tattoo, a tiny part of him that wasn't him. The impulse to peel the offending strip away was strong. He tried to work loose a tag and ended up bleeding.

Pressing a tissue to his mouth, he rummaged in his nightstand and came up with a mostly new ChapStick left by a long-ago one-night stand. Balmed, his lips felt bland and greasy, a sensation that turned his stomach.

He had a bourbon to steady his nerves, then called Divya Das, getting her voicemail.

"Hey. I'm back and I've got a present for you. It's not a commemorative shot glass. Drop by?"

He sent Mallick a one-word text—*unpacking*—and spent an hour organizing his findings and updating the murder book. At eight p.m., with no word from Divya, he left her another message, and texted Mallick that he was headed out for dinner.

Henry the convenience store clerk saw him and made hallelujah hands. "I was starting to get worried. I was gonna call the cops."

"I am the cops."

Updates the Commander wanted? Updates he'd get. Jacob sent step-by-step texts.

two premium quality all-beef frankfurters
relish
onions
jalapenos
ketchup
mustard

Henry rang him up. "Don't ask me to kiss you."

"Dream on."

The white credit card didn't work.

Walking home, Jacob answered a call from Detective Aaron Flores, who proudly announced that he had persuaded the events manager at the Venetian to dig into the old Outlook calendar. Bingo: the week of Dani Forrester's death, the North American Architectural Design and Drafting Society had occupied the Delfino Ballroom, on level four.

"I asked about the names you gave me," Flores said. "I didn't find anything, and I can't tell from the file if she met with any of them."

"Don't worry about it."

"What'd the other Ds say?"

Jacob recapped Maria Band's report. "New York and New Orleans I haven't heard from yet. Doesn't matter. Between her and you, it's enough for me to feel confident closing the noose."

"Excellent," Flores said. "Make it tight."

"Appreciate the help," Jacob said. He turned onto his block. "I'll be sure you get the credit you deserve."

"I'm not worried about credit. I'm worried about nailing the motherfucker."

A county Coroner's van was parked outside his building.

"Same here," Jacob said. "Listen, I gotta go. I'll keep you posted."

A young woman with red hair out of a box sat at the wheel, deep into her smartphone. Jacob rapped the glass and she jumped in her seat.

She buzzed the window down. "Damn," she said. "You scared the shit out of me."

"Detective Lev," he said. "Can I help you?"

She stared at his glossy lips. He folded them in. "Can I help you," he said again.

She snapped to. "You have something for me."

"I do?"

"That's what they told me." She handed him her ID: Molly Naismith, coroner investigator trainee.

"I called Dr. Das," he said.

"Well, you got me."

"Is she unavailable?"

"Not my wheelhouse," she said. "You got a problem, call the main line."

He glanced at the van. "A little overkill."

"They didn't specify what I was going to need." Leaving off *asshole*, but barely.

Kit in hand, she followed him upstairs. She transferred Reggie Heap's bloody loafers to an evidence bag and sat at his kitchen table to fill out paperwork.

"Do you know Dr. Das?" he asked.

"Not personally." She handed him the chain-of-custody form. "Sign, please."

"Is she going to process these personally?"

"No clue." *Bite me.*

He felt bad. He hadn't meant to antagonize her. "Sorry if I'm being a pain. I've been traveling for twenty-four hours and my head's a pipe bomb."

She softened somewhat. "I'll get this through as quickly as I can. Scout's honor."

"Were you a scout?"

She smiled and left, the evidence bag swinging at her side.

Jacob sat and composed an e-mail.

Hey Divya. Don't know if you're on vacation, wanted to give you a heads-up. Sent some shoes for DNA. There's blood on them I think might be from one of my suspects. The tech who picked up is named Molly Naismith, maybe you can touch base with her, make sure it's being handled properly.

He paused, gnawing his thumbnail.

I'm guessing you're busy, which is why I haven't heard back from you. If that's the case, just ignore the rest of this. I wanted to clear the air in case I've made you uncomfortable in some way. You're a pro and I like working with you, and I'd hate to feel I've done or said anything that could change that. I'm probably making too big a deal about it. Either way I'll lay it to rest.

He hammered DELETE until the entire second paragraph was gone. Mulling over what to replace it with, he settled on casual and brief and vague.

Like I said, don't know if you're around, but if you are taking off, and you haven't left yet, I'd love to

DELETE

it'd be nice to

DELETE

fun to get a chance to see you. Buy you dinner.

He reread it a couple of times, changed *buy you dinner* to *grab a bite*, and hit SEND.

THE MOST RECENT ONLINE PHOTO of Richard Pernath was a candid taken at a gala charity dinner. He'd aged well, the shelf of hair starting higher up on his forehead, elongating his face and counteracting a mild fleshing out of his features. The photographer had caught him among a group of tuxedoed men and gowned women chortling in various directions—except for Pernath, who had locked on the lens.

Jacob printed the photo and set it facedown on the desk. He needed it for reference, but he didn't want the SOB ogling him.

Additional clicking revealed that Pernath had taken a page from his father on how to conceal wealth. There were no cars registered in his name, no properties deeded to him. His office at 1491 Ocean Ave. listed business hours of ten a.m. to five p.m.

Tomorrow was another day.

He sent Mallick an e-mail summary and went off to bed, hoping for a few restful hours.

It wasn't to be. Caught between time zones, he got up at three-thirty and sat at his computer with the Prague letter spread on the desk, his chest prickling. He worked until the bruised sky began to heal, then went to his bedroom and yanked open his sweater drawer.

CHAPTER FIFTY-TWO

An airless basement room with mismatched bookshelves and a warping plywood Ark, the synagogue where Sam Lev prayed daily seemed anemic compared to the Alt-Neu's stony grandeur. A quorum and a half of codgers—Sam not among them—snoozed in metal folding chairs, waiting for the dawn service to begin. No one paid Jacob any attention until a voice behind him boomed, "My eyes deceive me."

Abe Teitelbaum had gotten his start as a deli counterman, heaving untrimmed briskets and thirty-pound crates of lox. Half a century later, he retained the physique of a circus strongman, chesty, thickset, low to the ground. Grinding the bones in Jacob's proffered hand, he said, "*Bienvenido*, stranger, to the land of the *alter cockers*."

"Great to see you."

Abe peered closer. "You're wearing lipstick now?" His chuck on the shoulder caused Jacob's rib cage to vibrate like a tuning fork. "Tell the truth: some girl hit you."

"They always do," Jacob said. "Thanks again for the help."

"What help? I helped?"

Jacob reminded him about the country club.

"Oh, *that*. That was my pleasure. Love to make em squirm. Only reason I keep my dues current."

"Do you know a member named Eddie Stein?"

"Nope."

"You should meet him," Jacob said. "You'd get along."

"I don't need any more friends. Fact, I'd prefer fewer." Abe thumbed at the white-haired men, lowered his voice. "That's why I hang out here. They're all gonna kick it soon. Very convenient." He grinned. "Speaking of people I like, how's your dad? I missed him yesterday."

Jacob frowned. "He wasn't here?"

"Not for davening and not later when we were supposed to learn together. Whatever, I'm not mad. Even a *lamed-vavnik* gets a sniffle every once in a while. A call would've been nice, though."

Jacob speed-dialed Sam. "Abba. It's me. Are you there? Can you pick up? Hello? Pick up the phone, Abba."

Abe looked distressed. "Nothing's wrong, I hope."

"I'm sure it's fine," Jacob said, dialing Nigel instead.

"I should've followed up," Abe said.

"Don't worry about it, really."

"You want, I can go over there."

Jacob held up a finger. "Hey, Nigel, listen, sorry to call so early, but is everything all right with my dad? I'm at *shul* and—"

Abe poked him in the arm and pointed: Sam had walked in.

"Never mind," Jacob said. "Disregard this message. Thanks."

Abe placed his hand lightly on Sam's bony shoulder. "The Messiah arrives. The kid and I were on the verge of bringing in the bloodhounds."

Sam stared at Jacob. "You're here?"

"That's the way you greet your son?" Abe said.

"I got back last night," Jacob said.

"Back?" Abe said.

"From Prague," Jacob said.

"Prague?" Abe asked. "What's going on? Why does nobody tell me nothing?"

Questions would have to wait: the retired-dentist-turned-*gabbai* banged the dais three times, the retired-lawyer-turned-cantor chanted the opening blessings, and Sam turned aside to put on his *tefillin*.

Blessed are You, Our God, King of the Universe, Who has given my heart the understanding to discern between day and night . . .

Jacob found his own seat and slung down his backpack. In it he'd packed a camera, junk food, sunglasses, flashlight; flex-cuffs and a Taser; his Glock, full mag plus one extra. To top it all off, the blue velvet bag, fished from his sweater drawer, containing his own *tefillin*.

How many years had it been? At least a dozen. He was afraid he'd forgotten how to put them on, but muscle memory guided him: he placed a black box containing the sacred writings on his upper arm, binding it there with black leather straps, mumbling the blessings as he went. He set a second black box at his hairline, centering it between his eyes, and finished by wrapping the arm-strap around his palm and fingers in the shape of one of the Divine names.

He glanced at his father and a chill came over him: Sam had settled into his seat, stock-still, in meditative silence, a life-sized version of the clay model. Then the cantor recited the *kaddish*, and Sam stood up, and the illusion dissolved.

PRAYERS PROCEEDED ROUTINELY: hymns of praise; declarations of faith; pleas for health, prosperity, and peace. During the recitation of the *Shema*, Jacob texted Mallick.

hear o israel the lord is our god the lord is one

After the song of the angels, the *gabbai* came around, rattling a tin charity box. Jacob fished out the hundred-dollar bill Sam had given him, folded it several times to conceal the denomination, and stuffed it into the slot.

During the final psalm, Abe excused himself, saying something about a breakfast meeting. Within a few minutes, the rest of the men had departed, leaving father and son alone.

"You didn't tell me you were coming," Sam said.

"Didn't realize I had to."

"Of course not." Sam smiled wearily. "You're back safely. That's what counts."

"What I said over the phone," Jacob said. "I didn't mean it."

"It's all right."

"No, it's not. I'm sorry."

"Don't give it a thought. You needed to speak your mind."

"That's the problem. My mind is a bad place right now."

A beat. Sam reached over and clasped Jacob's hand. Squeezed once and let him go.

"Abe said you missed learning with him. You okay?"

Sam shrugged. "Everyone deserves a day off."

Jacob had his doubts, but decided not to press. "I have something I want you to see," he said, unfolding his transcription of the Prague letter and his makeshift translation, placing them side by side on the table.

Sam picked up the Hebrew text and held it close. His failing eyes shuttled busily behind his sunglasses. "It's accurate?"

"I was going fast. But I think so."

Sam felt for the translation and compared the documents.

"I found a website with the Loew family tree," Jacob said. "There were several daughters and one son named Bezalel, but no Isaac. I'm guessing Isaac was Isaac Katz, who apparently was married to two of the Maharal's daughters."

Silence.

Jacob said, "'Joy and gladness' refers to a wedding, obviously." He leaned over to read. "'I say to you now, what man is there that has married a woman but not yet taken her? Let him go and return to his wife. But let your heart not grow weak; do not fear, do not tremble.' That's the priest's speech before the Jewish army goes to war."

Sam sat motionless.

"This business about clay and pottery, I found the source in Isaiah, but it doesn't make much sense to me. The last line, about disgrace, I couldn't find anywhere." Jacob paused. "Bottom line, Abba, I'm lost."

Sam adjusted his glasses, his chest cycling shallowly.

"On the contrary," he said. "I think you did fine."

He put the pages down. "The case is going well?"

"Pretty well. Can we talk about this for a minute, though?"

"I really have nothing to contribute," Sam said.

He picked up his *tefillin* bag and started for the exit. "Focus on your work."

"Wait a second."

"Don't get distracted," Sam said, and disappeared around the corner.

"Abba." Jacob grabbed the letters and his backpack and followed his father out to the pavement. Nigel had the Taurus curbside, the motor running. He got out to help Sam in.

"Abba. Hang on."

"I'm tired, Jacob. I had a hard night."

"Why? What's wrong?"

"I need to go home. Let me think it over." Sam climbed into the passenger seat. "I'll let you know if I come up with anything."

Nigel shut Sam's door, ran around to the driver's side.

"Where are you going?" Jacob said to him. "Hey. Man. Seriously. Come on. *Hey.*"

The Taurus pulled away from the curb, headed north on Robertson.

Half a block on, though, brake lights flared and Nigel jumped out and hustled back up the sidewalk, waving something.

"He wants you to have this," he said, handing Jacob another hundred-dollar bill.

CHAPTER FIFTY-THREE

Fourteen ninety-one Ocean Avenue sat on prime commercial real estate. The bottom three floors belonged to a laser dental clinic, a talent agency, and a private equity fund. Pernath had the penthouse.

The office had an open plan, poured concrete floors and high windows that took advantage of unobstructed water views. Jacob approached the reception desk, counting three women and four men, all trim and chic, sketching in the icy glow of outsized computer monitors. He picked through their faces one by one, wondering who was Pernath's current protégé.

The receptionist said that Richard was out with a client.

"I work for the city," Jacob said. "We're doing a zoning survey. I was hoping to talk to Mr. Pernath personally."

The receptionist smiled, returned Jacob's lie with one of his own. "I'll be sure to tell him."

Or you, pal. How bout it.

"Do you expect him in anytime soon?" Jacob asked.

"Gosh, it's so hard to tell. I'll make sure he gets the message, though, mister . . ."

"Loew," Jacob said. "Judd Loew."

The receptionist pretended to type. "Have an awesome day, Judd."

JACOB HAD MISSED SOMETHING while loading his backpack. He searched for the nearest camping supply store, found it close on Fourth Street, and bought a seven-hundred-dollar pair of Steiner binoculars, charging it to the white card.

He texted Mallick a photo of the receipt, adding *thanks.*

The Commander didn't take the bait: no reply.

Returning to Ocean Avenue by 11:15, Jacob parked adjacent to a strip of cliffside park offering an oblique but clear view of Pernath's building.

He switched on the radio, twiddled between sports talk and scratchy jazz, ate M&M's and a protein bar that claimed to taste like cookies 'n' cream.

It might have if he'd had some bourbon to chase it with. In a nod to responsibility, he hadn't had a drink since last night.

The problem with staying sober was that it felt to him like being drunk.

He raised the binocs at whoever entered or exited the building, killing time by guessing destinations.

Surgically enhanced bimboid briskly sashaying: talent agency, or a patient in search of perfect teeth?

Nerd in khakis and out-of-pants white shirt: the IT guy for the private equity firm.

Conspicuously well-dressed couple in their fifties: clients, either private equity, or checking on a remodel in Beverly Hills, Brentwood, Bel Air.

At 11:49, he propped the phone on the steering wheel, checking his e-mail to see if Divya had replied. She hadn't.

He sent Mallick a text.

outside pernaths office

The response shot back.

eyeball?

not yet he wrote. *will let u know*

do that Mallick replied.

How long was he supposed to keep up this bullshit? It was distracting, and pointless, and he put the phone away. He'd write when he had something to say.

At 1:16, he chanced a quick trip to a nearby public bathroom.

At 3:09, his phone beeped with a text from Mallick.

?

nothing Jacob typed.

then tell me that

At 3:40, a meter maid parked her motorized trike behind him and took out her ticket pad. He showed her his badge. Tacked on a smile for good measure. She made a face and putt-putted off in search of other victims.

Thinking about parking made him groan. The building was sure to have an entrance in the back. Jet lag didn't excuse being a dumb jerk-off.

His imaginary tweet to Mallick: *duh.*

Slinging his backpack over his shoulder, he jogged around the corner to Colorado, finding the alley that ran parallel to Ocean. There it was, a gated subterranean lot, accessed via numerical keypad. He pressed his face up to the steel latticework, squinting in at a maze of cars, any one of which could have belonged to Pernath.

He jogged back to the Honda. The meter maid had left him a ticket.

Crumpling it and tossing it in the gutter, he drove to a loading zone on Colorado with a sidelong view of the alley.

Circa five p.m., cars begin to trickle out, windshields muddled by a plunging sun. A headache that had begun an hour ago, a twinge born of squinting and alcohol deprivation, had blossomed into a throbbing monster. He popped Advil. His upper back hurt from twisting. His lower back hurt from sitting too long. His stomach rumbled. A cop on a bike rapped his window and told him to get moving. He opened his badge on his lap. The cop pedaled off.

Dusk arrived, salty and electric. Sodium vapor lamps dyed every driver orange. Squawking tweens flocked the Santa Monica Pier. The Ferris wheel came alive, a smoldering neon saw. Jacob sent a series of identical texts to Mallick—*waiting, waiting, waiting*. It took considerable restraint not to embellish.

Waiting . . . for Godot.

Waiting . . . for a girl like you.

He'd just about made up his mind to head home when, at 8:11 p.m., a metallic-green BMW coupe rose up from the sub-lot, left turn signal stuttering.

Richard Pernath in the driver's seat.

The architect swiveled his head, checking for other cars. For a moment his gaze lingered in the Honda's direction, and Jacob was sure he'd been made.

But Pernath's long face gave nothing away, and he raised a friendly hand to the driver of an SUV that had stopped to let him in.

Jacob jotted down the BMW's tag. He waited for a Volvo station wagon to set a screen, then pulled out.

Pernath went east on Colorado, south on Twentieth, east again on Olympic, passing beneath the 405, at this hour frozen with red brake lights. As predicted, he proved himself a conscientious driver, deferential to jaywalkers and shy of yellow lights—qualities that made him a rare bird among the froth-mouthed street gang known as the L.A. Commuters.

Good behavior also made him a major pain to follow. Jacob, fighting back predatory excitement, had trouble maintaining the distance. Several times he lost his screen car and had to pull over and wait for another to overtake him. He might've lost Pernath, too, if not for a pretty solid theory about the architect's destination.

His phone chirped: Mallick, wanting an update. The law demanded that Jacob ignore it, so he did.

———

THEY KEPT ON OLYMPIC as far as Century City, where Pernath signaled right and got onto the half cloverleaf that ramped up to Avenue of the Stars north.

The street was wide and divided into six lanes that terminated at Santa Monica Boulevard. The BMW's detour into the pickup lane for a glass office building caught Jacob off guard. He had enough presence of mind to keep the Honda moving, roaring through a right at Constellation and flipping a U-turn to await a green arrow.

When the light changed, he reversed direction onto Avenue of the Stars south. Cruising opposite the office building, he spotted the BMW among the scrum of cars vying for position.

Driving another half block, he U'd again, returned for a third pass. He'd completed the same circuit twice more when he saw the green car nosing from the end of the pickup lane, preparing to turn right.

Jacob slowed, waiting for Pernath to pull out ahead of him. The architect stayed put, ever so politely, so as not to cut Jacob off.

No, please, I insist: you first.

No, you.

You.

Alphonse, Gaston . . .

Damn your manners, mon ami!

Jacob rolled past, allowing himself a peripheral glance at the BMW.

There was a second person in the car.

Speed and glare and darkness reduced the figure to a vaguely human shape. He couldn't tell if it was male or female. Nor did he have time to work through the implications of either, because the avenue was about to end and he had to make a turn.

He guessed a right on Big Santa Monica.

Pernath came along behind him.

It was stop and go for several blocks through Beverly Hills. Crossing Rexford, Jacob looked back and saw the BMW shifting into the left turn lane.

Jacob jerked left onto the next side street, Alpine Drive, disregarding boulevard stops and eliciting the finger from a woman walking a Yorkie in a sweater.

He waited at Sunset Boulevard, praying his intuition would come through.

Fifteen seconds later, the BMW zipped past, a luminous green vapor trail.

Pernath wasn't driving so casually anymore.

Now he was in a god-awful hurry.

Jacob turned onto Sunset.

His phone continued to nag him as he worked his way eastward behind Pernath. More traffic as they entered West Hollywood, the Strip shimmying and glittering like a whore, pedestrians seizing the right-of-way whether or not it was theirs.

Jacob did not dare get close enough to see the passenger. Could be that it was Pernath's wife, and he was tailing a dutiful couple headed home to watch DVR'd *Jeopardy!* Web searches had produced nothing about the architect's family, but that didn't mean he didn't have one. Jacob, eager beaver, hadn't looked very long or hard. A more cautious cop might've taken a couple more days to gather intel, get to know his subject, identify weak points.

A more cautious cop would've missed this chance.

If the passenger was an innocent, Jacob had to make sure nothing bad happened.

If the passenger was an accomplice, he could grab them both.

The boulevard stabbed rapier-straight into the soiled heart of Hollywood. Any doubt as to where they were headed evaporated as Pernath slotted into the left turn lane at Highland.

Jacob hooked left on Cahuenga and ran parallel to the 101. South of Barham, he veered eastward into the hills, skirting the reservoir, switch-backing minor roads, scaling the night.

He kept his speed moderate. They would arrive well before him, but he had no choice: the road was isolated and unlit, and it was an un-usually clear night, his headlights bleeding everywhere. He cut back to parking lights, creeping along in a weak amber bubble. Anyone coming down the hill toward him wouldn't see him until it was too late. A small risk, worth taking.

The phone spit out a text.

He shut it off.

The intervals between houses lengthened—civilization gasping for breath, and dying, and he was alone, finding his way forward without aid. Far below, the diminished city gassed off a jaundiced haze. He kept driving, stalking, counseling himself patience, until he edged around a hairpin and his faith was rewarded: half a mile ahead, a pair of cherry-red holes appeared in the landscape. They swished left and right and left and were swallowed up in gray folds.

He realized that he'd begun to speed up again and eased off on the gas. No sense slaloming through the flimsy barrier. He'd get there soon enough. He knew. He'd been this way before. They were going to Castle Court.

THE SHATTERING OF
THE VESSEL

The thought of the tall men—terrible serenity—haunts her as she and the Rebbetzin hurry to the *shul* and ascend to the garret.

She sets the box of fresh clay beside the pottery wheel. Perel unpacks her toolkit and begins rolling up her sleeves.

"Oh, oh, oh. Curse me. We need water."

Dazed, she reaches automatically for the bucket and starts toward the ladder.

"Wait," Perel cries.

She freezes.

"You can't go out there." Then, soothingly: "They can't come in here. It's not allowed. Do you understand, Yankele? Here, you're safe from them. I promise you that."

She nods. The Rebbetzin's certainty bewilders her.

"It's not them you need to worry about. Yudl doesn't know you visit me here, does he? Has he ever asked you about it?"

She shakes her head.

"Good." Perel rolls down her sleeves and snatches up the bucket. "I'll be back soon."

The floorboards whine as she paces.

I said he'd get attached, and I was right.

It's not them you need to worry about.

And her mind fills with images: a nodding tribunal; black fire on white fire.

One thing at a time.

The implication devastates her.

They are not the danger.

Rebbe is the danger.

He who has been a father to her; who has blessed her like a son.

What awful power do they have over him, that they can turn him against her? She tears at her hair in grief, beats her breast like a penitent, yearning to bolt and run as fast and far as she can.

The outline of the arched doorway dims from purple to inky black. To get water shouldn't take this long.

She pictures the Rebbetzin lugging the heavy bucket through the street, those slender arms straining. Thoughts shift to catastrophe. The tall ones have caught Perel. What horrible fate awaits her? Will Rebbe intercede? He must. He is a good man; he loves his wife.

But he loves her, too, or he claimed to.

At long last she hears a creak and a slam, and uneven footfalls blunder down the stone corridor and through the women's section—a person bearing a tremendous burden, knocking into chairs, coming for the garret, coming for her.

"It's me, Yankele."

She peers down through the trap. Perel straggles into view. She sets down the brimming bucket and bends, hands to knees, breathless.

"My arms are going to fall off. Come, take this up, while I immerse."

When the Rebbetzin returns to the garret, her wet hair lies flat.

"I'm sorry it took so long," she says. "I was trying to buy us time."

From her pocket, Perel produces Rebbe's *shul* key—then a second exactly like it. "I had Chana Wichs give me her husband's copy, too, just in case. I swore her to secrecy. We'll see how long that lasts. Nobody likes to lie to the Rebbe, and Chana's lips aren't exactly the tightest. But at least for now, poor Yudl's going to think he's lost his mind, looking for that key . . . All right," Perel says, clapping her hands together, "think, think, think. We must be precise, we don't have time for error. First we must make some room. Help me, please."

Under the Rebbetzin's direction, she moves bookcases, clearing a wide circle.

"The wheel I won't need, you can put it over there." Perel rolls her sleeves up again and sweeps her skirts under her. She kneels before the box of clay and scoops a largish handful, then four more, mounding them together on the floor. "While I'm getting started with this, you"— Perel pats the remaining clay—"handle that. I'm going to need all of it. You know what to do?"

She nods uncertainly.

"Well? What are you waiting for?"

Throwing her faith in the Rebbetzin, she upends the box in the middle of the circle. Clay slops out.

Perel bites her lip. "I hope it's enough. But—go on, now. No time to waste."

She does what she has seen Perel do night after night, first compacting the loose clay and squeezing out excess water; then lifting the mass and wedging it against the floor to drive out air. Riverbank beetles, kidnapped and entombed, crunch as she presses down with her full might, folding, turning, repeating. Perel—the long muscles of her forearms rippling beneath her rippling silver skin—does the same with her own smaller block of clay, reaching over periodically to check the texture.

"Remember: overworking it is as bad as underworking it."

She goes about her job numbly, trying to drive out the memory of Rebbe's words.

It will be done.

"That's good. Now, two piles, one about so—oh. Oh, Yankele. You're trembling."

Perel crawls over to clasp her hands. Warm mud oozes between their palms.

"You're frightened. Of course you are? Who wouldn't be? But you must be brave."

She looks into the Rebbetzin's glistening green eyes.

"He doesn't want to do it," Perel says. "He has no choice. Anyway, I won't let him. You must trust me, Yankele."

She does. She must. Other than the Rebbetzin, she has no one else left.

They resume work.

"Two equal piles, please. A rectangle, like so. The second pile, make it into four logs. Two of them about this wide, two a bit fatter. Each pair, try to make it the same length, if you can. They don't have to be perfect."

Meanwhile, Perel has rolled her own clay into a sphere.

"That's fine. Put them at the corners—yes. Just so. Don't worry. As I said, it doesn't have to be perfect yet. I'll fix it. Tell me: do you see, now?"

She nods. She is excited. And terrified.

They're making a person.

On hands and knees, Perel moves about the figure, coaxing joints together, forming hollows, using the tip of the knife to render the tracery of veins and hair and skin. The aura flares in ecstasy, scalding the room and subsiding. The rough block slims miraculously to a torso; uneven stumps smooth to limbs, slender arms and long legs twine with muscles like a braided candle. Hillocks of breasts and open plain of stomach; soft grassy sex and valley below—the magnificent body of a woman.

The thrill of memory courses through her.

Her body.

The face requires patience, love, and mercy. Perel does not find it beneath her dignity to bend over, contorting herself, balancing on one elbow as she scrapes out the seashell contours of an ear. Nostrils open, lips part, ready to draw breath. Consternation tightens the brow—bad dreams, to which a determined jaw refuses to surrender.

She sees. And remembers more.

The Rebbetzin descends the garret to the ritual bath, immersing herself a second time. She returns full of agitation, rubbing her fingertips together as she walks circuits around the body, examining every last crevice and detail until she is satisfied.

"Are you ready?" Perel sits. "Lie down, please. Put your head in my lap."

She obeys, careful not to disturb the beautiful clay body.

Perel smiles at her upside down. "Thank you for everything you have given me."

Thank you.

"I'll miss you."

I'll miss you, too.

"You'll always have a home here." A sad laugh. "Although I'm sure it goes without saying that it might be wise to stay away for a while."

Perel strokes her head. "It won't hurt. It will be easy, like drawing a hair out of milk."

Soft touches smooth the distortions of her lumpy skull, her crumpled ears. Her eyes close. She had forgotten what sleepiness feels like. It's lovely, a pillowy fall from a great height, a descent that never ends. She feels heat on her face, the charge that fills the infinitesimal gap between two skins, and Perel's lips touch hers, and her mouth opens, and though she has been warned never to do this, though she knows what will happen, she trusts, and parts her lips wider, and brings forth her tongue.

The knot begins to loosen.

She can feel it unraveling, dissolving, and she exhales and sleep wraps her in a cloak of clay.

"You are here."

Stunned and numb, stomach greasy, chest thudding, ears ringing, she lies on her back, gazing through fuzzy infant eyes at Perel's shining face, doubled and cloudy and swimming in the gloom.

"How do you feel?"

"Tired."

The sound of her own voice stuns them: then the Rebbetzin bursts into tears, and then into laughter, and then they both do, the two of them trembling and whooping and hugging.

"Blessed are You, O Lord, Our God and King of the Universe," Perel says, "Who has given us life and sustained us and brought us to this time."

"Amen."

It's no less shocking the second time around. They explode in a round of giddy peals.

Perel helps her to a sitting position. "I'm going to let you go, all right? Will you fall over?"

"I won't fall." The cloak itches against her back. She's naked. The realization causes her to shiver violently. Perel fetches an old prayer shawl and covers her with it. "Better than nothing."

"Thank you."

"Can you stand?"

"I think so."

They are roughly the same height now, a shocking equality. Together they shuffle around the garret, her watery limbs firming up, regaining their intelligence, until she moves smoothly, gracefully, exploring her body in space, examining herself, top to bottom.

Blue veins underlie the silky pale flesh of her arms. She spreads her toes in the dust, shrugs her shoulders, twists at the waist. Everything feels familiar, and comfortable. She runs her fingers over her head. She has hair. Long hair, thick and soft. She brings the ends around to see what color it is. The lantern light paints in tones of linen and earth. Her eyes—what color are they? She trips over to the bucket, landing on her knees.

Perel lunges to grab her arm. "Are you all right?"

"Yes, fine." The water reveals eyes of indeterminate hue. Her face appears even more lovely than she had hoped for, the features finer and softer than they were in clay.

"Are you happy with how you look?"

She nods. It is a lovely face, yes; but more important, it is hers—the face she remembers.

Perel says, "I modeled it after my Leah."

She knows not what to make of that. But she's certain of what to say.

"She must have been a beautiful girl."

A silence.

"There is one more thing," Perel says. "The knot that stilled your tongue."

She sticks out her tongue, touches it, finds smooth, yielding tissue—no parchment. She looks at the Rebbetzin, who hesitates, and blushes, and then inclines her head downward.

Toward her pubis.

"I had to put it somewhere," Perel says. "It shouldn't come out. It's deep. But you should be careful, of course."

"I will."

"Don't look so surprised," the Rebbetzin says. "It's the source of life, and you are alive."

Her heart swells with gratitude; the back of her throat aches.

"Do you have a name?"

She smiles. Of course she does.

It's . . .

What.

She says, "My name is . . ."

Silence.

Perel frowns. "Yes?"

"It's . . ."

Ridiculous. She has her body back. She has her voice back. And yet the only name she can come up with is a man's name—the name she's been living with.

Yankele.

Her mind coughs up words in a forgotten tongue.

Mi ani? Yankele.

Who am I? Yankele.

The letters of each word reassemble themselves.

מאי

A new name. She will own it.

She says, "My name is Mai."

Perel smiles, relieved. "Nice to meet you, Mai."

Before she can reply, a loud banging comes from the first floor—followed by a silence, and then a tremendous crash, an axe splintering wood.

They're breaking the front door down.

Perel runs to the trapdoor, kicks it shut. "Help me."

Not so very long ago, Mai could have managed the bookcase on her own; now it takes the two of them, working together, to drag it atop the trap. Moments later men's voices ring out, and boots mount on the ladder, and fists beat at the floor.

"Perele," Rebbe calls, his voice pinched and distraught. "Perele, are you in there?"

Perel seizes Mai by the arm. Together they tiptoe across the garret.

"Perele. Please open up."

They come to the arched door. Perel lifts the iron bar holding it shut, hauls the door open. Frigid air streams in.

Below, the cobblestones swim.

The Rebbetzin clasps Mai's hands. "Go."

Mai hesitates. She's still dizzy, not to mention barely clothed, and Perel's grip on her feels like the pull of ten thousand men.

"Go," Perel says, releasing her hands. "Go as fast as you can. Don't stop running."

Mai eases one leg down the side of the building, feeling with her toes in search of the first rung. The metal is freezing, her muscles jellied, and after three steps she slips, letting out a shriek, clinging to one rung, her new soft woman's body banging into the rough brick. The prayer shawl falls, leaving her exposed to the world. Above her, Perel hisses to go, hurry, go, and she regains purchase and starts again to climb, watching the brick in front of her so as not to get dizzy, and she thinks she's doing well until Perel screams for her to stop.

She looks up.

The Rebbetzin is waving her arms frantically. *"Come back."*

She looks down.

David Ganz is waiting at the bottom.

He appears thoroughly confused—as well he should be, for he has come seeking a giant man and instead finds himself staring up at a naked woman. For a moment no one moves. Then he sprints to the rungs and climbs up after her.

"Faster," Perel yells. "Come on."

It's almost funny: what she would not give to have Yankele's body back, just for a moment. Ganz is gaining on her, his fingers starting to close around her ankle—hesitantly, because in all his life he has never touched a strange woman, and she jerks free, awakening him to his duty, and he seizes her leg in earnest, dragging her down, the tendons in her wrists straining, her throbbing fingers starting to uncurl. What does he think he's doing? He's going to pull her off. That's precisely what he means to do. He's going to kill her.

In his raspy voice he asks her to stop; come peacefully; he will not hurt her.

She knows that story.

She's heard it before.

But her hands are slick and weak and she knows that she cannot hold out much longer.

If it's going to happen, she's going to be the one to decide.

It's not a bad way to die.

She's done it before.

She lets go of the rungs and surrenders herself to the air.

Her twisting form plummets past Ganz's sweaty, cringing face; Perel's screams echo interminably from above.

Then a strange thing happens.

The cobblestones rushing up to greet her begin to slow, as though she is falling through water, and then syrup, and finally glass, and then the stones stop at a fixed size, at a fixed distance, and she floats.

She looks at her arms.

She has no arms.

In their place she sees a gossamer blur, emitting a loud buzzing.

She can't find her legs, either. She moves them, trying to locate them, and to her astonishment receives an answer from not two limbs but six, wriggling with minds of their own.

Dimly she hears Perel imploring her to go, fly, go; she hears David Ganz's frantic voice and now Chayim Wichs and Rebbe have joined the mix; but they sound far away, and garbled, and she ignores them, focused on learning how to move in this new form, tilting her hard-shelled body, willing herself through clotted air, thick as broth, an intoxicating metamorphosis. The scale of the world has shifted, her field of vision a beaded mosaic, many thousand tiles compounded together, swirling wondrously. It is not seeing as she has ever known it and yet it is natural to her. The ground vanishes into meaninglessness. She feels so light that it is a wonder she ever could have thought she would fall.

She rises toward the stars, leaving Prague behind.

CHAPTER FIFTY-FOUR

The last milestone before the road deteriorated was Claire Mason's driveway. Jacob pulled over fifty feet beyond, cut the engine, braved switching on his phone. The screen flooded with texts and voicemails from Mallick, demanding to know where he was, what was happening, why he wasn't responding.

Strictly for ass-cover, he texted back four words.

on suspect stand by

He assumed they knew where he was; he assumed they'd been tracking him all along. If they wanted to show up and stampede in and trample his work to dust, so be it.

He restarted the car.

Headlights off, the Honda lurched over moonscape. Jacob felt his senses heightened, attuned to every wind-wicked twig, every crenellated shadow, every granule of soil.

A quarter mile out, he cut the engine again and assembled his gear on the passenger seat. Flashlight. Taser. Flex-cuffs. Binocs.

He rechecked the Glock, stuffed the extra magazine in his back pocket, got out of the car.

Bent low, he advanced over cackling gravel, reached the final crest, and lay on his belly, worming forward till the death house came into view.

Windows dark.

Parking pad empty.

No human movement. No human sound.

No BMW.

He panned the acreage.

To his left, a rolling wave of hilltop, studded with stone.

To his right, the crescent canyon, slanting toward the house and curving around its back.

No growth over knee height. No place to hide a car.

He'd seen the lights, though; he'd followed Pernath halfway across the city. He was here, had to be, no other destination made sense.

Nowhere else possessed the same lethal sanctity.

Had he, somehow, missed him? Pernath driving up here to enact his ritual and leaving?

Impossible. Insufficient time, one way in and out.

Where was he?

They.

Jacob felt sick, remembering Pernath's approach down the alley, the second of eye contact.

The architect had made him. Strung him along. Doused his own lights; taken an earlier turnoff, Eagle's Point or Falconfuck or whatever; coasted off, leaving Jacob to sniff a false trail.

Dance, monkey, dance.

And now the motherfucker was free to do his thing with whomever he'd picked up in Century City.

A woman, held down as she choked on her own blood, praying for a savior never to arrive.

Because here he was, her savior, prostrate in the dirt, a line of ants trickling over his hand.

But how would Pernath have recognized him? They'd never met before.

But then where was the BMW?

It wasn't a car made for off-roading. Pernath could have stashed it downhill and ascended on foot, as Jacob had.

But if reason dictated leaving the car behind, it also dictated taking it as far as it would go: the end of the asphalt, near Claire Mason's house. Nowhere to hide a car there, either. Jacob would have spotted it on his way up.

He stayed there for another twenty minutes, agonizing.

A slash of bats dirtied the clouds.

The death house lay in cold repose.

Drawing up to a crouch, Jacob broke across the open ground; steadied himself against the front door for a two count and twisted the loose knob and swept in, gun drawn, clearing room to room, his hope withering in square-foot increments.

Nothing.

Nobody.

A second sweep ended in the kitchen, where he paused, pinching the bridge of his nose disgustedly as adrenaline flushed from his system and his lungs began to burn.

He'd had him, and lost him.

Or he'd never had him. He'd gotten overconfident. Made assumptions.

Fucked up.

He hammered the countertop in frustration, received the rebuke of a sparse echo.

Massaging his hand, he stared at the spot where the Hebrew lettering had been. The smooth wood bore no sign of it.

He thought about the missing brick from the Alt-Neu.

Thought about Mai running from him, gone in an instant.

Women he tried to make love to, recoiling in agony.

Bugs.

If all that could happen, why not a magically vanishing BMW?

Straight down the rabbit hole.

Since his return to L.A., he had been singularly focused on making the arrest. He'd allotted no time or space for dwelling on his mental state, and that had kept him from experiencing the full extent of his wretched confusion.

Now it rushed out of him, spurting from every raw orifice, dissolving the surface of reality. His heart wouldn't shut up. He held his splitting head together between his forearms, walking around the kitchen in circles. He'd fucked up, and because of that, more people were going to die. Tonight, or if not tonight, soon.

He tottered from the house and clicked on the flashlight and wandered over the property in the rising wind. Knees popping, he traversed the eastern slope, chasing every feral whine that escaped the canyon's lonesome depth. He went as far as the horizon and felt the seduction of gravity and imagined letting himself fall. He remembered Peter Wichs's hand on his arm and scrambled back to higher ground.

He was wasting his time.

Covered in scrapes and sweat, he straggled back to the Honda and collapsed in the driver's seat. The phone flashed. Nine more attempts at communication by the Commander.

report progress ASAP

never mind Jacob wrote back *they arent here will revisit tomorrow*

He pounded through the return trip as fast as he could without snapping the chassis, composing a mental list.

Pernath's father's house.

The office in Santa Monica.

The office in Century City: source security footage and determine who Pernath's passenger was.

Piss-poor list, reeking of failure and futility. No item on it appealed to him as much as the default retreat to home and alcohol.

Crossing from dirt to asphalt, he stomped the accelerator. The Honda's wheels spun out and he shot forward and he sped toward defeat.

Then he saw Claire Mason's driveway and her CCTV cameras.

The woman was a gift from the paranoid gods.

Braking, he backed up, pulled to Mason's talk box, and punched the intercom button.

It rang seven times. Maybe even Claire had a social life.

A scratchy voice filtered through the speaker: "Who is this?"

"Ms. Mason? Detective Jacob Lev from LAPD. I don't know if you remember, but I was—"

"I remember you."

"Great. I apologize for disturbing you—"

"What is it, Detective?"

"I was hoping I could come in and have another look at your security footage."

"Now?"

"If that's all right."

"Are you aware of what time it is?"

He had no clue. He glanced at the dash clock—after midnight.

"I'm truly, truly sorry," he said. "I really hate to have to disturb you like this, but—"

"It can't wait until tomorrow?"

"I wouldn't ask if it wasn't urgent, ma'am."

Impatient exhalation. "Hang on."

He glanced at the black camera eye on the intercom box, pictured her shuffling off to consult her monitors. He smoothed his hair and wiped dust from his face and prepared a smile.

The box spoke: "Detective? What did you want to see?"

"The road. From a couple of hours ago. I'll be quick. Thanks."

The gate shivered and began to slide.

He released the brake, wound up the same crushed stone path, through the same spotlit xeriscaping, toward the same stern modernist silhouette.

The front door opened. Same tatty green bathrobe in a widening slice of yellow light. Same scowl; same steaming tankard of tea. Except this time she didn't offer him any.

They walked wordlessly to the security room. He stood behind her, averting his eyes as she typed in her password.

"I'm looking for vehicles en route to 446," he said.

She clicked. Eight panels, eight blank swathes, bathed in green. The time stamp counted 00:13:15, 00:13:16, 00:13:17 . . .

"How far back?" she asked.

"Three hours. Eight-thirty."

"That's three and three-quarters hours," she said.

"I know." Strictly speaking, a wider window than he needed. "I'm sorry."

She sighed and reset the counter to 20:00:00. The screen gave a pixelated flinch.

They sat silently as minutes passed at 8×. Jacob couldn't decide whether he was rooting for the car to appear or not. Stupid, gullible, or crazy: which title did he prefer?

The counter reached eight-thirty without anything happening. Claire Mason turned and arched an eyebrow at him and increased the playback to 24×. The counter began to reel. Nine. Nine-ten. Nine-twenty. He'd picked up Pernath's tail at about ten after eight. The drive to Castle Court took about an hour and a half. The counter hit nine-thirty and he tensed up in anticipation.

Nine forty-seven: a square flash.

"Stop," he barked.

She hit the space bar, pausing at 21:50:51.

"Can you go back a couple minutes?"

She stared at him impatiently.

"I saw something," he said.

"That was me."

His heart sank. "You're sure?"

"I went to dinner," she said. "I got home at quarter to ten. That was me, pulling in."

"You're positive," he said.

She drew up. "Anything else, Detective?"

"Just a few more minutes, please?"

She let the video run up to real time: nothing.

"Thanks. Sorry."

She stood up. "Should I be concerned?"

"Not at all. Thanks again. Really appreciate it. Have a good night."

Her expression said that was unlikely.

She escorted him to the constricted entry hall, where he paused to thank her once more.

Stopped, breathless.

"What," she said.

He was staring at a gilt-framed pen-and-ink drawing of a woman's body lying among undulant vines, energy radiating out from her headless neck.

"Where did you get that?" he asked.

She blinked once, then dashed the tea in his eyes.

IT HAD MOSTLY COOLED OFF; he was more startled than hurt, and in the millisecond while his hands went up, he actually thought *How rude.*

She brained him with the mug. He heard a crack that he hoped was ceramic and not bone and pain trumpeted and his inner ear sloshed and he swung at her warping outline and she hit him again with something else, harder, heavier and he felt himself bowing sideways, sinking to one knee with his palm pressed to the cold concrete. She continued to hit him, breathing hard, emitting strange excited little chirrups. Blood streamed into his eyes. He rolled over into a puddle of tea to protect himself and she brought a picture (he did not know if it was *To Be Brasher* or another picture) crashing down on his upraised elbow. Glass teeth opened his forearm. She chopped the frame down like an axe, the corner spiking his temple, until the wood splintered; then she tried to stab him in the back with it, but he scissored his legs on the slick wet floor and he caught her ankle and she fell.

Dizzy and half blind, he surged atop her and got his hands around her throat and squeezed. Spit burst from her mouth. Blood jetted from his gashed arm and mixed with the foamy sludge running from the corners of her mouth and ran down her neck. He was trying to find her carotid. He needed four seconds of pressure. She twisted and kicked and clawed. A shadow fell across them.

A man's voice said, "Enough."

CHAPTER FIFTY-FIVE

t was the only word he would hear Richard Pernath speak. Pernath was wearing pressed jeans and a charcoal polo shirt. He was barefoot and holding a pump-action shotgun, which he kept fixed on Jacob while Claire Mason crawled away, coughing and gagging. Jacob slid himself back toward the wall, pressing up against the plaster, gripping his wounded arm. The barrel of the gun moved with him. His sinuses were choked with blood. He spat. Pernath's face twitched with revulsion but he didn't blink.

Claire Mason stood to retie her bathrobe. She wiped saliva on her sleeve and said, "I'm sorry," a remark that prompted Pernath to shoot the same disgusted face at her. The shotgun never wavered.

"I was getting him out," she said.

Pernath did not answer her, and she told Jacob to stand up and turn out his pockets. He set his badge and phone on the floor. He took the spare ammo from his back pocket and placed it beside them. She asked where his gun was.

"My car."

She patted him down nonetheless. He stood with his arms raised and his legs spread while she ran trembling hands along his inseams. The gash in his forearm was deep and ragged and perilously proximate to major blood vessels. It did not clot but oozed steadily, running down his biceps and dripping onto his shoulder and ear. Looking at it made him light-headed. His feet felt miles away.

They marched him out the front door. He could see the keys dangling in the ignition of the Honda. Pernath prodded him in the spine with the shotgun and he kept going.

They followed the network of brick paths lacing the property, heading around the swimming pool, in the direction of the orchard. Claire Mason led the way, ten feet in front of Jacob. He kept his wounded left arm aloft, over his head, clasping his left biceps with his right hand, trying to slow the bleeding. Runnels of blood pooled in the hollow of his collarbone. His temple bled, too. He left a trail of spatter on the brick. It would be easy to hose down. Same for the house's concrete floors.

Pernath brought up the rear, keeping well back of Jacob, but close enough not to miss. Some of the shot might pass through his body and hit Claire Mason. Pernath wouldn't care; he probably intended to kill her at some point. Jacob would simply be shortening the timeline.

He could appeal to her sense of self-preservation—tell her what became of all of Pernath's accomplices. Jacob doubted she'd believe him. Whatever depraved magic the architect had worked on Reggie Heap and Terrence Florack, he'd done the same to her. Jacob read it in the way she kept glancing back at Pernath, her face green and rippling in the light of the pool, her expression drawn and fearful. She was appealing to him. For approval. For forgiveness. And without looking back, Jacob could tell Pernath wasn't giving it to her.

Even if Jacob somehow got through to her, she couldn't help him: she was unarmed.

They started around the orchard. It was larger than it appeared from the front, perfectly choreographed rows of lemons and figs and plums stirring heavily in the breeze. Their perfume made Jacob teeter. He considered lunging for the gun anyway; better than dying helpless.

Wanting to know how far behind Pernath was, he said, "I spoke to Reggie's father."

Silence.

"He wants that drawing back."

Not even an errant breath.

Jacob kept walking.

THE GREENHOUSE OCCUPIED the lawn beyond the orchard. It was vast and unlit, a glass hangar, its southern side reflecting the cityscape. Jacob wondered what they were growing, that they needed so much area. He wondered why they needed a greenhouse when it got so hot in the Hollywood Hills.

Claire Mason crouched down to fiddle with the numerical padlock on the door.

Jacob's left hand had gone numb, the fingers curling up like fruit rotting on the vine.

The padlock snicked open. Claire Mason opened the door and switched on the lights and lines of fluorescent tubes crackled to life and he saw what they were growing.

Nothing.

An empty grassy scroll, violently uniform in color; no pots or planters, no climbing vines, no irrigation system. Here and there the ground humped, and there was a disruption in the pattern of the grass. Jacob had counted six such patches before he felt the shotgun in his back again.

They walked him to a flat spot at the far end. It looked as good as any a place to die. Claire Mason tramped over to the corner and came back with a shovel. She tossed it down at Jacob's feet and told him to dig.

He'd seen that in movies, had deemed it silly. Why would a person consent to dig his own grave? The implied threat of torture, for one. But that was secondary, he realized, to the desire to prolong life. It was amazing, what the human spirit would accept: a few more minutes, even the wretchedest imaginable, were preferable to death.

He bent to pick up the shovel. It felt heavier than it should. His left arm below the elbow had gone the same chalky hue as his hand. The gash once again began to ooze as he gripped the handle and put his foot on the blade and sank it into the earth and pried up a hunk. He dug slowly, thinking about his phone and wondering if Mallick was monitoring its location. He almost laughed, remembering his annoyance at the Commander's nannying. He hoped they didn't waste time searching the house. He hoped they noticed the trail of spatter.

"Hurry up," Claire Mason said. She paced in a five-foot radius from Pernath, as though tethered to him, while the architect stood relaxed, hip cocked, the shotgun leveled at Jacob's midsection.

The shovel beat a funeral cadence. Its handle ran slick with blood. Jacob's vision effervesced. His head fuzzed with white noise. He was having trouble standing. With nothing to catch hold of, his heart beat fast and light. His back was clammy, his arm numb to the shoulder. Beneath the grass lay a vivid red clay, manic with worms and grubs, a sunken island in a green sea.

He dug six inches deep, seven, eight, nine, and counting.

The buzz in his head rose to a vengeful tide, loud enough to drown out the retch of splitting earth.

Stomping down hard on the shovel, he lost balance, steadied himself, paused, eyes closed, expecting retribution, a brief blast of noise before silence.

Instead, he heard Claire Mason's voice shrilling—*what is that*—and then all was lost to the churn of innumerable wings.

Jacob opened his eyes.

Richard Pernath was staring up at the greenhouse's glass ceiling with his head hatched back at a severe angle. The shotgun hung forgotten at his side.

Claire Mason, equally rapt, pointing upward, her throat open in a mute scream.

A black mass in the sky, widening, blotting out the stars as it swept down toward them. The gray pallor of the greenhouse lights gleamed fleetingly in a hard underbelly for an instant and Jacob saw six hairy jointed legs and wings like sails and a beetle the size of a horse exploded through the roof, plunging them into darkness, knocking Jacob flat on his back.

The drone vanished, replaced by silence, then the guttural register of anguish.

Jacob clawed himself upright.

The iron frame of the greenhouse was frayed like thread, every panel ruptured except the ones directly above him. He sat in a patch of clean grass while the ground around him glittered.

Claire Mason ran in circles, batting at the air, howling, her skin riddled with shards of glass.

Richard Pernath was on his hands and knees, a large triangular shard jutting from his back like a silvery dorsal fin.

The beetle was gone. In its place stood a woman of perfect sculptural symmetry, lithe and naked in the moonlight. She began to advance on Claire Mason, who backed away, mewling and clutching at the bent frame of the greenhouse.

"No. *No.*"

The naked woman raised her arms and the muscles in her back danced, and then, before Jacob's eyes, she convulsed, and changed, swelling to monstrous proportions, to a thing blocky as a tower.

A gnarled appendage grew out of the claylike mass, lifting Claire Mason's body from the ground. Another tendril coiled around Mason's neck and there was a hiss and sizzle as her head separated and pipped to the ground and bounced, the severed neck sealed clean.

Mason's still-bleeding body collapsed in a pile.

With another convulsion, the tower of clay was gone and the naked woman turned to Jacob wearing Mai's smiling face.

Richard Pernath had managed to crawl to a hole in the greenhouse wall and was worming his way through. Mai started after him, but changed course and came toward Jacob, striding heedlessly over broken glass.

Jacob tried to tell her to leave him, get Pernath. The sound that came out of him was weak and wet. Mai knelt before him and took his hands in hers and drew him close. The heat of her body made apparent the deathly cold of his own.

She kissed him.

The burnt strip of skin on his lips came alive and for one delicious instant her humid floral breath flowed into him; then it curdled and became mud, and he struggled against its bitterness until it turned sweet once more, rolling slickly across his tongue with the taste of sex, and he gave himself to her. The mud coursed through him, transfusing, replenishing. Reviving his limbs and streaming into the chambers of his heart, which began again to churn.

He could not breathe. He did not need to. Everything he needed, she gave him. He strained to open his mouth wider, greedy for whatever she desired.

He grabbed for her perfect body, certain she wanted him as much as he wanted her, past and present and forever.

But she broke away, and he surfaced, gasping and sucking newborn air.

She said, "I've missed you."

Varying strains of color wove through her hair to create a troubling, unstable melange. Her eyes were green tonight, mirroring his own.

He said, "I've missed you, too."

As he said it he realized how true it was. He felt her fingers stroking his forearm and he looked down at the wound—a hardened scab, rust brown.

Mai smiled. "I'm part of you, now."

She raised his face and kissed him again, softly on the lips.

From behind her came the sound of a great rumbling, and they turned to see three tall shapes looming at the collapsed entrance to the green-house.

Mike Mallick said, "We're here, Jacob Lev."

Jacob felt Mai's hand tighten in his.

Mallick and his companions began to glide across the grass toward them, heralded by a frigid wind.

He said, "This is good. Stay right where you are. Do not let her go."

There was trepidation, too, in the way they moved, although whether they were afraid of Jacob or Mai or the both of them together was not clear.

"We're almost there," Mallick said.

He held up a calming hand, and Jacob could see that his other hand held something.

From far to Jacob's right came a very human groan: Richard Pernath was limping across the lawn, headed for the orchard.

"Don't worry about him," Subach said.

"Stay right where you are," Schott said.

Mallick drew close enough for Jacob to see the object in his hand.

It was a knife.

"You're doing the right thing, Jacob Lev," Mallick said.

"The balance of justice demands it," Schott said.

"It'll be quick," Subach said.

"Merciful."

"Necessary."

"Correct."

They kept coming closer, speaking in turn, mesmerizing him, and Jacob watched the glint of the knife, a brand-new blade fitted onto an old wooden handle. He knew how it would feel when they put it into his hands—how comfortable. He looked at Mai and at the tall men and over the lawn.

Pernath slipped into the trees.

"Jacob Lev," Mallick said. "Look at me."

Jacob released Mai's hands.

The tall men cried out, helpless.

Her smile was a sweet and sour mix of gratitude and disappointment, and she said, "Forever," and sprang up into the air.

The three tall men howled their displeasure and rushed forth.

It was useless: she had already changed, a black buzzing dot that slipped through their large, clumsy fingers, spiraling up to freedom. Jacob watched her ascend.

Silence.

The three tall men turned on him, showing new and terrifying aspects, and Jacob was afraid, drawing his merits around him like a coat of armor to protect himself from their wrath.

Paul Schott rolled his boulder shoulders contemptuously. Mel Subach pursed his wet thick lips. Mike Mallick snorted gales and said, "You have done a great wrong."

"We needed you," Subach said.

"You failed us."

"A *great* wrong."

"He's like her," Schott said. "He's just like her."

They crowded him, drawing in on him, teeth gnashing, eyes burning like coals as they expanded to a furious chorus: three to forty-five to seventy-one, two hundred thirty-one, six hundred thirteen, eighteen thousand, a thousand by a thousand, swelling to twelve by thirty by thirty by thirty by thirty by thirty by thirty by three hundred sixty-five thousand myriads.

And Jacob seized the halves of his mind and forced them back together, rising up under his own strength.

The hordes shrank back, leaving a trio of middle-aged cops in bad suits and cheap ties.

Mallick's white hair in frizzy tufts. Subach's gut straining his shirt. Schott holding his hands up as though Jacob in his righteous indignation would annihilate all of them.

And Jacob spoke, and he said, "Please get the hell out of my way."

He pushed through their ranks and ran to collect the abandoned shotgun.

"You don't know what you've done," Mallick called. "You don't know."

Jacob picked up the gun and pumped a shell. He said, "I know what I'm doing."

IN THE ORCHARD it was windless, gloomy, and still. He could not see well, but his mind spread wide to welcome new sensations: the strivings of insects in the ground below, fearful prey taking refuge in the underbrush, the collective spirit of all living things.

Jacob stalked the soldierly rows, fixed on the sound of labored breathing coming from a stand of fig trees.

A watery gray light in the shape of a man slumped on the ground, propped against a tree trunk.

Jacob raised the gun. "Lie down on the ground and don't move."

Pernath didn't respond. For a moment, Jacob thought he was dead. But as he drew near, he saw the architect's chest fluttering, the gray outline moving with it.

"Down on the ground," Jacob said. "Now."

Pernath's head rolled toward Jacob and he sighed. His arm whipped over, taking his torso with it, and his body elongated and he sank a shard of glass into Jacob's thigh.

Jacob stumbled back, a groan swelling in his throat as he tripped over a fig root and the shotgun flew from his hands. He hit the ground and pain ballooned through his lower body and he began kicking at the dirt, scrabbling in the direction of the gun.

He reached it and saw that Pernath was making no effort to come after him.

The architect simply sat there, his head lolling, a contented smile on his lips.

Jacob looked down at the shard. At least eight inches long, half of that buried in his quadriceps. Blood dyeing the fabric of his jeans. Shivering, nauseated, he stripped off his shirt and tied his leg off at the groin. He slid a broken branch between the shirt and his leg, and twisted as hard as he could to cut off the flow of blood. Another wave of nausea coursed through him. He tamped it down and picked up the shotgun, approaching Pernath in a wide circle.

Pernath's hands were loose and open in his lap. His eyes were half shut.

Jacob said, "Reggie Heap. Terrence Florack. Claire Mason. Anyone else I need to know about?"

Pernath smiled wider, baring blood-rimmed teeth. Blood bubbled from his nostrils. The mucoid gray light surrounding him flickered. He was dying without regrets. Jacob thought about what he could say to take that away from him.

In the end he said nothing. There was nothing to say. His tourniquet had soaked through and he was starting to feel faint again.

He pressed the end of the barrel against Pernath's throat and leaned down with all his weight. Pernath's Adam's apple imploded. It sounded like a wet cardboard box getting stomped on. His eyes bugged and he suffocated and fought.

Jacob counted to ten and released the pressure, allowed Pernath a few thin breaths. Then he bore down again for another ten count.

He repeated the process eleven more times, once for each of the victims he knew about. He could hear the voices of the tall men coming through the trees, calling his name. *Jacob.* He placed the end of the shotgun on Pernath's throat. *Jacob, where are you.* He pressed down one last time for good luck.

Jacob. Jacob.

He pulled the trigger, severing Pernath's head from his body.

The recoil kicked Jacob back. He was falling as he answered them. *Here I am.*

CHAPTER FIFTY-SIX

The nurse came into his room to announce a visitor. Assuming it was his father, Jacob waved permission and continued spooning oatmeal. The curtain shuffled aside and Divya Das stepped in.

He sat up, wiping his mouth. "Hey."

She looked around for a place to sit, did not approach the unmade cot next to Jacob's bed.

"My dad's been sleeping here. Go ahead. He won't mind."

Sam's copy of the Zohar lay on the pillow. She moved it to the night-stand and sat down, setting her orange bowling ball bag on her knees.

Jacob said, "I take it we're going dancing."

She smiled. "How are you feeling?"

Jacob had no memory of his first night in the hospital. He'd sneaked a look at his chart and learned he'd walked into the emergency room on his own, ranting and raving. He assumed that Mallick, Subach, and Schott had dropped him off and left. The clinical notes said it had taken two doctors and three orderlies to wrestle him down. Now they had him on an array of barbiturates, along with B vitamins to ease his detox and IV fluids to counteract blood loss. The wound in his leg had been sutured neatly.

He was no longer having green dreams, which offered relief but also pangs of melancholy. His world appeared astringent and flat. Institutional linoleum, smudged bumper rails, oppressive overlighting. No matter how much he slept, he felt tired. He was relaxed and bored and doped up, unable to care very much about anything.

He felt better and worse, trapped and free, blessed and punished in equal measure.

He said, "Sore."

"May I?"

He nodded.

She lifted a corner of the thin hospital blanket, revealing his bandaged thigh.

"Missed the femoral artery by a quarter of an inch," he said.

She tucked the blanket back in and reached for the chart, paged through it. "They gave you six units of blood."

"Is that a lot?"

"You oughtn't to be alive."

He spread his arms: *here I am.*

She lingered on the page a bit longer, replaced the chart. "I'm glad you're coping so well."

"Thanks. I thought you'd left town."

"I was going to." She dug in her bag and came out with a folder. "I wanted to deliver the results of your request personally."

He chose not to question the about-face. He thanked her and accepted the folder.

DNA recovered from Reggie Heap's bloodstained shoes matched the profile of the second Creeper offender—a perfect nine for nine.

He closed the file. "So that's that."

"So it would seem."

"I'll have to get in touch with the other Ds," he said. "They'll want to know."

"I'm sure they will." Long black eyelashes fluttered. "I have a message from Commander Mallick. He congratulates you for your fine work in stopping two dangerous and violent individuals, and he wishes you a speedy recovery. He said not to worry about the paperwork. They've got it covered."

"I can handle it myself."

"The Commander feels that you could use a break, after the ordeal you've been through."

"Does he."

"He—the detail as a whole—feels it wouldn't be appropriate to keep you in a high-stress position."

"Why are you talking to me like that?"

"Like what."

"Like a suit."

"You'll have a month, paid."

"And then?"

Her mouth bunched. "You're being transferred back to Traffic."

Jacob stared at her.

She looked at the floor. "I'm sorry, Jacob. It wasn't my decision."

"I'd sure hope not," he said. "You're not my superior."

She did not reply.

"He couldn't tell me face-to-face?"

"Mike Mallick is a very dedicated individual," she said. "But he's stubborn, and his way of thinking isn't necessarily the most people-friendly."

"No shit," he said.

"We're not all the same, Jacob."

"Whatever."

"He's entitled to his opinion," she said. "And I'm entitled to mine."

"And what's your opinion?"

"As I said, the Commander can have trouble when it comes to predicting how a person might behave in the moment. Given what you've seen, it's hard for me to find fault with your actions."

Jacob said, "Who is she?"

Silence.

Divya Das said, "The Commander congratulates you for your fine work in stopping two dangerous and violent individuals."

"Seriously?" he said. "This is what we're doing? Do you have any idea what this feels like?" He tapped the center of his forehead. "What it's like in here?"

On the other side of the curtain, his roommate, a ninety-year-old man, gargled and snored.

"Please keep your voice down," Divya said.

"Is someone going to show up with a machine that erases my memory? Do I get a complimentary lobotomy?"

His heart rate monitor was chirping aggressively. She waited for it to slow, leaned in to speak. "It seems to me that you have a choice. You can live inside your experiences or outside of them."

"And so? What now?" he said. "I wait for her to come back?"

"She certainly seems attracted to you."

"I can't imagine why," Jacob said.

She smiled crookedly. "Don't sell yourself short, Jacob Lev."

Silence.

"It had to be Traffic," he said.

She tried a smile. "Consider it a vacation."

A soft knock at the door. The curtain swished aside, and Sam appeared with a grease-blotched bag.

"Whoops," he said. "I didn't realize you had company. I can come back."

Divya Das stood up. "I was just on my way out. You must be Jacob's father."

"Sam Lev."

"Divya Das."

"Good to see you," he said. "How's the patient?"

"Better than most of the ones I deal with," she said.

She turned to Jacob, laid a warm hand on his shoulder. "Be well."

Jacob nodded.

After she'd gone, his father said, "She seems nice."

"She came by to tell me I'm being demoted."

Sam's eyes creased behind his sunglasses. "Really."

"Back to pushing paper."

"Mm," Sam said. "I can't say I'm disappointed."

"I didn't think you would be."

"You're my son. You think it's easy for me to see you like this?"

"I don't think it's easy for you to see anything," Jacob said.

"Touché." Sam reached in the bag and unpacked a breakfast crois-sant. "I had Nigel stop off," he said, putting the food on Jacob's tray. "Hospital food is dreck."

"Thanks."

"So? How's the leg? You want to take a rest? I can be quiet."

"I'd rather talk," Jacob said. He took a bite of the sandwich. It was pure artery-clogging pleasure. "You remember to put my *tzedakah* money in?"

"I did. I kept you in mind the whole time. I hope you felt it."

"Oh, absolutely. An angel came down and touched me and now I'm all better."

Sam smiled. "Lucky you."

A NEW RESIDENT CAME BY to inspect Jacob's wounds and declared the leg to be healing "okay." He probed the scab on Jacob's arm, reviewed the chart, and offered the umpteenth lecture on the need for Jacob to cut back on his drinking.

"The good news is we're not seeing signs of infection."

"What's the bad news?" Sam asked.

"There has to be bad news?" Jacob said.

"It's not bad, per se," the resident said. "But everyone's puzzled by your bloodwork. Your iron is still pretty elevated, as are your magnesium and potassium, although not to the same degree. Iron overload can be a risk factor for liver disease. Do you eat a lot of meat?"

"Do hot dogs qualify?"

The resident frowned. Young and cranky. He'd age badly. "I can't recommend that one bit. Anyhow, we reran your blood twice more, looking for other anomalies. A few other things popped up that I'm having trouble interpreting."

"What's that mean?" Sam said.

"Do you take a silica supplement?" the resident asked Jacob. "Some people use it because they think it prevents hair loss."

Jacob ran his hand over his thick, dark waves.

"Uh-huh. Other supplements? Anything homeopathic?"

"Nothing."

"Hunh. Okay. Well. I asked some colleagues for their opinion, and Dr. Rosen in psychiatry had a thought."

Jacob stiffened. "What's that?"

"There's a condition called pica, where a person gets cravings to eat inedible things, like hair or dirt or plaster. It mostly happens in pregnant women, or sometimes in individuals with severe anemia. In very extreme cases, you can get unusual trace minerals showing up in the blood. What I'm seeing from you isn't exactly consistent—you'd expect lower than average iron, not higher—but I'm having trouble coming up with a better explanation for why you have so much silicon in your system."

Jacob said nothing.

"Aluminum, also," the resident said. "Unless you're bathing yourself in antiperspirant." He paused again, glanced at Sam, back at Jacob. "Is that something you've, uh, done?"

"Eating dirt?" Jacob asked. "Or bathing in antiperspirant?"

"Either."

Jacob said, "No."

The resident seemed relieved. "I'm sure it's a lab error. We'll definitely keep an eye on it, though. Rest up."

Jacob lay back, absently running his fingers over his scabbed arm. The taste of mud was faint in the back of his throat. He was thinking about Mai, and Divya Das, and his father saying to her *Good to see you* rather than *Good to meet you.*

He looked at Sam, inscrutable as always. "Abba? I think I'd like to sleep a little now."

His father nodded. He reached for the Zohar. "I'll be here when you wake up."

CHAPTER FIFTY-SEVEN

Four days later, his blood had yet to normalize, but as he was reporting no obvious ill effects, neither the resident nor his insurance could justify keeping him in the hospital any longer. They gave him painkillers and a follow-up appointment. A nurse wheeled him to the curb and he hobbled on crutches to the waiting Taurus.

Nigel got out to hold the door for him. "Lookin good."

"You should see the other guy."

THE PLAN WAS to recuperate at Sam's. They stopped by Jacob's place to pick up clothes.

The Honda sat in the carport, looking somehow different. As Nigel helped him limp up the steps, Jacob realized what it was: for the first time in months, the car had been washed.

Jacob asked Nigel if he'd done it.

Nigel laughed. "Nope," he said, fishing out Sam's copy of the apartment key. "Maybe some girlfriend did you a favor."

EVERYTHING SUBACH AND SCHOTT had brought—the desk, chair, computer, sat phone, camera, printer, router, battery pack—was gone. The TV had been restored to its original position and reconnected. The bookcase had been repatriated to the living room, the potter's tools neatly arrayed on the shelves.

Also gone were Phil Ludwig's boxes of evidence, along with the murder book Jacob had put together.

The bathroom smelled piney. The fridge had been purged. He didn't own a vacuum cleaner but there were outfield stripes in the bedroom carpet. A zip-top bag on his nightstand contained his wallet, keys, and badge.

His old cell phone was plugged in, fully charged and getting five bars.

His backpack sat on the floor by the closet. He looked inside and saw his *tefillin* bag; a bunch of candy wrappers; his Glock and the magazine. They'd left him the binoculars, affixed with a Post-it, two words written in a whispery scrawl.

You're welcome.

He had gotten used to the chaos. The reversion to form disoriented him. He packed hurriedly, stuffing items into a duffel. Nigel hoisted it over one shoulder, the backpack over the other, and went down to put them in the car. While he was gone, Jacob limped to the living room, stood at the bookcase, examining the tools. Combs, paddles, a wire cutter, a set of knives.

One of the knives, the longest one, was missing.

Nigel reappeared in the doorway to help him down the stairs. "Ready to go?"

"Hell yes," Jacob said.

DOWNSTAIRS, a white work van was parked across the street.

CURTAINS AND BEYOND—DISCOUNT WINDOW TREATMENTS

An unfamiliar man sat in the driver's seat. He was black, sitting up so tall that the top quarter of his head was out of view. He appeared not to pay them any attention, but as the Taurus eased into the street, Jacob raised a hand to him, and he waved back.

SAM INSISTED ON TAKING the pullout couch and giving Jacob his bed, and he proceeded to astonish Jacob by handing him the remote control for a brand-new thirty-inch flat-screen television on a stand.

"Since when do you have that?"

"I'm not a Luddite."

"You hate TV."

"You want to argue about it or you want to watch it?"

THE BARBITURATES CLEARED from his system within forty-eight hours, and withdrawal set in.

Sam watched from a chair by the bedside, a pained expression on his face, as Jacob shivered and leaked sweat. "We should go back to the hospital."

"N—nnnn, not a ch—chance."

"Jacob. Please."

"Juh—just got to ri—ride it . . . *out.*"

His hands were shaking so much that he couldn't lay his *tefillin* straight.

Sam said, "Don't feel obliged because of me."

"You want to argue about it," Jacob stuttered, "or you want to help me?"

His father got up and cradled him from behind, wrapping the leather straps in evenly spaced coils. They were close against each other, Jacob's nose pressed to Sam's scratchy neck, and the smell of Irish Spring made him aware of his own, stale stink.

"I'm so sorry," he mumbled.

Sam shushed him gently and reached for the head *tefillin*, smiling as he centered them between Jacob's eyes.

THE GOLEM OF HOLLYWOOD

"What," Jacob said.

"I was remembering the first time I showed you how to do this," Sam said. He adjusted the box to the left. "How big they looked on you. No more talking, please."

Flat on his back, Jacob recited an abridged service, getting through as many of the core recitations as he could manage before the prayer book slipped from his hands.

Delicately, Sam lifted Jacob's head off the pillow and loosened the *tefillin*. He removed them; removed the arm *tefillin*. He fetched a cold towel and sponged down Jacob's forehead, soothing the spot where the leather box had bitten into his skin.

TREMORS YIELDED to low-grade headache and fatigue, the harbingers of a coming downturn in his mood, emotional nausea to go along with the physical kind. Sam appeared to sense the change, too. He responded by seeking to fill the hours with mild distractions, idle chatter and endless streams of riddles and puns.

Jacob doubted he could stave off full-blown depression with word games, but it was hard not to be charmed somewhat by his father's enthusiasm for providing care rather than accepting it. It had been a long time since he'd seen how Sam actually lived, and the self-sufficiency his father demonstrated was eye-opening.

Shuffling to and from the kitchen, ferrying tuna fish sandwiches and Gatorade and ice packs, going to the bathroom to rewet the compress or wash out the puke bucket.

Knowing the TV set had been bought for him, Jacob tried to show his appreciation by sticking to programming his father might conceivably enjoy: sports and news. They lamented the Lakers' early exit from the playoffs, watched baseball without comment. Sam studied while Jacob dozed. Jacob's major accomplishment of the first week was summoning the energy to call Volpe, Band, and Flores to relay the good news. Grandmaison he didn't bother with. Let him figure it out on his own.

WHEN HE FELT WELL ENOUGH, he and Sam began going out for long, slow walks, building up to three times daily, their tempo set by the drilling pain in Jacob's leg. Along the way they would encounter neighborhood folks, many of whom greeted Sam by name. A soft-bodied woman pursuing a pair of rambunctious grandchildren; a young father wrestling with a stroller. It was as if they owed Sam a great debt of gratitude, as if the weight of his existence lessened theirs, and Jacob thought of Abe Teitelbaum's refrain about his father being a *lamed-vavnik*.

On a Thursday evening, near the corner of Airdrome and Preuss, a girl on a bicycle called to them as she whipped by.

"Hi, Mr. Lev."

Sam raised a hand.

"Popular guy," Jacob said.

"Everybody loves a clown," Sam said.

For his part, his father gave no indication of being burdened. Jacob reckoned that had to be true. If you thought you were a *lamed-vavnik*, you couldn't be a *lamed-vavnik*. The reason for that went beyond a lack of the requisite humility. A *lamed-vavnik* could never recognize the immensity of his obligation, because the instant he did, the crush of worldly sorrow he was required to bear would paralyze him.

Jacob glanced back at the girl, her pigtails streaming. "Who was that, anyway?"

"How should I know? I'm blind."

THEY TURNED DOWN AIRDROME STREET.

Jacob said, "Do you remember we used to have our Sunday morning study sessions?"

"Certainly I remember," Sam said.

"I have no idea what you were thinking, exposing me to some of that stuff."

"What did I expose you to?"

"You taught me about capital punishment when I was six."

"In a purely legalistic sense."

"I'm not sure a first grader can reliably make that distinction."

"Is this where you tell me how I've ruined your life?"

"You haven't ruined my life," Jacob said. "I take sole credit for that."

At Robertson Boulevard, the orange and green 7-Eleven sign loomed in the twilight, firing up Jacob's cravings for bourbon and nitrates.

"Can we turn around?" he asked. "It's too noisy here."

"Of course. Are you getting tired?"

"Another couple blocks," Jacob said.

They walked east.

"Abba? Can I ask you something else?"

Sam nodded.

"Did you know Ema was sick when you married her?"

Sam said nothing.

"I'm sorry," Jacob said. "You don't have to answer that."

"It's all right. I'm not angry. I'm thinking about it, because I want to say it right."

They walked in silence a moment.

"Let's consider the question from another perspective. If I could go back, would I do it again? And the answer to that is, yes, without a doubt."

"Even knowing what happened to her?"

"You marry someone for who they are, not who they could become."

In the silence, Jacob's crutches scraped the pavement.

You can live inside your experiences or outside of them.

He was having trouble choosing.

He was having trouble deciding if that was an authentic choice, or an illusion.

"I worry that it's going to happen to me," he said. "I worry that it's happening already."

"You're a different person, Jacob."

"That doesn't make me exempt."

"No. It doesn't."

"So what makes you so sure?"

"Because I know you," Sam said. "And I know what you're made of."

It had begun to get dark.

Jacob said, "I was thinking, maybe, we could try it again sometime, learning together."

"What did you have in mind?"

"I don't know. Pick something interesting. I'm sure as soon as I get back they're going to slam me with a bunch of busywork, so, I can't promise my attendance will be perfect. But I'm up for it if you are."

"I'd like that," Sam said. "Very much."

At La Cienega, traffic reared up. They retreated westward. It took them twenty minutes to make it back to the house. Sam didn't seem too put out; for the moment, at least, they'd found a mutually agreeable pace.

IT FELT WRONG to tell Phil Ludwig over the phone. On a Sunday morning, Nigel picked Jacob up and they drove down to San Diego, where they found the good D crouched in his front yard, optimistically installing geraniums beneath the inland heat.

Ludwig stood, blinking sweat out of his eyes. "This is either gonna be a real great day or a real fucking bad one."

Over lemonade, Jacob recapped the events and the evidence, lapsing into generalities in describing Richard Pernath's final moments. Ludwig listened stonily. In his curt verdict—"Good"—Jacob saw an honorable effort to conceal disappointment. His success made Ludwig's failure official.

"I haven't talked to any of the families yet. I was hoping you'd be able to help me out with that. Not the Steins. Them, I'd like to speak to myself."

Ludwig said, "Let me think about it." Then, perking up, he said, "I got something for you, too. When you e-mailed, it reminded me I never gave you an answer about that bug."

"Don't worry about it."

"Fuck don't worry about it. I was up half the night. You're gonna pretend to be interested."

Out in the garage, Ludwig cleared the tabletop of the work in progress, a pristine tiger moth mounted on a bright white mat. He took down a crumbling, acid-ravaged reference book.

"I forgot I even had this," he said, stroking the warped cover, red cloth stamped in black.

Insecta Evropae
A. M. GOLDFINCH

"I picked it up years ago, at a library sale. I don't think I bothered checking it before cause it's Old World species."

He had bookmarked the entry with a color printout of one of Jacob's photos. He aligned it with a pen-and-ink illustration of *Nicrophorus bohemicus*, the Bohemian burying beetle.

Jacob crowded the table to read.

Found along the riverbanks of central and eastern Europe, *N. bohemicus*, like other burying beetles, displayed a behavior unusual in the insect world: mates remained together to rear their young. In the Bohemian, the tendency was pronounced, with couples pairing for life.

"Here's the thing," Ludwig said. "This book's from 1909. I looked online for a color photo and Wikipedia comes back that the species went extinct in the mid-1920s."

Jacob continued to stare at the images—to his eyes, identical creatures.

"You've got to remember," Ludwig said, "insects, it's hard to say that definitively. They're small, they live underground, and most people see em and just want to smash em. There's this beetle from the Mediterranean nobody's seen in a hundred years, and last year it turned up in the south of England. So, it happens. My thought was we pass this along to my friend. If he agrees, maybe then we go to one of the journals."

"Go for it," said Jacob. "No need to include me."

Ludwig frowned. "They'll want to know who's making the claim."

"Tell them you took the picture yourself."

"I shouldn't do that."

"You're the one figured it out," Jacob said. "I never would've known."

After mulling over whether there was condescension in this offer, Ludwig nodded. "Fair enough. You're sure?"

"Couldn't be surer."

THE STEINS WELCOMED HIM at their mansion. Jacob was concerned they would react badly to the news that the men who had murdered their daughter would never face trial. Rhoda sprang up and ran from the room, and Eddie tottered toward Jacob with his hands up. Jacob braced to block an uppercut, but Eddie wrapped him in a bear hug, and Rhoda returned carrying a bottle of champagne and three flutes.

"You see?" Eddie told her, shaking him. "I said all along he wasn't such a schmuck."

BUYING GIFTS FOR SAM, a man with zero material lust, had never been easy, and it had gotten more challenging as Jacob grew up and realized that his father never wore ties. To thank him for the extended stay,

Jacob settled on making him a Sabbath meal, the last before he returned to work.

Making his way through a slice of store-bought chocolate cake, Sam said, "Delicious."

"Thanks, Abba."

"I'm sure you're ready to be back in your own bed. Don't be a stranger, though."

"I can't," Jacob said. "Believe me, I've tried."

WHEN HE GOT HOME, the curtain installer's van was there; the same man sat behind the wheel, reading.

Jacob waved to get his attention. The man closed his magazine and lowered the window.

"Look, I don't know what your shift schedule is, if it's always going to be you out here, but I thought I'd introduce myself. I'm Jacob."

"Nathaniel," the man said.

"You want a drink or something?"

Nathaniel chuckled. "I'm all set, thanks."

"Okay. You change your mind, just come by."

Nathaniel smiled and saluted and buzzed the window up.

MARCIA IN TRAFFIC SAID, "How was Hawaii?"

Jacob pried open a box of Bics. "I wasn't in Hawaii."

"Vegas?" She leaned over his desk. "Cabo?"

Jacob shook his head and stood the pens in a mug.

"I know you've been somewhere," she said. "You have that glow."

He laughed.

"Fine," she said, pouting. "Be that way."

"Love to tell you, but there's nothing to tell," he said.

"Top secret," she said.

"Smart woman." He grinned.

She grinned back. "Well, I'm glad to have you back."

"Thanks, hon."

"Lev," a man's voice barked.

He looked up. Across the squad room, red as a fire hydrant with in-flammatory bowel disease, stood his old boss, Captain Mendoza.

Marcia muttered, "Meet the new czar."

"You've got to be kidding me."

"I need you in my office," Mendoza called.

From R-H to Traffic was quite a fall. Jacob knew from personal experience. "Who'd he piss off?"

"We haven't figured it out yet," Marcia said. "Any guesses?"

"Lev. Did you hear me?"

"Right away, sir," Jacob called. To Marcia: "I might have one or two."

Mendoza had ducked back into his office and was sitting with his feet up, flipping through a four-inch binder. Jacob could see the work of stress: ten lost pounds, dark half-moons beneath the eyes, scattered pimples. The mustache, usually trimmed with precision, lay crooked.

"Hope you enjoyed your vacation, cause playtime's over." Mendoza's voice sounded strained, higher-pitched, as if his vocal cords had been ratcheted tight.

He slapped the binder down. "Fifty years of information about car versus pedestrian accidents. Your magnum opus."

"Yes, sir."

Mendoza stroked his mustache thoughtfully. "Did you consider where bicycles fit in this equation?"

Jacob hefted the binder and took it back to his cubicle.

ON THE BRIGHT SIDE, he was home by six-thirty most days, and weekends were light. He made the regular Monday and Wednesday evening

AA meetings at the Anglican church on Olympic Boulevard, finding his regular place at the back. It wasn't the first time he'd sat in a house of worship, mouthing words he didn't believe in. Without alcohol, he had little reason to stay out at night; he was early to bed, early to rise, diligent and uncomplaining, chaste and humble. Eventually Mendoza grew bored of harassing him.

When he stopped in at 7-Eleven for diet cola, Henry would clutch his chest. "Was it something I did?"

NOW THAT HE KNEW what to look for, he easily picked out the people who had been sent to watch him. No regular rotation he could discern; sometimes every couple of weeks, other times monthly, a vehicle would show itself within a two-block radius. Caterer, roofer, furnace repair, a piano tuner, weatherproofing installation. Some of the lone occupants were cordial, others glum. None of them displayed anxiety or prolonged the conversation.

They didn't worry Jacob, either. It wasn't him they were after.

Returning home from his meeting one night, he was oddly pleased to spot Subach, his chicken-finger fingers drumming the dash of a plumber's van.

"Hey, Jake."

"Hey, Mel. Moonlighting?"

"You know. Same old." Subach grinned. "Traffic treating you okay?"

"Very fucking funny."

"Ah, relax."

"Tell Mallick thanks a lot."

"The Commander, I guess you could say he was a wee bit. . . *vexed*."

Jacob smiled tiredly.

"Don't worry. Won't last forever."

"Nothing does," Jacob said. "Take it easy, Mel. No hard feelings?"

"None from me."

Jacob paused. "But?"

Subach laughed. "Hey now. Be realistic. The world's full of hard feelings. Without that, we'd both be out of a job."

For their weekly study sessions, Sam selected a tractate discussing criminal justice, including the chapter on capital punishment.

"I think you're finally old enough," he said.

Jacob ran up a streak of fourteen straight Sunday mornings without an absence, the two of them sitting on the patio, eating pastry and drinking tea, batting around arguments. The melody of Talmudic study returned to his lips; he reintroduced himself to the luminous personalities that adorned the pages, and he found them far more sympathetic at second encounter. They were men, very much in the grip of their own uncertainties, trying to figure out how to *be*. The ritual structure they'd established was a noble attempt to infuse life with dignity and meaning. They strove for autonomy, for self-worth, for holiness. And when they failed, they sought new strategies. Jacob had missed that lesson the first time around. He did not intend to miss it again.

The Sunday before Rosh Hashana, Jacob arrived five minutes early. As usual, Sam was waiting out on the patio, his magnifying spectacles pushed back on his forehead. Instead of twin volumes of the Talmud, the table held a single sheet of paper: Jacob's transcript of the Prague letter.

Sam gestured to the free chair.

Jacob sat.

Sam cleared his throat, lowered the spectacles, flapped the page to straighten it. Paused. "Something to drink?"

"No. Thanks."

Sam nodded. He began to read, translating from the Hebrew.

"'My dear son Isaac. And God blessed Isaac so may He bless you.' You're correct in identifying this as a term of endearment for Isaac Katz. He and the Maharal were close, not to mention that they were student and teacher, a relationship compared to that of son and father.'"

He looked up. "Shall I continue?"

Jacob nodded.

"'As a bridegroom rejoices over his bride, so may God rejoice over you. For the sounds of joy and gladness yet ring in the streets of Judah. Therefore this time I, Judah, will praise Him.'"

Sam righted his glasses. "Isaac Katz was married to two different daughters of the Maharal. First Leah, who died childless, then her younger sister, Feigel. The date here, Sivan 5342, corresponds to that second marriage. Isaac Katz is a newly married man, and that's why the Maharal feels the need to give him an out by citing the priest's speech to the troops. He's saying, 'Something's happening, and I need your help, but only if you can set aside your personal concerns.' The next paragraph discusses what the problem is."

He offered the letter to Jacob.

"'But now let us remember that our eyes have seen all the great deeds He has done,'" Jacob read. "'For the vessel of clay we have made was spoiled in our hands, and the potter has gone to make another, more fit in her eyes. Shall the potter be the equal of the clay? Shall what is made say to its maker, you did not make me? Shall what is formed say to the one who formed it, you know nothing?'" He put the letter down. "Sorry, Abba. I'm not getting anything."

"The Maharal was concerned that his son-in-law wouldn't understand, either. He put in a fail-safe. Here, in the last line. It's not very subtle."

For in truth we have desired grace; it is a disgrace to us from God.

"You couldn't find the biblical verse this alludes to," Sam said. "That's because there isn't one."

Jacob reread the line in Hebrew.

באמת רצינו חן הוא גנאי לנו מה'

"Take your time," Sam said. "Play with it."

The instruction Sam had used when amusing Jacob with gematria—the geometry of letters.

Jacob added up the numerical values of the letters, reversed them. Nothing.

He selected the first letter of each word and paired them together.

ברחהגלמ

"Barach ha-Golem," he read.

The golem has fled.

"There's nothing more hubristic than the impulse to create life," Sam said. "Children are the best example of that. The Talmud says three partners participate in the birth of every child: the mother, the father, and God. That equation raises people up to the level of the Divine. It's also a statement of faith, declaring that God involves Himself with the individual. And yet, no matter how we attempt to assert our authority— even if we appeal to the Divine—children go their own way." He paused. "Any sort of offspring seeks to find its own way. That is the fundamental joy of parenthood, and also its terror."

Jacob said, "She came for me."

Sam didn't answer.

"Because of the blood in your veins."

"You said it yourself, Jacob. She came for you, not me."

Jacob looked at him.

"If you don't mind," Sam said, "I'll wait here while you get the car."

FOR A LEGALLY BLIND man giving driving directions, his father exhibited remarkable confidence.

"You'll want to get over to your right."

"I'm not going to keep saying this—"

"Then don't."

"—but I can't help thinking it'd be simpler if you just told me where we're going."

"You're going to miss it."

Jacob checked over his shoulder, swerved to avoid the 110. "Do I get three guesses?"

"Slow down," Sam said. "There's a speed trap ahead."

Jacob touched the brake pedal.

Beyond the overpass, a radar gun glinted.

"I probably could have talked us out of it," Jacob said.

"No need to take chances," Sam said.

There was only one place Jacob could think of that was due east, one place Sam visited often enough to navigate there by sound alone. At the interchange with the 101, he signaled right, then bore left for the 60 East into Boyle Heights, toward the Garden of Peace Cemetery. He signaled again for the exit at Downey Road.

"No," Sam said. "710 South."

He thought his father must be misremembering, or miscalculating; perhaps he went with Nigel at different times of day, when the drive took longer or shorter, and they followed a roundabout route. "Abba—"

"710 South."

Off the freeway, a tawny hill heaved up into view, speckled white with monuments. "The cemetery's right there. I can see it."

"We're not going to the cemetery," Sam said.

Mystified, Jacob made the merge onto the 710 South.

Two miles later, Sam had him get on the 5 South.

"I have half a tank," Jacob said. "Is that going to be enough?"

"Yes."

They switched to the 605 South, exiting at Imperial Highway and heading west through the city of Downey. Jacob had little to no knowledge of the area, and it was all he could do not to reach for his phone when Sam instructed him to get on the 710 North.

"We just got off the 710 South."

"I know."

"We're heading in a big circle."

"Keep going."

Jacob said, "Is someone following us?"

Sam said, "You tell me."

Jacob glanced in the rearview.

A field of cars.

At Sam's behest, they changed lanes several times, feinting toward exits.

"I don't think there's anyone," Jacob said.

Sam nodded. "I'm relying on you for that."

They passed the cemetery again, this time on the east; from that angle, Jacob could not see anything except the nodding mop-tops of palm trees. Continuing on to the freeway's terminus, they turned onto West Valley Boulevard, in Alhambra. He obeyed blindly as Sam relayed a series of turns through residential streets.

"What do you think?" Sam asked.

Jacob glanced in the rearview mirror.

"Clear," he said. He was amused and perplexed and irritated in equal measure. "I'm down to a quarter tank, by the way."

"We can stop on the way back. Right on Garfield, then it's your first left. Three blocks down, number 456 East, end of the block."

It was a nondescript lower-middle-class street, ranch houses with concrete latticework and proud flowerbeds, pickup trucks in the driveways, powerboats on trailers.

Sam said, "There's a parking lot, but it's only five spaces and they're usually full. I'd take the first spot you see."

Jacob pulled over outside a reddish three-story stucco apartment complex with a Spanish tile roof. There was a small semicircular driveway and a tiled overhang, boxwood hedges and a wooden sign.

PACIFIC CONTINUING CARE
A DIVISION OF GRAFFIN HEALTH SERVICES, INC.

They sat in silence in the car.

Sam said, "I ask for your forgiveness."

Jacob said nothing.

Sam bowed his head. "You're right. I'm sorry. I shouldn't have—I'm sorry."

He got out of the car and started up the driveway. Sick with dread, Jacob followed.

HE KNEW. He knew the moment they stepped inside. The woman behind the desk smiled at his father. She was wearing Mickey Mouse scrubs. She said, "Good morning, Mr. Abelson," and Sam nodded and Jacob knew.

The odor of cleaning agents was strong. He looked at his father, scrawling messily on a clipboard, signing himself in. Why was he doing this now? Why was he doing it at all? He'd never known his father to be selfish. Just the opposite. Sam gave and gave and gave. He gave all; forgave all. Jacob had to wonder if that same generosity extended, in a perverse way, to himself. Because he could not imagine a more selfish permission to grant oneself.

"Here." Sam was offering the clipboard. He had signed his name as Abelson.

Jacob didn't know what to write. Was he supposed to lie, too? He wrote his real name.

He knew. He followed regardless, trailing Sam down a cracked tile corridor, ecru paint in drippy layers. Through doors left ajar he saw grungy carpeting, flimsy bedspreads. Two beds per closet-sized room. The cheer of a child's drawing amplifying the deadness of the rough vinyl wallpaper. A vase of failing sunflowers, the finger of water at the bottom luxuriantly scummed. The pain in his heart made room for more pain. This could not be the best they could do. They had to do better.

Glare budded at the end of the hall. DAYROOM.

Figures of men and women. Reading, snoozing, playing checkers. They wandered about in pajamas stained with marinara sauce and applesauce. They wore slippers at noon. They seemed ill-defined, as though the room was filled with steam. Obesity and tremulous hands and cloudy eyes testified to the long-term effects of medication.

Overwhelmingly their focal point was a television set, tuned to a talk show.

Two heavyset Latinas in pink scrubs (hearts, Hello Kitty) made up the staff. They were watching TV, too. They looked over when Jacob and Sam entered. One of them smiled at Sam.

"She's in the garden."

"Thank you."

Jacob knew, and still he followed, passing numbly through the mute ranks of the mad, conscious of their stares. They—the vacant and the reasonless—even they were judging him. The one who never visits.

What the nurse had called a garden was a lagoon of pink cement stamped to resemble flagstone; a plastic trellis overcome by star jasmine; a clump of home-improvement-store planters. Iron fence pickets rose way up high, ten feet or more. He wondered if anyone had tried to escape.

There was one actual tree, a fig wickedly gnarled, dominating the corner, throwing long tentacles of shade, splattering the concrete with uneaten fruit.

She was there, on a corroding bench.

Her hair was dry and gone to gray. Someone had taken the time to comb it and pin it back. The pin was age-inappropriate, a cute little ladybug. Withered pouches of skin replaced the slender neck he remembered; the doughy body, too, insulted his memory. But her hands were the same, wired with sinew, and her eyes were the same electric green.

Her fingers moved ceaselessly, manipulating phantom clay.

"Hello, Bina," Sam said. He sat down on the bench and put an arm around her, pulled her into him and kissed her on the temple.

One of her hands climbed the side of his face and rested. Her eyes closed.

Jacob turned and walked away.

Sam called, "She asked for you."

Jacob kept going.

"She hasn't spoken in ten years."

Jacob reached the door and grabbed the knob.

"Don't blame her," Sam said. "Blame me."

Jacob faced him. "I do blame you."

Sam nodded.

Their three bodies triangulated long and narrow, forming an invisible blade laid across the garden. Jacob heard the natter of the dayroom TV. A thin hot breeze awakened jasmine and sweet, rotting fruit. His mother gazed up at the branches, moaning softly, lost. His father gazed at her, lost. Time passed. Jacob took a step toward them. He stopped. He felt drunk. He didn't think he would make it. He left them there together.

EPILOGUE

Resting at the tip of a fig branch, she gazes down at the family, fractured into thousands of pieces, and she curls up in sadness, her legs folding in on themselves.

Her love—he stands still as a statue. She wishes she could go to him, and comfort him, and tell him that she meant what she said when she said forever.

A breeze passes over her, cooling her shell from the hot sun. The branch dances in space. Below, the woman raises her eyes to the heavens. They regard each other across a great distance. A mewling burbles up from deep in the woman's throat, her dry lips moving without words.

She wants to remember.

As for *her*, she needs no reminder. It is like they met yesterday. In the grand scheme of things, they did. Forever is a long time.

She watches her love turn and leave, and she prepares to follow him. Now that she has found him again, she will crawl over the dead gray deserts to be near him. She will swim gray lakes, descend into the gray valley where he resides. They are places she knows well.

She raises her wings, bends her joints.

Leaps.

It's the same as always: for one terrifying moment, gravity overpowers faith, and she plunges toward the earth. Then she remembers who she is, and she begins to rise.

ACKNOWLEDGMENTS

Rabbi Yonatan Cohen, Paul Hamburg, Faye Kellerman, Gabriella Kellerman, Daniel Kestenbaum, Amy Glass, Yana Flaksman, Marc Michael Epstein, David Wichs, Menachem Kallus, Lieutenant Jan Chrpa, Lieutenant Lenka Kovalská, Slavka Kovarova.